Into the Wonder
Book 5

Oathbreaker

Into the Wonder, Book 5:
Oathbreaker

Published by Puggle Press

ISBN: 978-0692968079

In memoriam
Nola Jeffers Pursiful

She always had our backs

Table of Contents

Chapter 1

Not the Most Wonderful Time of the Year

Taylor scowled at Bledrus Dingle. For his part, the spriggan didn't seem to notice. He looked at her from across the table and shoveled another bite of turkey into his misshapen mouth.

The Route 80 Diner in Manchester, Kentucky was a quaint little place. The décor might have been described as Early Modern Basketball: photos of local high school teams going back thirty years or more adorned the walls, along with donated jerseys and some autographed pictures of people Taylor would probably recognize if she cared anything at all about sports.

The place was mostly empty. Besides Taylor and her repulsive dinner date, the only other people in the tiny restaurant were a couple of county sheriff's deputies and a homeless guy the manager had taken pity on. It was Thanksgiving, and most people were enjoying the holiday at home with their loved ones.

Taylor was sharing the holiday with her personal jailer, who had glamoured himself to look like an angel-faced ten-year-old. But Taylor had no trouble discerning his true, hideous appearance behind the illusion.

"You're enjoying this," she said.

Dingle's face revealed nothing. "I'm just doing my job."

Taylor scowled at him and poked at her mashed potatoes.

The waitress approached them and asked if they'd like dessert. Her nametag said "Wanita."

"None for me," Taylor said.

"Do you have pecan pie?" the spriggan said. Even his voice sounded like a kid's. Most spriggans didn't have that much skill.

"Is that okay, Mom?" Wanita asked Taylor. Taylor wasn't any good at the kind of husks Dingle could project to mask his faery nature, but over the last thirty-six hours, she'd had plenty of practice honing her power of suggestion. Nobody in the diner questioned that she could be somebody's mom. As far as they were concerned, she was just an extremely young-looking thirty-something woman.

"Fine," Taylor said.

"You ought to have some, too," Dingle said. Sweet treats enhanced faery magic. William Matthews thought it might have something to do with boosting the level of serotonin in the brain.

"I'm good."

"Please, *Mom*?" Dingle said. Beneath his husk, he furrowed his brows: a subtle threat?

Taylor sighed. "Do you have pumpkin?" If she were home, she'd be digging into a slice of her mom's pumpkin pie about now.

"One pumpkin pie and one pecan, coming right up," Wanita said.

As soon as she left the table, Dingle said, "You've got to keep up your reserves. Mrs. Hellebore wants to see what you can do."

"Yes, she's made that quite obvious," Taylor snapped.

"Like I said, I'm just doing my job."

"Uh huh," Taylor said. "I go through these stupid tests, showing you how good I am at glamours. You watch me and report to Mara on my progress. And along the way, you make sure I don't do anything tricky." She wondered, though, if anyone was watching Dingle.

Two days ago, while she and her friends were still sailing down the River of Night, she could almost believe Danny Underhill's theory that Dingle was secretly helping them, tipping them off to the Winter Court's plans.

Then, just when they thought they were safe, her grandmother Mara Hellebore showed up. She said it was finally time for Taylor to repay her debt, the favor she owed her grandmother in return for sparing the life of her friend Jill two summers ago.

Now, she wasn't sure what to think. Maybe Dingle was on Taylor's side. Or maybe he was just full of bluster and didn't know when to keep his mouth shut. Kidnapped, with no way to contact her friends, it would be nice to think she had a secret ally—even one as unpleasant as the spriggan across the table from her.

Wanita brought the pies as well as the bill. Dingle dug into his dessert as soon as it landed in front of him.

"I want to go home," Taylor said.

"What you want don't figure into it," Dingle said. "You swore an oath."

"I know!" Taylor checked herself. That came out louder and angrier than was prudent. Thankfully, the cops were engrossed in their own conversation about how the Kentucky Wildcats were likely to fare this year. The homeless guy was half-asleep at his table by the kitchen.

"I just mean...how much longer is this going to take? Layla isn't going to be able to fool my parents forever, you know."

Mara had left a shape-shifter in Taylor's place. Her grandmother said Jill and William's Second Sight wouldn't detect her, but Taylor couldn't believe it would take Jill long to figure out something fishy was going on.

She wasn't sure that would be a good thing. What would Layla do if somebody confronted her?

Taylor had to get home, and soon.

"Eat your pie," Dingle said.

Fresh pumpkin pie never tasted so bitter, but Taylor finished most of it, glaring at Dingle the whole time, Christmas music playing through the speakers overhead.

It was most certainly *not* the most wonderful time of the year.

Finally, Taylor reached for her purse.

"No cash this time," the spriggan said. "Use one of those plastic cards the deathlings have."

"I don't have a credit card," she said.

"Improvise."

She glowered. "Whatever." Yesterday, Dingle had stocked her purse with slips of newspaper cut to the size of dollar bills. A little bit of glamour and a winning smile was all it took to make cashiers think Taylor was handing them real money. They hadn't had a bit of trouble on their trip north. She had bought three meals a day, convenience store snacks, and an extra set of clothes and a toothbrush from a Wal-Mart somewhere in South Carolina, all with nothing but some worthless scraps of newspaper.

Usually, her grandmother traveled with them, along with a staff of guards and attendants. For these "tests," however, it was just Taylor and Dingle.

Taylor approached the cashier's station, gathering magic and meditating on her true name.

Time to commit some more larceny, she thought. Over the last couple of years, it had gotten harder and harder for Taylor to flat-out lie to anyone, but subtle deception was pretty easy. Or it would be if she didn't feel so guilty about it.

Wanita took the bill and asked if everything tasted all right.

Taylor smiled and handed over her library card.

She threw all the presence she had at the waitress, projecting confidence, authority. At the same time, she tried to remember how this process worked. She'd seen her mom and dad pay with a credit card a million times. She would have to anticipate Wanita's actions at every step.

The waitress looked at the card, then flipped it over to check the signature on the back.

Taylor's mind reached out to Wanita's. *It's a perfectly normal card,* she thought. She held a picture in her mind of what she

4

wanted the waitress to see: name, expiration date, the magnetic strip on the back. For good measure, she bathed the image in her true name: the focus of all her most powerful magic.

I am Neunhirri. I am Laughter in Winter.

Wanita swiped the card in the reader. Of course, it didn't even register.

"Credit or debit?"

"Uh...debit."

As Taylor pretended to enter her PIN, she concentrated even harder. Wanita checked the screen. Taylor willed it to say, "Approved"—at least in Wanita's mind.

The next part was going to be tricky. With no transaction to process, how was the machine going to spit out a paper receipt?

Wanita waited, smiling, while nothing happened. A few seconds later, she gazed at the machine, puzzled. She frowned and gestured, coaxing the machine to hurry up.

Taylor drew up even more magic. She was suddenly grateful Dingle had forced her to have that piece of pie.

She let a wisp of magic pass between them, a subtle addlement that forced a hiccup in Wanita's memory. She closed her eyes and wobbled a little as Taylor grabbed back her library card and slipped it into her wallet.

The transaction went through fine, she thought. *You already gave me my receipt.*

Wanita shook herself out of her daze. "You all come again. Happy Thanksgiving!"

"The same to you," Taylor said, not nearly as enthusiastically. Dingle touched her elbow, but Taylor stayed put. "Wait a minute," she said. She still had her wallet in her hand. Every cashier she had tricked between Darien, Georgia and Manchester, Kentucky had given her back some change—real money. It was bad enough they'd given her free stuff, it was like they had paid her to take it!

"I forgot to add your tip." She laid a wad of bills on the counter. Then she added a few more. "And will this cover his meal?" She gestured with her eyes at the homeless guy.

5

"I believe so." Wanita smiled. In hushed, earnest tones, she added, "God bless you."

Taylor grunted noncommittally.

In the parking lot, Taylor pulled her black leather jacket tight. There was a freezing drizzle in the air. It wasn't enough to stick, but it made for a miserable night for anybody who had to be outside.

"You seem to enjoy helping deathlings."

"What I enjoy doesn't figure into it," Taylor said. "It's called being a compassionate human being. You should try it."

"I am not a human being, Miss Hellebore. And neither are you."

She let that pass without comment, mainly because she didn't have a witty comeback.

The road was deserted even though it wasn't terribly late. Back home, Taylor's dad would be engrossed in a football game on TV. With Mara's shape-shifting spy on the scene, he and her mom wouldn't even know Taylor was missing.

That was the problem with Mara Hellebore: she thought of everything, and she was always planning ahead.

The spriggan led Taylor off the parking lot into the trees. "Ready?"

"Does it matter if I'm not?"

"Not really."

Taylor followed the spriggan's lead. He trudged up a narrow footpath. Soon, even the sporadic sounds of traffic on Highway 80 fell away to nothing.

"I'll have to report what you did," Dingle said. "But I wouldn't worry about it. She's only interested in your skill with magic. She'll be pleased you passed the test."

"Woo hoo," Taylor said, rolling her eyes.

They proceeded through the woods a few more yards. The spriggan said, "You don't have to like her, you know."

"I can't tell you what a relief that is."

"Just do what you have to do. Like I said, you swore an oath."

And Mara's spy back home was insurance that she would keep it.

That very fact made Taylor wonder, though. Breaking an oath must not be exactly like telling a lie. She could probably do it if she had to. But lately she'd been thinking a lot about what the consequences might be.

The mushroom ring was located in a spot barely big enough to be called a clearing. Dingle gestured, calling its magic to life, and they passed through it. As soon as they stepped out the other side, Taylor's magical senses tingled. This part of the Wonder was the same patch of woods as in the Topside world, only different. The weather certainly wasn't any more pleasant.

"I don't even know what this favor is I'm supposed to do," Taylor said.

"You'll find out soon enough."

Mara Hellebore met them outside of camp. The Chief Matron of the Winter Court was tall, dark-haired, regal in bearing. She wore a gown the color of gunmetal that seemed entirely too lightweight for the weather, but the chill didn't seem to bother her. She was uncannily beautiful, yet detached. A tattoo around her left eye danced as she arched her brow in a wordless question to Dingle.

"She did fine, Ma'am," he said. "Shall I give you the details?"

"Not here, Captain. In my tent."

In the distance rose Cair Cullen, the capital of the Winter Court and—as Dingle described it—the most impregnable stronghold in the entire Chiefdom of Arradherry. Stone turrets rose above the trees, ominous stone giants standing guard over Crom Cornstack's windswept keep.

Taylor had been adamant that she would not enter Cair Cullen. She had sworn by her own true name never to set foot in any rath of Arradherry. Mara had been obliging on that point— so far.

They had arrived that afternoon in the shadow of the seat of Mara and Crom's power and began pitching their tents. Now, though, things had changed. The clearing was seemingly filled with smaller tents, at least a dozen of them. Fair Folk of every size and shape milled about. Cooking fires burned down to embers in every direction. Voices, mostly male, sang what might have been a drinking song in a language Taylor didn't understand.

This wasn't what Taylor had expected. She was used to Mara and her entourage; this looked more like a military camp.

"W-what's all this?" Taylor said.

Mara ignored her. "Take her to her tent," the Chief Matron told Dingle, "then report to me."

Dingle bowed stiffly and led Taylor forward. Most of the tents were simple two-person structures, though at the center of the camp were some larger shelters. Those were all Taylor had expected to see: Mara's pavilion adorned with rich, purple bunting along with two smaller structures on either side: one she shared with her own attendants (who would also probably double as jailers if Taylor tried anything) and another for Dingle and the rest of Mara's personal guard. In front stood two trolls with bronze-barreled muskets.

"What's going on?" Taylor asked again. Dingle ignored her question just as Mara had. They walked in silence a moment longer, then he flung his hand out, stopping her as a detachment of armed fae warriors marched past. They were half a dozen short and loathsome spriggans led by an officer whose features were feral yet staggeringly handsome. The leader gave Dingle a crisp salute.

"Well?" Taylor pressed.

Dingle said nothing.

"Fine, don't tell me. It doesn't take a genius to know something is up. These guys weren't here when we left for the diner."

"Mrs. Hellebore will tell you what she wants to tell you," Dingle said, stopping in front of Taylor's tent flap.

A thought came to her. It wasn't a very happy one. "I'm not the only one being tested, am I?"

The spriggan arched an eyebrow.

"Belas Wakefire has been weakened," Taylor continued. "Crom wants to know what he'll do under pressure. How close he is to snapping."

Taylor knew—or at least strongly suspected—that her grandfather Crom Cornstack had been undermining the Summer Court and its Primus, Belas Wakefire, for years. Her stomach leaped into her throat as she realized she was right. She had to be. Whatever these soldiers were up to, Belas was in their sights.

"I'm right, aren't I?"

Dingle scowled. "Not for me to say," he muttered.

"But I can't tell anybody. What harm would it do?"

"Good night, Miss Hellebore."

"*Just tell me. Please?*" She threw some presence into her words, but she didn't try to threaten or overpower the spriggan. She'd already learned he was immune to her threats—presence or no presence.

The spriggan's eyes began to lose focus, but he abruptly shook himself alert. Taylor's heart sank. She'd almost gotten to him that time.

He gestured vaguely at his surroundings. "This don't concern you," he said. "Get some rest. Long day tomorrow."

And with that he opened the tent flap and waited for Taylor to step inside. As soon as she did, he stalked away.

On the inside, Taylor's tent was more like a small hotel room with canvas walls. There were two tiny cots in one corner, a washbasin and dressing table, a small sitting area, and a copper stove in the center that warmed the entire room. A canvas partition separated Taylor's private room in the back from the common area.

Taylor's "maids" (for lack of a better term) were a pair of almost-four-foot tall women with ruddy cheeks, braided brown hair, and tapered, bat-like ears. Alva was the oldest, and her sister's name was Maisie. Maisie was turning down the bed while Alva slid a piece of firewood into the stove. Both paused to greet Taylor.

"Good evening, Miss Hellebore," they said in unison.

Taylor nodded distractedly and lumbered to a chair on autopilot. The sudden appearance of Winter troops did nothing for her mood. Something was definitely up, and she didn't like any of the possibilities she could imagine.

Winter was through playing around. That could only mean Crom and Mara thought they had all the advantages.

"I don't suppose you two know what's going on?"

The little women tittered like Taylor had made a joke. Maisie said, "Can I fix you some hot cocoa, Miss Hellebore?"

Taylor rubbed her eyes.

This was it. Crom and Mara were about to launch their plan, whatever it was. And Taylor was part of it, somehow. She knew she wasn't going to like it when she found out the details.

But maybe, if she was lucky, she could figure out a way to stop them. Or at least slow them down. She was no fan of the Summer Court, but she felt a lot safer knowing the two leading Courts of Arradherry were evenly balanced.

"Miss Hellebore?"

"What?" Taylor sat back up. "Oh. Cocoa. Yeah. Thanks, Maisie."

A little more sugar could only help.

If it was going to be a long day tomorrow, Taylor had no doubt it would be a bad one.

Chapter 2

The Gatehouse of Tobarty

Claudia shivered as she wound through the narrow streets of Tobarty. The cold breeze had picked up since sunset and it looked like it might rain. Given the temperature and the altitude, it might even freeze.

Claudia's discomfort had little to do with the weather, though. She had a job to do, and it wouldn't be easy. She shifted the weight of her shoulder bag.

She had guessed something was wrong at Tobarty even before Danny tracked her down yesterday morning in her office at Bisgarra Verry. The pooka looked rough. He walked with a limp, and his clothes were dingy and worn.

"Crom Cornstack's got a weapon inside Tobarty," he had said as soon as she shut the door behind him. "A quickened artifact in the Teyrnus's office."

As soon as he said it, the pieces started to fall together in her mind. She remembered the difficult weeks she herself had spent at Tobarty while Gwenllian Birdsong was running things. Something about the place was unsettling. Every Teyrnus the Summer Court had sent to oversee the rath had been a failure—and every one had to be recalled when the job turned out to be too much for them.

"A quickened?" Claudia said. That could be bad.

"Me and Taylor think it's the desk."

Claudia cursed under her breath. The great mahogany desk. The one piece of furniture in the Teyrnus's office left over from when the Winter Court was in charge of Tobarty.

A commotion on the street called her back to the present. She ducked out of the way as a detachment of Summer troops marched by: a band of pisgies and moss folk led by a bright-eyed hulder. They muscled pedestrians out of their way as they marched toward the lower town. Their eyes betrayed wariness, maybe even frustration. Half the town was still loyal to its former masters from the Winter Court. Many others whispered rumors of an impending nunnehi invasion from the east.

A posting at Tobarty must have been a nightmare. Belas Wakefire had given the rath to his cousin Aemeron after a string of Teyrnuses each became so agitated and paranoid that it impaired their fitness to rule. Now that the Primus himself has been overseeing the day-to-day operations for the past few days, things had only gotten worse.

Things were certainly worse than the last time Claudia was in Tobarty, and that was only a few weeks ago. Then, she had managed to steel herself against the atmosphere of anxiety and despair even as far as the Teyrnus's office. Now, that oppressive gloom was everywhere.

Those soldiers could push her out of the way if they wanted. If Claudia's plan worked, they could thank her later for making their job easier.

She held her breath until they finally passed. "Almost there," she breathed, and moved on.

At the gate, she strode confidently up to the guardsmen. Presence was not one of her gifts. She couldn't project an aura of authority like the daoine sídhe could, but she knew how to act like she was in charge—and she'd spent enough time around the Gentry not to be bowled over by their glamour.

There were four of them, tall and lithe daoine sídhe in green rain cloaks: the kind of fae the Summer Court liked for assignments that called for more savvy than the average giant or spriggan could handle. They wore swords on their belts— lethal in close quarters—but their main weapons were the blunderbusses that rested against their shoulders.

Claudia didn't intend to find out how good the men were with either weapon.

The closer she got to the rath, the more she felt its oppressive shadow. Her senses spiked. Every subtle movement, every unexpected noise, assaulted her mind. She couldn't decide if she wanted to fight or run away. Neither option would be productive.

She pushed the swirl of agitated emotions down into her gut and pressed on.

One of the guardsmen stepped forward. A biting wind blew back his cloak, exposing his sword. He rested his hand on the hilt. With the other, he conjured a golden orb of faery fire.

Claudia took a breath and stepped forward. "I have an urgent message for the Teyrnus."

"Name?" the guard's lips curled into a sneer. His eyes darted to and fro, alert to any tricks. He was feeling the shadow, too—no doubt more intensely than Claudia.

"Claudia Fountain. I'm the Chief Matron's personal assistant."

"I know who you *look like*," the guard said. In the Wonder, one rarely trusted outward appearances.

"I'm no shape-shifter," Claudia snapped. Her face grew hot. She bit back the urge to say more. *Patience, Claudia*, she told herself.

"We'll see about that. What's in the bag?"

Claudia's heart pounded. She adjusted her shoulder strap. "My duties for the Summer Court often require specialized equipment." Which was perfectly truthful...though not at all relevant.

The guard reached out his hand for the bag. The others flanked their leader.

"Let's see."

"I have vital information for the Teyrnus," Claudia said.

"The Teyrnus is busy getting chewed out by Mr. Wakefire," the guard said. "We've got plenty of time to search you. You want to step over here?" He motioned toward a tiny gatehouse.

Not especially.

"Your commitment to doing your job is commendable," Claudia said, "but I really don't have time for—"

"What's that?" a different guard said, pointing at the bag.

"I saw it, too!" A third guard drew his sword. "Something was moving in there!"

Now all four guards circled Claudia, swords drawn.

"I am the personal assistant to the Chief Matron," Claudia rumbled. It wasn't an aura of confidence but rather something more primal. Her words hit the guards with the dread of an impending disaster.

They backed off, but kept their swords drawn.

"If you'll excuse me."

The leader shook off Claudia's glamour. He took a step forward. "Now, just a minute. The rath is on high alert. We can't just let—"

"There it was again!" the other guard said. He pointed his sword at Claudia's bag.

"Come with me," the leader said. He grabbed Claudia by the arm and yanked her toward the gatehouse.

Claudia slouched her other shoulder, letting the strap of her bag fall to her wrist. She tried to back away, but the guards had her surrounded.

"I'll take that bag."

Claudia couldn't let that happen, no matter the consequences to her. She shook herself free from the lead guardsman and pushed the back of her hand into his chest, delivering a jolt of electricity that dropped him to the ground.

The other guards shouted and fell on her, but not before she sent her bag skipping across the flagstones toward the main gate.

"Get the bag!" one of the other guards shouted as he grabbed Claudia by the arm.

The other two guards stomped toward it.

A pair of long, black ears popped out, followed by a black rabbit with glowing yellow eyes.

"Run!" Claudia called. "Don't worry about me!"

The rabbit bounded away with two guardsmen on its heels.

The other two guards muscled Claudia into the gatehouse. Firm hands wrapped around her waist.

"Let go of me!" she shouted.

One redheaded guard lifted her off the ground and hauled her toward the gatehouse. She couldn't blink away—the guard's mass was tied to her own as long as they were in physical contact, and not even the most powerful fae could blink with a 200-pound weight on her back.

The report of a blunderbuss nearly startled her off her feet.

Through the smoke and confusion, Claudia watched a blur of black fuzz dart through the gate and into the keep.

"Get that rabbit!" a guard shouted.

Her heart raced. Danny was on his own.

The redheaded guard heaved her forward. "Come along!"

The other guard, a tall, dark-eyed fae with his brown hair in a ponytail, held open the door. "Watch her head, Murgo," he called. Murgo lowered Claudia with a firm hand to the back of her head. As she struggled, the two toppled forward into the tiny room just as another blunderbuss fired.

Inside the gatehouse, the only light came from the glowing embers of a dying fire in the fireplace. It did almost nothing to stave off the damp and drizzly night.

"I am the assistant to the Chief Matron!"

Murgo slammed Claudia into a rough, wooden chair and drew her arms behind her back, binding them with enchanted rope that snaked between her wrists and tied itself in a firm knot.

"And I am the chief of the night watch!" the dark-eyed guard snarled. He conjured an orb of faery fire and set it loose in the room. At last, Claudia was able to take stock of her surroundings. There was a small table with two wooden chairs, a modest cupboard, and a collection of weapons in a rack by the door. The stone floor was as bare as it was cold.

The captain set her bag on the table and peered in, cautiously. Let him look: Now that Danny had escaped, there was only one thing left in it—and Claudia doubted the captain of the night watch would have the first clue what it was.

She tested the rope. It didn't give, of course. Nor could she blink. She'd have had the job of any guard who bound a prisoner without an anti-blinking charm on the rope.

At least she wasn't injured. Her mind was clear, for the moment. But every slight move set her senses on edge. The same anxiety or paranoia that had overtaken the guards would dig its claws into her soon enough. She took a deep breath and tried to put that thought out of her mind.

She could hear the blast of alarm horns, the pounding of booted feet, and gruff shouts of command. All the guards knew was that an intruder was loose in the rath. Given the current mood, they would do whatever it took to stop him. She only hoped Danny could take care of things without her.

He's sharp, Claudia told herself. *He'll keep them busy as long as he can.*

But how long would that be?

"This is ridiculous! I'm trying to help you! I have vital information for the Teyrnus!"

"What's this?" the captain of the night watch said. He held up a gourd painted to look like a grotesque face.

"It's just a container," Claudia said. "A vessel."

She bit back her anger, her frustration at being detained. Danny needed her, and there she was, tied up in the gatehouse like a common criminal.

"That so?" The captain quirked a skeptical eyebrow. "Looks suspicious to me."

"It's none of your concern, I assure you." She gathered her thoughts. Things were only getting worse—and fast. She didn't have time to lose. "If you insist on holding me here, then I demand to speak to Mr. Wakefire."

The captain threw back his head and laughed. "Yeah, you'd like that, wouldn't you?"

"You're staying right there, lady," Murgo said.

"But don't worry," the captain said. "Your buddy the rabbit'll be joining you soon enough. If you're smart, you'll cooperate. Otherwise—"

He stopped abruptly and pulled a Seeing Stone from his pocket. He breathed across its dull, gray surface and allowed himself to be immersed in the vision of whoever was scrying him.

"Redsmith, what's going on?" he said. As he listened, his smirk turned into a frown.

"All right, all right," he said, cutting off his subordinate. "You'd better tell Mr. Wakefire—Both of them, you idiot! The Primus *and* the Teyrnus!" The captain gritted his teeth as he listened. "I know how late it is; tell them anyway! And double the guard at both their chambers."

Another pause.

"No excuses!" he bellowed. "Find that shape-shifter and bring him to me! Understand?"

He broke off the conversation with an exasperated sigh. He clenched his fists and struggled to compose himself.

"Trouble?" Claudia said, arching an eyebrow and suppressing a grin.

The captain cursed.

Claudia's lips formed a subtle smile, and her mind began to conceive a plan.

"Watch the prisoner," the captain said. "I'll be back in a minute." He stormed out of the gatehouse, leaving the second guard alone with Claudia. He unslung the blunderbuss from his shoulder.

Perfect, Claudia thought. She gathered magic. Bound with enchanted ropes, she couldn't draw much, but every little bit helped. A tiny jolt of dread added to the chaos already swirling through the rath might be all she needed.

"Where do you suppose the captain has gone?" she said.

The guard flinched when she spoke. He grasped his weapon, but kept it pointed at the floor.

"Why do you care?"

Claudia shrugged. "I was just wondering why he'd leave you to guard me alone. Does that seem wise to you?"

His eyes widened, confused and maybe—hopefully—a little scared. He leveled his weapon at Claudia's head. "What's that supposed to mean?"

Claudia smiled the kind of smile that says you're about to enjoy unleashing unspeakable fury on someone. "Nothing."

"No! What do you mean?"

She looked the guard in the eyes and bored into him with a wave of dread. "You seem like a nice fellow. You don't deserve this."

He backed toward the door. Despite the cold, sweat trickled down his cheek. "Captain?" But the captain was already out of earshot.

Claudia began to chant. Her voice was barely above a whisper, but she didn't take her eyes off the guard. She leaned forward in her chair.

He bolted for the door. "Captain!"

Claudia sighed. Now that she had some privacy, things could go faster. She continued her incantation, focusing all her attention now on the painted gourd on the table.

As a changeling, Claudia's innate magic was fairly limited. She had inherited her power of dread from her cymbee father. Almost everything else, she had learned from her Topsider mother: a powerful witch with a knack for conjuration.

Her father had told her such a gourd was called a *nkondi* in the Kikongo language. Her mom, born on a plantation in South Carolina, just called it a hunter. She had heard stories from her own mother about how folks would use them back in Africa to hound evildoers and bring them to justice.

Claudia had always prided herself on her ability to fashion hunters, to imbue them with the necessary magics, to call them forth when needed. This one would have to be her best work yet.

Fortunately, she had planned accordingly. Expecting she would have to conjure on the fly, she'd primed her hunter before she and Danny even arrived at the rath—when she was assured of having a full head of magical steam behind her. It only took another couple of seconds before the gourd shook, shimmered, and then erupted in a gray, ghostly fog that roiled and twisted on itself until it took shape: a stooped, vaguely human form with a wolf-like face, wielding a club set with shards of flint, and dressed in a loincloth and a necklace of jagged teeth.

"Untie me!" Claudia commanded.

The magical construct leaped to her side and snapped the ropes with its bare hands. Outside the gatehouse, Claudia heard voices: Murgo and the captain arguing, approaching the door.

"Break down the door," Claudia said. "Get us out of here."

The hunter complied. It threw its shoulder into the door and splintered it into kindling.

The guards yelped. One of them fired his blunderbuss, but the ball of elf-shot hurtled straight through the hunter's smoky form.

The hunter bolted forward as Claudia ran to what was left of the door, grabbing her gourd on the way out.

Half a dozen guards were converging on the gatehouse. Some still had their blunderbusses at the ready but others, seeing how ineffective elf-shot was against the hunter, had opted for swords instead.

The captain of the night watch's sword wasn't hardened bronze as Claudia had expected, but a silvery titanium alloy, stronger and lighter than steel with none of the disadvantages. Carrying a weapon like that was a mark of distinction.

The captain slashed at the hunter. The blade passed through it without slowing down—but this time the hunter registered the attack. It hissed in anger and staggered backward. Then, without warning, it leaped forward, tackled the captain, and threw him to the ground.

Captain Murgo aimed his blunderbuss at the hunter. Claudia jolted him with a stunning spell. There was a sudden crack of thunder and a blinding flash of light in a kaleidoscope of dizzying colors that lasted for a full three seconds and sent all the guards ducking for cover.

"Here!" Claudia called, raising the gourd. The hunter leaped into the air and turned back into a swirling tornado of smoke as it returned to its container.

The captain lay motionless. Claudia noted blood on the ground and the sleeve of his tunic. Even as she sped away, she feared for his fate.

The plan was in shambles, and she hadn't even entered the rath. She and Danny had been separated, and she'd had to conjure her hunter too soon. Hunters were nearly unbeatable, but they could only maintain a physical form for so long. If she had to conjure it again—and she couldn't imagine a scenario in which she wouldn't—it might give out at the worst possible moment.

She never meant to hurt anyone, but now she was responsible for wounding a guard—or maybe worse. At least now the guards had other things to occupy their attention. She covered herself in magic mist and passed without notice through the narrow passages of the keep. She wondered where Danny was, how they could join up again and do something about that quickened desk in the Teyrnus's office.

Claudia sighed. In addition to assaulting a guard, she'd turned a dangerously mischievous pooka loose upon the unsuspecting residents of Tobarty Keep.

If she was lucky, all this would cost her would be her job.

The worst part was that she was doing it all to honor her oath to the Summer Court of Arradherry.

How could she ever explain all this to the Primus?

All she could do was press on and hope that, despite all appearances, the plan would work after all.

Chapter 3

The Hunter

Danny should have known getting inside the rath of Tobarty would be tough. The last time he'd been there, the Teyrnus was pretty much out of his mind. Things had only gotten worse over the last couple of weeks.

Without Claudia, he was on his own. He wasn't completely sure how to get to the Teyrnus's office. What's worse, he wasn't even sure what to do about the quickened desk when he got there.

But he didn't have a choice. Claudia had been arrested; it was up to him now.

He had barely gotten past the guards at the gate. He'd spotted a vent for the keep's heating system that was just big enough for a rabbit to squeeze through.

No one peering into the vent could see him—which meant no one could reach him with any of the standard offensive spells. There were other tricks, though, and Tobarty was bound to be filled with folks who knew them.

Above him, he heard guards barking orders, clearing passages. Shrill horn blasts alerted the whole garrison that there was trouble.

Yep, trouble, Danny thought. *That's me!*

The vent soon split into a T. Danny inched into the leftmost arm. He had to keep moving. He had to find Claudia, make sure she was all right. More than that, he had to complete his mission.

Alone in a heating vent, he wondered how.

He wriggled along to the next grate and waited for a detachment of guards to jog by overhead.

When he thought they'd passed, he inched his way into the hall, at the same time taking on his two-legged shape. He pressed himself against the stone wall, drew magic mist over himself, and looked around.

He was in a wide corridor, thankfully deserted. The stone walls were covered with bright tapestries. Lanterns in copper wall sconces cast a warm, orange glow as well as dancing shadows. He stretched out his magical senses and found only the kind of low-level emanations he would have expected in a place that dozens of Fair Folk called home. The sounds of marching feet and the occasional shouts of guards told him he couldn't count on privacy for long.

Danny ducked into a narrow side passage to gather his thoughts. He would have to find the Teyrnus's office. If Claudia got free, that's where she'd go, too. Their best chance had always been working together. Now that their plan to enter the rath secretly had gone to pot, they would have to improvise the rest.

Story of my life, Danny thought.

Another detachment of guards stormed down the main corridor: a mixed group of green-clad hulders and moss folk led by a fair-haired tylwyth teg. Danny pressed himself against the wall and hoped his glamour would mask his presence.

"Fan out!" the leader called. "Find that shape-shifter!"

Danny inched down his current passage as quickly as he dared, all the while drawing even more glamour into his magic mist. His heart wanted to believe it would be enough, but his head knew better. He'd run up against castle guards before. They weren't so easily fooled.

Two moss folk strode into the hallway. In the lantern light, Danny saw the amber gleam of their eyes and their tousled green hair. They lifted their arms to waist height. It wasn't an offensive gesture; they were doing what Danny had done before—sensing the flow of magical energies.

They'd find him any second. He couldn't let that happen.

So he took a chance. He stepped out of the shadows and threw a stunning spell directly in front of them. They crumpled to the ground amid the chaos of flashing lights and thunderous explosions. At the same time, the pooka bounded off in the opposite direction, taking on the form of a dog as he ran.

The leader roared with surprise, then shouted "That way!"

But Danny had already turned a corner and was hurtling deeper into the keep. He'd be faster on four legs, especially with nearly everybody locked inside their apartments. As soon as he found a good hiding place, he'd shift again and try to get his bearings.

He lost track of how long he ducked and dodged through the keep's twisting corridors. As a rabbit, he took refuge in the heating vents twice more. Once, he got very lucky, avoiding detection under magic mist while an even larger group of guards passed by.

He tried to blink through the doors of storage closets, but they'd been warded against him: standard procedure when there was an intruder afoot. Still, a place to catch his breath would have been nice.

As best he could tell, he was making progress toward the Teyrnus's office. He'd been there before, but it wasn't under the best of circumstances. He wracked his brain to remember any landmark that would tell him he was close to the area where the city guards had dragged him a few weeks back when one of his pranks had backfired on him.

Footsteps approached from the right. He held his breath and threw as much magic as he could into his glamour.

He peeked around the corner and saw a woman creeping toward him. She didn't look like Claudia: she was short, white, and blonde. But that's who it had to be under a thick glamour that was almost perfect. Nobody else was in the halls; the whole keep was under lockdown.

Danny rested his eyes, squinted, then looked again. It was Claudia, alright. Before his eyes, the woman took on Claudia's familiar form. The water jug she'd been carrying morphed into a painted gourd. She looked tired, frightened. Danny couldn't remember her ever being afraid of anything. He wondered what she'd been doing the past hour or so.

He grabbed her and pulled her close, clapping his hand over her mouth.

She started to struggle, then just as quickly relaxed when she recognized who had her.

"You okay?" he whispered.

She nodded. "We can't stay here."

"How far to the office?"

"Not far. That way." She indicated a wider corridor to the left.

"So what's the plan?" Danny asked. "Find the Teyrnus?"

She sighed in resignation. "The Teyrnus isn't going to listen to me now. As far as he knows, I've turned on the Summer Court."

Danny hadn't thought of that. A shiver went up his spine. "You been with the Summers nearly forty years!" he said. Claudia shushed him. His whisper carried farther than it should have.

"We can't worry about that now," Claudia said. Her face darkened. "We've got to neutralize that desk."

"All right," Danny said. "Then maybe it's time for the direct approach."

Danny could hear the men arguing twenty yards away. He and Claudia approached the Teyrnus's office under a thick blanket of glamour, but stopped short at the final turn and peered to the left around the corner.

Four guards stood at attention outside the office door. It was shut and no doubt locked and warded, but anybody with two ears could tell that Belas and Aemeron Wakefire were frustrated—with the emergency, with conditions at the rath, and with each other.

"Do you *want* me to fail, cousin?" Aemeron snapped.

24

"Of course not!" Belas yelled.

"Then let me do my job!"

"I'd be happy to let you do your job, *cousin*, if I thought you were in any way—"

"Watch it, Belas. Just because you're the Primus doesn't mean I won't—"

They kept arguing. The guards shuffled their feet and looked anywhere but at each other.

Danny leaned back.

Claudia gave him a concerned look. "You sure about this?"

He nodded and bowed his head. Claudia stroked his head, twisted a few of his curly black hairs around her finger, and sharply yanked them out.

"Be careful," she said. Before he could answer, she kissed him. His face warmed and his heart did a little happy dance.

Danny pulled away. "You bet," he said. Then he bolted across the corridor as Claudia began to knead the hairs into a little ball of wax.

Following Claudia's instructions, he kept turning left until he was at the opposite end of the corridor with the Teyrnus's office. He inched up to the corner and became a dog. He leaned forward, wagging his tail, ready to run.

As if on cue, a fierce barking erupted from the other end of the hall. Guards shouted. The report of a blunderbuss reverberated up and down the stone corridors.

Danny leaned forward to spy around the corner. A black Labrador retriever hurdled past. He grinned. It was almost perfect: big and fast and as solid as any real-live dog, with Danny's own glowing yellow eyes and wagging tail.

Love that woman!

"There he goes!" a guard yelled. Another shot rang out. The hallway grew thick with the stench of black powder.

Claudia's dog construct bolted past Danny's position with two guards on its heels.

Conjuration took a lot of magical energy. To get a really life-like construct, especially on the fly, you had to sacrifice range or durability or both. The fake Danny wouldn't last long once it got out of Claudia's field of vision, but it did its job: two guards had been drawn away from the door.

It was time for the real Danny to get to work. He leaped into the hallway and sped to the right, passing in front of the remaining guards, who were still reloading their blunderbusses.

"Wha—?" a guard sputtered, dropping his weapon.

Danny barked but didn't slow down. He skidded and slipped on the flagstones and rounded the corner to the right.

"Get him!" the other guard shouted.

Danny bounded past Claudia, who stood defiantly in the middle of the hallway. Her stunning spell took out both guards as soon as they came into view.

"Let's go!" she called. Danny took on his ordinary shape and followed as she stalked toward the Teyrnus's office. The Teyrnus was already standing in the doorway.

"What's going on?" he shouted. The Primus peered over his cousin's shoulder.

"Teyrnus Wakefire!" Claudia called, "it is imperative that—"

"*Miss Fountain!*" the Primus shouted, shouldering past his cousin. His wave of presence nearly bowled Claudia over. Danny staggered backward. "I thought surely the guards were mistaken. Is this an insurrection I'm seeing?"

"Not at all, Primus," Claudia said.

"You gotta listen to her, sir," Danny spoke up. "There's something you don't know."

"And the pooka," Aemeron Wakefire said. His mouth twisted into a scowl. It looked as if he'd swallowed a mouthful of spider webs.

The first two guards, the ones who's chased Claudia's dog construct, reappeared in the corridor. They charged at Claudia and Danny, poking swords at their sides as they came up behind them. Claudia's guard wrested the gourd from her hand and tossed it away down the corridor.

The Primus stalked toward Claudia. Danny wanted to shield her from what was coming, but the guard's strong arm and his cold, sharp sword kept him in place.

Belas Wakefire wasn't his usual, affable self. He looked tired, haggard. Danny wouldn't have been surprised to learn he hadn't slept in several days. If anything, his cousin looked even worse. "I'll confess my wife and I have wondered about you, Claudia," the Primus said. "Where your loyalties truly lie."

"I serve the Summer Court," she said crisply. "I swore an oath." Danny's heart pounded in his chest. What Claudia said was true. What she left unsaid was that she was a double agent whose true loyalty was to the Nunnehi Lands, just across the border.

He kept his eyes on Claudia, partly to avoid eye contact with Belas Wakefire but mostly out of concern. She wasn't looking so good. She was probably feeling the same thing Danny was: nerves on edge, doubting herself, fearing the worst could happen at any moment. This close to the source of Tobarty's foul magic, its power was even stronger.

"Is this what you call serving my Court?" he said. His voice cracked with vexation. "Attacking my guards? Spreading mayhem?"

"The mayhem is my fault, sir," Danny said. "Claudia ain't—"

"*I'll deal with you in due course!*" Belas snapped. Danny crumpled under the power of his presence. Only the rough hands of his guard kept him on his feet.

"Primus," Claudia said, "Teyrnus. Please hear me out. There's a Winter agent working at Tobarty."

The Teyrnus bullied his way in front of his cousin. "What's that you say? A spy?"

"I'm handling this, Aemeron," the Primus said.

The Teyrnus scoffed. "Is that supposed to give me confidence?" He turned back to Claudia with a savage gleam in his eye. "Who is it? Who are you working with?"

"Excuse me!" the Primus said. "I am in charge here!"

"And a fat lot of good it's done!" the Teyrnus retorted. "I want answers!" He grabbed Claudia by the lapels of her suit coat and pulled her close.

Danny couldn't take it anymore. He fought himself free and lunged at the Teyrnus.

"Danny, no!" Claudia shouted. But she needn't have said anything: just then, the two other guards, now recovered from Claudia's stunning spell, bolted into the corridor and wrestled the pooka to the floor.

Still in the Teyrnus's grasp, Claudia whispered a quick incantation, a few harsh syllables that called forth a thick, gray smoke from her gourd at the end of the corridor.

The smoke congealed into the hunched, dog-headed form of Claudia's hunter.

"In there!" she commanded, pointing with her chin. The hunter surged forward, a swirl of smoke following in its wake. A guard braced himself to stop it, but it slammed into him with its shoulder and flung him into the wall with effortless grace.

It pivoted in front of the door, raised its misty war club, and barged in.

Danny became a rabbit and squirmed away from his guards. It wasn't too hard: they were both dumbfounded by the sudden appearance of Claudia's hunter.

The Primus and the Teyrnus had both turned toward the open door to the Teyrnus's office. Even the guard grasping Claudia's arm seemed dazed. He held his sword away from her side, pointed the direction the hunter had gone.

There was a vicious crack of stone against wood.

"What the—?" Aemeron Wakefire gasped. He was the first to stalk back toward his office door and peer in.

Danny bolted in between the Teyrnus's legs and dropped his rabbit form. On two legs, he crossed the reception area and peeked into the Teyrnus's private office.

The hunter was standing on top of the desk, wailing on it with its club. It had already left a couple of deep scars in the wood where flakes of flint had bitten into it.

The Teyrnus caught up to Danny and hissed a curse. "Miss Fountain, call off your—"

The desk began to shimmer. Then it began to shake. Then it lurched forward, throwing the hunter to the carpeted floor.

"Danu's blood!" the Teyrnus whispered, backing up.

The desk shuddered again. There was a loud snap of cracking wood, and it launched itself into the hunter, bringing down a colorful tapestry that had hung behind the Teyrnus's chair— which was now nothing more than a pile of splinters and some scraps of upholstery.

The desk had sprouted four legs ending in sturdy hooves that pushed it forward into the hunter a second time. The desk crouched. Its top now bowed up in the middle, giving it a pronounced shoulder.

The Teyrnus drew a flintlock pistol from his belt, took aim, and fired directly at what on a creature of flesh and blood would have been the desk's haunches.

It lurched clumsily with a roar of defiance.

Claudia's hunter leaped on its top. Hanging on to the lip, the dog-headed creature once again started hacking it one-handed with its flint-barbed club.

"Guards!" the Primus yelled.

The guards edged into the outer office. They gathered magic as they eyed each other warily.

"Aemeron?" the Primus said. He was also preparing a magical attack. He traded glances with his cousin, who nodded to him. As one, the Primus and the Teyrnus blasted the desk. It staggered backward, bellowing with the voice of a wounded bull.

A second later, the two guards in the room also let loose their blasts.

The desk backed into the far wall, trapping Claudia's hunter and leaving a pile of plaster and shattered rubble on the floor. It stalked once more to the doorway between the inner and outer offices. It shouldered through, cracking the doorpost, then stopped. The doorway was too narrow. Something told Danny that would only buy them a few seconds.

The artifact's middle drawer dropped open, exposing rows of jagged metal teeth. "Out of my way," it growled. Its voice was deep and rumbly and smoldering with hatred.

"C-Claudia?" Danny yelped.

"I can't keep this up," she called back in a strained, breathy voice. She'd kept her hunter going a lot longer than Danny had thought possible. It would give out soon—and then what?

The desk rocked back and forth, then slammed into the doorway again. This time, it took out the other doorpost. The lintel dangled over its shoulder for a second before dropping into the Teyrnus's office, followed by a trail of dust. It was now free in the outer office.

"Hey!" Danny called. "Over here, you son of a hutch!" He waved his arms. The desk pivoted to face him. As soon as it did, Danny cast a stunning spell. The room erupted with lights, smoke, and thunder.

The desk lumbered toward Danny, but the pooka was too fast. He dove to his right and rolled to a stop against the far wall of the outer office.

Just then, Claudia's hunter rejoined the attack. Rather than leaping onto the desk's top, though, this time it swept at its nearest leg. With a mighty crack, the leg snapped off and went flying in Danny's direction.

The desk staggered backward as the hunter slid underneath and came up in front. It roared, and the hunter crashed its club into its opened middle drawer. Splinters and metal fittings flew everywhere as the desk bellowed with outrage and pain.

The hunter was up again in half a second, but it no longer looked solid. Wisps of smoke trailed off it. Then, as quick as that, it vanished completely.

Claudia crumpled to the floor.

The mangled desk loomed over Danny, its weird, angular mouth now a gaping hole, its right hind leg an uneven stump.

"You'll be first," the desk rumbled. Though it didn't have eyes, at least that Danny could see, the pooka knew it was looking at him.

"I ain't in no hurry," Danny said. He pushed himself up the wall.

The desk chuckled. "You better be." It took another clumsy step forward. It raised its voice. "You'll all be fodder for the Winter Court before long!"

Another lurching step, then there was a flash of light. The desk reared up on its wobbly hind legs. It bellowed once more and laboriously turned its back on Danny.

The top of the desk was scorched. Through the dusty air, Danny saw Belas Wakefire holding a ball of flame in his hand: not faery fire, but the real thing. He lobbed his fireball, hitting the desk on what would have been the right shoulder of a living creature. Just as quickly, his cousin did the same to the artifact's half-demolished face.

It thrashed about and screamed in agony as it went up in flames.

Danny scrambled to get out of its way. He ran to Claudia, who was just getting to her feet in the corridor.

The desk thumped about and made the most hideous noises as it burned. Smoke billowed out the door. The Primus, the Teyrnus, and the guards backed out of the office.

The Primus approached Claudia, who was holding on to Danny for support.

"Miss Fountain," he said. "Would you care to explain what just happened?"

Chapter 4

Spying

"I don't have much time," Mara complained as she breezed into the room and took her seat at the round table. The other members of the Winter Triad glanced at each other.

"The burden of conducting the Triad's business must be terrible." The elder woman, a brown-haired fae in a voluminous indigo gown, let her words drip out in a bored drawl. The three women sat in the Triad's council chambers in the heart of Cair Cullen. The guards had been sent outside. Their only company was the tapestried stone walls and a half-dozen lanterns in copper wall sconces.

"We're less than a month into the Winter Assize," the woman continued. "Do you already need a vacation? Perhaps extend your little camping trip?"

The other Triad member—young, blonde, and dressed in red and black—stifled a laugh, but green fire danced in her eyes.

"Is there something you'd like to say, Wenhover?" Mara snapped.

The blonde woman sat up straight. Her eyes darted to her associate, but she said nothing.

"All right," Mara said. "It seems you're the appointed spokesperson, Aeora. Or should I say, 'self-appointed'?"

"We didn't summon you to debate semantics," Aeora drawled.

"Good," Mara said. She tapped her fingers impatiently on the table. Crom would be returning soon. She should be waiting for him in her pavilion. "Otherwise, I'd have something to say about that 'camping trip' comment."

Aeora folded her arms and turned up her nose.

"The girl refuses to enter the rath." Mara spread her arms. "It's as simple as that."

"I'm inclined to agree with the child," Aeora said. "She shouldn't even be here, Mara. Or are you unaware the Summer Court is mustering an army?"

"Of course I'm aware. As is the Primus."

"And yet you persist in this ill-conceived plan of yours."

"*You don't even know what my plan is,*" Mara said. She allowed her presence to permeate the room. It would have little effect on her fellow Matrons, of course. She just liked watching them squirm.

She also wondered how much they did know—or suspect. Surely not much. She'd only told Crom the barest essentials. Enough for him to muster the Ledogans and to demand a favor from his allies in New Avalon, but certainly no more. In the end, though, Crom would be as pleased as she was with the outcome, and no one else would be any the wiser.

There was no way the other members of the Triad could know the plans she had for Taylor Smart.

"You act as if we're the only ones to be curious," Aeora said. "Entering the Nunnehi Lands to collect the child—"

"As was my right! She swore by her own true name—"

"...the Primus's unexpected trip to New Avalon—"

"Crom Cornstack does not need the Triad's permission to—"

"...and freeing Lunso Butcher's gang from prison in Ledoga?" Aeora raised her voice on this last point. Mara swallowed. She knew about the...operatives...from Ledoga?

"Now you listen here, Aeora Twist. It is the Primus's prerogative to act in the interests of his Court."

"And it is in the Triad's interests to see that the Eldritch Law is observed. In *every* detail."

Mara breathed slowly. It was becoming clear to her now: the House of Twist was next in line of succession should the House

34

of Hellebore fall. Aeora saw an opportunity. Part of Mara—a very small part—admired her determination to pursue it.

She uttered her next words slowly, with a rumble of presence that would have reduced lesser fae to tears. "*Do you have evidence, Aeora, any evidence at all, that the Primus or I have transgressed the Eldritch Law?*"

"None," she admitted with a smirk. "Then again, the Drum Dancer likely has more resources at his disposal."

"And what does *he* have to do with any of this?" Mara's throat was suddenly parched. What did Aeora Twist mean, bringing *him* up?

"Word is, he's taken an interest in this matter."

Mara refused to let surprise or dread register on her face. She folded her hands in front of her on the table. "The Deep Council has a very clear policy against interfering in our internal affairs. If the Drum Dancer's minions have nothing better to do—"

"Not his minions, Mara," Aeora interrupted. "The Drum Dancer himself has been asking questions. In the Nunnehi Lands, at Tobarty—incognito, of course, but that's what my sources tell me."

Now Mara's mind was reeling. The last thing she needed was for the Deep Council to stick their noses in her affairs. What chilled her even more, though, was Aeora's admission that she had her own sources within Tobarty. As if her knowing about the Ledoga cateran and New Avalon wasn't bad enough!

"Then let him dig," Mara bluffed.

"Oh, it's quite beyond my power to influence the Deep Council one way or another," Aeroa said.

"Indeed." *And it always will be, by Danu!*

"It is not, however, beyond my power to challenge any actions you might take that would bring disgrace upon the Winter Court."

"Even if it brought down the House of Hellebore?" Mara clucked her tongue. "How selfless you are!"

"My Matronal oath was quite clear, Mara."

"No clearer than mine, Aeora. I wouldn't want to be in the shoes of *anyone* who dared to undermine this Court with Summer troops on the march."

"Nor would I," Aeora said.

"Then, if you'll excuse me, I'll be about my business."

"And Wenhover and I shall be about ours." Aeora bowed slightly, enough to signal Wenhover it was time to leave. They rose in unison, leaving Mara seated at the table.

Taylor tossed and turned in her cot but never managed to get to sleep. What were all those soldiers doing in the camp? From the River of Night all the way to Kentucky, it had only been her, Mara, Dingle, and the servants and retainers: a dozen people, tops. Now, Mara's entourage had grown into a small city—a city braced for battle.

She slipped her bare feet to the ground and tiptoed to the flap that separated her bedroom from the main part of the tent. She opened the flap a sliver and peeked out. Maisie and Alva were sound asleep on their cots.

She backed into her room, careful to avoid tripping over a small brass heater that burned wood pellets and gave her room a subtly smoky aroma. Two years ago, the smoke would have probably triggered an asthma attack, but Taylor's whole being had become suffused with magic since then. She couldn't remember the last time her asthma had given her any problems.

Outside, the sounds of marching feet had finally died down for the night. But if the camp was calm, Taylor was not. She paced her room, growing more and more agitated.

She had to find out what was happening, and there was only one way she could think of to do that. She knelt at the canvas wall by the head of her bed and probed the tent's bottom with her hand. She poked and dug until she could slip her hand through and touch cold, damp grass outside.

Then she sat cross-legged on the carpeted floor.

Taylor took several long, deep breaths, repeating her true name and trying to focus on a shape she had tried to burn into her imagination: a blackbird.

She had only practiced shape-shifting late at night, when she knew everyone else was asleep. It worked about half the time. When it did, she only remained a blackbird for a few minutes before changing back. She didn't think Mara knew she had learned that particular trick, and she wanted to keep it that way.

I am Neunhirri, she told herself. *Laughter in Winter.*

She imagined the bird floating above her knees, imagined its every detail: the slender bill, the gleam of its pale eyes, the softness of its gray-brown feathers. Which was apparently the color of female blackbirds. Go figure.

Breathe in. Breathe out.

She marveled at how easy Danny Underhill made shape-shifting look.

Breathe in. Breathe out.

Here goes.

And then she was a blackbird. She hopped out of the pajamas that had fallen in a heap where she'd been sitting. So far, she'd only managed to take her clothes with her once while shape-shifting, and that was deep in the Wonder where magic was much easier to access.

Her inability to repeat the trick frustrated her. She couldn't very well escape the camp and survive outside without something to shield her from the cold.

Then again, she didn't dare try anything fishy with Layla back at home ready to do who-knows-what to her parents and her friends if she got out of line.

But maybe at least she could find out what was going on. She hopped to the gap in the tent and squirmed her way out. The cold breeze ruffled her feathers. Hopefully, she wouldn't be outside long.

She took flight and darted around the camp, taking it all in. The cooking fires she'd noted earlier (from the air, she counted five of them) had all but died out. No one was around. The guards in front of Mara's tent flap leaned on their weapons and fought to stay awake.

Taylor decided that she hadn't been imagining it earlier: the place had really taken on the appearance of a military encampment. In addition to her tent and Mara's and a smaller set-up for Dingle and his guards, at least thirty two-person tents had been erected on an adjacent field. Three larger tents festooned with colored banners dotted the boundary of the smaller ones. Taylor guessed they were the officers' quarters.

Further on, the dark towers of Cair Cullen rose into the starless sky. Seeing it, she dropped from the sky and landed on a tree branch, where she stared at those towers for several minutes.

Even the thought of Crom Cornstack's domain sent shivers down her spine. It was where she was born, where she'd been torn from her mother's arms to be abandoned hundreds of miles away in a Topside hospital, seemingly with no hope of ever even knowing who or what she was. Her birth mother had spent fourteen years locked away somewhere in that rath, mourning the death of her husband and longing to be reunited with her child.

Taylor flew off in disgust. She sped back toward Mara's tent. If there were anything to learn, she would learn it there. As she flew in close, she spotted movement at the entrance: a dark, looming shape with a mane of white-blonde hair that flicked in the breeze like an unholy silver flame.

It was Crom. He was dressed as she remembered from the River of Night, in a blood-red cloak with white fur trim. He held something in his massive hand: a smallish object wrapped in black cloth. The guards, nearly asleep standing up just a few minutes ago, stood crisply at attention as the Primus of the Winter Court spoke to them.

"Look sharp, men," Crom was saying.

"Yes, Primus."

Taylor's claws would have been useless on the bare canvas, but the corded black and silver trim around the edge gave her a perfect perch. She gingerly crept toward the tent flap as Crom went inside.

"I was right," he grumbled. "The Summers know about Tobarty. They've destroyed the desk." Taylor strained to listen. Apparently, Danny had done his job. Her tiny heart pounded with a mixture of relief at the pooka's success and anxiety for what might happen next.

"Then we can expect them to respond," Mara said. "Impulsively."

Crom chuckled. "It's the only way they know."

Taylor shivered, this time from the cold.

"I trust this won't affect your plans for the girl," Crom continued.

"Why should it?" Mara said. "I expect the Summers will provide me the perfect cover. I see you've brought it."

"I've done as much with it as I could," Crom said. "It's a tricky piece of magic. It needs your gentle touch."

"That won't be a problem," Mara said. "I can have it ready by morning."

The tent flap opened. Taylor hopped backward, and Crom glanced out at the rows of tents. It didn't seem like her grandfather to pace, but that was apparently what he'd been doing.

He turned back inside. "I expect the Summers will soon find the artifact at Tobarty was the least of their troubles."

"Is the vessel still working?" Mara said. Taylor perked her ears. Vessel?

"Perfectly. Even if the desk is destroyed, the vessel is filled to the brim. It will be ready." Taylor could almost hear the arrogant smirk on her grandfather's face.

There was a long silence. Taylor wondered if they were through talking. Then she heard a gentle suction sound. With a shudder, she realized her grandparents were kissing.

Gross! she thought. There were some things old people just shouldn't be allowed to do—and Crom and Mara measured their age in centuries.

She flew away, as much to get out of the cold as to avoid hearing anything more from inside the tent. She didn't feel any closer to knowing what was in store for her.

What's more, from what she'd seen of the Summer Court, Mara was right. If they had learned the Winters had pulled one over on them at Tobarty, they would retaliate—quickly and maybe not too diplomatically.

She landed beside her own tent and wriggled her way inside.

Who am I kidding? she thought. *The Summers' reaction is going to be the opposite of diplomatic!*

And that, she realized, explained the massing troops. There were more than fifty of them, maybe as many as eighty. But they were only the first of the warriors Crom was mobilizing against a Summer offensive.

Come morning, Summer troops would probably be marching toward Cair Cullen.

The Chiefdom was about to be plunged into civil war.

And Mara Hellebore was going to use the confusion to pull off whatever she had planned for Taylor.

Taylor resumed her everyday form, put on her pajamas, and lay awake in bed the rest of the night.

Chapter 5

William Haggles
with the Help

William lay under the covers in the sweatpants and Green Lantern tee shirt he'd worn all day. He had hoped to get some sleep before the magical alarms he'd set went off. Instead, he tossed and turned until past midnight.

The wind rushed through the trees outside his second-floor window. The weatherman had warned of freezing rain in Kentucky and Tennessee—nothing that would reach as far south as Macon, Georgia. It was still a cold, cloudy night, though. William was glad to be inside, warm and dry.

At 12:30, he slipped out of bed, put on his tennis shoes, and tiptoed down the hall to Jill's room. She opened the door before his third knock. She was also fully dressed.

"Is it time?" she whispered.

"Maybe. I'm not sure," William said. He shrugged. "I couldn't sleep."

"Me neither. Wait downstairs?"

William nodded, and the twins crept down the stairs. Jill went straight to the living room. William took a detour to the kitchen to fix himself a cup of tea. He heated a University of Georgia mug full of water in the microwave, then stirred in a spoonful of dried berries. He stirred the mixture until the water turned rosy red, then added a generous squirt of honey.

Then he turned off the light in the kitchen and joined his sister in the living room. Above the front door was the horse-shoe he'd hung over a year ago at his grandmother's instruction.

It wouldn't stop a fae who really wanted in. Maymay said it was more like a No Trespassing sign, a declaration that these Topsiders knew their rights and weren't going to be walked all over.

There were four horseshoes in the house: over the front and back doors and both William's and Jill's bedrooms. They were all tied to the house's threshold, the magical barrier that even non-magical mortals could generate when their house became a home. The horseshoes couldn't keep anything out, but the threshold could bar the way to anyone—or anything—that hadn't been invited. On top of that, Maymay had added some additional protections to guarantee her kids and grandkids were safe from the Good Neighbors.

Those protections were still in place, but William's parents had tweaked them a few days ago when they agreed to accept food and housekeeping services from some of Silas Bludgitt's friends. William still couldn't believe his parents had said yes. Then again, maybe he could. William had disappeared into the Wonder after some of Taylor's many supernatural enemies attacked in a nearby park. Not long after that, Jill left with Danny Underhill to go find him.

He couldn't imagine what all that felt like for his parents. The church grim's offer of support must have broken the ice. It finally gave his mom a reason to think positively about the magical world he and Jill had become a part of.

Jill took her seat on the couch. William paced back and forth in the dark, looking out the front window.

"Are you sure they're coming?" Jill whispered.

"Mom left them cookies and milk on the back porch," William said. He considered his mug and frowned. "They'll be here."

He sat on the footstool, facing his sister. Having finally built up his resolve, he choked down a swig of tea. The bitter taste made his body shudder.

"Is that stuff really that bad?" Jill said.

"Not really," William coughed. "The honey helps." Maymay had told him that rowan berry tea would enhance his Second

Sight. He drank a little bit whenever he could. If he had to deal with the Fair Folk tonight, he wanted every advantage. Plus, the berries were supposed to be poisonous to the fae. If worse came to worst, maybe he could splash some in their faces.

He only wished he could be sure he wasn't wasting his time.

"Jill," William said, "are you sure about all this?" This was a lot of work for a false alarm, but Jill insisted something was up with Taylor. He studied his sister's troubled expression. "There could still be another explanation."

He waited for the eruption. Who was he to question his sister's intuitions? But it didn't come. That didn't mean Jill was less than 100 percent certain about the situation.

"You didn't have any doubts earlier," she said defensively. "How long have Taylor and I been best friends?"

"A long time. But you told me yourself, your Second Sight—"

"I know," Jill said. "She's not using glamour. But I know what I feel. I can't explain it, but that's not Taylor."

Jill was a lot better at Second Sight than William was. She was so good the images could be overwhelming. She usually avoided using her ability to see the true nature of things. Rowan berry tea was off-limits to her, to William's consternation. The last thing she needed was anything that would crank her Second Sight any higher.

But that was also why William took it so seriously when she'd used her ability on her best friend.

Taylor had brought dessert over that afternoon. Mrs. Smart's pumpkin pie had been a Thanksgiving tradition in the Matthews house for three or four years now. She made a bunch of them and sent them to all her closest friends.

Sure, Taylor had seemed aloof. Did that really mean anything? But what first set off Jill's alarms was that she had called ahead to make sure it was okay for her to come over—as if she ever had to ask permission before! And as soon as she dropped off the pie, she barely said hello before excusing herself to run back home.

William had chalked it up to Taylor having a lot on her mind. William knew he did: the last few days had been as intense an experience as he'd ever had in his life. And Taylor was right beside him for almost all of it.

But Jill had thought there was more to it. Later, after dinner and during halftime of the last of the Thanksgiving day football games, she had coaxed him down to the basement to talk privately.

There, she laid out her suspicions: Taylor might not be Taylor at all.

"She looks like Taylor. That's obvious," Jill conceded. "But something's not right."

"But if it's not really her...who is it?" William countered. "*What* is it?"

"How should I know?"

They sat across from each other at the card table in the basement. Maymay had taught them magic down there, and it had mostly become "their" room ever since. Between them lay William's dracontia, the magic crystal wrested from the forehead of a dragon he had stabbed Tuesday night. Apparently he'd killed the beast, though he had been too busy having a near-death experience to remember most of it.

Could Taylor really be an imposter? It didn't seem possible.

Then again, William had seen plenty of impossible things over the last couple of years. He had learned a lot of magic, at least in theory, but he didn't know of any way a Good Neighbor could impersonate someone without using glamour.

He had to admit, however, that there was still plenty of magic he didn't know. So he had to work with what he had. He scouted the room. The circle of power he and Jill had drawn and redrawn on the floor. The workbench in the corner was laden with all the magical tools and implements he and his sister had accumulated: his grandmother's blasting rod, the dozens of bottles and packets of spell ingredients, his sister's wooden scrying bowl...

Of course. "Let's try something," he said. "Stay right there."

He strode to the workbench and picked up Jill's scrying bowl. "Okay," he said. "First things first." He ducked into the laundry room to fill the bowl with water, then set it down in front of his sister at the table.

He returned to the workbench and found a little beeswax sculpture, a rough representation of Taylor with her name carved into the side. Inside it was a tooth that Taylor had lost two years ago: an unexpected gift from Danny Underhill when Jill needed to track Taylor a few days back.

He sat back down and gestured toward the bowl. "See if you can find Taylor."

"That tooth might not have much juice left," she said. She shivered. "These kinds of things have an expiration date."

"Just try."

"I'm not sure, William."

Jill could do twice as much magic as William, but she didn't always have confidence in herself. "Didn't you tell me you once got a vision of Taylor when you two got separated in Louisiana?" he said. "And that was a long time before Danny brought you that tooth."

"But she was only like fifty yards away!" Jill protested. "Now she could be anywhere. She might not even be in the Topside world."

William grinned. "That's the beauty of it," he said. "Think about it: The Smarts' house is probably fifty yards away, give or take. If that girl over there is Taylor, then you shouldn't have any trouble finding her."

Jill's eyes lit up as she realized what William was getting at. "But if she's not..."

"If she's not, then not getting a vision of Taylor probably means you're right."

Jill nodded agreement. She peered into the bowl for several long, silent minutes. She grabbed the beeswax sculpture and passed it over the water.

"Just take your time," William said.

Jill nodded to him and took a long, measured breath. Clutching the figurine to her chest, she stared some more.

She sat silently, peering into the bowl, for a solid minute.

"Anything?" William said.

More silent staring. William began to believe Jill had been right all along.

She looked up with an expression of weariness and concern. "I can't find her," she said at last.

William's stomach turned into a big ball of lead. "Then... whoever is over across the street...."

"It's not Taylor," Jill said, shaking her head. "No matter what she looks like."

And that was when they hatched a plan. Mom and Dad had explained about the faery housekeepers; maybe they could help. But it was one in the morning, and there was still no sign of them.

"I don't think they're coming," Jill said.

"They're coming," William said. "Just be patient."

Jill was about to say more, but William held up a hand to shush her. The back door creaked open. He could hear whispered conversation, but the speakers talked too softly to be understood.

William stood back up. For a second, he wished he'd brought his staff with him or even his Pawpaw's gold ring—any kind of magical tool in case the brownies didn't appreciate being discovered. But it was too late for that. He crept to the entryway with Jill right behind him. He ducked his head to the left, toward the kitchen. Holding out his hands in a gesture of surrender, he stepped around the corner.

Even in the dark, William could see the little person's eyes flashing panic. She squeaked and took two steps backward, nearly bowling over her partner.

William put his finger to his lips and shushed like his life depended on it.

"Don't be afraid," Jill whispered. "We live here."

The woman conjured a warm, orange ball of faery fire that gave enough light for everyone to see clearly.

She stood a little over three feet tall, clothed in a simple homespun dress and apron with a kerchief to tie back her curly, black hair. It made her pointed ears seem even bigger than they were. Behind her, the man wasn't much taller, also in work clothes. He hefted a wooden toolbox packed with dust rags, furniture polish, and other cleaning supplies.

"You ain't supposed to see us," the woman hissed. Her round face flushed. "It's against the rules!"

"And I'm sorry about that," William said. "It won't happen again—but it's kind of an emergency."

"Emergency!" she said, louder than William would have liked. He shushed her again. He'd rather not wake up Mom and Dad.

The woman lowered her voice but set her hands on her hips and glared at William and his sister. "What kind of emergency calls for sneaking up on honest, hardworking brownies? You just about gave me and Ocky a heart attack!"

"We're really sorry," William said. "Just hear us out, okay?"

She glanced back at Ocky. He nodded warily. "Make it quick," he said. "We still got two more houses to clean."

"Thank you," Jill said. She nudged William when he didn't speak up.

A second later, he took the hint. "We think something has happened to our friend Taylor," he said.

"Taylor Smart?" the woman said. "That's the Gentry kid, ain't it? Across the street?"

"We just came from there," Ocky said. "She was asleep in her room. Ain't that right, Fern?"

William bit his lip. If there was anything to Jill's suspicions, then someone had gone to a lot of trouble to plant an imposter in the Smart house—and he had no idea why. It might not be wise to tell these little folk everything he suspected.

"Well...we're not sure what's going on," he said. "We were hoping some of her friends knew something."

"We're looking for three little folk," Jill said. "They hang around here sometimes."

"Wasko, Haggler, and Pete?" Ocky said. "I know 'em."

"Do you...do you think you could get them a message?" William said. "We'd really appreciate it."

Fern sniffed. "Depends on your definition of 'appreciate.'"

Right. The Fair Folk traded in gifts and favors. It must have been in their DNA. But William was ready. He reached into his pocket and pulled out a tiny stoppered vial. It glowed with dim, silvery light.

"Would a vial of moonbeams be enough appreciation?"

William had carefully divided the moonbeams, which Maymay left behind when she went back to New Orleans last summer, into two containers. He didn't know everything they could do, but they'd surely be enough payment for delivering one simple message.

Fern took the vial and held it up to her face. She extinguished her orb of faery fire to see it clearly by its own light.

"This come from a full moon?" she said.

"That's what the original label said," William said. "I copied it over exactly, see?"

She turned the vial on its side to read the label William had stuck on it.

"New Orleans, huh?"

"That's right," William said.

Fern frowned. "Says here these are nearly two years old."

"All we want is for you to pass on a message," William said.

"There's some pumpkin pie in the fridge," Jill added hopefully. "You're welcome to help yourself."

Fern stood silently, considering the offer and staring at the vial.

At last, Ocky spoke up. "Wasko and the boys are in town. I reckon we could send word you're trying to find 'em."

"That would be great!" Jill whispered. "Thanks!"

"You gonna drop the wards around your house so they can get in?" Fern asked.

"No!" William blurted. Given the circumstances, he didn't want to create any more loopholes that might let something through that didn't belong. It was bad enough their mom had given the fake Taylor permission to come inside when she called about the pie. "We'll meet them tomorrow. Say about noon?" He turned to Jill. "That'll give us time to work things out with Mom and Dad."

Jill gave him a skeptical look. *You think it'll be* that *easy?*

"Where you want to meet, then?" Fern said.

He thought about the mushroom ring behind the Smarts' house, but he didn't like being that close to whoever was pretending to be Taylor. In the end, there was really only one choice.

"Oak Hill Baptist Church," William said. "It's just a few miles north of here on Gray Highway."

"I know the place," Ocky said. "Silas Bludgitt's hangout."

"Good idea," Jill said. She patted William's shoulder.

"We'll get out of your hair now," William said. He glanced at Jill, who nodded back to him.

"Thanks again for doing this," Jill said.

"Thanks for the moonbeams," Fern answered. "And the pie."

William tiptoed up the stairs with his sister on his heels. Wasko and the boys were bound to know something. And if they didn't, maybe Silas would.

Either way, he and Jill had to do something. Somebody had kidnapped Taylor, and that didn't spell good news for anybody.

Chapter 6

The Magic Mirror

Taylor must have eventually fallen asleep, because she woke up feeling miserable. It was still dark outside, which didn't surprise her. She was usually up by five or six o'clock. Something about her fae nature made her most energized around dawn and dusk.

From the sounds outside her tent, she wasn't unique. The troops she'd seen last night were marching about. Officers were shouting orders. Occasionally, there was the sound of wood striking wood, the whoosh of canvas falling softly to the ground. The army was breaking camp.

She wondered if she'd be going with them...wherever they were headed.

No, she decided. If they were already breaking camp, that meant they'd had breakfast even earlier. But she was still in her pajamas. Maisie and Alva would have awakened her if she was supposed to get moving that early.

She splashed water in her face at a washbasin in her room. After brushing her teeth and combing her hair, she dressed in some of the clothes she'd acquired on her journey northward: jeans, tennis shoes, and a black, long-sleeved Imagine Dragons tee shirt.

Halfway through getting dressed, she began to smell bacon frying in the outer tent. Maisie and Alva were up, then. Taylor decided to join them before they called her to breakfast.

They were hard at work. Maisie was frying bacon and scrambling eggs at the stove while Alva was setting the table with fine linens and porcelain china. Like the day before, it was a table for one; the servants would eat their breakfast after Taylor had finished hers.

"Good morning, Miss Hellebore," Alva said as Taylor entered the room. "Did you sleep well?"

"Morning," Taylor said. She ignored Alva's question, though. Her own questions were more pressing.

"It sounds like the army's moving out," she continued.

"Oh?" Maisie said, noncommittally.

"Do you know where they're going?"

Maisie turned back to the stove top. "Milk or orange juice?"

So they weren't in a mood to talk. Mara had a way of damping people's moods. Taylor accepted the challenge. "Coffee," she said. "And plenty of sugar." She stepped toward her seat. Alva pulled her chair out for her before she could do it for herself.

"As you wish, Miss Hellebore," Maisie said.

She gathered magic and breathed a little bit of presence into her next words—not enough to overwhelm her servants, just to make them agreeable. "I guess soldiers are always passing through Cair Cullen?"

"You might say that," Alva said. She poured Taylor's coffee while her sister plated eggs, bacon, and toast.

"Routine patrols? That kind of thing?"

"Apple butter for your toast?" Maisie said as she set Taylor's breakfast in front of her.

"Thanks," Taylor grumped. Maisie and Alva weren't cooperating. She ramped up her presence. "It's just that I've never seen an army on the march before. It's all very interesting."

"It ain't as exciting as it looks," Maisie said.

Alva nodded knowingly. "Our brother Dermit is part of a cateran over in Tobarshamn."

"What's a cateran?"

"Irregular troops," Maisie explained. "Little folk and trolls and woodwoses and such. Not a war band like—" She slapped a hand over her mouth. Taylor tried not to smile. Just a little more presence...

"Those guys outside are a war band? Sídhe warriors?"

52

"Please forgive my sister, Miss Hellebore," Alva said with a sidewise glance at Maisie. "She talks too much."

She doesn't say nearly enough! Taylor thought.

But she had heard of war bands. Gwenllian Birdsong had once said that Taylor's dad, Aulberic Redmane, might have been the leader of a war band by now if he were still alive. She had made it sound like a great honor.

Taylor started to say she didn't mean to pry, but couldn't get the words out. Prying was exactly what she meant to do! Her tongue wouldn't cooperate to form the polite lie, so she settled for, "I'm just trying to understand. If Mara wants a favor from me, I need to be up on all this, right?"

"Not necessarily," Alva said.

"And at any rate," Maisie said, "such questions are best answered by the Chief Matron herself."

Taylor didn't respond. This wasn't the first time she'd seen her grandparents' employees shake off her power of presence. People who couldn't do that probably didn't last long at the Winter Court.

Even so, she was frustrated at being kept in the dark. A Winter Court war band was on the move to parts unknown. For all she knew, there were others as well, maneuvering for position in whatever chess game Crom and Mara were playing.

The one thing she knew for sure was that Crom's gambit with the enchanted desk at Tobarty had been discovered. She shuddered to think that Danny might be in trouble, but that was only the tip of the iceberg. She guessed Belas Wakefire was steaming mad about Crom pulling one over on him. A sídhe nobleman would never let that kind of insult to his honor slide. Once more she imagined the Summer Court's response. For every Winter war band or cateran on the march, she bet there was a Summer counterpart out there somewhere, demanding satisfaction.

"Hey there!" a familiar voice growled from the other side of the tent flap. Bledrus Dingle had arrived.

Alva padded to the flap and cracked it open. "Can I help you, Captain?"

"The girl is to come with me as soon as she's ready," he said. "Mrs. Hellebore says it's time for her to get to work."

"She's just set down for breakfast," Alva said.

"Make it quick," Dingle said. "We're on a schedule."

Alva closed the flap and approached Taylor at the table. Before she could say anything, Taylor said, "I heard."

She had lost her appetite, but she choked down her breakfast anyway.

Dingle stood silently outside the tent until Taylor was ready to go. She deliberately took her time, just so she could listen to him huff and grumble. When she finished thoroughly chewing her last bite of toast, she reclaimed her black leather jacket from the bedroom, said goodbye to Maisie and Alva, and stepped outside.

The rain had finally let up, and the sun was beginning to rise. As Taylor suspected, her new neighbors had been busy. The city of tents had been packed up, leaving a bare clearing. Only the doused cooking fires gave evidence that a war band had camped there last night. Her tent, Mara's, and Dingle's remained.

"What's on the schedule for today?" Taylor asked. "More shoplifting?"

Dingle scoffed but kept his eyes forward and said nothing.

Mara's tent was only a few feet away from Taylor's. The guards at the entrance gave Dingle a crisp salute and parted so he and Taylor could go inside.

Mara Hellebore sat in a padded wicker chair beside a small desk near the back of the room. She wore a floor-length dress of purple and silver, with an ornate silver pendant around her neck. Her own servants, a little person and a tall, blonde elfin woman, were cleaning the breakfast dishes, packing them into a huge trunk as they went.

Her grandmother was heading out, then. That probably meant Taylor would be moving on as well.

"Good morning," Mara said. Her lips drew back into an icy smile.

"Your goon here isn't telling me anything. I take it we're leaving?"

"My 'goon,' as you call him, has served the Winter Court faithfully for over two hundred years and has been captain of the Primus's guard since before your deathling grandparents were born. I will thank you to extend to him the respect that service has earned."

Taylor sensed frost forming at her feet. She turned to Dingle and gave him a slight bow. "How rude of me. I'm sure when it comes to breaking things and bullying people who are smaller than you, you're at the top of your field. My apologies."

Dingle puffed up his chest like he missed Taylor's insult entirely. He nodded back and said, "No offense taken, Miss Hellebore."

"I still don't know what we're doing today," Taylor said.

"For my part, I shall be returning to Cair Cullen," Mara said. "I'm leaving you in Captain Dingle's capable hands."

Clutches, more like. But Taylor kept that thought to herself. If Mara was sending her off with Dingle, then things had changed. Had she finally seen enough of what Taylor could do?

"Does that mean I've passed your little tests?"

"Impressively."

"Oh, joy. Do I get a gold star on my report card?"

Mara sighed. "Must you always be so flippant?"

"Yes, actually. So, what's the plan?"

Mara crossed her legs and shook her head. "Your mother always had an attitude," she muttered. Taylor fought not to grin.

"As soon as some of Captain Dingle's associates arrive, you'll be moving on."

"Moving on? Where to?"

"Patience, Selena." The Chief Matron rose from her chair and strolled toward Taylor.

Taylor wondered about that name, "Selena." It was the name her mother gave her as a baby, but the Hellebores were better than most Fair Folk about using her Topside name. That made sense: they'd disowned Taylor's mother, so why would they claim any connection to Taylor herself?

Lately, though, it seemed they had started calling her by her fae name. That made Taylor nervous.

Taylor looked up into her grandmother's dark eyes and said, "I'm not sure how I'm supposed to repay the favor I owe you if I don't know what you want me to do."

"And I'm not sure I can trust you to fulfill your oath once you learn what I demand."

That made Taylor's heart skip a beat. She'd known from the start that this favor—whatever it was—wouldn't be easy or pleasant. And Mara had had a year and a half to work out the details.

"I'm not an oathbreaker," Taylor said.

Mara considered that. She walked in a lazy circle around Taylor, sizing her up from every angle. "Then you at least have some sense," she said. "Perhaps the fate of the former Chief Matron of the Summer Court was instructive in that regard?"

"Just call her by name. Anya Redmane." She was Taylor's other grandmother, the mother of Taylor's father, whom Crom Cornstack murdered for eloping with his daughter.

"We do not speak the names of oathbreakers," Mara said. Her eyes flashed pure hatred. "We leave them to fade."

Anya had broken an oath long before Taylor was born. She'd hidden away her other son, Lorcan, rather than letting him be sacrificed to satisfy the Fair Folk's twisted concept of honor. But that had only become known two summers ago. Since then, she'd been stripped of her position and hounded by the Wild Hunt. Maybe worst of all, she had indeed begun to fade.

The Fair Folk could be killed, but they didn't die of disease or old age. If they got old enough, though, they could grow tired of their bodily existence. When that happened, they faded.

Taylor didn't fully understand what that meant. She only knew that the last time she'd met Anya, she was a pale reflection of her former self: older, frailer, less powerful and imposing.

Then she put something together she hadn't before.

"Anya's husband faded." Taylor tried to work out the chronology, but Mara beat her to it.

"I told you we do not mention the names of oathbreakers!" Mara snapped. Composing herself, she continued. "But yes. Vergosus Bright discovered his wife's deception forty years ago. Crom and I tend to think it was the last straw for him."

Taylor shuddered. Could a broken oath really result in the demise of an innocent fae?

"For all his faults—and trust me, they were many," Mara continued, "Vergosus was an honorable man. Trapped between his duty to his Court and to his wife…fading must have seemed like the only option."

"I see."

"What you need to understand is that breaking a solemn oath has consequences." Mara leaned into her. Taylor took a half step back, then regretted it. She should have stood her ground.

"We Gentry folk are among the most powerful of fae," she continued. "Our words shape reality to our whim."

"Full of yourself much?"

Mara glared. She set her hands on her hips and took a step toward Taylor. "Tell me, Selena." She grinned savagely, a cat ready to pounce. "Have you ever kissed a boy?"

"*What?* What does that have to do with anything?" Her face reddened as she clenched her fists.

"Well, have you?"

"N—" the word caught in her throat, and her pulse pounded in her temples. She took a breath, grit her teeth, and answered, "No." She'd kissed William Matthews just a few days ago, and almost immediately realized it was a mistake. As soon as she told the lie, though, something wrenched in the pit of her stomach. "It's complicated."

Now Mara smiled openly. She was having fun torturing her rebellious granddaughter.

"If you haven't learned already," Mara continued, "you soon will, that even speaking an untruth can create small disturbances in the Wonder." She paused, no doubt for dramatic effect. "The Wonder tends to fight back."

"So tell me, Selena," Mara continued. "Is there a boy you'd like to kiss?"

Thoughts of Jared McCaughey niggled their way unbidden into the back of her mind. She shoved them down. Her classmate had no defenses against her powers of glamour. A casual word in the heat of the moment had once turned him into a fawning, lovesick puppy. Taylor had vowed never to let anything like that happen again.

It was past time to change the subject. "Is this your plan?" Taylor spat. "Are you going to embarrass me to death?"

Mara rolled her eyes derisively. "I only wish to remind you that a fae's words have consequences."

"I already know that," Taylor said, defensively. "I'm not stupid."

"And yet you do such stupid things," Mara said. She shook her head. "I know I've said it before, but I just don't think you're as smart as everybody says you are."

Taylor bristled.

"But if you understand about the power of words, you know that breaking an oath violates the connection between you and the Wonder. Have you ever heard the story of the Gentryman and the Ogre?"

Taylor remembered the tale from a story book Shanna had given her. A Gentryman swore a foolish oath to an ogre and then faded on the spot when he was forced to break it. She gulped.

"I see from your expression that you have." Mara paced back to her seat. "I will admit the story is somewhat exaggerated," she said. She took her seat and bore into Taylor with an expression of pure evil. "A morality tale for impressionable children."

She leaned back and folded her arms across her chest. "I expect you to honor your oath. Are we clear?"

Taylor stood, mouth open. Sweat trickled down her neck. Her stomach was suddenly full of lead.

"Selena, are we clear?"

In fact, the idea of breaking an oath revolted Taylor—even an oath she had every reason to break. Something about the way her faery brain was wired made it sound like the worst thing she could possibly do. Worse than stealing clothes or food with imaginary money. Worse, maybe, than killing somebody.

"Crystal," Taylor said.

"Then sit with me for a while." Mara gestured to another chair, not as big or ornate as her own. "Soon, Captain Dingle's associates will be here. And then, you're going to take a little field trip."

Captain Dingle appeared at the tent flap. "Chief Matron, the cateran from Ledoga is here." He didn't look enthused by this development. Then again, he rarely looked anything but disgusted with life in general.

"Have them gather on the green," Mara said. "I'll attend to them shortly."

"As you wish, Ma'am," Dingle said. He gave Taylor a glare. Then he bit his lip and slouched away.

Mara rose from her wicker throne and glided toward her private chamber, leaving Taylor alone in the outer portion of the tent. Taylor sat still, wondering what to do. There was no way she could escape, and she wasn't invited to join her grandmother. Apparently, she was supposed to sit still until... something happened.

On the other side of the partition, Mara began to chant a slow, melodious song. It wasn't English—or any language Taylor recognized. It seemed like an ancient tongue, perhaps nothing ever heard on human earth. The incantation rang through the tent, not loudly but firmly, with a subtle pressure of magical energies being brought to bear.

Taylor tried to sense what was happening. She didn't feel any magic directed toward her, only the ripples of whatever Mara was doing in her inner chamber.

Along with the sound of Mara's chanting came a gentle rumbling that Taylor felt more than heard. It reminded her of distant thunder, though the sky had begun to clear. She looked around, saw no indication that Mara's servants might be returning, and quietly stood up.

She crept to the entrance to the inner chamber and slowly pulled open the flap by a hair. Mara stood before a small table. Taylor could see her in profile, her eyes gleaming with intense concentration. She held her hands in front of her, palms down, focusing magic on something on the table: a small hand mirror rimmed with twisted brass knot work. It had to be what Crom had brought her the night before. But what was it for?

The mirror shimmered. It might have shaken, but that could have been Taylor's imagination. She jumped back, afraid the movement—if it was movement—would alert Mara to her presence.

But the Chief Matron continued to chant, seemingly oblivious to Taylor spying on her. The magic continued to build. Taylor drew back the tent flap once more. She found herself holding her breath, waiting for something to happen. Surely the mirror was going to explode, or fly around the room, or turn into a purple platypus at any second!

But nothing happened. After another minute, the magic in the room began to subside—though the mirror itself continued to shimmer. Mara picked it up by its handle and ran her long, pale fingers over its rim.

She glanced in Taylor's direction. Taylor gasped and ran back to her seat. A second later, Mara rejoined her in the outer chamber. Rather than being upset, she wore a wry smile.

"Does this trinket interest you?"

Taylor looked at the floor. "I didn't mean to..."

"Of course, you did," Mara said. "I don't blame you, it's an impressive piece of magic. The Primus acquired it from the Holly King of New Avalon."

"I see."

"I suppose you're curious about what I'm going to require of you." She stood in front of Taylor. Her fingers continued to play against the edge of the mirror.

Taylor looked up, meeting her grandmother's icy gaze. Her heart raced. Her mouth grew suddenly dry.

"It's quite simple, really. Well within your proven capabilities."

"Y-yes?"

"I simply want you to deliver this." She raised the mirror for Taylor's consideration.

It was obvious there was a catch. But at the moment, Taylor couldn't guess what it might be.

"W-where to?"

Mara smiled. "In due time. Come with me." She swept off toward the outer tent flap. She passed through, leaving Taylor to open the door for herself.

Outside, a group of Fair Folk had gathered. They were some of the ugliest, evilest creatures she had ever seen. There were about twenty of them. Taylor could identify the ugly features and short stature of three spriggans. An impish-looking fae with light brown skin and wooly, cinnamon-colored hair was bound to be part pisgy. He was dressed all in green and he scraped underneath his fingernails with his dagger.

The two tallest members of the group brushed seven feet. They had huge noses, watery yellow eyes, and knobby bumps all over their skin. Taylor guessed they were trolls—though they didn't seem affected by the sunlight, unlike the other trolls she'd had the misfortune of running into.

There were also half a dozen women who kept to themselves. They all had blonde hair, pointed ears, and eyes that gleamed with malice. They carried bows and sported quivers of arrows at the waist.

Rounding out the group were three fae and three little folk. One of the fae was a short, stocky man with black hair and glowing yellow eyes that reminded Taylor of Danny Underhill. He stood next to a taller, skinnier Native American fae who played with a tiny fireball he made to weave between his fingers. The pooka—he had to be a pooka—said something to his neighbor and then let out a high-pitched, cackling laugh.

The last of the fae was another redhead with a bushy beard and a finger missing from his left hand. He shot a glance at the pooka, who quickly shut up.

Finally, there were three little folk: two Native Americans and one white guy who was taller than the others. This last was a bearded old man dressed in a shabby red coat and matching flat cap, black trousers, and a pair of brand-new boots that looked way too expensive for the rest of his outfit.

All but the women carried firearms: mostly shotguns and trumpet-barreled blunderbusses. In addition, most of the band wore hand-to-hand weapons at their belts: short swords or daggers.

As soon as Mara emerged from her tent, Dingle bellowed for his charges to stand at attention. They complied after a fashion, and without haste. Dingle fired his own blunderbuss into the air to hurry them up.

"Look alive!" he bellowed.

The band only snapped to order when they noticed Mara approaching. Then they couldn't form ranks soon enough.

Dingle bowed curtly as the Chief Matron drew near. Taylor kept her distance as best she could.

"This is the Ledoga cateran?" Mara said. She arched an eyebrow. Taylor couldn't blame her: they looked like a pretty unsavory crew.

"As you say, ma'am. They call themselves the Red Fangs."

Mara frowned. "Of course they do. I take it they've been thoroughly briefed?"

"Aye!" the bearded redhead snarled. His self-confident swagger marked him as the leader. "And we ain't sure we like what the spriggan's told us." Others murmured agreement. The leader eyed the mirror in Mara's hand.

Mara cast a glance at Dingle.

"That's Lunso Butcher, ma'am," Dingle said under his breath.

"I see," Mara said, turning directly to face the leader. She studied the rounded tops of his ears. "The terms of our agreement are simple enough, Mr. Butcher. One mission, in exchange for which your various obligations to the Winter Court will be considered settled. Once your service is concluded, those of you who are still alive will be free to go. That I have sworn by my own true name."

"But that mirror," the leader said. He shuddered as he gave the object another look.

"*Do you have misgivings, Mr. Butcher? Doubts about my competence?*" Mara was a good three or four inches taller than him. She leaned over him, making the most of her height advantage. Taylor could tell she was applying presence as well.

"I-it ain't exactly that, ma'am." His eyes widened. He took a half-step backward.

"Good."

"I-it's just... If anything went wrong. Me and my gang..."

"*Nothing will go wrong,*" Mara said, "*if you and your troops will simply follow orders.*"

Mara's glamour was working on the whole gang. They stared at her in rapt attention. The two Native American little folk hugged each other. A troll and two of the women fanned themselves to keep from fainting.

"*Do you have any further questions?*"

"N-no, ma'am," Butcher said.

The Chief Matron addressed the entire band. "*If any of you still have reservations, kindly inform me now.*"

No one said a thing.

Mara looked each member of the Red Fangs in the eye. She spread her hands and said, "Do you swear to complete this mission to the best of your abilities?"

She waited. At last, Butcher spoke up. "We swear." He swallowed. "Don't we, guys?"

The others nodded and muttered.

Mara set the mirror face-up on the ground. "Then gather around."

"All right," Butcher grumbled. "Team one, team two. Front and center."

The trolls, the women, the fire guy, the two Native American little folk, and one of the spriggans huddled close and stretched out their arms to each other. Their expressions revealed their nerves.

The others backed away, and so did Dingle. Taylor decided that was a good idea and did the same.

Mara raised her hands over the gathered criminals and began to chant, presumably in the same ancient language she had used before in her tent.

A troll cursed. One of the women shut her eyes tight and drew her neighbor close.

Magical energy swirled. To Taylor it felt like a massive sub-woofer that you felt as much as you heard, only there was nothing to hear but agitated murmers from every member of Lunso Butcher's team one and team two.

Taylor tottered to one side as she momentarily lost her balance. There was a sudden WHOOMP as the air pressure shifted. Then the designated members of Butcher's band vanished, sucked into the mirror.

Butcher gasped.

Dingle swore.

Taylor sucked in a breath. Her eyes darted between Dingle and Mara.

Steam or fog rose from the mirror's face. The air gave off the subtle smell of ozone.

The Chief Matron stooped and retrieved the object. Taylor stood on tiptoes to look at the glass. As she expected—or maybe feared—terrified faces stared out of it: the spriggan, two or three archer women, and the little folk, with the others pushing and shoving in the background.

Butcher swallowed. "And that's it, then?"

Mara ignored him and handed the mirror to Dingle. "Wrap it well, Captain. We don't want it to break."

"No, ma'am."

At last, Mara turned to Butcher. The rest of his team stood behind him: the pisgy, the two spriggans, the pooka—whose eyes blazed with amber fire—and the old, red-clad little person. "You will escort Miss Hellebore and see to her safety. Captain Dingle will accompany you as far as the border."

Dingle nodded, still shaken by what had just happened.

Mara then addressed Taylor. "I've instructed Maisie and Alva to pack you a light traveling bag. Fetch it now so that you may on your way."

Taylor didn't know what to say.

It was too much to take in: her grandmother was sending her to deliver that mirror to somebody. Which meant she was sending her to smuggle a band of murderous criminals to somebody.

Who might it be? An ally in need of support? Somebody the Winter Court couldn't back openly?

More likely an enemy the Winters had in their sights.

Either way, it put a lump of cold lead in Taylor's stomach. Thoughts of her unsavory "escort" didn't help matters. Butcher gave her the creeps, and that wild-eyed pooka looked like he might explode at any second.

"This way," Dingle said.

Taylor drifted after him in a daze, leaving a trail of frosty footprints in the grass.

Chapter 7

On the Road

Jill woke up in a pristine house. Ocky and Fern had dusted, swept, run the vacuum (how did that not wake everybody up?), folded the laundry and stacked it on top of the dryer, and even set a fresh bowl of potpourri on the coffee table in the living room.

It took most of the morning for Jill and William to explain things to their parents as they sat at the kitchen table after breakfast. Jill insisted on doing most of the talking. She allowed her Second Sight to open just enough to get a clear sense of all the emotions swirling through the room as she explained her fears about Taylor.

"What do you mean, 'in trouble'?" Her mom asked. Her anxiety spiked right away, bathing her in a roiling blood-red aura. She almost looked on fire to Jill's supernatural perception. The dismal, gray hole in her middle churned with displeasure. It was a psychic wound Mrs. Matthews didn't even know she had—the remains of a tragic episode that happened when she was just a toddler.

"We're not sure," Jill said. She didn't want to tell the whole story. If her parents had to interact with the fake Taylor anymore before all this got sorted out, she didn't want them freaking out and spilling the beans.

"We know somebody who can help," William added. "I think you might have met him. Silas Bludgitt?"

Mention of Silas's name seemed to calm things down. Mom's aura settled into a ruddy glow. Their parents had met Silas while

Jill and William were sailing down the River of Night. He was the one who had arranged for the cleaning crew and even sent a pretty tasty casserole as a show of kindness.

Jill's parents asked a ton of questions, and Jill and William tried to answer them as honestly as they could. "Have you talked to Taylor about this?" I don't think she's free to say anything—and if you see her again, you probably shouldn't bring it up. "Are she or her parents in any danger?" Maybe.

Finally, Mom asked the one question Jill and her brother both knew was coming. "How are *you* going to stay safe?" Her aura surged. Jill chose her words carefully.

"I wish I could promise that nothing bad will happen," she said. "But something bad has already happened. Taylor...she's like a sister to me.... Mom, you'd never forgive yourself if something ever happened to Aunt Odette, something that maybe you could have stopped."

"We can do things," William said. "Things other people can't. And like they say, with great power comes..."

"What I was going to say," Jill interrupted, "is, 'To him who knows to do good and does not do it—'"

"To him it is sin," her mom finished the Bible verse. Her aura shifted from angry red to bright magenta. Feelings of love and pride blended with fear and resentment.

"Maymay taught us what to do," William said. "So far, everything she showed us has worked just like she said."

"So, what are you telling us?" Dad said. "What are you wanting to do?"

"We want to go talk to some folks who might be able to help." Jill said. "Silas and some others like him."

Dad exhaled a long, deep breath. "I suppose you'll need a ride?"

Hopefully, Wasko, Pete, and Haggler would know something helpful. If they didn't—and William grimaced at the thought—another field trip might be in the works. Nobody said that out loud, but everybody was aware of the possibility.

For now, Dad was okay with that...at least in theory. And surprisingly, Mom was coming around. Jill had been smart to appeal to her sense of moral obligation. Maybe it was dawning on Mom that Jill and William's gift could be just that: a gift they could use to do some good.

Even so, William didn't want to make a big deal of it. He and Jill just had a job to do, and they were the only ones around who could do it. So he gathered some supplies from the basement and both of them got in his dad's Toyota before their parents changed their minds.

They drove out of town on Gray Highway, his dad never taking his hands from ten and two o'clock, never looking anywhere but straight ahead or into a mirror.

Soon, densely packed city buildings gave way to more open country with scattered buildings: a church, a garden center, a real estate business, a gas station. After ten minutes, Mr. Matthews turned onto a county road, drove another half mile, and pulled into the parking lot at Oak Hill Baptist Church.

Jill was riding shotgun and said, "This shouldn't take long."

William collected his staff and his backpack full of supplies. He was the first to open the door and get out. Jill followed close behind. Dad didn't cut off the engine.

William scanned the trees across the street. "What's that?" he whispered, leveling his staff.

"Where?"

He frowned. "Never mind. Just a squirrel in that tree over there."

Jill squinted. "That's got to be a hundred yards away. You're imagining things."

"I guess," William said. "So where to?"

Jill looked around, probably scanning the area with her Second Sight. "Let's try the graveyard."

They walked away from the church building, away from where their dad sat waiting for them, into the old cemetery grounds.

"This is where Taylor and I came before," Jill explained.

"It looks so...normal."

"Maybe to you." She studied the arrangement of gravestones like there might be a hidden pattern in them. Whatever she saw, it prompted her to point toward the back of the property and start walking that way.

All of a sudden, William's ears popped and his head got fuzzy. He stretched out his arms to keep his balance. When he was sure he wouldn't stumble, he took a look around and took note of how things were now different. The graves were still there, the old wooden church still stood in the distance, its steeple piercing the sky. But there were lots of subtle changes. The sky was no longer a wintery bluish gray. It had acquired greenish highlights to make it a dull turquoise. The trees at the edge of the church property seemed to stretch upward at odd angles, contributing to William's sense of dizziness. There was a sweetness in the air, a subtle blend of aromas barely perceptible unless he shut his eyes and focused on them.

"That's it?" he said. "It's that easy?"

"Taylor talks about swirling lights," Jill said, her voice trembling. "I've never seen them. But you feel it, right?"

"Yeah," he said. "We're in the Wonder all right." He glanced at his sister. Her face had gone listless, like she might pass out. "You feeling okay? Jill?"

"Huh?" she said. She shook herself awake.

"Just take deep breaths," William said. Something about being in the Wonder always did a number on Jill. Maybe like an addict getting the slightest taste of the poison that could kill them. He didn't like the idea of Jill being here. But with any luck, they'd be heading home soon.

The church building was still there in the Wonder. The twins headed toward it, eyes open for anything unusual.

But where was everybody? It was twelve o'clock; Wasko and the others should have been there.

William was about to say something when Jill stumbled forward. She'd tripped over a cord stretched low to the ground between two gravestones and set half a dozen cowbells jangling.

She jumped back up, but the cord had wrapped itself loosely around her legs. It wasn't so much binding her as clinging to her. With every move, the cowbells continued to clank. They moved on their own, bouncing over the grass and clanging with no one rattling them.

"What the—?"

That's when the dogs bounded into view. There were two of them: redtick coonhounds, mostly white but with splotches of orangey rust. They were barking like crazy, but William could only hear the faintest whisper of it—and the closer they came, the quieter they got. Soon, William couldn't hear them at all.

He dropped into a crouch and prepared to beat them off with his staff.

Jill saw what was happening and said, "Bro, it's okay."

A second later, a harsh voice rang out. "Goodness! Mercy!" A gray-skinned little person appeared at the edge of the graveyard, skittering toward them. He wore dark trousers, suspenders, and a white dress shirt with the sleeves rolled up. Despite the chilly weather, he wasn't wearing shoes. "Back off, you mangy beasts!" he growled.

The dogs came up short. They circled around Jill and William, tails wagging, silently barking their heads off. Jill backed away, still clunking and clanging.

"Jill!" a second voice called. "William!" There was another flutter of movement behind the first little person. Three more scrambled to join him. The first was a brown-skinned man with a turkey feather in his bowler hat. It was he who had called their names. Following him were a husky, bat-eared guy, the tallest of them all at about three foot six, and a slender albino with wooly silver hair.

"Silas!" Jill called, recognition in her eyes. "Guys!"

"Let me get that tripwire," the albino said. He snapped his fingers, and the cord dropped lifelessly to the ground. The cowbells fell silent.

"Haggler," William said. He remembered him and his buddies, Wasko and Pete, from when they'd met a few weeks ago. "It's good to see you—all of you."

"You too, kid," Wasko said, pushing back his bowler. He wiped his hand on his shabby jacket and offered it to William.

William shook his hand while nodding toward the string of cowbells. "What's that all about?"

"Just a precaution," Haggler said.

Wasko nodded. "Word is, there's been some kind of trouble up north. It don't hurt to be ready."

"And the cowbells?" William said.

Silas chuckled. "The Gentry hates 'em," he said. "Not as much as a big ol' church bell—" he gestured toward Oak Hill's bell tower "—but they'll still do the trick in a pinch."

"It's the vibrations," Haggler explained. "Messes with their magic. I set them out in case there was any trouble. They're not much more than a distraction, but sometimes that's all you need. At least they'll give Mr. Bludgitt time to get to the bell tower."

"I remember," Jill said. She looked at her brother. "Taylor nearly passed out the last time."

"What's this I hear about Miss Hellebore being in trouble?" Wasko said.

"She's disappeared," Jill said. "We're afraid somebody took her."

Wasko, Haggler, and Pete's mouths dropped open. "Oh, Brother Mike," Pete said. "That ain't good."

Silas scowled. "It's what I've been telling you," he said. "Something's going down. I don't know what, but I don't like it."

"Maybe we ought to go inside," Haggler said. He looked up at Jill and William. "We need to hear what you have to say."

Silas led everybody to the church and opened a tiny doorway hidden in the wooden molding. Haggler re-set his tripwire and came down last of all. Everyone slipped inside and inched down a narrow stairway into a homey one-room apartment with hardwood floors and a Ben Franklin stove in the corner.

By the time Haggler entered, everyone had already pulled chairs from the kitchen table to sit in a circle around the couch. The dogs lounged on the floor in front of the stove.

William and Jill walked them through the events of the past few days, how they'd emerged from the Wonder near Darien, down on the coast, how Taylor had gotten them back to Macon via ring-travel, and how Jill couldn't shake the feeling that the girl they'd come home with wasn't really her best friend.

"But I Saw her," she said, frustrated. "It's not an illusion. It just...isn't Taylor."

"Probably a face-shifter," Haggler said.

"Makes sense," Silas agreed.

"A face-shifter?" William said. The name pretty much gave it away, but he had to ask. "You mean, like a shape-shifter?"

Silas grunted. "Shape-shifters mostly do animals. Face-shifters do people. With a little bit of blood or hair to make a connection, they can be a perfect match for whoever they're trying to impersonate."

William blew out a breath. "And you can't detect them with Second Sight?"

"It ain't a glamour trick," Haggler explained. "The form they take is a hundred percent real—even though it's temporary."

"Who would be able to do something like that?" Jill asked.

"Most Fair Folk could probably learn how," Wasko jumped in. "But not many do."

"Why not?"

Wasko shrugged. "Too much trouble," he said. "It's a whole lot easier just to wear a husk—a glamour trick, like Haggler said."

"But Jill can see through glamour tricks," William said. "Me too, sometimes." He wasn't liking the conclusion he was coming to. "It looks like whoever it was that took Taylor knew about us."

"That's got to be the worst thing I've heard today," Jill said.

"Uh huh," William said.

Pete scratched his head. "It sounds like she's in trouble."

"Right," Wasko said. His eyes darted from Jill to William. "And you've got no idea where she could be?"

Jill pulled her wax effigy of Taylor from her purse. "I tried to use this. It's got one of Taylor's teeth in it." She slumped backward. "It's just too old."

They sat in the circle, not looking at each other.

"She was always so nice to us," Pete said.

"Can we not talk about her in the past tense?" Jill snapped.

Pete hung his head, apologetic.

"There's got to be something we can do," Haggler said.

"We're open to suggestions," William said.

"Hm," Silas said. "Can I see that?" He pointed to Jill's effigy. She handed it over. "Goodness. Mercy," he called. The dogs leaped up and padded over to where he stood in the middle of the circle.

"No offense to your powers, Jill, but if there's anything of Taylor's in this thing, my dogs can smell it."

William watched, his eyes wide. The dogs sniffed the little statue. They wagged their tails. Then one of them, the female with a face and back of mostly red, let out a silent bark. The other joined in a second later.

"Are they really smelling Taylor from a two-year-old tooth?" William said. He fought the grin off his face.

"Kid, these are *cwn annwn*, the hounds of the Underworld. There's nothing they can't find." He patted Goodness's back and commanded, "Go get her!" Now everybody was on their feet. The dogs barreled out of the apartment, up the stairs, and down a narrow passageway before bursting out onto a second-floor hall decorated with bulletin boards and paintings of Bible scenes. They scrambled to an open door five feet away, still barking wildly, but William couldn't hear a thing.

"This is Taylor's Sunday school class," Jill said. She had visited with Taylor a few times through the years when Oak

74

Hill had special events. The dogs had entered the room and had taken up positions on either side of a lime-green sofa.

"That's where she usually sits," Silas said. "And she hasn't been to Sunday school in about a month." He called his dogs to him and scratched them both behind the ears. "Good job, you two. I might keep you around after all."

"Silas," William said. "If your dogs could sniff around at the last place we know Taylor—I mean the real Taylor—was with us…"

"They shouldn't have any problems tracking where she went."

"Awesome," Jill said. "When can we leave?"

William broke out in a cold sweat. "You can't go," he said at once. As soon as he did, he flinched. He knew the storm was coming.

"Excuse me?" Jill said, clenching her fists. "Was there an election I didn't know about that made you the boss?"

William wondered if Taylor had been secretly giving his sister death-glare lessons. But he wasn't about to back down. "Jill, think about it. Too much time in the Wonder…it's not good for you. You know that."

"I'll take my chances. Taylor—"

"And don't forget: there's a fake Taylor on the loose. Taylor's folks could be in danger." He looked his sister in the eye. "*Our* folks could be in danger."

Jill sighed. She gritted her teeth and stood her ground. "I do *not* like the idea of you going off by yourself."

Wasko piped up. "Don't you worry about that none! Me and the boys'll go with him. Won't we, guys?"

Haggler and Pete nodded. Pete said, "We're used to living on the road. We'll take good care of him."

"Silas?" Jill said.

The church grim frowned. "I don't like the idea of a Topside kid tramping around in the Wonder…. But I don't like the idea of Taylor being in trouble, either." He looked up at William. "Take Mercy. She's the best tracker." Goodness hung his head as if he understood the slight. "I'm staying here with Goodness. We're almost a month into the Winter Assize. It wouldn't be smart for me to leave my post right now."

"I understand," William said. "We'll take good care of Mercy, won't we, guys?"

William and Jill returned Topside long enough to explain things to their Dad. Mr. Matthews gave him a firm hug but didn't put up too much of a fight. When Jill hugged him, though, William almost lost it.

"How do we keep in contact?" Jill said. "Your phone got trashed."

He broke off the hug and wiped his cheeks. His phone had gotten soaked in the River of Night. Then again, there were no cell towers in the Wonder anyway.

"Do you have a mirror in your purse?"

"Yeah."

He pulled his own scuffed, brown compact from his backpack along with a Swiss army knife. He unfolded the main blade and used it to carefully pry the mirror loose. Then he folded that blade away and found a smaller one, more like an X-acto knife. He gritted his teeth and poked his thumb. A tiny bubble of blood rose on the skin, and he smeared it on the back of the mirror.

"Now you," he said, handing Jill the knife.

Her mouth dropped open. "You can't be serious."

"We need a strong relic," William said. "I don't like working with blood, but it's the strongest connection we've got."

Jill grimaced but poked her own thumb and then let her droplet of blood fall onto the back of William's mirror, merging with his own.

He took Jill's mirror and rubbed the two together, back to back, chanting a simple incantation. "*Semea. Semea. Chiiii.*"

Jill joined in. William could feel her far more impressive magical power ramping up the spell. They repeated the incantation over and over, eyes on the two mirrors but also watching each other out of the corners of their eyes.

William could feel the swirl of magic in the air, but he and Jill kept chanting, kept imbuing their essence into the mirrors. He felt something tug at his chest, a magical connection suddenly springing into being. Jill must have felt it too. In unison they shouted, "*Eseshopi!*"

On the final syllable, a wave of vertigo overwhelmed William. Both siblings staggered backward. Jill ended up holding both mirrors. She pulled them apart and returned William's

"These should work like Taylor's Seeing Stone," William said. "If we did it right."

"We did it right. Now go before I change my mind and keep you here."

"You got it," William said. He waved one last time at his dad, then approached to give him a firm handclasp. Mr. Matthews patted him on the shoulder. William was fairly sure his dad's barrel chest stuck out a little more than usual.

He turned around and walked toward Silas's secret doorway. He was about to enter the Wonder in search of his kidnapped friend. Jill would have to take care of things at home without him, and he'd have to survive the Wonder without her. Memories of his last trip blurred together in his mind: deer women, ape men, tie snakes—freaking *dragons*, for crying out loud! And above them all, the somber, brooding face of Taylor's grandfather, Crom Cornstack....

He shook himself alert. He couldn't let himself worry about everything that might go wrong, and he didn't have time to make a list anyway.

He kept telling himself that he had done this before. Sure, he almost died...but he didn't. He came out on top. And with three little folk and a magic bloodhound at his side, he could do it again.

Chapter 8

The Drum Dancer

Carl's Catfish House was mostly empty. The normal lunch crowd was probably at home eating turkey sandwiches or other Thanksgiving leftovers. The only people in sight were Sandra, the waitress; the regulars, Kenny and Darryl, arguing politics in their usual table by the window; and an unassuming man in a corner booth. He had dark brown skin and wavy black hair. He could have been in his forties, but still full of youthful vigor. He was dressed in khakis and a plain white button-down shirt.

Moe Fountain slid into the seat across the table from him. He had a drum at his side: a traditional Native American instrument with a single drumstick resting on top. Of course, the man had glamoured it to look like a briefcase.

"Oronyatekha," Moe said with a subtle bow. "You're taller, I see. Close to six feet, I imagine. Good of you to try to fit in."

"Five-ten," Oronyatekha said. "A lot more room for fried catfish than my usual size." He patted his stomach.

"The height suits you." Moe studied his guest and wondered what his presence might mean. "It's been a while."

"And that's a shame." Oronyatekha tapped the laminated sheet of paper that served as a menu. "You can't get this stuff up north."

"It's the seasoning," Moe said. "Carl's is famous around here."

Oronyatekha folded his hands on the table. "The fish itself is excellent, as I remember. Is it local?"

"That's right," Moe said.

79

"My compliments." Oronyatekha took a sip of his sweet tea.

Sandra arrived to take their order. When she left once more, Moe watched her go, making sure she was out of earshot. He lowered his voice. "I hope you don't plan on doing any drumming while you're here. The Topsiders get antsy about sights and sounds they can't explain. An ogre took a wrong turn around Ridgeville about eight, ten years ago, and folks are still talking about a 'Bigfoot sighting.'"

"The last thing I want to do is make trouble for you, Moe. You know that."

"Then, if I may be so bold," Moe leaned in. His slit-pupil eyes flashed. "Why are you here? And don't tell me Carl's catfish is the whole story."

Oronyatekha returned Moe's stare. "Deep Council business."

That was no surprise, of course—although Moe didn't like the implications. Relations had been worsening between the Nunnehi Lands and the Chiefdom of Arradherry for years. The nunnehi had been amassing troops across the border from Tobarty as if they expected an invasion any day now.

But Tobarty was nearly three hundred miles away. Something else was going on.

"Then shouldn't you be on the border?" Moe said. "At Danuwayi...or perhaps Tobarty?"

Oronyatekha chuckled. "I wish I could tell you," he said. "Or more to the point, I wish you were privy to Deep Council matters."

"Alas, I am not."

"I'm serious," Oronyatekha continued. "Your nomination has never been formally rescinded. I could—"

Moe leaned back. "I've told you before, old friend, I don't get involved in politics."

"And I—" Oronyatekha stopped when the waitress brought Moe a cup of coffee. When she left, he said, "And I don't share Council secrets."

"I would never ask you to," Moe said. "Though I'm sure you understand I'm protective of everyone who lives in my domain.

If I were to get blindsided by something..." Moe allowed his presence to rumble. "*I would hate to find out you might have prevented it.*"

"Your domain has nothing to fear, *old friend.*" The Drum Dancer seemed only slightly discomfited by Moe's display. "Though I might be forgiven if I questioned your total commitment to it. A seat on the Deep Council—"

"Would be a distraction and an aggravation," Moe said. "You know I don't like to leave my valley. I'm bound to the land, and the land is bound to me. If I were to take off chasing the four winds, the plants and the animals would pay for it. And then where would you go for catfish?"

Sandra brought two plates of Carl's specialty along with fries and hushpuppies. Moe thanked her and asked for a bottle of hot sauce.

"So there's nothing you can tell me?" Moe said.

Oronyatekha thought for a moment as he squirted ketchup on his plate. "There are certain factors I can't quite account for," he said. "Certain elements that don't add up to anything that makes sense."

"That's what brings you to Grubb, South Carolina?"

"This delicious catfish brings me to Grubb, South Carolina." He forked a bite into his mouth.

"So you just happened to be in the neighborhood?"

Oronyatekha shrugged. Moe pondered where the Drum Dancer might have come from. Some place further south, like the River of Night? Or maybe Ichisi to the west? How could either figure into a Deep Council investigation?

"I'll figure it out soon enough," the Drum Dancer said.

"Of that I've no doubt."

"If you get word of anything...out of the ordinary..."

"I'll be sure to let you know."

"I'm glad to see you're willing to cooperate." Oronyatekha's pained expression belied his jovial tone. Something was definitely afoot.

"Stay safe, old friend," Moe said. "The Deep Council needs you."

"I will," the Drum Dancer said. "I'll get to the bottom of this. And when I do," he grinned, "you may rest assured I'll never breathe a word of it to you."

"I wouldn't respect you if you did," Moe said.

"I'm glad we understand each other." He gestured with his fork. "But no more shop talk today. I want to enjoy this excellent lunch. My treat, by the way."

"Much obliged," Moe said. "We really need to do this more often."

Chapter 9

Unexpected Reunions

"Mr. Underhill," a woman's voice said.

Danny opened his eyes. Thick forest-green drapes held the sun's glare at bay. He sat up in bed, still wearing the clothes he'd had on the night before.

"I would like to speak with you as soon as possible," the woman said. She stood at the door, almost but not entirely respecting Danny's privacy. She was tall and blonde, obviously well-born by the commanding way she carried herself. And Danny recognized her.

"Gimme just a minute, Mrs. Birdsong," Danny said.

The newest member of the Summer Triad pulled the door closed behind her. Danny threw his legs over the side of the bed and eased himself up, his back creaking. Last night had taken a toll on his muscles. He padded across the room to splash water in his face at a brass washbasin.

What do they want now?

The Teyrnus had drilled him and Claudia with questions half the night. In the Primus's guest suite, he explained how he had been clued in to the quickened artifact at Tobarty, and Claudia shared her earlier suspicions that something like that was afoot. She also reminded the Teyrnus that the mahogany desk had been in place since before the Summer Court took over the rath. It was, in fact, the only piece of furniture left over from the Winter Teyrnus that wasn't unnervingly grotesque.

Aemeron Wakefire seethed at a slow burn as Danny and Claudia spoke. Belas Wakefire sat and listened and only occasionally interjected a question of his own. Both men's eyes brightened as the conversation progressed. Their minds, it seemed, were clearing—but this only made them angrier as they pieced together how the Winter Court had been undermining them.

"This cannot be countenanced!" Aemeron hissed.

"Nor shall it," Belas spat. He slammed his fist on his own desk. "I shall muster my most trusted war bands immediately."

With that, Danny and Claudia had been ushered from the room. Claudia left for Bisgarra Verry right away—Dubessa Fairchild would need a full report on the night's activities—but she left Danny the key to an apartment at Tobarty that the Teyrnus reserved for visiting Summer officials.

He had slept fitfully the entire morning until Gwenllian Birdsong woke him up. The mantel clock said it was a bit past noon.

He brushed his teeth, ran his fingers through his thick, curly hair, and slipped on his moccasins. As promised, Mrs. Birdsong was waiting for him in the living room.

"Have a seat, Mr. Underhill," she said. She had taken a high-backed chair near an open window looking out over the lower city and the gray-green mountains beyond. That left Danny with the couch, where he would have to look almost into the sun to speak with the Matron.

"Claudia said I could use the apartment, Mrs. Birdsong. I'll be sure and straighten everything up before—"

"We have brownies for that, Mr. Underhill. Giving you a place to stay is the least we can do after you helped uncover the Winter Court's plot."

That was a relief, but Danny still felt nervous. What more could he tell the Summers than he already had?

"You seem to have come out relatively uninjured," Mrs. Birdsong said.

"Just a little sore, ma'am" Danny said, squinting in the sunlight. "I've had worse."

84

"I see." The Matron nonchalantly examined her fingernails. "My husband the Teyrnus tells me you were quite helpful last night—or should I say this morning? Your information, though distressing, explains much about what has been happening at Tobarty."

"Glad I could help, ma'am."

"There is one more question I would like to ask you. Then, I expect we can send you on your way."

"Ma'am?"

She sat upright, suddenly demanding Danny's full attention. "Not long ago, Claudia Fountain negotiated your release from my husband. Something about a spontaneous explosion of vegetables in the town market?"

"Y-yes, ma'am?"

"He says she traded a very costly vial of dragon's blood for your freedom. She said it was vital to the Summer Court's purposes that you be let go."

A swarm of butterflies blinked into Danny's gut. Claudia had indeed traded the dragon's blood for his release, but it wasn't for Summer Court business. She needed him to get word to the nunnehi about the mess in Tobarty.

Danny shaded his eyes with his hand. "Well, she's the assistant to the Chief Matron. I reckon she keeps all kinds of magical ingredients and whatnot."

"The dragon's blood isn't the issue," Mrs. Birdsong said. "As you say, Claudia travels with a selection of such substances. She is free to use them as she sees fit in the course of her duties. The issue, however, is that neither I nor the Chief Matron have any knowledge of this supposed business for which Claudia needed you."

And Danny really wanted to keep it that way!

"Why did Claudia require your services, Mr. Underhill?"

Because she's a nunnehi spy and she needed to get a message to headquarters. "Well, Mrs. Birdsong," Danny stalled, "if you don't mind my saying, having a shape-shifter around can be pretty handy...".

"That isn't what I meant," Mrs. Birdsong said. Her tone was sharp but not angry. Accusatory, but not beyond reason. "I'm asking about the task to which Miss Fountain recruited you. What, precisely, did she need you to do?"

"Oh!" Danny said. "You mean the task!" He paused to gather his thoughts. He had to keep Claudia from getting in trouble.

"Yes, Mr. Underhill, the task," Mrs. Birdsong said again.

Danny gulped. "Well, you see...," he began, "Claudia suspected something was up at Tobarty."

"Yes?"

"So...she sent me to investigate." As soon as the lie left his mouth, Danny felt a quantum of magic siphoning away. The butterflies in his gut started tickling his insides, but he tried not to show it.

"She needed to work with somebody outside the Summer Court." That much, at least, was true. "I could go places she couldn't, you see?" That was also true, but it didn't keep a trickle of sweat from finding its way down the pooka's neck.

"And that was why Claudia negotiated your freedom," Mrs. Birdsong said. "So you could help her investigate the issue at Tobarty."

Danny braced himself. "That's right." He looked at the floor, shielding his eyes from the sun, to cover for the twinge of pain his face no doubt betrayed. Even more magic drained out of him. He'd lied to the Matron twice now. He couldn't do it three times.

"And this investigation led you to the River of Night?"

That was a tricky one. It was on the River of Night that he and Taylor figured out about the quickened desk, but Jill Matthews got him there, not Claudia.

Mrs. Birdsong's eyes bored into him. He felt the power of her presence washing over him. Then she sat back and smiled.

"I'll be frank with you, Mr. Underhill," the Matron said. "The Chief Matron has had reservations about Claudia from the start. There are things in her file that don't entirely add up."

Danny gulped.

"You wouldn't lie to me, would you, Mr. Underhill?"

"Mrs. Birdsong, ma'am" he said, his throat dry, "if you don't mind my saying, I've had a rough couple of days. Is there anything else you wanted to ask me about?"

"I'm simply trying to find clarity about why you were traveling the River of Night. Do I understand correctly that you were acting as an operative of the Summer Court? There is no other reason Miss Fountain may have contracted your services?

Danny kept his eyes on the floor, and only partly because of the glare from the window.

"Mr. Underhill?"

He cleared his throat. He couldn't tell her the truth. It would expose Claudia. She could be tried for treason!

"I...uh..."

"Yes?"

He took a deep breath. "That's right, Mrs. Birdsong," he said. "I'm proud to have been of service." The butterflies drew red-hot knives and started slashing at Danny's insides. He felt lightheaded. Nauseated.

By oak, ash and thorn, what have I done?

"I believe that will be all," Mrs. Birdsong said. "I expected the matter would be cleared up easily enough."

Danny's shirt was damp with sweat and his stomach writhed in anguish.

"Mr. Underhill?"

With difficulty, Danny looked her in the eye. He flashed her what he hoped was a cocky smile. "I'm pretty much the best at what I do." He set his hands on his knees.

The Matron regarded him for several seconds before saying, "So I hear."

Danny let go of the breath he'd been holding. "If you need me again, C-Claudia knows how to find me."

The Matron rose to her feet and gave Danny a subtle nod. "Thank you for your time, Mr. Underhill. Good day." She glided silently to the door.

As soon as she shut it behind her, Danny collapsed in his chair. His head swam, and his stomach felt like he'd caught about a dozen flaming nunnehi arrows.

He didn't cry out, though. For all he knew, Mrs. Birdsong could be listening at the door. After a minute, he permitted himself to slump to the hardwood floor and pound it in agony. Danny usually had no problems telling a lie once. But three times!

He climbed to his feet, woozy and sore. He took a deep breath. He opened his right hand, palm up, and tried to summon faery fire.

It didn't come.

An hour later, Danny weaved his way through the narrow streets of Tobarty. On the green at the edge of the lower city, the city garrison was mustering. Soldiers—a collection of elves, pisgies, and spriggans led by Gentry officers—marched in formation with muskets at their shoulders.

The city folk kept their distance. Many of them still harbored sympathy for the Winter Court. But where in recent months they might have stopped to jeer or work some mischief against the Summer troops, today they thought better of it. The mood in the city had changed. The Summer soldiers displayed a clarity of thought, a sense of determination, that hadn't been there before.

Danny absorbed all these details, but he didn't dwell on them. He had more pressing concerns. *No need to panic*, he told himself. *I'll just find me some cookies, maybe a piece of carrot cake....*

An hour after his interview with Gwenllian Birdsong, his magic still hadn't returned. The best he'd been able to manage was a lackluster orb of faery fire that was barely worthy of the name.

Just got to give it time...

The houses of the lower city gave way to farmland, but Danny kept walking. A ring of standing stones at the edge of the settlement came to life with a swirl of gold and silver lights. From it emerged a ragtag band of warrior wannabes: little folk, field folk, woodwoses, and such. They were led by a loud-mouthed, blond-haired fae who brandished a rapier as he spurred them toward the city.

If the caterans were mustering too, that was bad news. With a shiver, Danny remembered what it was like seventy years ago, the last time the Summer and Winter Courts plunged Arradherry into all-out civil war. The vibe he got back in town was eerily similar.

Danny let the cateran pass before approaching the ring. He raised his hand to summon the portal to life...and nothing happened. He hung his head.

The closely-packed farmsteads nearer the city had blended into a more rural geography. At least, he thought, he was free of the city. If he was going to be weakened for the foreseeable future, he much preferred to convalesce on a farm. Surely somebody would take him in for a day or two in exchange for some honest work. It didn't take magic to chop wood, butcher hogs, or re-chink a tobacco barn.

So he kept walking. He'd already settled on a farmhouse close to the road a few hundred yards away. He planned to knock on the door and hope for the best.

When he finally got there, the farmer discouraged that plan with a warning shot from his twelve-gauge. Danny bowed away, apologizing for bothering him.

He'd about given up hope when he caught the smell of apple pie baking. He followed his nose and his rumbling stomach to a smaller farmstead at the edge of the woods. An auburn-haired fae was chopping wood out back. A woman hummed a lilting tune inside.

Here goes, he thought. He walked up to the door and gave it a rap.

A beautiful blonde fae woman swung the door open, and Danny's jaw dropped open.

"Danny?" she said, wide-eyed.

"Bryn?"

Danny had met Brynhilde Delling a few decades ago when he was in the service of the Summer Court. The huldra had even accompanied him on a couple of switch-outs—the last being the time Anya Redmane had sent him to collect Taylor Smart and bring her into the Wonder. Like all huldras, she was tall and beautiful. Her beauty had a graceful wildness to it, like a lioness or a unicorn. Even in bib overalls and a plain white tee shirt, she set Danny's heart thumping.

She twitched her cow-like tail and scanned the road behind him. "What are you doing here?"

"I...I didn't realize this was your place," he stammered. "I smelled the pie and... Bryn, I could really use a place to rest for a while."

"Of course," Bryn said. She glanced out the window toward the fae chopping wood. "It's just, we're trying to keep a low profile." She invited him in. It was a simple farmhouse, one large room with a loft, over a third of it packed with barrels and canvas sacks—provisions for winter. There was a big bed decked with colorful quilts, a dressing table, and a simple stone fireplace beneath the loft. A table and chairs, cupboard, oven, and washbasin filled the rest of the room.

"We?" Danny said. Then he put it together. He mouthed an "Oh."

"My boyfriend's had a rough time lately. We've only lived here a couple of months."

"Yeah, you might want to think about moving," Danny said.

Her green eyes flashed. "More trouble in town?"

"War bands are moving." Danny quickly explained about the Winter Court's plot to confound the Summers at Tobarty, the quickened desk and its apparent abilities to darken the minds of the Teyrnuses and their staff.

As Danny spoke, she took her pie out of the oven and set it in the window to cool. She came back to the table and regarded her houseguest in somber silence.

Danny had just finished describing last night's adventure when a young male fae entered through the back door. He was taller than Bryn and just as good-looking. He wore his flannel shirt open to the waist despite the chill outside.

"Who's your friend, chère?" he said. His accent from the bayous of New Cephalonia sounded out of place in the mountains of eastern Arradherry.

Bryn looked at the newcomer and then at Danny. She really did look worried, like she'd been caught doing something. "Look, Bryn, I understand about huldras and their gentleman-friends. I ain't gonna judge—"

"It's not that," Bryn said. "It's just that...this is sort of a delicate situation." She bit her lip.

Danny furrowed his bushy eyebrows.

Bryn took a breath. "Danny Underhill, I'd like you to meet Évastre du Marais."

Chapter 10

Taylor Asks
a Lot of Questions

Taylor, Dingle, and "team three" of the Red Fangs took short ring-jumps eastward. They remained Topside between portals, either stopping to rest or hiking from one mushroom ring or ancient ruin to the next. Danny had once told her it was harder for the Fair Folk to track people's movements when they weren't in the Wonder. Taylor wondered whom the Red Fangs were trying to evade.

The team stepped out of a pure mountain stream onto cold, damp earth. They followed a twisty footpath down the side of a mountain, hiking through what was probably still someplace in the backwoods of Kentucky. The sky remained clear, but the temperature hadn't warmed much throughout the day. Taylor didn't mind. She was already sweating from the hike.

No one wore husks to mask their appearance. Dingle and the two Red Fang spriggans trudged across human earth in all their unsightly glory. Taylor had learned that the shorter and fairer one was named Arthek while the taller—almost five-six—and darker one was Treeve. Apart from the occasional pointed ear, bulbous nose, or extremely short stature, Taylor's other traveling companions would almost pass for human—at least from a distance or in the dark.

The fact that no one tried to mask his true appearance told Taylor they wouldn't be visiting any Topsider towns along the way. If they ran into anyone in the woods, they'd get an eyeful: you don't often see a gang of faery-tale monsters hiking through the woods. Everyone carried backpacks with a few supplies. Dingle had buried the magic mirror deep in his pack.

Every so often, Dingle would make her repeat a phrase she didn't understand.

"*Ha zudeia virdiga*," he prompted.

"*Ha zudeia virdiga*," she answered. "What does that mean?"

"Do I look like I speak Esrana?"

Esrana was an ancient language of the daoine sídhe. Taylor got the impression it was kind of like Latin in her world: nobody really used it, but it made what you said sound important. Her mother had given her an Esrana true name—Neunhirri, "laughter in winter."

"It's some kind of spell, isn't it?"

Dingle grunted.

"Something to do with...my mission?"

"Do you think you could say it and pour some magic into it?" Dingle said.

"Maybe."

"Try."

So she did, whispering the phrase to herself over and over as they hiked through hills and hollers until her feet were sore.

"Slow down!" the wizened little person grumbled. He was red in the face and struggling to keep up.

"S'matter, Fergus," the pooka jibed, "legs too short to keep up?" He let out another annoying cackle of a laugh.

"I'll shorten *your* legs, you miserable puke!"

The pooka rounded on him, eyes blazing, a malicious grin spreading across his face. He summoned balls of fire in both of his hands.

Dingle's sword flashed between them. "Enough of that!" he yelled.

Just as quickly, Butcher shoved Dingle out of the way. "I'll handle this!"

Taylor backed away, instinctively gathering magic.

"I'm in command here!" Dingle said, scrambling to regain his footing. He surged up to seven feet in height. Arthek and

94

Treeve, the Red Fang spriggans, did the same, and balled their fists.

Butcher just laughed a mirthless laugh. "You ain't nothing but a babysitter."

The Red Fangs chuckled.

"That's what the lady said," the pooka crowed. "Soon as we get to the border, you're out of here."

"It's gonna be a short mission without your buddies to help," Dingle said. He hefted the strap of his backpack with his left thumb. "What d'you figure your odds are without your friends to help you?"

Butcher glowered.

Dingle turned to the pooka. He sheathed his sword, but jabbed at him with his finger. "You don't like the leprechaun, you save it till after the mission," he said, gesturing to the old, red-clad fae.

Leprechaun?

"Got it?"

The pooka nodded. "I was just teasing," he said. He let out another cackle, less enthusiastic than before. "No hard feelings, Fergus?"

"You better sleep with one eye open, Ian Shagfoal," Fergus growled.

Fantastic, Taylor thought. *My first leprechaun, and he's homicidal.*

After another murderous glare at the Red Fangs, Dingle resumed his usual size. Arthek and Treeve did the same. Taylor breathed easier, but only a little.

Dingle and Taylor led the march. The other spriggans took up the rear, with everyone else in between.

"Don't mind Shagfoal," Dingle whispered to Taylor. "A pooka ain't himself if he ain't stirring up trouble."

"Some pookas have a little more sense," she muttered. She cast a wary glance behind her. "Those guys are all criminals, right?"

Dingle nodded.

"And we trust them because...?"

"They're oath-bound to Mrs. Hellebore." Dingle chuckled. "As soon as this mission's over, I wouldn't trust 'em outside of blasting range."

"Okay," Taylor said. "That's kind of what I figured."

And that just made her even more nervous about what she had gotten herself into.

"When are you going to tell me where we're going?" She brushed away a low-hanging branch. Birds flitted through the trees.

"I ain't."

"So...I'll just recognize it when I see it?"

"Maybe."

"And we're not going straight there in one jump because...?"

"You ask a lot of questions."

"You noticed that, huh?"

Dingle sighed. "Too much magic for a long jump."

"Too much..." Then she figured it out. "All those people in the mirror, right? Their magic weighs us down—if that's the right word for it."

"Close enough," Dingle said. "More powerful portals could handle it better, get us there in a snap. But people watch them more carefully."

"And we don't want to be seen."

Dingle chuckled. "You figured that out all by yourself, did you?" They had come to a fork. At Dingle's direction, they took the path to the right with the Red Fangs following close behind.

"We need medium-sized portals," Butcher interrupted. "Big enough to bear the load, but not so big they're well-traveled. Even then, long jumps strain the system. It's better to make little jumps. Slow and steady."

"What he said," Dingle added, though he gave the leader of the Red Fangs a scowl for butting in.

"I see." But she wanted to know more. Where were they headed? And dare she hope that Bledrus Dingle was secretly on her side?

Taylor tried to put together everything she knew about him. When she and her friends had been trapped in the domain of Osaa the tie snake, the spriggan had given Jill all her magical supplies back, which they'd used to escape. And he'd dropped enough hints that they figured out about the quickened desk at Tobarty and how her grandfather was using it to undermine the Summer Court.

But he was also the captain of Crom Cornstack's palace guard! He was practically his right-hand man.

Nearly everybody else in positions of authority in Arradherry were either daoine sídhe or their cousins, the tylwyth teg. Taylor got the impression it would take a lot for a spriggan to rise through the ranks as high as Dingle had. He must have been especially loyal to Crom. He wasn't the type to knowingly help the enemy.

And yet, she couldn't help but remember his expression two summers ago in Louisiana. Mara was demanding that Jill pay the debt of honor she'd incurred. She was ripping the magic out of her—and none too gently, either. Taylor offered to pay Jill's debt for her. She could still see Dingle's mouth drop open as he realized what Taylor was doing.

Dingle might have been a loyal soldier, but Taylor wondered how much he actually liked his job.

She feared her own survival might hinge upon the answer being "not much."

She listened for bird calls. She didn't understand much of the language of birds, but she was getting better at it. Unfortunately, the local nuthatches, wrens, and cardinals were only talking about nests and worms and loud, two-legged ginseng harvesters. Taylor may have picked up a couple of wrennish swear words at that point in the conversation.

Still, maybe that could be a start. "It sounds like the birds haven't caught on yet that anything is up."

"Nope."

"Do you think they will? I mean, do Topside birds ever hear about things happening in the Wonder?"

"Sometimes."

Well, this isn't getting me anywhere, Taylor thought. "You know these woods pretty well."

Dingle grunted and shot her a wary glance.

Slow down, Taylor. She let several seconds pass before she spoke again.

"I mean, you're not even using a map."

"Maps can get stolen," the spriggan said.

"By the Summer Court?"

"Or nosy kids." He stopped long enough to turn and glare at Taylor.

Taylor opened her arms in a gesture of surrender. "Fine. No more questions." *For now.*

"Ain't it about time for lunch?" the cinnamon-haired pisgy called from behind.

"You're always ready for lunch," the pooka teased.

"Mervin's got a point," Fergus the leprechaun said. He was breathing hard. "We should stop to rest."

Dingle studied the sun's position and furrowed his brow, probably making mental calculations of some sort.

"What do you say, *Captain*?" Butcher said.

Dingle glared at the leader of the Red Fangs. "Fine."

In the shadow of a vast oak tree, everybody reached into their packs and pulled out sandwiches wrapped in brown paper.

Taylor sat next to Dingle at a distance from the Red Fangs. The pooka, Ian, was arguing with Butcher. He had been for at least half an hour.

"So what's wrong with toads?" he demanded for the seventh or eighth time.

"We can't use your tupping toads as a diversion on every tupping job, Shagfoal!"

"Lunso's plan'll work," Arthek the fair-haired spriggan chimed in. "Just give it a rest, why don't ya?"

"Use your toads on your own time," Treve added, "when I don't have to look at 'em. The tupping things are uglier than you are!"

Everybody laughed at that—everybody but the pooka.

"Fine," Shagfoal said. "We'll do it Lunso's way. It don't matter: Once we're through with this mission, Eelick and me got plans. Big plans, d'you hear?"

"The troll gonna set you up with his sister?" Mervin the pisgy jibed. Everybody laughed again, and this time the pooka cackled along with them.

The Red Fangs continued to grumble and snipe at each other, but the mood had changed. The tension had lessened, giving way to loud, crass joking. Taylor simply shook her head and tried to ignore it. At least with them occupied with something else, she had another chance to talk to Dingle instead. She had to get him to open up. What was going on? What did her favor to Mara Hellebore really mean, especially if it took such unsavory traveling companions to do it?

She hated being in the dark. As she ate her ham sandwich, she thought of another angle to try.

"Does Crom really think he can win?"

Dingle looked up from his own lunch. He furrowed his bushy brow.

"I mean, his one advantage was the enchanted desk at Tobarty. Take that away..."

Dingle chortled and coughed bread crumbs and flecks of liverwurst. "Look who's the master strategist," he said. After a moment's reflection he added, "So you heard about that, huh?"

Taylor's face reddened, but she didn't stop. She gave her words the tiniest impulse of presence—not enough to raise the spriggan's defenses, but hopefully enough to make him feel like talking. "Well, you tell me: how does he expect to beat the Summer Court if they're not preoccupied at the border?"

"You don't know what you're talking about."

"Then explain it to me. Because it sounds to me like Belas Wakefire has a perfect chance to hit back hard at the Winter Court."

Dingle chugged a drink from his canteen. "Did it never occur to you that Crom's running more than one plan?"

Yes, as a matter of fact, it did. Perhaps we could discuss that?

"I don't see how anything can top that desk. I mean, it was the perfect spy, right?"

Dingle waved off the question and took another bite of sandwich.

"Right?"

The spriggan shook his head and glanced at the Red Fangs, deep in their own conversation. He lowered his voice. "You ever been to Tobarty? You can just about spit across the border into the Nunnehi Lands. It was hard-won territory, and the nunnehi would take it back in a heartbeat if they could."

"Then why—"

"The Winter Court held Tobarty before I even came to work for Mr. Cornstack," the spriggan continued. "The Primus knew from the start he'd need to know fast if the savages got it in their heads to try anything."

Taylor bit her lip or she'd have laid into him about that "savages" remark. These were her friends he was talking about. And if he wanted to talk about savagery in the Wonder, she could tell him a few things about his boss. But she needed information, and that meant she needed to keep her cool. "So the desk was there from the start?"

"Two desks," Dingle explained. "One in Tobarty, the other in Cair Cullen: a matched set. They gave Mr. Cornstack a direct line to the Teyrnus of Tobarty."

"And when the Summer Court took over..."

"Nothing changed," Dingle whispered. "Except now Mr. Cornstack didn't send messages or instructions. He sent glamour."

"Confusion," Taylor said. She remembered Danny's description of what things were like in Tobarty. "Paranoia, fear."

"You got it."

"But...Belas Wakefire knows about the desk now. It's no good if it's been destroyed, right?"

Dingle chuckled. "Like I said, it was a part of a matched set. It didn't just receive magic."

Then what *did* it do? What was the spriggan getting at?

"You mean it took something? It stole something from the Teyrnuses?"

"Little by little," Dingle said, "not enough for anybody to notice. But after five hundred years, it adds up."

Taylor started putting the pieces together. She didn't like the shape things were taking. "You mean...the desk stole other people's magic?"

"Magic, courage, clarity of mind. All stored up in a trophy on the Primus's favorite desk."

Taylor shivered—and not from the cold. Her mind shot back to a vision she'd had on the River of Night. Crom had invaded her mind, imposed an image that the two of them were sitting in his trophy room. He was seated behind a huge mahogany desk that must have been the one Dingle was talking about. On it was a severed head preserved with a lacquered coating. That had to be the trophy Dingle was talking about.

She wanted to be sick, but she forced herself not to. Her mind reeled. She struggled to put what she was thinking into words. "But...," she said. She didn't want to think it, but she couldn't avoid the implications. "But, what can Crom do with that?"

Dingle scoffed. "What *can't* he do?"

Just then, Fergus snarled a curse at Shagfoal, who then pushed the leprechaun onto his backside.

"Settle down!" Butcher yelled. In a heartbeat, he was standing between them with a ball of roiling magical energy in each hand. Fergus was on his feet just as fast, with a bronze knife drawn. "You wanna fight, you save it for the—"

"Butcher!" Dingle sprang to his feet and grew to over eight feet tall.

The bearded leader of the Red Fangs growled at the spriggan. He turned back to his men. "Save it for the mission, d'you hear?"

"Right," Fergus said. "Assuming the puke is up to it."

Shagfoal's eyes glowed with amber fire.

"Just do your jobs," Dingle snarled. "All of you!"

The Red Fangs settled down, after a fashion. When it was clear the brawl had been averted, Dingle shrunk to his usual five and a half feet. Everyone finished lunch in silence, packed up, and moved out.

But Taylor's mind was a jumble. Crom Cornstack had been siphoning magic off of his closest lieutenants for five hundred years. And then he started doing the same to the Summer Teyr-nuses of Tobarty. He was like some kind of vampire, storing up all the magical energy he could ever need, keeping it stored inside the severed head of some ancient rival—and driving his enemies insane in the process.

And there she was, stuck in the middle of nowhere, on her way to fulfill her sworn duty to Crom's wife. She took a deep breath. She willed herself not to break down, not to collapse into a puddle of tears at the realization of just how diabolical her grandparents really were.

She had to do something—but what? There was no way she was going to violate her oath. The very thought made her sick to her stomach. She had made a promise to Mara in order to spare Jill's life. It felt like an insult to her best friend to go back on her word: like her life wasn't really worth the sacrifice.

And even if she was willing to trample on Jill's honor, she didn't dare break her oath. It would strip her of her magic when she needed it most. It might even kill her.

The Fair Folk kept their word. Like it or not, that was who she was.

She plodded along woodenly, trying to think of any way out—any glimmer of hope that she could turn her situation around.

The trail they followed opened onto a mountain spring practically bubbling with magic. Dingle raised his hand, and a vortex of lights erupted above it. He offered Taylor his hand, and the two stepped into the portal with the Red Fangs right behind them.

Chapter 11

Heading Home

Danny sat at Bryn's table, nervously trying to summon faery fire while Évastre du Marais peered out the window. Bryn sat on the edge of the bed.

The pooka hadn't heard the sound of tromping feet—a sure sign he was preoccupied with his own problems. But as soon as Évastre came inside, he drew the curtains shut. Soldiers had begun marching out of the woods. Évastre looked nervous.

"You're being paranoid," Bryn said for the third or fourth time. "You've lived here since July. The Summer Court knows where you are. Don't you think they'd have come looking for you by now if they'd wanted to?"

Évastre let go of the corner of the curtain. The heavy crunch of booted feet trailed off into the distance. He turned back to Bryn and Danny.

"I reckon you're right. Are you okay, there, bougre?"

Danny snapped to attention. "There ain't no reason to call me a bug!"

Évastre chuckled. "Bougre. It means buddy, pal. I'm sorry, I'm just trying to be friendly."

"Yeah," Danny said. "I guess I'm a little preoccupied." He stared at his hand, which produced the dimmest flicker of orange light. It only lasted a second and then it went out. "And you're really Taylor Smart's cousin?"

"I reckon so," Évastre said. "I only met her once, though." He took a seat across from Danny at the table.

"Évastre's been on the road for a while," Bryn offered.

Danny remembered the story. The boy's dad was Lorcan Redmane, who was supposed to have been put to death over seventy years ago to satisfy a debt of honor. But Mrs. Redmane had other ideas. Breaking a solemn oath, she had spirited him off to New Cephalonia instead and let a fetch take his place.

Eventually, Lorcan grew up and fell in love with a wood nymph. Évastre was Lorcan's son: a satyr not yet forty years old, though he looked closer to seventy. He had a young, impish face, upturned nose, subtly pointed ears, and tousled auburn hair. Even though he was obviously concerned, he projected firm self-assurance. He seemed to have completely skipped the gawky, self-conscious phase most fae boys go through about halfway through their first century.

"When Mrs. Fairchild found out what your grandma had done," Danny said, tentatively, "it must have been rough. I'd have made tracks, too, if I was you."

"Thankfully, the new Chief Matron chose not to pursue the matter," Bryn said. "It was enough for her to replace...Évastre's grandma. She could afford to be benevolent."

"But you've only been here since summer?" Danny gave up on the faery fire and tried something else. He formed an image in his mind: a lanky, black Labrador retriever.

"I spent the better part of a year looking for my dad," he said.

Danny screwed up his face and tried his best to pour himself into the shape of a dog, but he couldn't. *I could be a dog since I was a kid!* he thought. *What's Mrs. Birdsong done to me? What have I done to* myself?

"Are you sure you're okay?" the satyr said. "You look distracted."

"What? Sorry, I'm just...not myself right now." He looked at Évastre. "So you was looking for your dad. Did you find him?"

"I heard a rumor he was up in Windhame, but I never saw him. Last I heard, he'd had a run-in with a tribe of bow walkers."

Danny's jaw dropped. "Bow walkers? That's...really bad."

Évastre looked at the bare, wooden floor. "Yes, sir. That they are."

The room went silent for several uncomfortable moments. At last, Bryn said, "Anyway, that was where we met." She glanced at the satyr. "I grew up in Windhame. I'd gone back to visit family, and before I knew it, along came Évastre." She smiled at him.

"And she convinced me to come back south," Évastre said. "Said it was time to get on with my life. That a change of scenery would do me good."

"And I was right, wasn't I?" She grinned. Then she turned toward Danny, and her expression turned serious. "But what's happening? Why are there soldiers on the march? And what's the matter with your magic, Danny?"

Danny was afraid to offer too many details. He explained how Belas Wakefire had discovered the Winter Court had pulled one over on him by giving him Tobarty. He dodged questions about how he was involved, and kept Claudia's name out of it altogether.

When Bryn asked about the soldiers, he guessed they figured into the Primus's plan to even the score. He didn't know precisely how, but anybody could see it wasn't going to be pretty.

"Things are heating up," he said. "Just like seventy years ago."

"That was before my time," the satyr said. "But I've heard the stories."

"The stories ain't half of it," Danny said. "Living through it...." He shuddered. The Courts were going to war again. There were no two ways about it. Only this time, Claudia had a front-row seat—and him, too, if he wasn't careful.

Then he thought about his new home in Tsuwatelda. Seventy years ago, the nunnehi got drawn into it when Summer and Winter clashed. Would the same thing happen again?

One thing was sure: they needed to know what was up. Claudia, bless her, would want Chief Tewa to get a report.

"I gotta get out of here," he said. Maybe it sounded cowardly to Bryn and Évastre, but he didn't care. He had to tell Chief Tewa everything he and Claudia knew.

"Danny, something's wrong," Bryn said. "What aren't you telling us?"

He thought about his meeting with Mrs. Birdsong, how he had to lie to protect Claudia—and how it had robbed him of his magic. Surely it was just temporary! But one way or another, if anything happened to Claudia....

"I'd rather not say. That way, you can't say nothing, either."

"This is bigger than the mess with Taylor a couple years ago, isn't it? When the former Chief Matron got hold of her?"

Danny nodded. "I think so."

Bryn looked at the satyr but she spoke to Danny. "What can I do to help?"

"Bryn," Évastre started.

"Now now," she said. She and her boyfriend traded glances.

"You gotta think this through, chère."

"No." She turned to Danny. "What do you need?"

"Really, Bryn?" Danny said. "You'd help me out? I can't pay you nothing."

"Danny, hush. We used to be partners. Everything I know about switching, I learned from you."

"Bryn," Évastre said, a little more forcefully. "You don't know what he's asking. It could be dangerous." He stood up. "You can stay here as long as you need, bougre, but please don't ask us for more than that."

"You're right," Danny said, deflated. "I don't mean to burden you with my problems."

"It sounds to me like your problems kind of spill over," Bryn said.

Danny looked at her and decided to take a chance. "I...had to do some stuff. Earlier. And now I'm not really at a hundred percent."

"Yes?" Bryn encouraged.

"I could use some of that pie," he said, forcing a laugh. Just as quickly, he hung his head. "And then...I ain't sure I can open a portal home."

Bryn and Évastre looked at each other again. Évastre shrugged.

Bryn was the first to speak. "I heard you live in the Nunnehi Lands now."

"That's right."

Évastre turned his back on the conversation. "Oh, for crying out loud!"

"Évastre!" Bryn said. "Hush!"

"He's talking about crossing the border, Bryn. In case you haven't noticed, that might not be the smartest thing to try to do right now." He drew closer and stroked her arm.

"Then you can stay here," Bryn said, springing from the bed. Évastre took a step back.

"Look," Danny said, "I don't want to cause no trouble."

Bryn rounded on him. "You hush, too! You're hurt, and I'm going to help you."

"But—"

Bryn raised a finger to cut Danny off.

"Judaculla Rock is still neutral ground," Bryn said. "We'll head that way." She looked at Évastre. "I can be back in a few hours."

"I never said I wouldn't go with you, chère," Évastre said. "We just gotta be smart is all. Ain't no telling what...what my relatives could be up to."

Bryn slipped into Évastre's arms and whispered, "I know." They traded some more words, but Danny worked hard not to overhear them, and even more so when they started kissing.

He sighed and wondered where Claudia was. At Dubessa Fairchild's side, no doubt. Maybe that meant she'd be some-place safe when the fighting started.

He tried once more to conjure faery fire. This time, he got a good, bright yellow ball that lasted about five seconds before flickering out. It wasn't much, but it was better than he'd managed all day.

"D'you folks think I could have some of that pie now?" he said.

As it turned out, Bryn wasn't that great a baker. Her apple pie was a little burnt and kind of dry. It was also way too sweet, but Danny hoped that would work to his advantage. He ate the slice Bryn had cut for him, and then agreed to seconds.

The sun was low in the sky by the time he, Bryn, and Évastre left the farmhouse and headed into the woods. The soldiers they'd seen earlier had come from that direction, and Bryn explained there was a ring of standing stones in a nearby clearing. It stood in the center of a manicured clearing.

The guards had heard them coming. A dozen soldiers—mostly pisgies and other, lesser kindreds—leveled their muskets at them as soon as they came into view.

The pooka, the huldra, and the satyr stopped and raised their hands.

One of the guards, a blonde woman in a green tunic, approached. By her fair skin, upturned nose, and pointed ears, Danny took her for an ellyll, a kind of forest sprite that sometimes fell in with the Summer Court. She leveled a javelin at them; her musket was slung over her shoulder.

"State your business," she said.

Danny tried to work out what version of the truth would get them the least dead. He was about to say something, when Bryn beat him to it.

"Andred?" she said. "Andred Thornberry? It's been ages!"

The guard warily sized up Bryn. She didn't seem especially pleased to meet them. "Brynhilde?"

"Brynhilde Delling. You remember! We met at Dulauny about fifteen years ago, at Luey Heath's installation ceremony. You were in Mrs. Fairchild's honor guard."

"And you were being a bit too friendly with Bacary Lalo," Andred said.

"Bacary...," Bryn mused. "I remember him! He was pretty cute—Oh!" She blushed. Évastre gave her a sidewise glance. "Was he...I mean, were you...?"

"We were—and still are, no thanks to you."

Bryn cringed. "I wish I had known. I mean, it's not like I'm a deer woman out to steal somebody else's guy."

"No," Andred said. "You're not." The message in her tone was clear: *And don't even think about trying.*

"Well, water under the bridge, I guess," Bryn said. She leaned a little closer to Évastre. "We were just on our way to our friend Danny's place." She nodded toward the pooka.

"I gotta get back before my boss has my hide," he added. He tried to look desperate and put-upon—which wasn't much of a stretch.

"Your boss?"

"I'm behind on my fall chores," he explained. "I still got a lot of wood to chop, and the tobacco barn's in pretty bad shape, and then—"

"I don't need to hear your entire schedule, Mister...?"

Danny's heart picked up its pace. What would this woman do if she knew who he was? "Yeah, you're right," he said. "It's pretty obvious you've got some important work to do. Don't let us bother you."

Andred looked at each one of them in turn, weighing her options. Danny tried to look as innocent and unthreatening as possible. Évastre gave her a disarming smile. If Bryn had anything else to say, she thankfully kept it to herself.

"Make it quick," Andred said at last.

"You bet," Évastre said. Andred signaled to her team to let them pass. Évastre turned to Danny and Bryn. "Let's go."

Bryn gestured, calling the portal to life in a maelstrom of gold and silver sparkles. "How do we want to do this?"

"You two just supply the power," Danny said. "I'll nudge us in the right direction." Bryn and Évastre each grabbed one of Danny's arms above the elbow. He was shaking in spite of himself, but he stepped up to the portal.

"Ready?" he said.

"Ready," Bryn and Évastre answered, and the three of them stepped into the chaos.

Chapter 12

The Wal-Mart Incident

William thought ring travel was bad enough with Taylor. He didn't know it would be ten times worse holding on to the leash of a faery dog in full bloodhound mode. It had gotten even worse once Mercy picked up Taylor's scent in Darien. Then they hurtled yet again through a vortex of flashing lights and disorienting visions of woodland springs, standing stones, and dilapidated cemeteries. Mercy dragged all of them through the swirls and currents of the Wonder at breakneck speed.

They landed on a hillside underneath a turquoise sky. The grass was damp with recent rain. White clouds zipped by overhead.

Mercy strained at her leash. She sniffed the ground and growled and pulled William forward, over the hill and into a patch of flat land surrounded by trees.

She looked up at William and barked. Of course, he didn't hear anything. At a distance, though, he understood she sounded like she was right behind you.

He turned to Wasko. "How far does her bark carry?"

"A hundred yards, maybe two hundred. It'll taper off pretty quick after that."

William wondered how many monsters might be hiding within a two-hundred-yard radius.

"Looks like somebody camped here recently," Haggler said. "There's trampled grass all over, see?"

Wasko pointed to a small, blackened heap near the center of cleared-off circle. "And there's where they built a fire."

So they must have been on the right track. At the same time, it wasn't entirely good news. It looked like a lot of people could have camped there, and as far as William knew, Taylor didn't even know how to build a fire.

"Who do you figure she's with?"

"Could be anybody," Wasko said.

That's what made William nervous. Wherever Taylor was going, it was against her will. Shadowy images of Taylor's grandfather flitted through his memory. Crom Cornstack was huge—built like a linebacker—and despite his white-blond hair and full beard, he didn't look much older than William's own dad. The guy could probably bench press a water buffalo.

He didn't want to say it out loud, but if he had to guess who had kidnapped Taylor...

"Bound to be Crom Cornstack," Haggler said. "The Summer Court's too busy these days trying to hold itself together, and the nunnehi wouldn't do anything like this in a million years."

"Yeah," William said. Mercy barked silently and strained against her lead. "Come on, girl," he said, barely staying on his feet as Mercy explored the campsite. "Where'd she go from here?"

Mercy stalked to the edge of the clearing, then charged headlong into the forest. It wasn't long before she made a beeline for a pool of still water. She barked at the pool, wagging her tail furiously.

Haggler stepped forward and summoned the portal to life. William still couldn't see the flurry of gold and silver sparkles that Taylor had described, but he trusted the little folk knew what they were doing. Wasko and the others grabbed on to William, and soon all of them were once more lurching into the chaos.

They stepped out of the vortex into the narrow mouth of a cave, barely noticeable on the side of a hill. Everybody piled out, nearly tripping over each other, as Mercy dragged them down a steep slope.

William's stomach turned somersaults, but he managed not to lose his lunch. He should have been worn out, but he wasn't. If anything, the chase was invigorating. He was on a mission, and his sense of purpose pushed him forward. In an instant they had reached the bottom of the hill and stepped out of the woods.

They soon came out onto a highway. With a moment's reflection, William realized the sky was its normal color. They had arrived in the Topside world, a fact that was proven by the sound of an approaching car behind them.

Thankfully, Haggler was thinking fast. He threw a glamour over himself and Mercy so they looked like a second- or third-grader and his preschool-aged brother. At the same time, Pete and Haggler turned into normal-sized adults in khakis and polo shirts.

A half-mile jog brought them to the edge of a small town. A few hundred yards ahead, William spied the familiar blue sign of a Wal-Mart. Mercy tugged them straight for it.

It looked clean and new. The open land around it was mostly dirt and weeds until it met the woods a few dozen yards away. William saw birds flitting through the trees, but otherwise the forest seemed empty.

As soon as they lurched through the doors, William could sense people furtively looking in his direction. He tried to act calm. Just heading to Wal-Mart for some stuff.

The place was crowded with shoppers, and William remembered it was the Friday after Thanksgiving. Stores like this always had huge sales on Black Friday. All the best deals would have been grabbed up that morning, but even in the late afternoon, the place was bustling with activity.

The inside looked like every other big-box store on the planet. The racks of Clemson Tigers tee shirts and sweats told him he was somewhere in South Carolina, but not much more.

Navigating a Super Wal-Mart with an overeager hunting dog and three little people proved to be a challenge. Haggler kept a tight hold on Mercy's leash, and William tried not to worry about what the shoppers around him might be seeing. He brushed the side of his pants leg, reminding himself of his jet amulet. The longer he carried it, the easier it seemed to get for him to see through faery illusions. But if he concentrated, he could see what everybody else saw.

Haggler had chosen to look like a little black kid, which made sense. Even though his skin and hair were milky white, his features were more African than anything else. He made Mercy look the same, just a few years younger. Maybe William could pass for their older brother if nobody studied them too closely. It apparently didn't occur to the other two little folk to coordinate: Wasko was a tall Native American while Pete was a short, dumpy white guy.

William loved the fact that race wasn't a big deal among the Fair Folk. But for the benefit of all the normal human bystanders, he still kind of wished they all "matched."

Of course, Mercy was as oblivious to William's concerns as his two-footed companions. The dog bounded through the women's clothing section, sniffing at blue jeans and tops of a style that William could imagine Taylor wearing. They had all arrived in Darien wearing clothes borrowed from the stores of an all-male poleboat crew. It made sense that Taylor— or whoever was with her—would look for something more appropriate for her to wear.

A mom wheeled her cart past them. It was filled with kitchen appliances, pull-ups, and little girl's clothing. The toddler in the baby seat broke into wide-eyed amazement. "Goggie!" she squealed, pointing at Mercy.

Wonderful, William thought. *Little kids can see through glamour.*

Haggler cast a worried glance back at Wasko. He looped Mercy's leash around his hand to keep the dog close to him.

The mom was busy studying the prices on flannel shirts, so her daughter tried again. "Goggie! Goggie!" She giggled with glee.

"Are you a doggie, Sarabeth?" the mom teased, crinkling her nose and kissing the little girl's forehead.

William pretended he didn't notice any of this. Haggler stuck close to Mercy with his hand on her collar. He guessed they probably looked like two little kids holding hands as they walked through the store.

Mercy led the team out of the clothing section and around toward the front checkout lines. There, workers were directing traffic and fixing a knocked-over Christmas display.

A white guy in a button-down shirt, dress slacks, and a name badge strode toward them. He was maybe in his fifties, with thinning brown hair and a little too much weight around his belly. He must have been a manager, and he looked worried about something.

He stopped in front of them and looked at William. "I'm sorry, son, but you need to leave your backpack outside."

"What? Oh!" William's heart raced. He cursed his stupidity. How had they even gotten into the store with his backpack full of magical tools? He must have looked like a shoplifter.

"I'm sorry, sir. It must have slipped my mind."

The mom and the toddler swung back around. "Goggie! Goggie!" the little girl cried. Mercy wagged her tail and silently barked "hello."

"I'm gonna have to take a look inside your bag," the manager said. "Is your mom or dad around?"

Pete stepped forward. "Is there a problem, sir?" William's heart sank. *Let me handle this!*

Wasko slapped his hand on William's back. With a wink, he said, "Now, William, let the man see your backpack."

"Wait a minute," the manager said. His eyes darted between Pete and Wasko. "Which one of you...?" He knitted his brow. William could practically see the wheels turning inside his head.

"Yes?" William said. Haggler was trying his best to keep Mercy calm, but the little girl in the shopping cart wasn't helping. They had to get out of there. William wondered if it would be worth it to let the manager go through his backpack. After all, he hadn't stolen anything. He had nothing to hide—though what might the manager make of all the trinkets and odds and ends he was carrying?

"Right." The manager said. "If you'll just hand it over..."

"Can we just get this over with?" William said. He shrugged his bag off his shoulder, steadying his staff as it stuck out of the top. "We're gonna be late for a...thing."

"Goggie! Goggie! Goggie!" the little girl yelped. Mercy wagged her tail so hard her whole backside nearly took flight.

"What is that, some kind of weapon?" The manager took a half step back.

Nothing gets past you, does it? "It's called a hanbo," William said. "I'm taking tae kwon do classes and—"

Mercy leaped up, rested her front paws on the shopping cart, and licked at the little girl's face. The girl squealed and danced in her seat.

"Hey, buddy, please don't climb on the cart," the mom said, her expression more concerned than angry. "It might tip—"

William reached out his hand to steady the cart.

"You know," the manager said, "maybe we ought to do this in my office."

"No!" William, Wasko, Pete, and Haggler all said at once—though Haggler said it in the voice of a seven-year-old. William felt a throbbing pressure at his temples.

"Goggie! Goggie! Goggie! Goggie! Goggie!"

"We're really going to be late for that...thing," William said. Sweat had begun to plaster his tee shirt to his chest.

"What thing?" Pete said. Wasko gave him an elbow to the ribs. "Oh! The thing!"

"I'm afraid you're just going to have to be late," the manager said. "All of you, come wi—"

The lights flickered.

William glanced at Wasko, who looked just as surprised as he was. All the while, he and Haggler tried to pull Mercy away from her new friend.

"Hey, Buford," a voice squawked on the manager's walkie-talkie. He pulled it from his belt.

"What is it, Sheila?"

Haggler and William finally got Mercy down on all fours.

"It looks like we got a dog in the building," Sheila answered.

William sucked in a breath. He definitely felt a headache coming on.

"We ain't seen it," Sheila continued, "but we can hear it barking."

"Where at?" Buford asked.

"Carl says he heard it in sporting goods, but Rachel heard it over in the dairy aisle."

Buford the manager looked at the ceiling and rubbed his eyes with his free hand. "Well, that's all I need!"

The lights flickered once more.

"Okay, Sheila, meet me in layaway." He glared at William and his cohorts. "I'll be back there as soon as I can. And get somebody to check the breaker box! I'm afraid the lights are about to—"

And then the entire store went dark. Shoppers gasped. The toddler screamed. Buford said a bad word.

"Guys!" William called. But they had the same idea. In the confusion, he lunged for his backpack, wrenching it from Buford's hand. He and the little folk bolted for the exits almost faster than Mercy could lead them.

William summoned light into the gold ring on his hand and held it in front of him, pointing the way.

Haggler dropped his glamour. Instead of projecting the illusion of being a small child, he gestured wildly toward anyone who might have gotten in their way as they ran. People stopped in mid-stride with expressions of bewilderment, like they had forgotten what they were supposed to be doing.

Mercy barked furiously, though the only people who could hear her were apparently at the back of the store. At least it looked like she still had Taylor's scent.

As soon as they reached the front doors, they veered to the right, past the automotive bays, and into the open field beside the store. They must have run a hundred yards or more through the weeds and bramble, finally stepping out onto a crossroads with a gas station and a fast food joint.

Mercy bounded toward the restaurant, nearly yanking William's arm out of its socket.

"Mercy, heel!" he called.

The dog kept charging forward.

"Mercy!"

Haggler and the others re-applied their glamour, and once again they looked like the weirdest non-traditional family in the history of wherever they were. William planted his feet on the blacktop. It was the only thing to keep Mercy from breaking down the door to get inside.

The others quickly caught. "I guess Miss Hellebore stopped to eat here," Wasko said, wheezing.

"Say," Pete said, eyes longingly fixed on the hamburger poster in the window, "do you think we could—?"

"No," William said. He could already hear sirens in the distance. There was no telling what was happening at the Wal-Mart "We better keep going."

Mercy led them to a mushroom ring thirty or forty yards off the road. As before, everyone held on tight as the dog bounded into the mystic portal.

They emerged beside a stream. River sprites frolicked in the water, but quickly dove under when they saw William and his cohorts appear. Pete braced his hands on his knees and gasped for breath.

William gazed at the turquoise sky, now quickly on its way to purple as the sun set in the west.

"Hold up!" Pete croaked. "I gotta...catch my breath...before we...."

"I second that!" William said. He was once again in charge of Mercy's leash, and his arm was numb from the punishment it was taking.

"Five minutes," Wasko said. "We don't want the trail to get cold."

It didn't seem like Mercy was having any trouble with the trail, and she still had every bit as much energy as when they started three or four hours ago. But the two-footed members of the rescue party were exhausted.

"Let's say ten," William suggested. "Pete's right. It's nearly time for supper."

"Thank you!" Pete said. He produced a paper bag filled with trail mix: nuts, dried fruits, and...crickets?

William drew out Mercy's leash to its full length and tethered it to a tree branch, then slid down the tree's trunk and sat under its shade. He reached in his backpack for some scraps of ham and biscuits for Mercy and a bologna sandwich for himself.

"Does anybody want to tell me what happened back there?" he said.

"You mean with the kid?" Haggler said.

"I get what happened with the kid. I'm talking about the lights. Was that you?"

The albino little person shook his head. "I figured it was you."

"Me?" There's no way William could pull off anything like that. He wasn't sure how he'd even try. "That was definitely not me."

"You sure?" Haggler pressed. "Not even by accident?"

"Huh." He hadn't thought of that. "You mean my witch's aura?"

His grandmother had explained how witches generated a kind of magical turbulence around themselves. This aura caused things to happen beyond their control: milk turning sour, fires burning in strange colors. About a year ago, he and Jill had even overloaded the wiring in their family's washing machine.

William thought about it for a second, then gestured dismissively. "I don't think so. That took a lot more magical juice than I've got. Maybe my sister could do it if she were worked up enough, but not me."

"Maybe the lights just went bad," Pete said.

"Just when we needed them to?" William said. "That was a pretty new building. Unless the electricians didn't have a clue what they were doing…"

He took another bite of his sandwich.

"Well, whatever happened, it saved our bacon," Wasko said. "I hope Miss Hellebore stayed off of human earth for the rest of this trip. Too many Topsiders make me nervous—no offense."

"None taken." William chuckled. "That's how Taylor's felt as long as I've known her."

As they ate, William pulled his dracontia from his coat pocket and studied it in the waning light. The dragon it had come from was massive and had a hide like an elephant, but the stone set in its forehead was clear as glass and weighed almost nothing. It carried some of the warmth of William's body from being in his pocket, but it didn't glow or hum or do anything else magical—and yet Danny and Taylor had acted like it was the greatest magical tool he owned.

Did you do that? William thought. *Did you blow out the lights?*

His face grew warm, and he looked around to see whether anybody had noticed. They were all scarfing down their food. William shook his head. *I'm talking to a rock. How messed up is it to talk to a rock?*

Wasko shared the water in his canteen with Mercy, who was still sniffing around the trees and wagging her tail. Then they packed up and got back on the move. They dove once more into the vortex, hanging on for their lives as Mercy bounded on. They stepped out of a mushroom ring, sprinted across a fallow field, and then dove back into the Wonder through a portal anchored to an ancient gravestone. Flashes of color, snippets of alien sounds, and bizarre and beautiful vistas assaulted William's senses as he hurtled along.

Another jump dragged them past a dollar store in another little country town. Yet another jump, and they were nearly run over as they bolted across the driveway of a fried chicken place.

Then, at last, the vortex emptied them all onto a patch of knee-high grass.

William fell forward and rolled on the ground. As he sat up, Wasko was at his side in a heartbeat, shushing and urging him to stay down. Haggler was patting Mercy's flank, keeping her calm.

They were higher in the mountains now, and they had landed in front of an outcropping of rock that bore primitive markings: ancient petroglyphs of hunters and prey animals.

William rolled onto his side. Twenty yards away, men were moving through the trees. There must have been at least fifty of them, maybe more, marching in neat rows down a wooded gravel road.

He pulled himself to all fours while ducking behind a boulder. Haggler firmly guided Mercy to take cover.

William peered over the crest of the rock to get a better look. Pete and Wasko joined him, only they stood on their tiptoes while William crouched.

The glint of brass gun barrels caught the last rays of the sun before it sank beneath the trees. Muskets, William thought, no doubt loaded with elf-shot. As he looked closer, he noted this nearer group of warriors all had swords at their sides as well.

"Oh, Brother Mike!" Pete whispered.

Wasko stared, wide-eyed. "This ain't good."

"Nope," William agreed.

The men, and a few women, were grim-faced but possessing the eery comeliness he had come to associate with Taylor's people. Everyone was tall and well built, and dressed in cloaks of green, brown, or gray. At the head of the column were at least a dozen men on horseback.

They kept coming. Maybe twenty had passed before William thought to count them. He lost count after a hundred when his cramping calves demanded he stop crouching and sit down. But it was definitely an army: maybe two hundred strong, row after row of them marching toward the east.

In the distance rose four gray spires of an imposing castle set on a gently sloping hill.

Haggler had moved on from patting Mercy's side to rubbing her belly. "Ain't much we can do till this war band passes."

And hope they didn't completely erase Taylor's scent.

A horn sounded from the front of the column. The soldiers broke formation and began to spread out on either side of the road.

"What are they doing?" Pete whispered.

"Perfect," Wasko said through gritted teeth. He turned to the others. "They're making camp for the night."

Chapter 13

The War Band

Over the last few days, a rule of thumb for dealing with the Fair Folk had crystallized in William's mind. Average to good-looking: proceed with caution. Ugly: run away. Impossibly beautiful: run away *fast*.

One look, and William was pondering the best escape routes. The war band that had begun setting up camp less than twenty yards away revealed a mixture of faces and forms, from the grotesque to the stunningly, unnervingly handsome.

The little folk had the same idea. Wasko and Pete skulked backward around the side of the hill toward where the rock painting was located. Haggler patted Mercy's back and coaxed her to follow him. William passed him the leash and then pulled his backpack off his shoulder. He grabbed a zip-top bag full of reddish-orange powder. Crouching low, he backed away while strewing the powder on the ground. With each throw, he backed away, following his companions and covering their tracks.

He'd never tried hot foot powder before, but Maymay swore by it. A little sprinkle was supposed to make unwanted people go away. Maybe if any soldiers came that way, they'd change their minds about going further.

William and the others rounded the hillside and climbed higher. Wasko and Pete had already conjured a veil of magical mist to mask their presence. At the top of the hill, they lay on their bellies and peered out over the valley. They had a good look at the war band and could hopefully remain unseen.

The castle a mile or more away captured William's attention. The only castles he'd ever scene were in movies. This one stood tall and imposing on the top of a hill. William could just make out the bustle of people moving this way and that outside the walls.

Pete's face was white with fear. William had to admit, the army looked awfully scary.

"It's okay," William whispered.

Pete shook his head. "You don't know where we are!" he hissed.

Haggler nudged his chin toward the castle in the distance. The war band had camped at the edge of a vast plain that stretched almost to the outer walls. "That's Cair Cullen," he said. William didn't respond.

"Capital of the Winter Court," Wasko said.

"You mean that's where Taylor's grandparents live?"

"It's the evilest place I ever been." Pete leaned back against the rock, dazed.

"Pete spent some time there a few years back," Haggler said.

"You used to work for the Hellebores?" William said, wide-eyed.

"He used to be their prisoner," Wasko explained. He shook his head. "If Haggler and I hadn't broke him out...."

William shook his head, bewildered. Whoever had kidnapped Taylor had taken her to her grandparents' castle. Now there was an army setting up camp practically in its shadow.

The soldiers moved quickly but not hurriedly, pitching tents and building fires. Groomsmen took care of the officers' horses. Others gathered firewood near the edge of the road.

At the back of the train were a couple of mule-drawn wagons driven by two tall, eerily beautiful fae, one man and one woman. A half-dozen other fae and little folk bustled around each. They didn't unpack much except for an embroidered rug and a bird in a cage—a crow or a raven as far as William could tell—from the fae woman's wagon.

William's eyes drifted to the officers, who strode around the edge of the camp in the direction of the two wagons. They were also tall and good-looking. The leader's cloak was fastened at his neck with a copper brooch that caught William's attention.

"What's an apple tree mean?" he whispered to Wasko, who lay beside him at his left.

"Means we're in a forest."

"No, I mean the leader's got an apple-tree brooch. Does that mean anything?"

Wasko squinted to where William was pointing.

"How do you know that's an apple tree?"

"Well, it's got apples on it, doesn't it?"

Wasko squinted again. "It's got some kind of design. If you can see any more than that…"

"I think I see branches," Pete commented from William's right. "It might be some kind of tree."

"Apple tree's a symbol of the Autumn Court," Haggler said.

William looked back at the albino little person. He hated not knowing things.

"Cornstack's flunkies."

Wonderful.

Haggler and Mercy remained behind the crest of the hill. It was all Haggler could to do keep Mercy from dashing down into the valley. The dog's eyes were fixed on a spot in the distance, on the other side. It was obvious that's where she wanted to go, and she didn't seem to care that the whole place was crawling with soldiers.

"For what it's worth," Haggler said, "Mercy isn't looking toward the castle. Something over that rise has her attention."

William considered that. "Is it too much to hope that Taylor just stopped here for lunch or something before moving on?"

"Maybe not," Haggler said. "Word is, she's sworn to never enter a rath of Arradherry."

"I've never known her to break her word," William said. He hoped that still held. He had no intention of getting any closer to Cair Cullen than he had to.

"We gotta do something," Wasko said. "They'll be sending patrols out before long. And I don't like the looks of that magery unit." To William's curious expression, he added, "Those wagons down there? They'll be full of equipment for those two battle mages. One of 'em's gonna have eyes in the sky before long."

William looked back down into the valley. The female battle mage was seated cross-legged on the rug, eyes closed in meditation. One of her attendants stood ready with his hand on the door of the birdcage he'd unloaded earlier.

William thumped his forehead on the cold ground. They had to follow Taylor's tracks, and that meant crossing to the other side of the valley. To do that, they'd have to sneak past about two hundred troops loyal to Crom Cornstack. They'd have to somehow avoid their patrols, not to mention the fae witch down there getting ready to fare forth in the body of a crow to literally get a bird's-eye view of the entire area.

Haggler shushed Mercy, who had let out a silent, impatient yip. Remembering how the folks at the back of the Wal-Mart heard her when nobody near her could, William lifted his head to spy on the camp. Thankfully, it didn't look like anybody heard her there. Maybe a yip didn't carry quite as far as a full-on bark.

Still, he didn't see how they could stay put much longer.

Wasko was apparently thinking the same thing. "We gotta get to the other side," he said.

"You ain't serious," Pete hissed.

Mercy wrestled with Haggler, who kept patting her and scratching her behind the ears.

The battle mage's attendant released the crow. It cawed as it spiraled up into the sky, then veered off across the valley to the east, toward Cair Cullen.

They were just going to have to risk it. William turned toward Haggler. "Can we stay invisible if we're moving?"

Haggler shrugged. "Wasko and Pete and me'll be fine. You and Mercy'll each have to stick close to one of us. And we can't make any noise."

William sighed. "I don't see any other choice."

"Me neither," Haggler agreed.

William pulled his staff from his backpack.

Wasko looked at each of his compatriots in turn. "We'll circle around behind 'em—make as wide an arc as we can."

"Will Mercy pick up the scent on the other side?" William asked.

"No problem," Haggler said. "As long as we're quick. All those extra people down there mean a bunch of new smells she's gonna have to navigate."

"Then we'd better hurry," William said, and rose to his feet.

They followed the ridgeline west. William stuck close to Wasko, who led the way. Pete followed behind them, and Haggler brought up the rear, tugging on Mercy's leash.

The dog knew this wasn't the right direction, and she apparently didn't think of a valley full of armed Fair Folk as an obstacle. Still, Haggler was able to keep her quiet, except for a few low grunts that William hoped wouldn't be heard over the sounds in the camp.

They didn't run into any patrols. At one point, though, they were forced to stay frozen for several tense minutes as the crow circled overhead.

As soon as it veered back to the east, they faced the trickiest part of the plan: crossing a gap in the trees literally wide enough to march an army through. How far, he wondered, would the little folk's glamour extend?

"Maybe we shouldn't all go at once," William whispered.

Wasko looked across the open space, then toward the camp. It was out of sight a hundred yards to the right. William couldn't hear any activity, but the little person's ears perked up as he turned his attention that way.

Finally, Wasko nodded and guided William slowly across. When Wasko sensed the coast was clear, he motioned for Pete to follow. Another thirty seconds passed before he signaled for Haggler and Mercy.

"I don't get it," William said when they were once more safe behind the treeline. "I've seen how ring travel works. Can't they just...pop all the way to where they're going?"

"It ain't that easy," Pete whispered. "A portal can only handle so much magic running through it."

"Right," Wasko agreed. "They can get overheated. Send a couple hundred fae through a portal—assuming it can even handle the weight—it's gonna seize up."

"You Topsiders have an expression," Haggler said. "Don't burn your bridges behind you."

That made sense. "They don't want to take the direct route there—wherever 'there' is. But they might need a direct route back home."

"That's about the size of it," Wasko said. "They're leaving themselves a straight shot home in case things get—" He cut himself off and pulled William deeper into the trees. Pete and Haggler followed suit.

The commander had sent a patrol westward after all. Four mounted fae rounded the bend, two on William's side of the gap and the other two on the side he had just left. They carried brass-barreled cavalry pistols at the ready, and William could see the scabbards of their sabers tapping against their thighs. They rode in almost perfect silence—it was a miracle Wasko noticed them in time. Their bright eyes scanned in every direction.

William held still and tried not to breathe. The little folk did the same. Haggler rubbed Mercy's back and leaned in to make a gentle shushing noise in her ear. William prayed the dog could understand.

The scouts didn't seem to notice them though they were only a few feet away by that point. They peered into the trees, but gave no indication they saw the place where William and the others were trying to hide. The tree trunks weren't thick enough to shield them completely, but that didn't seem to matter. William really wanted to ask the little folk how their glamour worked, but now wasn't the time.

The patrol continued on. As soon as they were out of sight, William and the the rest headed further into the trees and then veered back toward the east, toward Cair Cullen.

William kept his staff ready, but rested his left hand on Wasko's shoulder to make sure he—and his concealing mist—stayed close. As they inched closer to the camp, he began to make out sounds: chopping firewood, sharpening swords, the grunts of men hauling heavy loads, the muffled clop-clop of other scouting parties coming back from patrol.

Mercy wagged her tail furiously. She must have picked up Taylor's scent again. But then she opened her mouth and let out a single, silent bark, and William's stomach churned. Wasko looked back at Haggler with fear in his eyes. Haggler pulled Mercy close and patted her back, but the damage was done. The proof came a second later, when William heard someone in the camp ask, "What was that?"

Wasko urged everyone on. They would have to hurry now. The soldiers knew someone was out there, even if they didn't know where.

A faery dog's bark seemed to come from everywhere and nowhere. It would be nearly impossible for them to get a clear idea of what direction to search. Even so, now they knew there were people skulking about. The next portal had better be close by!

They picked up the pace, even as Mercy led them around the edge of the war band's camp. The sun had ducked beneath the trees. With luck, the growing darkness would protect them even if their glamour failed. They silently rushed along, and William couldn't help but cast anxious glances at the rath as it loomed in the distance.

Someone stepped on a twig. It snapped, clear and crisp, making William wince. They dropped down off the ridge line, away from the camp—and even closer to Cair Cullen.

Mercy yanked Haggler forward, and all of a sudden, their entire marching order was reversed: Mercy led the way with Haggler, followed by Pete, Wasko, and William.

Mercy barked again. She was far enough ahead of William that he picked up the sound as a distant whisper, somewhere down around the lower threshold of his ability to hear.

A crow cawed overhead. He glanced up, and sure enough, a black shadow flitted above them. Had the battle mage seen them? He couldn't be sure, but the way things were going, he had to assume scouts would soon be tracking them on foot.

Mercy bounded off, following a narrow foot path deeper into the woods. It was all Haggler could do not to be dragged along behind her. The others struggled to keep up.

They emerged in a much smaller clearing centered on a ring of mushrooms barely ten feet across.

It had never occurred to him that soldiers might already be guarding any portals in the area.

"Don't shoot!" Pete shouted. He looked on the verge of tears.

"What he said!" Wasko agreed.

William cursed under his breath.

"Halt!" a guard yelled, leveling his musket on Haggler. Three more guards did the same, taking aim at William, Pete, and Wasko.

William had read that you couldn't really aim those old-fashioned muskets. That's why Revolutionary soldiers stood in a line and all fired at once: with that many weapons, something was bound to hit. But in 1776, they were firing from forty or fifty yards away, not ten or twenty feet. William figured he must have been inside dueling range—and those muskets looked a lot more accurate than pistols.

Haggler raised his arms in surrender, keeping the end of Mercy's leash wrapped around his right hand. William and the others lifted their hands as well.

The first guard eyed everyone warily. Surely a teenager, a dog, and a trio of little folk didn't look like a threat...

"This is a restricted area!"

"We're just passing through," Wasko said, his voice wavering. "We don't want no trouble."

Mercy wagged her tail furiously and let out a stream of unheard, plaintive barks. She tugged against her leash, forcing Haggler to lurch forward.

The musket's report seemed to crack open the clearing.

Haggler fell, clutching his side. As he let go, Mercy bounded toward the guard.

Two other soldiers fired, missing both Pete and Wasko. Just as quickly, Wasko unleashed a stunning spell that bathed the clearing in flashing colored lights and the sounds of firecrackers.

William ducked back from the soldier who still had him in his sights. Time seemed to slow down as the scruffy young fae squeezed the trigger, and a jet of green light traced its way toward William with a cloud of smoke in its wake.

William flinched and turned away. He felt the musket ball slam into his right shoulder and then evaporate.

His heart pounded, but he was still on his feet. He peered down the end of his sleeve, catching sight of the protective sigils he'd worked into the fabric months ago. They still worked!

His hope surged and he spun around, aiming his staff at the soldier who'd shot him.

"*Bazagra!*" A pulse of magic arced toward the fae, hitting him square in the chest and draining his magical reserves.

"Get Haggler!" he shouted as he swung his staff toward the next soldier.

They didn't have time to reload; they'd have to either draw their swords or use magic—and the latter wasn't an option for the one William had blasted. William and the others had a chance to get away, but they'd have to act fast.

The soldier he'd bazagra'ed reached for his sidearm, but William smacked him on the hand with the end of his staff. The soldier wailed and dropped the weapon.

William didn't wait for it to fall. He shouldered this fae to the ground and struck the second one on the back before he could unleash the blast he was aiming at Pete.

Meanwhile, Wasko had hoisted Haggler up. The albino didn't look good, but Wasko managed to get him on his feet, with an arm draped limply over his shoulder.

"Mercy!" William called. "Here!"

A third soldier, still reeling from Wasko's stunning spell, weaved toward Willam, sword in hand. He lunged, but William parried and drove the butt of his staff into the center of his chest. As the soldier staggered backward, William trained his staff on the fourth soldier, five feet away and moving his hands in a tight circle, readying a spell.

"*Bazagra!*" William cried. Once more, magic arced toward his target, who fell back, stunned.

William wasted no time before starting on another spell. "*Sharba pesharba flammante fayah pyripeganyx,*" he intoned. He felt the wood of his staff grow warm to the touch.

"*Sharba pesharba flammante fayah pyripeganyx.*" The tip of the staff began to glow. He spun in a circle, daring any of the fae soldiers to come closer.

Wasko guided Haggler around to Pete, who had managed to grab the end of Mercy's leash. The three held Mercy back at the edge of the mushroom ring while they summoned it to life.

William repeated the incantation twice more, and the end of his staff burst into flames.

The soldiers' faces fell. They scrambled back down the footpath toward the camp.

William laughed in spite of himself. He turned back to the little folk and saw that they were all staring at him, wide-eyed and open-mouthed.

The turkey feather on the band of Wasko's bowler hat drooped, almost on cue. "Uh...what was that?"

William realized he was breathing hard and grinning from ear to ear. He took a long, slow breath. He felt invincible!

"No idea," he admitted. Everything had happened so fast. He couldn't believe what he had just done.

But invincibility gave way to self-consciousness. The tip of his staff was still on fire. He hurriedly blew it out.

He looked toward the mushroom ring. "I'd rather not be here when those guys come back."

He came up behind Wasko and Haggler, stooped down, and wrapped his arms around both of them.

"You heard him!" Wasko croaked. He helped Haggler to his feet. "Let's get moving!"

That was all the encouragement Mercy needed. She pulled them into the ring. A second later, only their footprints gave evidence they had ever been there.

Chapter 14

Dingle Spells It Out

Near sunset, Taylor, Dingle, and the Red Fangs stopped beside a ring of standing stones somewhere high in the mountains.

"All right," the spriggan announced. "This is it."

The Red Fangs gathered around him. Dingle gave them all a wary look as he dug the magic mirror from his pack. "Team three, you know what to do."

Butcher grinned. "About tuppin' time!" he said.

"I still got my toads ready," Shagfoal the pooka said, hefting a small leather bag.

"Enough with the toads," Butcher growled. He turned to his team. "Anybody that's gonna shift, do it now."

"What about team one and team two?" Mervin the pisgy said. At that, all eyes fell on Dingle.

"Leave that to the girl," he said. He passed Taylor the mirror. Her heart pounded. Her head told her it only weighed a few ounces, but it somehow felt much heavier than that. It seemed to vibrate with energy like a living thing. She didn't dare unwrap it—the last thing she wanted to see was all the anxious faces it contained staring up at her.

"She knows what to do?" Shagfoal challenged.

"I'm about to explain it to her," Dingle said. "It's a little too late to back out."

"Ain't nobody backing out!" Shagfoal hissed. "I swore an oath, Dingle! We all did!" His body melted and contracted until he was a black cat. His fur full and bushy, he might have looked cuddly if it weren't for the demonic glow of his eyes and the self-important attitude his posture projected. At the same time, Arthek and Treeve shrank smaller and smaller—down to three feet, two feet, one foot, six inches.

"No more than two at a time through the portal," Butcher called.

Arthek and Treve were the first to go, followed by Shagfoal in cat form, who entered the portal alone.

A minute later, Mervin and Fergus wrapped themselves in magic mist. At Butcher's signal, they, too, stepped into the vortex.

Finally, Butcher was left alone with Dingle and Taylor. His lips curled into a derisive sneer as he stepped up to Taylor. Dingle interposed himself, but Butcher shouldered him away and jabbed a finger at the center of Taylor's chest. "I'm gonna lose some men in the next couple hours," he grumbled. "It better not be your fault when it happens."

"The girl swore an oath, too!" Dingle snapped.

Butcher turned his attention on the spriggan. "She better know what's expected of her."

"*Can we not act like I'm not here?*" Taylor spat. Butcher barely flinched at her impulse of presence. "I promised Mara a favor. I don't like it, but Our Kind keep our word."

"You better," Butcher said. Then he vanished. But from somewhere nearby, he said, "If you know what's good for you, you better."

The portal snapped shut, and Taylor was left alone with Dingle.

"All right," he said. "Put down the mirror."

She set it carefully on the grass with a shaky hand.

The spriggan bore into her with his beady eyes. "Say it again. The words I taught you."

Taylor stared at him. When her mind jolted back into gear, she mumbled, "*Ha zudeia virdiga.*"

Dingle extended his left hand, palm facing outward. "Again. And put some magic behind it."

She repeated the phrase, more confidently this time, and doing as Dingle had instructed by adding a pulse of magical energy. Dingle sneered at her, either pleased or contemptuous— it was hard to tell with a spriggan.

Taylor's throat was dry, and her heart bounced around her rib cage.

"Not bad," he said.

"When are you going to tell me what this is all about?"

"My orders were clear," Dingle's own expression, such as Taylor could read it, suggested anxiety. "I wasn't to say anything until now, understand?"

"So you're finally going to tell me?"

"I wasn't supposed to give you time to think about it." He looked toward the spring, its portal now dormant. "Team three'll be in place by now. If you don't come through the portal in the next minute or two, they'll figure something's wrong."

"Y-yes?"

"I wish you'd have figured it out for yourself..."

"Just tell me, already!"

"You're good," Dingle said. "Anybody can see that. Most children your age don't have your kind of power, not even daoine sídhe. But you're still just a kid, understand? You've got plenty to learn. There's nothing you can do that a hundred other Winters couldn't do better." The spriggan's voice had climbed half an octave. Taylor could see a trickle of sweat making its way across his hideous face. He was nervous, and it was starting to show.

"So, what—?"

"There's only one thing you can do that none of Crom or Mara's minions can. That's what Mrs. Hellebore wants."

"I don't understand..."

Dingle took a breath. He nervously tapped his fingers against his thigh. He looked at the ground, like he couldn't look Taylor in the eye any longer.

"What?"

He lifted his scraggly brow, though he still didn't make eye contact. Instead, he seemed to focus on a spot just over Taylor's shoulder.

He took another breath. "Nobody from the Winter Court can walk into Tsuwatelda, no questions asked."

The silence in the woods was absolute. It was as if even the birds and the deer were shocked by what Dingle had said.

Taylor looked down at her feet, where the mirror still lay wrapped in cloth. She imagined the brutal warriors trapped inside it. She imagined them springing forth, weapons ready.

A lump of ice-cold lead dropped into her gut. She clenched her fists to keep her own hands from shaking. Everything suddenly made sense.

"M-my mom..."

The spriggan said nothing for the longest time. He just looked at that same spot over Taylor's shoulder.

She looked up. Her eyes were bubbling with anger. Presence rolled off her in waves. *"They want to kill Shanna?"*

"No," Dingle said defensively. "They just...want her home."

"I don't see how that's much better!" Crom and Mara had kept their daughter imprisoned for fourteen years. Taylor couldn't imagine what they'd do to her if they got her back in their power.

The ground began to spin. Taylor took a deep breath. "Still," she whispered. How could Crom and Mara hold a grudge for so long? How could they do this to their own daughter?

"Mrs. Hellebore," Dingle began. He stopped, then started again. "She wants you to take the mirror to Shanna. She figures you know how to get there. Then... Then you're to summon the other two teams with that incantation I taught you."

Taylor stared at him. The initial shock was wearing off. Seething rage took its place.

"You're not to go to anybody else, understand? You're not to tell anyone why you're there."

"No!" She felt her stomach tying up in knots as soon as she said the word.

"But your oath—"

"I can't just—Ungh!" She doubled over.

Two summers ago, she promised she'd do anything to spare Jill's life—and she meant it! Even thinking about breaking her oath felt like she was spitting in her friend's face. How could she back out of her promise?

A wave of nausea surged through her. The magic of her sworn oath reached up from somewhere deep in the Wonder, wrapped itself around her insides, and nearly wrenched her in half.

Anything but this! she prayed.

"You ain't got a choice!" Dingle said. His surly exterior had all but melted away. He looked at her—or rather, past her—with something like pity. "You've got to deliver Mrs. Hellebore's package," he said, his voice barely above a whisper. "Do that, and you've repaid your debt."

With a shudder, Taylor realized why Crom Cornstack was so pleased when she publicly and dramatically repudiated the Winter Court a few days back. He'd made her look like a victim. She'd put her foot down and refused to have anything to do with him.

And everybody knew it. From Ichisi to Tsuwatelda.

Nobody would question her showing up unannounced. She'd already visited Shanna before. The guards would just let her walk in, probably give her an armed escort. She shuddered with horror.

"They close the gate at sunset," Dingle said. "Team three is waiting." He gestured toward the mirror.

"*Let them wait!*" Taylor snapped. Her insides screamed in defiance. She rocked back and forth. There had to be a way out, a way to keep her oath without endangering Shanna. If only she had time to think!

"You...don't want to make Mrs. Hellebore angry."

"*You don't want to make* me *angry*," Taylor hissed. Presence rolled off her in roiling waves. Even Dingle shrunk away from her.

But she knew she was beaten. Gritting her teeth, she stooped to pick up the mirror. As soon as she did, her stomach began to settle.

"This isn't over," she muttered. And it wasn't. She vowed to herself that, if she managed to survive the night, she would be Crom Cornstack and Mara Hellebore's worst nightmare. She even had a faint glimmer of a plan.

She glared at Dingle. "*Crom's desk. It channels magic into some kind of vessel, right? That's what you said.*"

"Th-that's right." The spriggan's eyes grew wide.

"*A head? Is it a severed head?*"

"Yeah," Dingle said. "It's called a sacrum. It's...like a receptacle for magical energies. Very ancient magic. Very powerful. The head was from one of Mr. Cornstack's rivals, centuries ago. But how did you—?"

"*You don't ask the questions!*" She wrapped her hands tightly around the mirror as if trying to strangle it.

"M-miss Hellebore," Dingle said. His voice cracked.

"*What?*"

"I'm sorry they're putting you through this."

Taylor looked him in the eye. For the first time, he returned her gaze. "Then help me."

"I can't," Dingle said, deflated. He studied the ground in front of Taylor's feet. "I ain't got any more choice about this than you do."

"*But you know this isn't fair! You know this is evil!*"

"What I know don't matter. Mr. Cornstack is still my bounden lord." He pointed a gnarled finger toward Taylor. "And if you don't think I'm going to honor that oath till my dying breath—"

"*I think you're a coward*," Taylor spat.

She stared at Dingle. Dingle stared at Taylor's shoes.

"I better go," Taylor said. Her breath rose in a billowing fog. "Thanks for nothing."

Dingle shivered and brushed flecks of frost from his nose.

Taylor turned her back on him. She gestured, and the portal sprung to violent life in front of her.

She imagined Shanna looking for her years ago after she had escaped from Cair Cullen. Now Mara was using her to get Shanna back, and she could barely contain her fury. Only her oath kept her from hurling the mirror into the trees.

"You'd better hope we never meet again, Bledrus Dingle."

Shoving the mirror into her pack, she stalked to the edge of the spring and stepped into the vortex.

Chapter 15

A Present Darkness

"How about a banishing spell?" Jill asked into her cell phone. She paced in front of the picture window in the living room, glancing toward the Smarts' house. The setting sun cast long, brooding shadows over Knottingley Drive.

"Honey, I don't think it'll be strong enough." Maymay's voice sounded anxious, agitated.

"It worked on that three-headed buzzard thing." Jill remembered how her brother had improvised a banishing-spell attack two Halloweens ago against a monster that Mara Hellebore had sent after them.

"That's because William threw it at close range," Maymay countered. "A banishing spell isn't meant to work that way. And anyway, I don't like the idea of you getting close enough to use it."

"I might not have much choice about that," Jill said. Why couldn't William be there? He was the resourceful one.

And why hadn't he called? It had been hours since he left with Wasko, Pete, and Haggler. If he was in trouble somewhere deep in the Wonder....

"No," Maymay said. Her voice shook Jill back to the present. "I don't suppose you do."

Jill had explained to Maymay what she and William had found out about the Good Neighbor impersonating Taylor. If her parents knew, they'd tip the fake Taylor off for sure, but Maymay couldn't spill the beans all the way from New Orleans.

"And your friends are coming over at two tomorrow?"

"That's right," Jill said. Last weekend was William's birthday party; tomorrow was hers. "Taylor" and a few more of Jill's friends from school and from church were getting together for snacks and a Netflix movie. Now, the whole thing sounded like a terrible idea. What if fake Taylor decided to do show up? What if she tried to do something? Jill felt a headache coming on.

"You'll want to make sure the house is protected," Maymay said.

"I'm already on it," Jill said. She pinched the bridge of her nose. "But Mom already invited the fake Taylor in, so there's not much I can do."

"You can keep out any party-crashers she decides to bring along."

Jill hadn't thought about that. A lump formed in her stomach as she considered it. One Good Neighbor was bad enough!

Keep it together! Jill told herself. Her parents, the Smarts, her friends: everybody was counting on her, if they knew it or not. There had to be some way she could keep everybody safe.

"We still don't know why she's even here," Jill said. The only hope she could hold onto was that the imposter had been laying low at the Smarts' house.

Jill had kept an eye on the place all day, opening her Second Sight as much as she dared. The symbolic images she saw mostly made sense to her: The dark, twisting shadows and the flitting, ghostly bat-like shapes most likely meant danger. That was obvious enough. She guessed the icy fog that had settled on the lawn might have something to do with the Winter Court, Taylor's family on her mother's side. She didn't have a clue about the buffalo she saw walking down the street. It was probably just her own nerves, though, because it disappeared as soon as she blinked her eyes.

"The Good Neighbors always have a plan, baby," Maymay said. "Usually more than one. It's best to be ready for them."

"I know." She just didn't like it. Not for the first time, she wondered how her best friend could be related to these creatures who had turned her life upside down.

If only she'd told Mara Hellebore where to go when she'd first invaded her life two years ago. If only she'd been smarter. Stronger.

"I could bind her in a circle of power," Jill offered.

"You'd have to trick her into stepping into it," Maymay countered.

She was right. Jill realized it was a dumb idea as soon as she'd said it. There's no way fake Taylor would just stupidly walk into a magic circle and let Jill trap her there.

"I've still got your blasting rod."

"Then you'd best keep it close by," Maymay said. "And your jet amulet."

"It's always in my pocket."

"Good. How's your supply of rowan berries?"

"I'd have to look, but I don't think William has used them all up. Do you have an idea?" She heard pages turning on the other end of the phone. Her grandmother was rummaging through her notebooks.

"If you could whip up some protective amulets for your friends, make them look like party favors..."

"That's a great idea!"

More pages turning. "Most amulets take time," Maymay said. "Ingredients have to be harvested at the right phase of the moon.... Mixtures have to marinate.... But if I'm not mistaken... Here it is! This is a recipe I've used before when I was in a hurry. I'll email it to you."

"Thanks, Maymay!"

"You'll need rowan berries...and salt..."

"Right."

"And St. John's wort?"

Jill grimaced. "I'm pretty sure we're out."

Then there was silence on the other end. "I don't know where you'd get more at this time of year."

"Would something else work? We've still got plenty of fern blossoms, and some—"

"No, honey, it has to be St. John's wort."

Rats.

Shadows gathered on Knottingley Drive. Not sinister, supernatural ones this time, just the ordinary ones that stretched across the pavement on an autumn afternoon.

"Jill?" her mom called. She turned around. Mrs. Matthews was wiping a pyrex pie plate with a dishcloth.

"Yes, Mom?"

"When you get off the phone, would you run this back over to Mrs. Smart? And tell her thank you."

Jill's mouth went suddenly dry, but she tried to keep the concern off her face. "Okay. Just set it on the counter, please."

Jill had kept her distance from the imposter ever since she figured out something was up. Normally, she and the real Taylor would have spent the day after Thanksgiving goofing off together. Jill wasn't ready for that—and she figured fake Taylor wasn't either.

"Something we agree on," she muttered, rolling her eyes.

"What was that, honey?" Maymay said.

"Nothing, Maymay. Just thinking."

Then Jill remembered something. Two things, actually. Earlier that week, she'd used one of Maymay's spells to converse long-distance with Danny Underhill. She'd used a simple mirror to anchor the pooka's consciousness. And not long after that, she'd had a vision of her grandmother. When Maymay was young, she went up against a roomful of Good Neighbors with nothing but a mirror, a staff, and a cat.

"Aren't there ways of trapping a fae in a mirror?"

She could almost hear Maymay frowning through the phone. "You're asking about some pretty powerful magic. Very complex—and very dangerous if you don't do it right. It would put my mind at ease if you wouldn't try anything like that, baby."

"I can do it," Jill said. She hoped she was telling the truth.

"Do you know this girl's true name?"

Jill cursed to herself. She didn't even know fake Taylor's everyday name.

"Not exactly."

"Then we've got to think of something else. Please?"

Deflated, she said, "Okay. You're right." She gazed across the street and two doors down. Without Second Sight, everything looked perfectly normal at the Smart house.

"If you think of anything else...."

"I'll call right away," Maymay said. "You be safe, you hear?"

"I will, Maymay," Jill said. "Love you. Bye." She ended the call and got ready to pay the Smarts a visit. It was hands-down the most unsafe thing she could imagine.

There was no answer when Jill knocked on the Smarts' door, but both of their cars were in the driveway, and the light was on in the front room. The sun was setting, but Jill didn't think that had anything to do with the chill in the air she felt as she stood on the stoop, waiting.

Eventually Mrs. Smart opened the door.

Jill forced a perky smile. "Here's your plate back, Mrs. Smart. The pie was great."

Mrs. Smart mumbled something. She smiled back at Jill, but something wasn't right. It was like she was struggling to remember what she was supposed to do next. The two stood and stared at each other for a long, awkward moment.

Not good, Jill thought.

She held out the pie plate, her hands trembling. "C-can I come in?"

Mrs. Smart accepted the plate and wandered toward the kitchen. She left the door open, so Jill quickly stepped inside.

Mr. Smart was watching a football game on TV. At least, he was making a halfhearted effort at it. His glazed eyes were glued to the screen, but there was no sense of engagement. Fred Smart wasn't as big a football fan as Jill's own dad—no one was, as far as she knew—but he enjoyed football, and one of his favorite teams was playing.

"Mr. Smart?" Jill said. "Hi there. Mr. Smart?" She waved her hand in front of him, but he didn't even blink.

"Holding," he said to no one in particular.

There was still no sign of fake Taylor. Where could she be?

On the TV, the referee said, "Holding. Offense. Ten-yard penalty."

So at least Taylor dad wasn't completely out of it. He was following the game, but that was all. It gave Jill the creeps to see him this way.

Jill took a breath and let her eyelids close as she took another one, slow and shallow. Then, as she opened her eyes again, she also opened her Second Sight.

Now there was a haze in the room, indistinct but no less real. It was like beginning of an allergy medicine commercial: the bright, crisp colors Jill was supposed to see were replaced by muted tones. Nothing was dark or foggy, but nothing was as clear and sharp as it should be, either.

She studied Taylor's dad, sitting in his easy chair. He still hadn't acknowledged her presence. His eyes were locked onto the TV screen. As Jill peered deeper, she saw something like a ghostly cloak or blanket draped over him. It wafted on an unfelt breeze, slowly undulating like the fins of a manta ray.

Something to deaden their senses? Jill pondered. *To keep them from noticing that anything is wrong? Something to keep them out of fake Taylor's hair?*

Jill glanced into the adjacent kitchen, where Mrs. Smart was putting away the pie plate. The same heavy shroud lay over her.

She watched as Taylor's mom shuffled about, pulling out leftovers to heat up for supper. There was something hypnotic about the slow, measured way in which she moved. It was like she didn't have a care in the world. She just went through the motions of what she imagined she should be doing.

The aroma of the turkey and dressing made Jill's mouth water even though she'd already eaten. The whir of the microwave became a soothing hum that drowned out the cares of the world. So peaceful...

Jill shook herself. Fake Taylor's glamour had almost gotten to her. She passed her hand over the jet amulet in her jeans pocket, and her mind cleared at once. She let go of her Second Sight, though, just to be on the safe side.

She couldn't leave Taylor's parents like this. There had to be something she could do.

After a quick mental inventory, Jill decided her best bet was a steel washer she'd taken from her dad's toolbox. The iron in it might ground a faery's magic if she could figure how to use it to anchor a protective spell. In her mind, she replayed her grandmother's lessons about charms and amulets. Maybe she could remember enough.

Here goes, she thought. She slipped the washer into Mr. Smart's hand and folded his fingers around it. With her own hands wrapped around his, she whispered the same incantation she used to summon the full power of her jet amulet: "No faery takes, nor witch hath power to charm."

Mr. Smart blinked and grunted, but his eyes still refused to move from the TV.

"Mr. Smart?" Jill whispered.

"Is something wrong?" Taylor's voice snapped Jill to attention. She stood up quickly and backed away. Taylor—no, the fae imposter doing a perfect impersonation of Taylor—stood in the doorway leading to the bedrooms at the back of the house.

"Oh, there you are," Jill said, feigning innocence. "I was just..."

"Just what?" fake Taylor said. She arched a skeptical eyebrow, but her voice remained light and friendly.

"Just...visiting with your dad."

At that instant, the washer fell from Mr. Smart's limp hand and rolled across the floor.

Fake Taylor jumped back like it was a snake. Though she regained her composure in a heartbeat, she shot a withering glare at Jill. *Not good!* Jill thought. She had blown her cover: Jill could see it in fake Taylor's eyes. The imposter's face darkened. Jill's started to panic.

"I'm sorry, I..." Fear and shame bubbled to the surface of her consciousness. What was she trying to do, pull one over on the imposter. It was useless, it was—

She blew out a breath and shook her head. What did she have to feel guilty about? Fake Taylor was trying to get inside her head! Jill concentrated on her amulet.

"Is that yours?" fake Taylor asked, pointing to the washer in front of her on the floor. All pretense of friendliness was now gone from her voice.

Crap. Now what?

Mr. Smart was still oblivious. From the kitchen came the drone of the microwave.

There was no point pretending anymore. Fake Taylor had seen Jill working magic on Mr. Smart. Jill had seen fake Taylor jump away from the steel washer. She imagined what the real Taylor would do in her situation.

Pushing the fear aside, Jill planted her hands on her hips. "So, how are we going to do this?"

Fake Taylor smirked. Jill's feigned bravado must have amused her. "How about this?" she said. "You go home and leave me to do my job."

"And leave the Smarts alone with some kind of evil faery?"

The imposter's face flickered. For half a second, the veneer of Taylor was gone, replaced by a dark-haired young woman with malevolent fire in her eyes. Taylor's face returned as quickly as it had vanished, and the imposter jabbed at Jill with her finger. "What did you call me?" she snapped.

Jill's stomach churned. Too late, she realized she'd just called fake Taylor an ugly name. But there was no point apologizing, even if she felt like it. "I can't let you hurt Taylor's parents," she said.

Now fake Taylor's smirk became a wide, bemused grin. "As if you had any say in the matter."

"I'm serious!" Jill's voice cracked. She clenched her fists. She wished she had brought Maymay's blasting rod.

"Oh no," the imposter deadpanned. "The little girl who thinks she's a witch is serious. I wonder what she'll do." She took a step toward her. "Maybe she'll open her mind and let me take a stroll through her memories. Or send her friend on a wild goose chase that helps me bring down my bitterest enemy. Or maybe," she said with obvious glee, "she'll take food from my hand and eat it." She crossed her arms. "That was incredibly stupid, you know. People in the Winter Court are still laughing about it."

Jill's face warmed and her eyes widened.

"Yes, Jill, I've read your file," fake Taylor remarked. From her tone, she wasn't impressed. "I am a professional, after all." Jill's mind swam to learn that she had a file in the first place!

"Frankly," the imposter continued, "it seems to me the Smarts are in greater danger with you trying to 'help' them than if you'd just leave. Now." She eyed the floor. "And take that vile piece of iron with you."

Jill's temples throbbed. This imposter had done her homework. She knew everything about her, all her mistakes, all her weaknesses. Her throat went dry.

"Got to go long," Mr. Smart mumbled. He was completely engrossed in the game....but without the slightest hint of emotion. Jill cringed as she saw the blank expression on his face. She had to get the Smarts out of there, but how?

She scooped up the washer and slipped it back into her purse. "Why are you doing this?"

"I'm only doing my job, Jill," fake Taylor said. "I take my job very seriously. You do not want to get in my way."

"This isn't over." It was an empty threat, but Jill had to say something.

"It will be soon enough," fake Taylor said. It didn't take magic for Jill to hear the utter confidence in her expression. "And then you and I will have a little talk about manners." She jabbed her finger at Jill. "Nobody calls me the f-word."

Jill gritted her teeth. Fake Taylor had the Smarts in her power. She had more magic, more time to prepare—and fewer qualms about harming others. She had all the advantages, and they both knew it.

"Another day or so, I'd wager, and I'll be on my way," she said. "Unless..."

Jill's temples pounded. "Unless what?" Her imagination crowded with unpleasant possibilities.

Fake Taylor smiled. "This is a nice neighborhood," she said. "It's quaint, in a backward sort of way. Maybe I'll just stay a while. I mean, it's not like Taylor is actually going to survive her little errand."

"If you think you can just take over Taylor's life—"

"I'll do as I please," the imposter said. Her eyes—Taylor's eyes—flashed blue fire. "And anyway, it's been ages since I've had so many deathlings to play with."

Chapter 16

Going through Customs

The first time Taylor traveled via the the faery ring system, it was one of the worst experiences of her life. Her stomach churned, and she was certain she was going to throw up all over Danny Underhill.

Of course, that was before she fully embraced the faery world by eating a faery apple at Moe Fountain's place. As soon as she did that, it was like someone flipped on the lights. Her senses sharpened—not just her sense of sight or hearing, but the way she became attuned to the subtle ebb and flow of magical energies around her.

Her health got better, too. She'd struggled with asthma the first thirteen years of her life. Now, she couldn't even remember the last time she'd had an attack. She had started working out for the first time in her life—and even though she hated the grueling routine Ayoka and her cousin Tsisgwa had set for her, she soon began to thrive.

As her magic matured, she grew accustomed to the previously blood-curdling chaos of flinging herself into the Wonder. She bounced between mushroom rings, standing stones, hidden grottoes, cemeteries, and battlefields. Any place that inspired awe, any place of natural beauty or great antiquity, could potentially be a door into the Wonder. She had progressed to the point that she hardly noticed the disorienting kaleidoscope of sights and sounds. The wildest reaches of the Wonder had become like home.

None of that mattered as she hurled herself toward Tsuwatelda. Bledrus Dingle's words tore her in two. She found herself stripped of every familiar landmark, everything that made the Wonder, as strange as it was, a place she could feel at ease.

They want to kidnap Shanna.

A myriad of scenes flashed through Taylor's vision: ancient petroglyphs, an artesian spring, a ring of mushrooms.

They want me to help them kidnap Shanna!

It was a cruel joke. Crom and Mara felt Shanna had betrayed them to elope with Aulberic Redmane. Now they'd arranged to get Shanna back in their clutches by using her own daughter to betray her.

Her mind raced. What could she possibly do to avoid being part of this? She wanted to rebel, to escape to Ichisi and forget about the whole thing. But in the deepest recesses of her heart, she knew that wasn't an option.

The Fair Folk keep their promises. She wanted to back out, but her whole body shook in revulsion at the very thought of it. Shame and dread sent shivers up and down her spine. What would happen if she put her foot down and refused to go along with Mara's plan? Would her magic go away for good? Would the strain harm her in some other way?

Mara had reminded her of the Gentryman and the Ogre. The Gentryman had gone back on a promise, and it cost him his life.

Would the same thing happen to her?

She landed at the edge of a ring of standing stones that she recognized well. She was in a valley with bald mountain peaks all around. A quarter of a mile ahead was the wooden palisade around the nunnehi town of Tsuwatelda. She could see the central mound rising above the valley floor with its Council House and the homes of the chiefs and their families.

A nunnehi warrior appeared before her out of nowhere. He was dressed in buckskin trousers and a cotton trade shirt adorned with black and red ribbons. He had five or six hoop earrings in each ear and feathers braided into a topknot of straight, black hair. He carried a war club and had a bow and a quiver of arrows slung over his shoulder.

Three others in similar attire appeared behind the first a heartbeat later. Where daoine sídhe like Taylor specialized in fooling the mind, the nunnehi were masters of invisibility. For all she knew, there were two or three dozen more warriors all around, guarding their town beneath the cover of their magical veils.

She thought of Lunso Butcher becoming invisible before her eyes. Was he nearby as well? Her mind darted this way and that, searching for a way to warn the guards without tipping off the Red Fangs.

"*Osiyo*," the first warrior said. "Hello."

"*Osiyo*," Taylor answered. Her mind went blank. What was she supposed to do now? She tried to remember the little bit of Cherokee she'd picked up when she'd visited Shanna over the summer. "*Dohitsu?*" How are you?

The warrior didn't answer. Instead, he asked, "What is your business in Tsuwatelda?"

Taylor spied a big, black cat lurking in the tall grass. Ian Shagfoal the unhinged pooka. Arthek and Treeve, each as small as a mouse, were probably hiding in the nearby trees. The others were bound to be somewhere close, shielded from the guards by their various forms of magic.

"I've...come to visit my friend Ayoka. Chief Tewa's grand-daughter?" Chief Tewa was very cautious about Shanna's safety. No one spoke openly about the fact that he was harboring a fugitive from Arradherry's Winter Court. Even if these warriors knew about Shanna, they would never admit it. That's why Taylor had been instructed to always say she was here to visit Ayoka. It wasn't a lie: Ayoka lived in Tsuwatelda, and the two girls liked to visit when Taylor came to town.

She hoped that by the time she made it to town, she'd think of some way out of this.

"Ayoka?" the warrior said.

"Th-that's right. If you'll excuse me..."

He interposed himself between Taylor and the road into town. He wasn't trying to be threatening—though most nunnehi warriors did just fine without trying.

"Please forgive me," he said. "But I'm afraid I'll need to ask you a few more questions."

Of course you do, Taylor thought.

She took one step toward town, but the warrior wasn't budging. Something had put him on the defensive. Maybe he and his buddies had a clue that Butcher and his men were afoot. Not enough to order the area swept for intruders, but enough to make them wary of an unexpected visitor.

Part of Taylor hoped they would detain her. It was the only way she could see to get out of this mess. She'd have done her best, but failed.

But even entertaining that thought made her stomach queasy. She'd made a promise. It was turning out to be a horrific one, but she just couldn't bring herself to renege on it.

The warrior studied her for no more than a second, though it felt like the better part of a day. When Taylor spoke again, she smiled and put the slightest bit of presence into her voice.

"So...if that's all...?"

The warrior looked at his cohorts. Their shrug said, *You're the ranking officer* and *Don't blame us if something goes wrong*.

"Do you mind showing me what's in your bag?"

Taylor swallowed. Her throat was suddenly parched. She felt a presence behind her—or maybe it was just her imagination: Lunso Butcher's unseen presence quietly warning her not to mess things up.

But what if they saw the faces of the other members of the Red Fang cateran in the mirror? Would they take her into custody or kill her on the spot?

She realized with a start that Mara expected something like this might happen. All of a sudden, her "training" made sense.

"Of course," Taylor said. She shrugged her satchel off her shoulder and handed it over.

"Would you open the bag for me, please."

She complied, all the while projecting presence, drilling it into the nunnehi warriors with her eyes, her smile, her posture.

She held the pack open for him. He peered in, warily at first, but then more relaxed. Her presence was working—the nunnehi were starting to warm up to her—but friendly feelings weren't going to be enough.

Sure enough, his eyes landed on the mirror wrapped in its cloth. He prodded it with his finger.

She pushed even more glamour into her words. *"That's a present."*

He pulled out the mirror. "For your friend Ayoka?"

Taylor chose not to answer. The warrior didn't seem to notice.

She formed an image in her mind of a perfectly ordinary hand mirror. She'd convinced the waitress in Kentucky that her library card was actually a credit card. Now, she'd have to convince three nunnehi that an enchanted mirror wasn't enchanted at all.

The warrior unfolded the cloth. A corner of the mirror came into view—and in that corner, a wide-eyed spriggan peered out, panicked.

Taylor gave the nunnehi everything she had. She watched as his face relaxed from curiosity to dull lethargy.

He folded the cloth over the mirror's face and slid it back into Taylor's pack. Neither of his companions protested. They hadn't seen the spriggan, either.

"Off you go," the warrior slurred. He looked like he might fall asleep with the slightest encouragement. "They'll be closing the gate soon. You'd better hurry."

"Thanks," Taylor said. She slung her pack back over her shoulder and stepped away before he could change his mind.

The town was about about a quarter of a mile away. Taylor counted her steps out as she walked. Every one of them made the leaden lump in her gut the slightest bit heavier.

159

She was on her way to see her birth mother. And when she saw her, she was going to unleash the Red Fangs so they could take her away to be punished for a fifteen-year-old act of disobedience.

Not for the first time, she wondered how Crom and Mara could treat their own daughter this way. Her lip quavered to think they'd managed to involve her in their twisted sense of revenge. Shanna had supposedly betrayed Crom and Mara; now Taylor was on her way to betray Shanna.

"This is sick," she muttered. She'd traveled 200 paces.

"Just follow your orders," Butcher's voice whispered behind her.

So he was following her. She didn't turn around to look: she knew he'd still be invisible. That was apparently his thing, and he did it as well as any nunnehi she'd ever met.

Butcher's presence didn't surprise her; Mara wasn't the type to leave anything to chance. She'd tricked Taylor into owing her this so-called favor, but she would want some assurance Taylor wasn't going to back out at the last minute.

Not that she had a choice. Now that she was close, even the idea of backing out made her sick. Whatever magic compelled the Fair Folk to honor their oaths had burrowed into her stomach and threatened to slice it to ribbons every time she even thought about running.

She stopped to wipe sweat from her forehead. Two hundred and fifty paces. She expelled a breath. Butcher or no Butcher, she couldn't go through with this. As soon as the thought passed through her mind, her gut twisted.

I'm sorry, Jill.

The Fair Folk keep their promises. Even if it kills them.

I'm sorry, Shanna.

She started walking again.

Shanna was the only one of her faery relatives she had any kind of affection for. Her surviving grandparents were all manipulative monsters. Anya Redmane had been willing to destroy her just to spite Shanna. Even after she'd been deposed

160

as Chief Matron of the Summer Court, she'd managed to meddle in Taylor's life, appearing to her in a laundromat in Macon to announce that a loved one was going to die within a year or two.

Taylor shuddered. It was almost exactly the anniversary of that encounter, and here she was, getting ready to unleash the fury of the Winter Court upon her mother.

Crom Cornstack and Mara Hellebore weren't any better. If anything, they were worse. They were trying to take over the world—or at least their corner of it—by bringing down Anya's successor, creating chaos so they could swoop in to restore order as undisputed rulers of Arradherry.

Somewhere out there, she had a cousin, a satyr named Évastre du Marais. She'd only met him once, and he seemed nice enough. Maybe a little...cowardly? No, that wasn't fair. He'd just led a sheltered, pampered life in the mansion his dad had built in the Louisiana bayou.

Taylor wondered if Évastre's dad—her uncle, Lorcan—was out there somewhere. If he was, did he know what was happening in Arradherry? If he thought his niece were in trouble, would he run to help her or would he stand by and watch as everything came crashing down around her?

Would he applaud her for keeping her oath, as terrible as it was?

Four hundred paces. No more than another hundred or so to Tsuwatelda. Taylor could see the warriors guarding the gate, patrolling the wall.

She hadn't heard anything from Butcher after that one curt sentence. Was he still following her? Was he getting ready to play some other role in Mara's plan?

The mirror weighed down her bag, which didn't make any sense. It was only a few ounces of bronze and silver, but it seemed to have a life of its own. She couldn't decide if it was her imagination, or if the mirror was vibrating at her side.

At 480 paces, she found herself holding back tears. Who could do this to their own daughter? Their own granddaughter? It didn't make any sense.

The morality of the Fair Folk rarely did.

At 500 paces, she nodded respectfully toward the warriors ahead of her at the gate. She choked back her tears, took a deep breath, and prepared herself to twist their minds to her will if they gave her any trouble.

One of the guards raised his arm and shouted something to people inside. The gate was being pulled shut for the night, but at the warrior's signal, progress stopped.

There were four guards standing watch, plus however many were tending to the gate. She recognized one of them from her last visit, a young man somewhat shorter than the average nunnehi, but well-muscled and with a winsome smile. She regretted that she'd never learned his name.

Taylor jogged the last fifteen paces. If she looked flustered about nearly missing the gate, maybe they wouldn't noticed how flustered she was to part of a suicide mission.

"*Osiyo!* Thanks for holding the gate," she called. Her presence beamed.

"It's...not really allowed," the warrior said.

"I understand." Taylor tried to look contrite. "I wasn't supposed to be this late. I hate to be a bother."

The warrior looked her over. The sun had set, but Taylor assumed the nunnehi's night vision was at least as good as hers.

He waved her through, and the gate creaked closed. The warriors slid a huge wooden beam across it. It made a harsh smack as it lodged into place. For Taylor, it was the sound of the last nail hammered into a coffin.

There could be no turning back now—if there ever had been.

Mara had her right were she wanted her, literally. The mirror in her pack seemed to hum expectantly.

People milled about. There weren't as many as might have been in a Topside town; life among the nunnehi, and among the Fair Folk generally, moved at a slower pace. Whenever Taylor visited Tsuwatelda, she was reminded of things the Topside world had mostly lost: closeness to the earth, the rhythms of days and seasons, simple pleasures like food and music and unstructured play—things even her mortal grandparents barely remembered.

There were no agendas or appointment books in Tsuwatelda. There weren't any streetlights, either—though most people could conjure any light they needed. When the sun went down, people put down the day's work and ate supper with their families, or else gathered with their neighbors to sing and dance into the night.

In the distance, across the stickball field, was the upper city with its Council House and the homes of Tsuwatelda's elite. In the lower city, the common people laughed and shared stories about their days.

A feeling of dread brought Taylor up short as she thought about what would happen to these people's lives once she unleashed the Red Fangs. Her pulse pounded, and her hands were sweaty. Her knees faltered, resisting her brain's command to keep on walking.

The tears she'd held back earlier began to flow in earnest, and she was glad there were so few people on the street to notice her. She let out a sob and forced herself on.

Then she caught a glimpse of something out of the corner of her eye. It was only there for a second, and then it was gone: a slim, dark shape in an alley.

Was it Butcher again? He or one of his men was bound to be somewhere close by.

She turned the last corner and headed down Shanna's street. With every step, her legs grew heavier, more resistant to where they were taking her. Tears streamed down her cheeks, but she refused to give in to them. She could only hope and pray that somehow she could warn Shanna before she did was she had to do.

She stopped twenty feet from the door. There was a light on inside; Shanna was home, probably eating supper alone.

I can't do this, Taylor thought, and her insides squirmed. *I won't do this!* A stabbing pain tore into her guts, and she let out a chastened whimper.

There it was again: movement in the shadows, but as soon as Taylor looked, it went away.

She had no choice. She took one laborious step and then another. Gathering magic, she knocked at the door.

"Who is it?" Shanna called cheerfully.

Taylor couldn't find her voice to answer.

The door swung open. There was her mother, young and beautiful, in a pair of jeans and a cotton trade shirt cinched at the waist with a beaded belt. In the half light, Taylor could see the shock of electric blue highlights in her short, black hair and the dangly silver earrings in her ears.

Shanna's eyes were wide: surprised but also wary.

"Taylor?"

Taylor brought out the mirror and pulled the cloth from around it. It seemed alive in her hands, itching to break free of her grasp. "I'm so sorry," she whispered. "So sorry."

"I...I don't understand." Shanna gestured for her to come in.

Taylor willed her magic to infuse the mirror. Her voice broke as she shouted, "*Ha zudeia virdiga!*"

Chapter 17

All Netherworld Breaks Loose

The mirror shook so violently Taylor couldn't hold onto it. It jerked itself free from her hand and landed face-up on the ground, glowing with crimson light.

The first of the Red Fangs to appear were the two trolls and the spriggan, who instantly grew to over ten feet tall. All three carried muskets that might have been small cannons. Taylor got ready to blast them, but before she could, one of the trolls grunted and stumbled backward.

Taylor's eyes darted up to see the nunnehi warrior poised on Shanna's roof, bow in hand. Her heart did a somersault. They knew!

More arrows rained down from other warriors who appeared out of nowhere on rooftops and out of alleys. But the remaining troll and the spriggan were smart: they conjured shield spells that gave cover as the rest of the Red Fangs emerged from the mirror.

The skinny Native American fae had appeared before the first arrow hit the troll. He leaped clear of the mirror and thrust his arm forward, throwing a fireball at the house next door to Shanna's. Its thatch roof began to burn.

The two little folk were next. They scampered away, one to the right and the other to the left. They weaved to and fro, cackling and throwing spells at everyone they saw, warrior and civilian alike—and ducking or conjuring shields whenever anyone took a swipe at them.

A troll finally fell after the third nunnehi arrow got him between the eyes. He fell backward, and Taylor had to leap back to keep from being crushed. The arrow had vanished without leaving a wound.

The remaining troll and the spriggan opened fire. Two nunnehi warriors fell as jets of green light slammed into them.

By this time, both trolls and one of the little folk were down. Three nunnehi converged on the spriggan with their flaming war clubs. The spriggan had discarded his firearm—no time to reload—and was wailing away with a nasty bronze-bladed axe with a haft like a tree branch.

The fire-carrier fell when a nunnehi cracked his skull with a war club, but not before he had set three more houses ablaze. He wouldn't have gotten so far, but wherever the little folk had worked their magic, people seemed bewitched. Some broke down, weeping and pounding their fists on the ground. Others cried out as if in agony. Two warriors had actually begun fighting each other.

Taylor gulped back tears. I did this. *It's all my fault.*

The archers had emerged by this time. Two of them rushed toward Shanna, standing stunned in her doorway, while the others started picking off the nunnehi, who were now converging on the house from the ground.

Taylor blasted one of the women, but she conjured a shield that deflected her attack.

"Shanna!" Taylor called. She sprinted forward, grabbing the cloak of one of the women and yanking her backward.

Shanna blasted the woman in the lead, who crumpled to the ground. Two others converged on her, pushing her back inside.

The houses on either side were in flames. The families that lived there had emptied into the street. They and some of the warriors did what they could to keep the fires from spreading further.

"Shanna!" Taylor called again. There were sounds of a struggle inside her mother's house. A familiar voice shouted,

"Let go of her!" A second later, Danny Underhill flew backward out the front door and landed in the middle of the melee.

The sight of Danny shot her with courage.

Taylor gasped, but she kept her head down. Arrows were flying everywhere. The female Red Fangs were as deadly with their bows as the nunnehi. They each held two or three arrows at a time in their bow hands and got off a shot every few seconds. All the while, they leaped and danced in the street, avoiding the arrows of the town's defenders. Wherever they stepped, a trail of black smoke followed them as if their feet were about to catch fire.

Taylor grabbed Danny and helped him to his feet. She was about to try to pull him to safety when she heard Shanna screaming.

"Behind the house!" Danny said, standing shakily. He and Taylor sidestepped the melee, nearly tripped over an unconscious and bleeding little person, and ran to the sound of Shanna's voice.

The women who had rushed the door were there, also billowing black smoke. Now, however, the smoke was taking form: two broad, black wings; a round head with a nasty beak and empty eyes. Giant ravens.

One of the women had Shanna, bound with a gleaming silver cord, draped in front of her on her raven's neck. She lay on her belly, her legs kicking furiously but ineffectively.

The woman uttered a visceral grunt, and the raven took flight. The second woman did the same a heartbeat later.

"No!" Taylor cried.

A nunnehi loosed an arrow, but Shanna's abductor was ready with a shield spell. The arrow twisted away and landed harmlessly on another neighbor's roof.

Taylor cursed. She understood the plan now. The teams in the mirror came in with guns blazing to capture Shanna and create as much chaos as possible. Now they were making their escape.

167

She turned to Danny. "They're heading for the standing stones! We've got to catch them!"

Danny groaned. He seemed tired, but he took off toward the city gate as soon as he processed what Taylor had told him.

Above, two more archers on their smoky, flying mounts joined the two from behind the house. The one carrying Shanna took the lead; the others loosed arrows toward the ground seemingly at random. Townspeople, emerging from their homes because of the commotion, crumpled as elf shot drove them to the ground in agony.

Warriors overtook Taylor and Danny, sprinting for the gate. Others flanked them, leaping from rooftop to rooftop.

Smoke tickled Taylor's nostrils. She turned back and saw a whole city block ablaze. Amid the chaos, two huge, darkened figures surged forward: a troll and a spriggan, advancing with giant strides and shrugging off any who stood in their way.

"Horse!" she cried.

"What?"

"We've got to catch up to them! Be a horse!"

Danny paled at the suggestion. "We're almost there!" he yelled.

The gate loomed ahead of them, ajar. As they got closer, Taylor spied cracked timbers and scorch marks darkening the wood. Team three had apparently been busy, clearing the way for the others to escape.

The remnants of team one were gaining on them. Team two soared overhead on their ghostly giant ravens.

Warriors at the gate loosed their arrows, but the enormous spriggan waved them aside with a shield spell. The troll aimed his musket and fired. The warriors dove for cover—along with Taylor and Danny.

She had to do something! But even if she could settle herself enough to become a blackbird, what good would it do? She might catch up to Shanna, but then what?

The spriggan threw fireballs at the guard house inside the palisade. A second later, he ripped through what remained of the gate, sending splinters in every direction. He wasn't running, but his enormous legs took five feet or more in a stride.

The troll came up behind, and then one of the little folk, still cackling and working his bewitchments on every bystander.

Taylor blasted him so hard he fell flat on his back.

She didn't have time to think, so she didn't. She bolted toward the troll and threw herself upward, grabbing him by the belt and kicking the backs of his legs.

The troll spun around, whipping Taylor, who was hanging on with white knuckles.

"Over here, you big oaf!" Danny called. He advanced on the troll with balls of faery fire blazing in each hand.

What's that *going to do?* Taylor wondered.

The troll swung the butt of his musket like a baseball bat. Danny barely ducked in time, extinguishing his fire orbs as he hit the ground.

"Eelick!" the spriggan growled. "Quit goofin' around!"

"Coming, Santo!" the troll answered. He whipped around again, but Taylor wasn't about to let go. She concentrated all her magic in her hands. Frost began to form between her fingers, in her palms. With another surge of will, she forced everything she had into the troll's back.

He yelped and spun around again.

"Get her off me!" he hollered.

"We gotta get to the standin' stones!"

"But—"

An explosion cut him off. The troll staggered to one side, and Taylor saw a charred patch of ground where a fire ball landed between him and the spriggan.

There was a flash of light, and then a third voice. "We couldn't hold 'em off!" It was Ian Shagfoal, the Red Fang pooka, sprinting toward them.

Santo, the spriggan, cursed.

"Head for the caves!" Before he could break away, Danny bowled into him. Both pookas wrestled on the ground.

Taylor felt huge, rough arms grab her waist. Santo pulled her off the troll's belt and dropped her to the ground. Then the two brutes turned away.

She spun in the dirt, looking for Danny. Shagfoal had him pinned to the ground. She scrambled to her feet and lunged toward them, screaming.

Shagfoal flared his fingers in Danny's face. Taylor jumped on him, and his blast jetted harmlessly into the grass.

Shagfoal's eyes glowed with yellow fire as he crouched on all fours and glared at Taylor. He looked like a short, ugly football lineman waiting for the snap. "Damn spriggan threw away a perfectly good hostage," he said.

Then he sprung, plowing into Taylor, grabbing her arm and flinging her body over his shoulder. At the same time, his body expanded, until he had the form of a sleek, black pony. He took off at a gallop.

No matter how hard she tried, Taylor couldn't pull her hands from his shaggy mane.

Danny rolled onto his belly. He launched himself forward, hoping he'd regained enough magic to become a dog—but it didn't work. He slammed face-first into the grass. By the time he'd regained his feet, he knew there was no way to catch up to Taylor and the other pooka.Over his shoulder, black smoke billowed from the lower city. Warriors, now converted into a fire brigade, shouted orders as commoners streamed to safety outside the palisade.

In the other direction, a small but resolute band of nunnehi warriors shot arrows from the ring of standing stones into the retreating assault force. A cinnamon-haired pisgy fell beneath a hail of elf shot. Another figure, a blonde woman dressed in black, sat dazed on the ground.

Someone called his name. He spun back around to see Bryn and Évastre sprinting toward him.

"What's happening?" Bryn said.

Danny met her wide-eyed expression. "Snatchers!" he said. "At least a dozen of 'em!" He slapped his hands on Bryn's shoulders. "They got Taylor—and her mom, too!"

Bryn gazed at the ongoing battle over Danny's shoulder.

"Wait a minute," Bryn said. "Taylor, the girl I impersonated that one time?"

Danny nodded.

"What's she doing here?"

Danny swallowed. He didn't have a good answer for that one. It seemed like she came with the snatchers—but what would she be doing with a gang of no-accounts like that?

"Hold up," Évastre said. "Taylor's *mom* was here? My aunt? Shanna Hellebore? I thought she was..."

"That was kind of the plan," Danny said. With a sigh, he added, "Looks like it didn't work."

"So what happens now?" Bryn asked.

Danny didn't answer. Instead, he turned and jogged toward the rocky slope of one of the peaks that surrounded Tsuwatelda. Bryn and Évastre called after him, but he just kept going until he arrived at the back of the nunnehi line. The snatchers were pushing toward a tall, narrow gash in the rock.

The pooka stopped and sucked in deep, labored breaths while resting his hands on his knees.

"Get back!" a warrior called. Danny was close enough to see there were ten of them in two ranks of five. He skidded to a stop on the damp grass.

"They're heading for the tunnels, ain't they?" Danny wheezed.

The warrior loosed an arrow, but it was swept away by a troll's shield spell. The squad advanced, the rear rank moving to the front as the former forward rank drew handfuls of arrows from their quivers. They were now less than sixty yards from the mouth of the cave.

Another warrior looked him in the eye as he nocked his arrow. "You're the pooka, aren't you? I've seen you at Chief Tewa's house." He sprung to the front as the ranks shifted again.

"That's me," Danny said. He'd almost gotten his breath under control. "They got prisoners."

The forward rank loosed a volley of a dozen arrows in a matter of seconds. As the ranks advanced once more, the warrior said, "We saw."

The last of the snatchers, a scowling spriggan, ducked into the cave entrance. He fired one last ineffectual shot from his musket before vanishing into the darkness.

"But you're gonna get 'em, right?"

"Half of us," he said. "Half will have to guard the standing stones until reinforcements come."

Danny looked back toward the town. Smoke and flames gutted upward into the night sky. It was going to be a while before reinforcements got there. Bryn and Évastre were sprinting toward him.

In front of the cave, a red-clad leprechaun lay unconscious in the grass.

Danny's muttered a curse.

The warrior—he must have been the leader—barked orders in Cherokee. Two men sprang forward to secure the prisoner. Five others discarded their bows and arrows and drew war clubs from their belts.

"I'm going with you," Danny said.

"Danny, no," Bryn said as she reached his side. "Not until—"

"She's right," the nunnehi leader said. "We can handle this."

"I'm going!" Danny said. He'd never forgive himself if anything happened to Taylor. "I've been in those tunnels before. Have you?"

The leader said nothing.

"They wind around so much you're liable to meet yourself on the way out."

"And you can guide us?"

Danny bit his lip. "Let me try."

The leader sighed. "A little knowledge is better than none at all—if you can keep up."

"Just watch me."

His eyes glowed—dimly, but surely. He clenched his jaw, closed his eyes, and forced himself to concentrate. The change seemed to take forever, and it was as disorienting as the first time he'd done it nearly two hundred years ago. His head swam as he felt his body contracting, his bones rearranging themselves, his skull compressing to half its size.

He fell to all fours in the form of a big, black dog. It had taken every ounce of his will, but he'd done it.

He sniffed the air and bounded forward.

Chapter 18

The Tunnels

The last time Taylor visited the tunnels on the outskirts of Tsuwatelda, she had been thrown into a sack and carried away by a belligerent dwarf. This time, with her hands bound with magical silver cord, she was pushed downward into the darkness by a murderous pooka.

By the light of half a dozen floating will-o'-the-wisps, she could make out the remaining members of the Red Fangs cateran. Lunso Butcher led the way, musket in hand. Next came Eelick the troll, followed by three hedge-riders. Shanna, still bound with magic ropes, stumbled between two of them, who looked so much like each other they must have been sisters.

Next came Taylor herself. Ian Shagfoal shoved her on, and she scraped her shoulder against the rock. She hoped Shanna hadn't given much for the leather jacket Taylor wore; it had seen a rough week.

Taking up the rear were Santo and Arthek, the spriggans, now shrunken down to their normal, unimpressive height. They scowled and peered over their shoulders. Every thirty or forty yards, they dropped little paper packets along the trail—magical traps for anyone who came after them.

The nunnehi will come for us, she told herself. If not for her, then at least for Shanna. Her mom was the biggest prize in the Wonder: the Winter Court wanted her back, obviously, but stealing her from Tsuwatelda was a slap in the face to the nunnehi. They'd rescue her to defend their honor, if nothing else.

175

There were eight Red Fangs and two hostages. Taylor wasn't sure how many nunnehi would be coming, but she knew they'd come. They had to.

She tried to gather magic, but her bonds made that impossible. The cord been laced with iron, or else imbued with some other kind of enchantment that drained her power. All she could do was keep stumbling forward beneath the pooka's rough hands.

"This would go faster if I could get my balance!" she spat.

"Quiet back there!" Lunso Butcher hissed.

"You heard him," Shagfoal growled. "You wanna wake the neighbors?"

The thought had, in fact, occurred to her. The dwarves who lived in these tunnels wouldn't appreciate uninvited visitors, especially if they threatened to drag them into a battle between the daoine sídhe and the nunnehi.

The tunnel leveled off, then forked. Butcher pulled a crinkled piece of paper from inside his vest. He unfolded it and studied it by the blue light of his fire orb.

Eelick the troll set his hand against the wall and bowed his head in concentration. Rather than glowing, his eyes went utterly black. "Go right," he said.

"Lemme think!" Butcher snapped. He flipped the map right-side up.

"Go right," the troll repeated. His eyes went back to their normal, watery pale green.

"I got this!" Butcher re-folded the map and trudged down the rightmost path.

Just then, an explosion rocked the tunnel behind them. Somebody had sprung one of the spriggans' traps.

Please hurry, Taylor thought.

"Look alive!" Butcher shouted. He picked up his pace down the right tunnel. Santo and Arthek unslung their enormous muskets.

The tunnel forked again. This time, Butcher led them down the leftmost passage. This passage was no longer a simple crack in the rock but a rough-hewn corridor, wide enough for two or three to walk through side by side.

They hurried on. Taylor fell to her knees, forcing Shagfoal to drag her. Anything she could do to slow them down...

"Stop right there!" someone called. The wheezing, nasal voice came from somewhere up ahead. A dwarf stood at the other end of the corridor. He was nearly six feet tall, broad-shouldered and barrel-chested, with a jet-black, greasy beard. He wore overalls stained with coal dust and held an axe in his meaty hands.

Behind him, two other dwarves filled the passageway.

Eelick fired his musket without even aiming. The boom of exploding black powder reverberated through the hall, and the dwarves hit the floor.

Butcher called for the Red Fangs to retreat. They double-timed back up the corridor to the last fork. There, they swung around the bend at breakneck speed and shot up the other corridor. This was a narrower way, but still shaped by dwarven tools. Butcher and Eelick led the way.

Taylor heard a dog barking. She turned back to see a handful of nunnehi warriors gaining on them, led by the glowing eyes of a sleek, black Labrador retriever.

Danny!

One of the archers loosed an arrow, and a hedge-rider crumpled to the ground.

"Keep going!" Butcher yelled.

The corridor ended in a T. Two dwarves, different from the first three, were waiting for them. Eelick plowed into them with a blood-curdling howl. The troll grabbed one dwarf by the collar—Taylor recognized him from the eyepatch he wore—and flung him away to the left. The other fell back to the right.

They entered this new corridor with the dwarves regathering to their left and the nunnehi behind them and gaining fast. There was no choice but to go right.

Butcher led them on. Soon, they came to a stone staircase leading upward, into the heart of the mountain.

Angry shouts echoed behind them. Nobody had had time to explain to the dwarves what was going on. All they knew was that their home was being invaded. The nunnehi would have to stop at least long enough to assure them that they were there to help.

The dog barked once more, his voice ringing through the bare, stone tunnels as if coming from every direction at once.

Butcher pulled out his map. At the top of the stairs was another long corridor that ended at a set of double doors. This corridor was a wider than the previous one, and its vaulted roof rose ten or twelve feet high. Lanterns hung unlit in brass wall sconces.

"That way! Then left!" Butcher thundered, pointing toward the doors. The Red Fangs bolted forward.

They'd covered over half the distance when the doors swung open. Twenty yards away, a handful of nunnehi warriors poured into the room, their flaming war clubs crackling. They'd somehow circled around to head the Red Fangs off.

A woman suddenly gasped in pain. Shanna had stomped on a hedge-rider's foot. She whipped around, straining against her cords. Taylor bit Shagfoal's arm so hard it brought blood. The pooka wailed and shoved Taylor to the floor.

At the same time, the nunnehi sprang into action. Butcher and one of the two remaining hedge-riders fell in the first few seconds. Eelick roared and stomped. Where his foot hit the paving stones, they cracked away from him, gouging a deep rift in the floor that sent three nunnehi diving for the side walls.

At the same time, the spriggans grew to giant size. They filled the corridor nearly to the ceiling. They kicked and grabbed at anyone who came near, keeping the nunnehi off balance. One of them crumpled unconscious under Arthek's size-thirtysomething foot.

Taylor felt movement above her, then there was a snip, and her hands were free. She rolled over to see a nunnehi warrior standing above her, deflecting a blow from Santo's massive fist.

The dwarves appeared at the top of the stairs, with Danny in dog form leading the way. The tall dwarf with the axe was the first one into the fray. With an inhuman grunt, he slammed his weapon into Ian Shagfoal's side. The pooka's shield spell deflected the blow, but he was unprepared for the dwarf's savage follow-through. He buried his shoulder in the pooka's chest and drove him into the wall.

The dwarf backed off just enough to swing his axe again. This time, though, Shagfoal let out a cackling laugh and blinked away. The axe struck stone, and the handle snapped.

The Red Fangs were cornered, with nunnehi blocking one exit and dwarves blocking the other. Taylor crawled and stumbled to Shanna. Kneeling beside her, she tried to undo the cords around her wrists.

Just then, the two hedge-riders grabbed Shanna and Taylor and heaved them to their feet, shoving them toward Eelick and Arthek. Taylor unleashed a blast, but it hardly slowed Eelick down at all. He had his rough, warty arms around her in no time. She couldn't tell if she'd loosened Shanna's bonds.

The hedge-riders cast stunning spells that filled the corridor with smoke, flashing lights, and the sound of a dozen bombs going off. In the confusion, they made for the doors with the troll and the two spriggans, bearing their prisoners, close behind.

Following Butcher's previous instructions, they turned immediately to the left. After a few feet, this way led them once more into a rough, natural tunnel. Not far past the door, the way sloped downward and and the tunnel itself narrowed—though it was still tall enough for the spriggans to maintain their giant size.

Danny barked, the sound bouncing off the rocks like a ghostly warning.

Shanna doubled over, grunting against Arthek's vise-like grip. When she looked up, her eyes blazed with blue fire. Her body was suddenly bathed in blue-white light. As she let out a triumphant scream, the spriggan let go of her. The insides of his forearms were thick with frost.

Taylor had done it! Shanna's hands were free, and she was able to use magic.

Now it was Taylor's turn to make the most of the opportunity Shanna had given her. She'd already seen that her blasts did next to nothing against the troll, so she turned her attention to the two hedge-riders. A well-placed kick forced Eelick to drop her to the ground. She threw every ounce of magic into a blast aimed directly at the head of the nearest of the women. She was unconscious before she hit the ground.

The second hedge-rider drew her knife, but Shanna already had her hands on either side of her head. Waves of cold poured off her. The woman jerked in pain, then shrieked, then fell, blue with frostbite and unconscious, next to her sister.

Arthek took a step toward them when Danny barked once more. He had slipped between Santo's legs and chomped on Arthek's heel. The spriggan howled and kicked him off. Danny hit the side of the tunnel with a yelp.

Taylor tried to blast Arthek, but with no effect. She hadn't had enough time to recharge. Beside her, Shanna looked like she was in the same shape.

Santo lifted Danny by the scruff of his neck. "Get the hostages!" he called. Eelick and Arthek did as they were told.

The nunnehi and the dwarves appeared at the top of the tunnel, stopping abruptly when they saw Shanna, Taylor, and Danny held fast by their captors.

"Don't come no closer!" Santo yelled. His monstrous arm was wrapped around Danny. In his other hand, he held a knife to the pooka's ribs.

The nunnehi's flaming war clubs crackled—the only sound in the tunnel besides everyone's labored breathing. But they held their position.

The two hedge-riders groaned and slowly got up.

Danny whined and shivered in Santo's iron grip. It took him longer to resume his two-legged shape than it should have— which probably kept him from stabbing himself with Santo's knife. The spriggan held him fast, though, and growled into his pointed ear.

Once Danny had shifted, Taylor could see more clearly that his left arm hung limp at his side. He seemed tired, dazed. A little spot of blood appeared under his right sleeve where Santo's knife had nicked him.

"We're leaving, and you ain't following," Santo said. "Got it?"

"Leave the women and the pooka," the leader of the nunnehi said.

"Not tupping likely," one of the hedge-riders muttered.

"Eelick?" Santo said.

The troll shoved Shanna toward the two women, who grabbed her and wrenched her arms behind her. He set his warty hand against the tunnel wall, and all at once the whole cavern shook.

The spriggans and the hedge-riders retreated deeper into the tunnel. A second later, the ceiling collapsed between them and their pursuers. Dust filled the narrow passage, but the Red Fangs forced their captives to plunge deeper into the earth.

Taylor kicked against Arthek's knees, accomplishing nothing. They were cut off from the only people who could help them. Soon they'd be free of the tunnels and on their way back to Cair Cullen.

Taylor's birth mother must have had the same thought, and had no intention of going back to her parents. Shanna stumbled, dragging a hedge-rider down with her. She and the hedge-rider wrestled for a second. Then Shanna shoved the heel of her hand into the archer's face and let loose a blast.

The other woman dropped as if dead. Shanna grabbed her knife and swiped at the other one, who leaped back with a curse.

Danny growled and twisted in Santo's arms, digging his foot into the most sensitive spot he could find. The spriggan loosened his grip, more from surprise than pain, but it was enough for Danny to drop to the floor and scurry away on his hands and knees.

He charged straight for Arthek, howling.

Turn into a dog and bite him! Taylor thought. *Why aren't you shifting?*

Arthek shrugged Taylor to the floor. The hedge-rider and the troll loomed above her. She blasted the hedge-rider, who fell backward and struck her head against the rocks. Taylor grinned with satisfaction, but just as quickly the troll scooped her up and held her fast.

She watched in horror as Danny faced off against the two spriggans. At over ten feet tall, they practically filled the tunnel. She'd seen Danny take on spriggans before. In the open, he could use his speed and agility to gain the upper hand. But in an enclosed space like this?

Taylor struggled in Eelick's warty arms.

She expected Danny would become a rabbit and scamper free any second. He could escape and go for help. Instead, he pulled a little bronze knife from his belt. It wasn't much of a weapon, and the look on his face said he knew it.

Why doesn't he shape-shift?

Danny took a swipe at Arthek, then backed away before the spriggan could reach him with a massive fist.

Santo came on him from behind. Danny twisted around and bolted for the far wall.

He wasn't fast enough. Arthek caught him by the collar and shoved him up into the ceiling. Danny gasped harshly as he hit the stone with a *thunk!*

Arthek slammed Danny to the floor with all of his giant strength. As soon as he did, Santo stomped on his chest.

Danny spat blood.

"The pooka's tough," Santo commented.

"This'll be fun," Arthek said, then kicked Danny all the way to the opposite wall.

"*Stop it!*" Taylor screamed.

Eelick shrieked and dropped Taylor. The troll fell to the ground, clutching the back of his thigh. Taylor rolled on the ground to see Shanna standing over him with a bloodied knife in her hand.

"*Back off!*" Shanna yelled, and Taylor could feel her presence roll through the tunnel like a thundercloud. Eelick curled up into a fetal position. The two spriggans stumbled backward toward the place where the roof had caved in.

It barely registered when the dwarves broke through the cave-in and the nunnehi swarmed into the tunnel, quickly taking charge of the remaining members of the Red Fangs. Eelick used his earth magic to open a hole in the floor. He disappeared with three nunnehi on his trail.

Taylor didn't care. She didn't take time to stand up. She scrambled on all fours to Danny's side, tears welling up.

"Oh, God," she whispered.

His face and his shirt were covered with blood, and one leg bent the wrong way. He coughed weakly, then winced at the effort.

"Danny," Taylor said.

He didn't open his eyes. Taylor knew that if he had, they wouldn't be glowing.

He coughed again. Blood and spittle spattered his chin.

"Taylor," he rasped.

Taylor set a finger on his bloody lips. "Just rest," she said with a sniffle. "Save your strength."

"Tell...Claudia..." Danny collapsed in another coughing fit. He clutched his side and scrunched is face in agony.

"We need help!" Taylor shouted. "*Now!*"

At some point, Shanna had joined Taylor on the floor, wrapping her arms around her shoulder. Now Taylor pushed her away so she could stand and get help.

The dwarf with the eye patch was by their side in an instant. Blain. For some reason, she remembered his name was Blain.

He stooped down and pulled open Danny's eyelid. As Taylor feared, there was no fire there.

"You've got to save him," she said.

He didn't look at her, but he answered, "He's pretty beat up."

"*You've got to try, damn it!*"

He sighed. "Dwally? Guys? Some help here?" The other dwarves gathered around.

"What's his name?"

"D-Danny. Dandan, that is. Dandan Underhill."

"You wouldn't know his true name, would you?"

"No."

Blain frowned. "He defended our home. We'll do what we can." He began to hum an alien, dwarfish tune. His four friends gathered around and joined in. Shanna helped Taylor to her feet and shepherded her away. Blain needed room to work.

The hum became an eerie, savage howl that filled the tunnel and vibrated in Taylor's ribcage as it rose to an almost unbearable volume. Taylor could feel powerful waves of wild, primal magic washing over the tunnel, rebounding against the walls, taking up every open space.

Shanna set a steadying hand against the wall and held Taylor in her other arm. The nunnehi stood nearby, braced, as if ready for the floor to give way beneath them.

"He shouldn't have come after me," Taylor whispered.

"He came after both of us," Shanna said. "I think he's too loyal to have done anything else."

"But...." Taylor gazed to where the dwarves continued their bizarre healing ritual. "But why didn't he shape-shift?"

"He told me something happened at Tobarty," Shanna said. Her faced showed concern. "He wouldn't tell me the details. He just said he had to...tell a lie." She shuddered as she said it.

Taylor's heart sank. Danny had sacrificed his magic, and she had a good idea why. He had planned to find Claudia so she could help him in Tobarty. But that could have gotten dicey. If somebody asked him the wrong question and he couldn't weasel out of answering....

Her gaze returned to the pooka, fighting for his life as the dwarves droned, howled, and chanted. The minutes ticked by.

Then, the tidal wave of magic subsided the same way it had built up.

And it was over.

Taylor took a step forward, shrugging off her mother's embrace.

Blain rose, staggering. He looked so tired, so pale—paler, if possible, even than his normal chalky complexion.

Taylor asked the question with her eyebrows. The dwarf shook his head and frowned. He staggered again. He'd have fallen forward if one of his friends hadn't caught him.

A ball of lead dropped into Taylor's stomach.

Her breath came in short gasps. The room spun.

She fell to her knees, and then to her face.

She did nothing for the next five minutes but pound the ground and sob.

Chapter 19

A Faery Funeral

William pulled his covers tighter. He and the guys were exhausted. They'd spent all afternoon and half the night tracking Taylor. At least they were long past those Autumn Court soldiers, and thankfully it didn't look like they'd been followed. Haggler rested peacefully. He had fought to stay lucid all the way here, fighting off the effects of the elf-shot. He'd fallen asleep almost before Pete could spread out his bedroll for him. Wasko and Pete both assured William that Haggler would be good as new in the morning. They all needed to rest.

There was no telling how many miles they'd covered. William had no clue where he was except that it was somewhere in the mountains. It had to be hours past midnight; the starry night was crisp and clear and black. All he knew as the cold wind blew across his face was that his limbs burned with fatigue. He wanted to find Taylor. Mercy's agitated state earlier that night told him she was close. But even the thought of seeing her safe and sound could barely compete with the prospect of shutting his eyes for just a little while.

His dad always said you can't give your all when you're running on empty. As he lay on the hard ground and his legs and back throbbed, he appreciated the wisdom of that.

It had taken all of his cajoling, not to mention a sleep charm courtesy of Wasko, to get Mercy to settle down for the night. William got the impression the dog would track Taylor to the end of the earth, no matter how long it took, and never even slow down.

William rolled over on his side. As much as he wanted to rest—as much as he needed it—the events of the day kept him awake. What had happened with those Autumn soldiers? How had he pulled off that fire magic? How was he able to keep his cool in the heat of battle? He'd been in some pretty serious scrapes in the last few hours, but as he thought back on what had happened, he realized he hadn't even been scared.

And how was he able to recognize the apple trees on the soldiers' brooches? There was probably a spell for super-vision, but he certainly didn't know it.

He yawned. Maybe tomorrow he'd start finding answers.

He turned on his other side, rearranging his bedroll as the covers fell off his shoulders. Just as he closed his eyes, though, something caught his attention: pinpricks of light higher up the mountainside. They moved slowly in a single file from left to right, edging down the slope.

William sat up.

The wind carried the sound of a bell to his ears. It wasn't the usual clear ringing sound he associated with bells. This one sounded dull and heavy, as if muffled.

"Guys," he whispered. He reached for his staff as he kicked his covers off.

Pete snored.

"Guys," William whispered again, a little louder this time.

"Wh-hrrm-huh?" Wasko said, rolling over. He reached blindly for his bowler hat.

"Something's going on."

Haggler poked his head up. He still looked vaguely disoriented, but better than earlier. William pointed into the distance. The procession of lights was coming nearer, but they weren't headed directly for them. Instead, they were following a mountain trail that curved downward and away.

William peered intently. Despite the near-total darkness, the scene soon resolved itself into something he could understand.

It was indeed some kind of procession. There were dozens of people walking two by two, either holding orbs of faery fire or allowing the lights to circle around them.

They were a curious mixture of fae of seemingly every race, both little folk and regular-sized. Leading the procession were six nunnehi warriors carrying someone on a stretcher, covered, it seemed, with snow.

It looked like a funeral. The mourners wore grave expressions, but they were dressed in ordinary clothes. They were, however, wearing wreaths of flowers or carrying them in bouquets: pansies, violets, snapdragons, and mums. They also carried slim tree branches that reminded William of riding crops, or maybe of his Maymay's blasting rod.

They slowly wove down the side of the mountain. If they knew they were being watched, they didn't let on. The wind shifted, bringing the sound of faery music: a slow, mournful vocalizing that pierced William's soul. He'd never heard anything so beautiful—or so plaintive. He wanted to weep, but he didn't know why.

Careful, he thought. He took a breath and reached for his jet amulet, passing his thumb over the etched markings on its face.

He watched as the procession moved on. Even in the dim light, William found himself zeroing in on subtle details. The body on the stretcher—he was sure it was a funeral procession now—wasn't covered with snow at all but with heaps of white flowers. They partially obscured the curly black hair and the simple buckskin jacket without totally masking the human-like shape of the deceased.

Soon he could make out the pained expressions on the people's faces. Near the front was a pretty Native American girl—Ayoka!

Then his eyes focused on the person next to her, tears streaming down her cheeks as she sung with all her heart.

"T-Taylor?" he whispered.

Taylor's eyes met William's. What in the world was he doing there? She wanted to run to him, to let him to hold her tight and assure her everything was going to be okay, but she didn't dare. Instead of gesturing for him to approach, she cast him a wary look and waved him away with her stick.

He got the message. He nodded and stayed put, though by his expression, he didn't know why.

He didn't know what Ayoka had explained to Taylor mere minutes before, that faery funerals could be dangerous for any Topsiders who got too close.

Ayoka was one of the first people to reach Taylor when the nunnehi brought her, Shanna, and the captive remainder of the Red Fangs out of the tunnels and back to Tsuwatelda Valley. The dwarves followed behind, exhausted from the fight and from their failed attempt to save Danny.

The nunnehi reported to their superiors. Others led Taylor and Shanna away and threw blankets over them to stave off the chill of the night. Taylor huddled with her birth mother in a state of shock. When Ayoka came and sat beside her, it was all Taylor could do to look her in the eye.

The dwarves offered to dig Danny's grave. The captain of the nunnehi accepted this as an expression of their gratitude. "An honor," he said with a crisp bow to Dwally Wormfield, the dwarven leader. They slumped back toward the entrance to their underground domain while Shanna filled in Ayoka about everything that had happened.

Taylor offered details about her travels over the last few days, but she didn't trust herself to say much. Thinking about anything took too much out of her.

The three sat beneath the town's standing stone portal. The fires in town had been put out and the injured were being attended to. No one had died—no one *else*, Taylor thought as she fought back another wave of tears—but many had been injured, and it would be days before the townsfolk had a clear sense of how extensive the property damage was.

The Fair Folk apparently didn't believe in postponing a burial. It was still hours before dawn when the nunnehi captain approached Taylor and Ayoka to escort them to the ceremony.

By fae custom, Danny would be buried in the Topside world. The dwarves had found a suitable location on the side of Pilot Knob. The nunnehi blinked Taylor, Shanna, and Ayoka to where the procession was supposed to start. Ikegwa was there, a young boy Taylor had met on her first visit to Tsuwatelda. A yunwi tsunsdi couple and their three children took the time to introduce themselves as the Cloud family. They had been Danny's employers for the past two years.

Others came to see her. Bryn, the girl who had been Danny's partner two years ago when Taylor first met him. She was with Taylor's cousin Évastre, of all people! She hadn't seen him since Louisiana, when she'd gotten into this mess with Mara in the first place.

Why does it take a funeral to get everybody together?

Then another thought came to her. "Claudia should be here!" she sobbed.

Her absence was just one final insult. She and Danny went back a hundred years or more, and it was obvious they cared about each other. Now, she'd have to learn what had happened and mourn alone with no chance to say a proper goodbye.

Taylor cursed.

Mr. Cloud offered her a garland of violets and purple mums. Others wore similar necklaces of flowers, so Taylor followed their example.

"It's customary," Ayoka whispered. "And this." She held out a wooden switch cut from a tree branch. It was as thick as Taylor's pinky and longer than her thigh.

She asked the question with her eyes: *What's this for?*

"You'll see," Ayoka said. "It's...not really a nunnehi thing. More like...I mean...." She gestured helplessly, not wanting to offend.

"Pookas come from Europe," Taylor guessed. "This is what white fae do. What...*we* do." There was still so much about her

191

heritage that Taylor didn't know. Most of what she'd learned, she hated. Preparing for Danny Underhill's funeral, that hatred bubbled dangerously close to the surface.

The procession began. The nunnehi from the tunnels carried the simple wooden bier on which Danny's body lay, festooned with white flowers. The mourners summoned faery fire and marched slowly, side by side, behind the pall bearers. The leader of the procession, an elf to judge by his blond hair and lithe features, rang a muffled bell. Someone began to intone a funeral dirge—an anguished tune in a minor key, rendered in wordless vocalizations that set something vibrating at the core of Taylor's being. It reminded Taylor of a poleman's holler, only more relentlessly despondent.

She thought of her grandpa Smart's funeral years ago. Everybody was sad, of course, but there was also a sense of completion. He'd lived a good life, and his loved ones sent him on with hymns and Scripture readings that brought them comfort.

There was no comfort to be found in Danny's death. She didn't know much about faery beliefs, but she couldn't ever remember any of her friends in the Wonder ever talking about heaven or reincarnation or anything like that. They weren't sending Danny on to something else, she realized. He was simply gone.

When Taylor spied William crouching behind a hillock, her heart skipped a beat. He must have come looking for her, which meant he and Jill had figured out about Layla. She needed to know what was happening back home.

But not right now. First, she had to say goodbye to Danny. She marched on, adding her own strained voice to the dirge.

Her thoughts drifted far from Pilot Knob, to the day in the park when Danny ran off the bogeyman who'd tried to kidnap her for the Winter Court. Further images came to her, unbidden. Danny's fumbling attempts to teach her to shape-shift. The look on his face when she was thrown into his prison cell in Osaa's underwater domain. The twinkle in his eye whenever he pulled

192

off a really good prank. Did he *really* drive a chicken stampede against Mara Hellebore?

He always found a way to keep Taylor going when she wanted to give up. He never complained that she asked too much of him.

He had no business trying to save me!

The ball of blue-white flame in Taylor's hand flared.

Stupid pooka! Let somebody else save the day for a change!

Taylor's song became a miserable descant that forced jarring, discordant harmonies against the other voices.

They arrived at the spot where the dwarves had dug a pit. They stood around it, hands still dirty, shovels at their sides like soldier's weapons at parade rest. They added their animalistic growls as an undertone to the dirge of the other mourners.

With every note, Taylor felt more magic swirling around her, disorienting her. She watched everything happening as if from outside herself, as if standing just over her own shoulder and observing dispassionately while at the same time feeling like her heart was about to explode with pain and fury.

The nunnehi set the bier on the ground beside the grave. Two of them lifted Danny's body and held it over the hole. When they let go, it drifted slowly down as if on a cushion of air.

Without a signal from any conductor, the song changed key: still minor, but higher pitched. The whole group of mourners gathered around, at least two dozen of them. Mr. Cloud pulled off his flower garland and threw it in pieces into the grave. One of his sons did the same.

The song shifted again. Now it was less a tune and more a wild cry of utter desolation. Others tore off their garlands. Some landed in the grave, others fell to the ground to be trampled.

Taylor howled with rage and ripped the flowers from her own neck. All around her, fire orbs blazed with renewed intensity—red, white, orange, green, and blue.

Around her, people snapped their branches in two and shook them at the starry night in defiance.

Then one of the dwarves pitched a shovelful of earth onto Danny's body.

If it hadn't been real to Taylor before, that single act drove everything home. He was truly gone. It was no prank, no illusion. He was never coming back.

Taylor was so full of hurt and anger that she nearly floated out of her shoes. She gripped her broken, frost-covered branches so tightly her knuckles turned white.

Her whole body shook. The shriek of the crowd reached a fever pitch. Her voice was scratchy and broken, but she didn't back off, she wasn't ready to settle down. She refused to let up until she had shouted out every last drop of grief if it took her all night. If it took her a hundred years!

She howled louder than anyone—even the dwarves. There was something cleansing, renewing, in the feeling of animalistic abandon.

Suddenly, all the lights went out at some unspoken signal. There was movement all around. Mourners rushed off in every direction. Some blinked away in a flash of superheated dust. Most simply ran pell mell across the frosty grass, lashing out with their branches at who knows what.

Taylor ran as well, barely watching where she was going. She screamed curses into the darkness until she blacked out.

Chapter 20

A Ghost from the Past

Taylor was barely aware of her actions or her surroundings. She certainly couldn't have explained why she ran howling from Danny's grave, stumbling over rocks and roots, slashing at anything—or nothing—with her wooden switches.

In her berserker frenzy, she might have whipped William silly, but a redtick coon hound slammed into her before she could get to him. It set its paws on her shoulders and silently yelped and wagged its tail.

She took a swipe at the dog, but only succeeded in knocking it off of her. By the time it had circled around her a second time, she was coming to her senses.

She fell to her knees, coughing with every labored breath. Her screaming had torn her throat to pieces. It was hot and raw, and she needed something to drink. Her head swam. Her temples pounded. She'd drawn up every ounce of her anger and frustration and hurled it to the night wind. Now her whole body shuddered as she drew in each agonizing gasp of frigid air.

Faery funerals were not for the faint of heart.

She threw her head back and gazed into the starry sky. For an instant she thought she might lash out again, but she was spent.

"Taylor!" William called. Golden light beamed from the ring on his right hand. She struggled to contain her smoldering fury.

"Miss Hellebore!" another voice added. A round little person peeked his head over the hillock.

"Pete?" she croaked. She took deep breaths. Her chest heaved. All her energy had drained away like water down the drain. The dog licked her face. She fell onto her back, exhausted. She dropped her switches and tried to push the beast off of her.

Two more little folk appeared: Haggler and Wasko.

Taylor fought her way to her knees. Her head swam, and the dog wouldn't leave her alone. She braced herself to keep from getting pushed down again. Then she recognized the dog.

"Mercy?"

The dog silently barked at the sound of her name.

"Mercy, heel!" Haggler called. The dog kept licking Taylor's face.

"Mercy!"

It finally got down on all fours and trotted over to Haggler. The albino little person offered the dog a treat. "Good girl," he said, patting her flank.

Taylor stayed on her knees, looking for the strength to stand.

William knelt in front of her. Wasko, Pete, and Haggler came up behind him.

Taylor sniffled. She must have looked like a mess. She coughed again, and puffed out in an icy breath.

"Taylor?" William whispered. She met his eyes, and all her emotions came back again. She tilted to one side and let out a defeated moan.

"They killed Danny," she said. She bit her lip. She had to keep it together.

William's jaw dropped. He gazed over Taylor's shoulder in the direction of the grave. Taylor could hear the dwarves shoveling earth, patting it down.

Before she realized she was doing it, she waddled on her knees to William and wrapped her arms around him, squeezing him tight.

"They killed...? Who...?"

Taylor didn't know how to begin. Before she could even start, Shanna and Ayoka arrived. Good. They could tell the story.

Shanna and Ayoka and the little folk circled around Taylor and William. It was a long time before Taylor pushed William away and stood up. Her legs were stiff from kneeling. Her whole body felt heavy and worn, like she'd just lost a stickball game to a team of angry giants.

"I'm just going to...." She didn't finish her sentence. She just wandered away from the circle. William started to follow her, but somebody held him back.

"Give her a minute," Ayoka said.

"Yeah," William said, distracted. Taylor didn't precisely storm off, but it was obvious she didn't want company.

Ayoka gave William a sidelong hug. "Good to see you again."

Her touch brought him back to reality. In the distance, the grave diggers finished their work. With heads bowed, they trudged up the side of the mountain without further ado.

"Taylor said...Danny..." William looked around, disoriented. It was hard to process everything.

"They attacked the town," Ayoka said. Her voice was shaky. "They'd come for Shanna. Taylor and Danny tried to..."

"Wait, who's Shanna?"

A woman approached, tall and fair skinned. A pinprick of silver light floated around her black hair, trimmed short on the sides and bushy on top with electric blue highlights. The faery orb bathed her in its glow. Other than her hair, she looked an awful lot like Taylor. "I'm Shanna," she said.

"Taylor's mom?" William's head spun when he put two and two together. That had to be who she was, even though she didn't look any older than twenty.

Shanna nodded. "You must be William, is that right?" Her icy blue eyes fell to the three little folk gathered around him. "And more of Taylor's friends."

Quick introductions were made. Wasko, Pete, and Haggler shook hands with Shanna and Ayoka. Mercy, having finally found her quarry, fell fast asleep at their feet in a matter of minutes.

Two others joined them: an older teen guy in blue jeans and a flannel shirt, wearing a panther's pelt for a cloak; and a blonde girl about the same age who, if anything, was even prettier than Taylor's mom.

Shanna, William thought. *Not "Taylor's mom." Taylor's mom is not allowed to be a hot twenty-year-old!*

The newcomers were escorted by a pair of nunnehi warriors who bowed stiffly and then excused themselves.

"William? Is that you?" the blonde girl said, a bemused smile stretching across her face.

"Uh... have we met?"

"Not officially, I guess," she said. "I'm Bryn. But I was Taylor for a few days a couple years ago." Her features changed, and her hair darkened until it was the color of honey. Her body slimmed until it matched Taylor's slender form. "We talked at that Jared boy's birthday party. Does he still have a crush on Taylor?"

William looked across the way to double-check that the real Taylor was still sitting on an outcropping of rock thirty yards away. The girl in front of her wasn't a perfect copy, but she was awfully close.

"Whoa."

Bryn resumed her original form. "And this is Évastre." She pulled panther-boy forward. He had brilliant green eyes and auburn hair and the slightest trace of a dimpled chin. His smile, though subdued, would have made half the girls at Riverview High School swoon. William was starting to feel self-conscious in the presence of so many good-looking Fair Folk.

"Pleased to meet you," Évastre said, extending his hand. "Though I reckon we'd both wish it was under different circumstances." His backwoods Cajun accent reminded William of folks he'd met in Louisiana visiting his grandmother.

"Évastre is Taylor's cousin," Bryn explained.

That brought William up short. He'd gotten the impression the only one of Taylor's magical relatives she wanted anything to do with was her birth mother.

"I'm sorry about your friend," Évastre said. "I only met him yesterday, but Bryn speaks very highly of him."

Once again, William was brought down to earth. Could Danny really be dead?

"What happened?"

"The nunnehi and the dwarves were trying to rescue us," Shanna said. "Danny was with them. He—" She sniffed. "He just...jumped into the middle of the fight. But he slowed them down. The nunnehi might not have caught up to us without him."

William felt his fists clenching around his staff. He hung his head. If only he and the little folk had been there!

"And who were these people again?"

"Hired thugs," Shanna said, her eyes flashing. "Taylor says my mother sent them."

"Your mother—?" William's eyes darted to Évastre.

"No relation," he said. His expression was pained.

"Évastre's kin to Taylor's pa, not her ma," Wasko spoke up. "At least, I think that's the way it is."

Whatever the case, it was all William could do to accept that parents would ever treat their kids like that. "This is intense," he said.

"It's about to get worse," Ayoka said. "Those monsters nearly burned down Tsuwatwelda. My people are going to demand satisfaction."

William looked around. The nunnehi had vanished along with everyone else from the funeral.

"I never dreamed it would come to this," Shanna said.

"Nobody blames you." Ayoka assured her. "But William," she said, eyes wide. "What are you doing here?"

He quickly told her the story of how Jill figured out the "Taylor" back in Macon was an imposter, and how Mercy had tracked the real Taylor all day long and into the night. He finished by looking at Shanna and saying, "So I really need to get home. My sister's still in trouble."

"That imposter is bound to be Layla Silk," she said.

"You know her?"

"She's one of my mother's attendants. A jinni—or a jinniyah, if you want to use the proper feminine term."

"I don't know that it matters," William said. He scrounged in his jacket pockets for a pen and a blank index card. "What's the story on her?"

"She's a little older than me," Shanna said. "One hundred ten, maybe 120."

William arched an eyebrow at that, but he wrote it down.

Shanna continued. "And she's an expert face-shifter, but you already know that. She can impersonate practically anybody if she has enough time to prepare."

"Okay," William said, scribbling notes. "What else?"

"She's a shape-shifter; most jinn are. Pit viper, I think."

"Wonderful," William muttered.

"And, of course, she can whisper."

He looked up from his index card. "Come again?"

Shanna scrunched her face, figuring how to explain it. "It's something jinn can do. Sort of like presence, only subtler. It has to do with the power of suggestion."

"Mind control?" William's throat was suddenly parched.

"You could call it that," Shanna said. "Jinn are able to put ideas in a person's head. They don't know what's real anymore and what's just their imagination."

"My sister told me a little about that," William said. "When she was in Louisiana with Taylor, she says the Good Neighbors made everybody start snapping at each other."

"Something like that would be child's play for Layla," Shanna agreed. "She's very good, William. She could probably make a Topsider imagine any number of things, maybe make them forget who they even are."

William sighed. He wished he were with his sister. It sounded like she could use all the help she could get. "Okay. Anything else?"

"Just the usual things nearly all Fair Folk can do: blinking, blasting, and the like.

William wrote it all down. He flipped the card over and started writing on the back. "And I take it she has all the same weaknesses?"

Shanna nodded. "She's a jinni, so she'll probably be even more sensitive to iron than Taylor or me. The rest, you know: she's averse to salt and rowan berries; she can't tell a lie three times; loud, clangy bells will make her dizzy or even nauseated."

"Got it," he said. He looked up at Shanna and then Ayoka. Ayoka gave him an affirming nod. "I've got to get this info to Jill. Excuse me." He turned and walked five or six steps away.

...and pray it's not too late for her to use it.

Taking a deep breath of cold, mountain air, he pulled his mirror from his pack. He wasn't sure what time it was, but it was bound to still be hours until sunrise. But Jill needed to know what was going on—and he needed to know that everything was okay back home.

He assumed Jill would sleep with her own mirror under her pillow. Their incantation, not to mention their blood, had bound the two mirrors together. Now it was time to see if the magic had worked.

"Jill!" he called. Nothing. "Come on, Jill, wake up!"

He looked around. Taylor was still sitting by herself, fuming over everything that had happened. The others milled about, obviously ready to get moving, but unwilling to interrupt Taylor's solitude.

Good call, William thought.

"Jill, can you hear me?"

Something shifted in the mirror. A fog rippled across its surface then dissipated, leaving the clear image of Jill's darkened bedroom. A light flicked on, and William scrunched his eyes shut against the glare. The image in the mirror wobbled around, like a handheld video camera in shaky hands, before settling on Jill's sleepy face.

"William!" Jill cried, suddenly awake. "Where are you? We've been worried sick!"

"I'm okay," he said.

"You found Taylor?"

He nodded. "She's with me. They were using her to get to her mom. Her birth mother, that is." He bit his lip. The next part was going to be hard. "But I've got some bad news."

Jill's face fell. "What's the matter?"

He took another deep breath. His hand trembled, and it wasn't from the cold.

"They got Danny, sis. He's...he's gone." He retold the story as he'd heard it from Shanna. With every word, Jill's expression grew more and more distraught. Soon, she was visibly weeping. Her mirror-cam wobbled around again, and William told part of the story to the lamp on his sister's night stand.

Then he reported what he'd learned about Taylor's imposter, Layla. He insisted that Jill write it down, and he waited impatiently while she found pen and paper. He hoped having something to do would take Jill's mind off of the bad news he'd told her.

When he finished, Jill said, "We know her name now. I guess that's something."

"I hope it's enough," William said. "Do you think she'll show up at your birthday party?"

Jill shuddered. "I don't know. If she comes, at least I'll know where she is. But I don't like the idea of her being inside our house. After seeing the Smarts yesterday..."

"What? What's up with the Smarts?"

"She's done something to them. Some kind of glamour. I don't think it'll harm them, but...." Jill trailed off. William had feared something like that might happen. But what could one underage witch do about it? He wished he was there, especially now that Taylor had managed to escape without his help. He wondered if his sister looked tired because he woke her up or because she'd been up all night worrying.

"Just...hang in there, okay? There's bound to be a way to stop her."

"I'm open to suggestions."

"Maybe you should call Maymay."

"I already did."

"And?"

Jill grimaced. "Were you aware there are a whole bunch of things that won't work?"

William hung his head. If Maymay didn't have any good ideas.... "Maybe now that Taylor's free, they won't need Layla any more. We could be worried for nothing."

"William, do you believe it'll be that easy?"

He watched his sister wipe tears from her eyes. "Not really."

"Then get back here as soon as you can, okay? With you and Taylor here, we've got a shot."

Movement in the distance had distracted William. Someone was hiking up the side of the mountain, a wispy, red-haired figure with a dark green cloak pulled tight around her.

"Danu!" Shanna cursed behind him. William whipped around to see her frozen in place.

"What?"

"Of all the...." She clenched her fists and stalked toward the approaching figure. Évastre noticed her moving a second later. He also gazed into the distance, and his face blanched white.

"It can't be," he muttered.

"What?" William asked again.

Shanna and Évastre strode past him. They seemed wary but not frightened. Shanna's expression was one of barely contained anger; Évastre seemed simply bewildered.

William looked again at the red-headed woman stumbling toward them over the rough terrain.

The little folk muttered among themselves. Bryn knelt down to whisper something to them.

William trotted back to join them. "What's going on?"

"It's her," Bryn said, eyes wide. "I guess I just assumed...."

"You assumed...?"

"That she'd already faded," Bryn said.

"Who?"

"That's Taylor's other grandmother," Bryn said, pointing to the woman. "That's Anya Redmane."

Chapter 21

Family

Shanna didn't notice her mother-in-law's arrival at first. Her skin tingled as the cool winter air subtly warmed around her. Then she saw her and cursed.

What is she doing here?

Scarcely realizing what she was doing, she drifted down the slope of the mountainside. Évastre followed two steps behind.

She passed Taylor, who sat on the frosty ground. Then she noticed the approaching figure too and jumped up to join her mother and her cousin.

Shanna's pulse throbbed in her temples. For several seconds, she forgot to breathe.

The former Chief Matron of the Summer Court slowly advanced. She walked with a plain wooden staff, puffing with each step, hand on the side of her back as if the aches and pains of old age had finally caught up with her after a centuries-long pursuit. Her hair, once flaming red, was frosted with silver highlights. Her face, once young and bright, had lost none of its beauty even though she seemed to have aged far more than the handful of years since the last time she and Shanna had met.

Most arresting was the fact that she wasn't entirely solid. Shanna could see the shadows of trees whipping in the wind behind Mrs. Redmane's slender form. When she stopped to rest, her body solidified. It was as if it took effort for her to remain on human earth.

Shanna blew an exasperated breath and watched the fog waft up into the night.

"Mrs. Redmane," she said with an icy glare.

Évastre kept back, eyes wide and mouth agape. "You're...the former Chief Matron?" Not "Anya Redmane," Shanna noted, or even "my grandmother." He'd learned his lessons well, apparently: the daoine sídhe didn't utter the names of oathbreakers, and they certainly didn't claim them as family. Shanna had gotten over such formalities fifteen years ago.

Taylor approached the trio. Shanna wondered what she thought in this company. Everyone present was a member of Taylor's family, yet their lives couldn't have been more different.

"*What are you doing here?*" Taylor challenged. Waves of presence surged out from her, making Évastre flinch. Even Mrs. Redmane took a step backward as Taylor stalked nearer.

Shanna remembered what Taylor had told her about the coin laundry a year ago, how Mrs. Redmane had predicted the death of one of her loved ones.

"*You killed Danny!*"

"I did nothing of the kind, Selena." Mrs. Redmane's green eyes were watery and weak. They had none of the vibrant fire that Shanna remembered. "I only warned you. Our Kind face death at a disadvantage. You no doubt realize that now. By and large, we lack the requisite firsthand experience."

"*By and large,*" Shanna repeated. She might have reined in her feelings—that was the Winter Court's trademark, after all—but she didn't want to. Instead, she let her presence flow. Her expression was as cold and hard as steel. She was at least as agitated as Taylor. Between the two of them, the temperature hovered just below freezing. Mrs. Redmane glowed faintly, projecting barely enough warmth. Évastre seemed not to notice the cold—apparently satyrs were built for inclement weather.

Mrs. Redmane turned her watery eyes toward Shanna. She opened her mouth as if to speak, then stopped herself. Her hands trembled.

"Is there something you want to say to me?" Shanna said. She took a defiant step forward. Before Mrs. Redmane could respond, she turned to Évastre. "So what do you think of the great Anya Redmane—the woman who disowned her son for marrying beneath his station? If she hadn't thrown him out, he'd be alive today! *My husband* would be alive today!"

She balled her fists. It was all too much—the attack, the fire, the chase through the dwarves' tunnels...and then Danny....

"But she couldn't have that, now could she?" Shanna continued. "Couldn't let 'that Hellebore tart' into her house? Those were your words, weren't they?"

Her presence reached fever pitch. Mrs. Redmane took another step back. She showed no fear, but she said nothing. Why wasn't she saying anything?

"Do you see why your father wanted nothing to do with her, Évastre? She single-handedly destroyed her entire family. Aulberic. Your father Lorcan. I'll bet she's the reason her own husband faded as young as he did."

She breathed hard and fast. Frosty mist swirled around her head, reflecting the light of the silver will-o'-the-wisp that floated above her.

Mrs. Redmane's lips quivered. Her face and body phased, losing opacity for a second and then returning to normal.

"Do you hear me, Mrs. Redmane?"

"Of course I hear you!" she whispered, and her voice cracked. She wiped tears from her eyes.

Shanna jerked backward. She'd never thought it possible for her mother-in-law to be broken; that's why she didn't read it in her face. But suddenly it was plain as day.

No longer did she see the officious bully so preoccupied with politics and blood lines that she was willing to disown her son. Here instead was the woman who had given up her eldest son, Lorcan, rather than hand him over to the teind of the Winter Court. Here was the woman who lived for seventy years with that secret gnawing away at her, privately shaming her, threatening to expose her at any moment.

Here was the woman whose younger son, Aulberic, caught the eye of the daughter of the Chief Matron of Winter. The woman who couldn't let go of her hatred for those who'd already robbed her of one son, who'd guaranteed she'd never see her grandson.

Here, at last, was the woman who watched in horror as Shanna's own father smashed her son—her last remaining son—into a bloody, mangled mess.

"Danu," Shanna whispered. The memory hadn't faded in fifteen years. She and Aulberic had been hiding in a cabin in the woods that Aulberic's friend Nat Bundlestraw had found for them. Winter forces found them. Aulberic tried to fight them off, but Crom conjured an ectoplasmic boar that gored Aulberic to death and trampled his body until he was unrecognizable. Shanna could do nothing but watch helplessly and scream in a hill troll's iron grip.

She remembered the shriek of grief and outrage coming from the trees. The Summer Court had arrived, too. Anya Redmane had been too late to retrieve her errant son, but not too late to watch him die.

The standoff was little more than a blur. Harsh words were spoken, threats made, and finally blasts and volleys of elf-shot exchanged, but Crom Cornstack had done what he'd intended and saw no need to stay around. The whole savage business was over in minutes.

Shanna breathed deeply, filling the air with frost.

"*I hear you,*" Mrs. Redmane repeated. She projected presence, but weakly, half-heartedly. She spread open her arms. "I'm in your power now. What are you going to do to me? Shame me? Blast me? Conjure a boar to trample me like your father did to my Aulberic?"

Taylor's eyes widened at that last one. Shanna had never gone into detail about how Taylor's father had died. She had hoped to spare her the nightmares she endured.

There would be plenty of time for that later. Now she had to deal with Anya Redmane, who was, she realized with a start, no longer a threat—to her or anyone else.

Taylor's eyes darted from Shanna to Mrs. Redmane. She looked more confused than angry. Évastre was even more perplexed. He rocked nervously back and forth and pulled his panther-skin cloak tight around his shoulders.

The ground around them was covered with a thick coating of frost.

But Shanna didn't want to unleash her fury against this old woman anymore. There would be no satisfaction in it. She could never do more to her than she'd already done to herself.

Mrs. Redmane fell to her knees. She bowed her head. Her shoulders heaved.

Shanna stood shyly, not sure what to do.

"What...?" Taylor began, tentatively, her voice barely a whisper. "What is she doing here?"

"I do as I please," Mrs. Redmane said. She hung her head. "Or is that too much to ask?"

And Shanna understood, though the idea made her tremble. Her mother-in-law had come to make peace. While she still could.

"How did she even find us?" Taylor asked.

"My magic isn't *entirely* spent," Mrs. Redmane croaked.

"But you used most of it to find us, didn't you?" Shanna said. "You don't have much left."

Mrs. Redmane shook her head.

Without thinking, Shanna knelt beside her mother-in-law and tentatively reached out a hand to touch her shoulder. She didn't know why she did it. She had no idea what to expect in return. But for a brief moment, she felt a connection. For all their differences, they shared common grief in the loss of Aulberic. The next thing she knew, they had embraced. She felt hot tears on her neck.

Taylor and Évastre joined them. Mrs. Redmane cupped her grandson's cheek in a semi-transparent hand, then turned to brush a stray hair out of Taylor's eyes.

"I wish I could forgive you," Taylor said. "I want to forgive you...but I don't know how."

"Forgiveness doesn't come easily for Our Kind," Mrs. Redmane said, resigned. "If at all."

She took a deep breath and expelled it slowly.

"Live well, Selena Hellebore." Another deep breath. Mrs. Redmane glowed slightly, and Shanna felt a warm breeze against her cheek.

The glow subsided.

And then she was gone. She simply vanished into nothingness.

Taylor gasped. Her eyes darted all around. "Is...Is she...?" she stammered.

Shanna nodded. "She's faded."

"Just like that?"

"Apparently."

They all collectively held their breaths as if waiting to see what might happen next. Taylor broke the silence.

"She's gone for good?"

Shanna nodded again.

They sat in silence for half a minute. Shanna held Taylor close and thought about Aulberic, about the life the three of them might have had.

Eventually, Taylor glanced over her shoulder at Danny's grave. "Shanna. Do we...? I mean, do Our Kind...?"

"Yes, Taylor?"

She sighed. "William's grandmother... Well, some people believe... I mean, according to Google... A lot of Topsiders say that Our Kind don't have souls."

Shanna had wondered when that subject might come up. She could only imagine what Taylor was thinking, being raised by Topsiders with their strange customs and beliefs. "What would you do with a soul if you had one?"

That brought Taylor up short, as was obvious from her expression. She furrowed her brow, perplexed at the very question. She took another glance at Danny's grave. "Go to heaven?"

"Is that what Topsiders do with their souls?"

"I...I don't know."

"Have you ever heard Topsiders talk about soul food? Or soulful music?"

"I have," Évastre jumped in. "We got those things by the bucketload where I grew up."

"Or baring their souls when they share some deep secret?"

"Y-yeah?" Taylor said.

"So," Shanna said. "Enjoying good food—and the company of the folks that made it. Making and listening to music that moves you. Down here." Shanna patted her chest. "Feeling something so big, so terrible, that you've got to find a friend to help you bear it. Those are also things Topsiders seem to do with their souls, wouldn't you say?"

"But...I do those things, too. We all do."

Shanna smiled tenderly. "Then maybe you've answered your own question."

"But...when my friend Jill uses her Second Sight on me...she doesn't see anything."

Shanna shrugged. "Maybe our souls just work differently."

Taylor considered this in silence.

Nobody wanted to move, but the ground was cold and hard, and Taylor's friends were waiting for them.

"We should go," Shanna said. "People are going to need our help in Tsuwatelda."

"I reckon so," Évastre agreed. He stood up and then helped Shanna to her feet.

"And I need to talk to Chief Tewa," Taylor said. "There's something he needs to know about Crom Cornstack."

That got Shanna's attention. "Something about my dad?"

"I found out how he's gained and kept his power all these years. I found out—" Taylor jumped back. Something dark and slimy bounced off her face, leaving a red welt. Shanna peered at the ground where it landed. A toad jerked and quivered in the grass.

"What the...?" Taylor marveled.

Another toad thumped to the ground over by Danny's grave. Then a third slapped Shanna on the back. It fell near the first, then started hopping off down the mountain. From somewhere in the distance echoed sounds of cackling laughter.

"Oh, no!" Taylor said, her eyes darting in every direction.

William shouted in the distance. From the way he jumped around, a toad had hit him, too.

"What are all these toads…?" Évastre began. He, Shanna, and Taylor all searched the sky, trying to figure out where they were coming from.

"I don't like this," Taylor said. "Get ready." She flexed her fingers, gathering magic.

"Ready for what?" Shanna said.

Toads continued to fall from the sky. The initial trickle soon became a deluge. Taylor darted toward William and the little folk, her arms over her head. Évastre and Shanna followed close behind.

That telltale cackle had to mean Ian Shagfoal was nearby. Something magical was afoot, and Taylor didn't like it. The welt on her face burned like dragon's blood.

William used his staff like a baseball bat to swat at the rain of toads. Mercy snarled and danced about, nipping at the toads already on the ground.

"Ayoka!" she called. The nunnehi girl was already braced for action. She had no weapons, but she had fallen to a crouch with her arms spread wide, gathering magic, getting ready to respond…but to what?

Wasko, Pete, and Haggler marched forward in three separate directions, eyes wide. A toad had already knocked Wasko's bowler hat from his head, and Pete kept his hand to his left eye, nursing an inflamed bruise.

Évastre ran to Bryn's side. Both the satyr and the huldra looked perplexed.

A toad thudded against Taylor's forehead, stopping her in her tracks.

"Everybody, on your guard!" Ayoka called.

William swiped at another toad and sent it soaring. Ayoka pulled off her buckskin jacket and used it to swat toads away from her.

There was a flash of light. Suddenly, a dark shape was bounding toward her. Ian Shagfoal's gleaming yellow eyes pierced the darkness. Taylor got off a blast, but the pooka veered hard to the left at the last second, and her pulse of magic fell harmlessly behind him.

He blinked away, reappearing behind Wasko and William. He gestured, and a volley of red and yellow fireworks streamed from his hand.

Just then, the earth began to shake. The rock outcropping where she'd sat earlier moved, jutting upward and then collapsing on itself. A hole opened up in the earth, and a gigantic, warty form climbed out of it and stalked across the mountainside.

Taylor looked in the direction Eelick the troll was headed, and cursed that she hadn't figured it out at once. Ian and Eelick hadn't abandoned their mission. They'd just realized they were outnumbered in the tunnels.

And now the troll was barreling straight for Shanna!

A toad hit her in the back of the head, singeing her hair. She cried for Ayoka, who was groaning and digging a toad out from the back of her collar. She threw it at last to the ground, then winced and shook her blistered right hand.

Shanna made to blast the troll, but it shrugged it off. He grabbed her, flung her onto his back, and dropped into a second hole he had opened in the earth.

"Get them!" Taylor screamed.

William trained his staff on the troll and opened his mouth to cast a spell. Just as quickly, the troll and Shanna were gone. He swept toward the pooka, but he blinked away with one last taunting laugh.

The ground was littered with the croaking, quivering bodies of acidic toads. The only sounds on the mountainside was their forlorn croaking and Taylor's own labored breath.

Shanna was gone.

Chapter 22

Preparing for War

Taylor thought she'd reached her breaking point before.

Danny's funeral still left her shaking with anger and despair. The pooka was the first of the Fair Folk to show her any kind of compassion, the one who'd first taught her about glamour and true names and Courts and shape-shifting. He was the one who taught her the wisdom of oak and ash and thorn.

Losing him was devastating. But now she'd lost Shanna, too. It was too much to take in. A wintry breeze swirled around her, and she could feel her nose growing cold. A thick coating of frost formed at her feet.

She screamed a curse into the night, loud and long and charged with presence. The little folk fell to the ground. Mercy howled silently in obvious agitation. Bryn and Évastre turned away, huddling in discomfort. Only William and Ayoka seemed unaffected. Their faces revealed anguish, sympathy, but no discomfort under the onslaught of Taylor's explosion of magic.

Once you cared for somebody—really cared for them—presence no longer worked on them.

Her whole body shook. Slowly, deliberately, she marched up the mountainside to rejoin her friends.

Ayoka ran to meet her. "Are you alright?"

"No." Taylor glowered at her. It wasn't anything Ayoka had done; Taylor was just so full of fury that she could barely contain it. Évastre, Bryn, and the little folk kept a respectful distance.

"We'll tell the warriors," Ayoka offered. "As soon as things settle down—"

"They took her," Taylor said. Her voice was even, barely a whisper, but electric with unbearable anger.

"I know," Ayoka said. "And I'm sure my grandfather—"

Taylor spun and slapped her hands on Ayoka's shoulders. "They took her!" she repeated.

William raised a hand in a soothing gesture. "That's right," he said. "And I know it looks bad, but—"

"I'm going to get her back."

William shivered, like the wind had suddenly turned and he'd caught a blast of freezing air.

"But you don't even know where he's taken her," Ayoka said.

Taylor looked out over the mountains. "Cair Cullen," she said. "That's where he took her. The place where I was born."

"But you can't go there," Ayoka said, her voice low and soothing. "You can't enter a rath of Arradherry. You know that."

"I'll do whatever I want!" Taylor snapped. "By oak, ash, and thorn, I'm going to Cair Cullen to find Shanna and bring her back."

"Okay," William said. "I get it. You want to help Shanna, but don't you think—?"

"I *am* going to help Shanna," Taylor said. She took another step forward.

"And then I'm going to bring down the House of Hellebore."

William felt warm in spite of the frosty air. He was still breathing heavy from batting away all those toads, and what Taylor had said made him sweat. "Taylor, you've got to think this through."

"*Are you with me?*" Taylor said. Her voice was as hard and cold as her eyes. It wasn't a request, William realized. It was a command—or maybe a threat. That was what was making him sweat. It wasn't what she was saying, it was how she was saying it.

Ayoka appeared at William's side. "You can't enter Cair Cullen," she said. "You swore an oath."

"*Then I'll break it*," Taylor said through clenched teeth, like her stomach was suddenly in knots. Something was twisting in William's own stomach, warning him to proceed with caution. He was mostly immune to Taylor's presence, but he was still aware of when she was using it.

He wondered if she was aware that everybody left on the mountainside—Bryn, Évastre, and the three little folk—were slowly backing away from her.

"*I'm getting Shanna back*," Taylor said. "*I'll do it by myself if I have to.*"

"You don't have to," William said. "But can't we just...think about this for a minute?"

"William is right," Ayoka said, stepping forward. "Breaking an oath is serious business. There's no need to sacrifice yourself. Let's all calm down for a minute and figure out—"

"*There's no time!*" Taylor thundered. "The last time Crom and Mara captured Shanna, they locked her up in a dungeon. Who's to say they won't do something worse this time? We've got to get her out *now*!"

"Then let's do it smart," William said. "Let's make a plan that doesn't involve marching up to a faery castle and pounding on the door."

Taylor turned away. She paced back and forth. Haggler, Pete, and Wasko darted around her, trying to keep out of her way.

The black of night was slowly fading into the steel gray of a cloudy morning.

Taylor cursed under her breath. William took a step toward her, but Ayoka held him back.

"It's *ulonasti*," she whispered. She bowed her head, almost in reverence.

William glanced at Taylor and then back at Ayoka. "Yeah, it may not be nasty now, but I've got a feeling it's about to be."

"No, *ulonasti*," Ayoka said. She shifted on her heels, looking at the ground as if to find the words to explain herself. "You probably know this. Any magic directed at another creates a

217

bond between the caster and the target. That makes combat magic especially dangerous."

"Right," William said. In his mind, he ran through his grandmother's notes on combat magic. "To be effective, you've got to reach down deep, find a dark place inside you. Anger, hatred, primal aggression."

"Exactly."

"But that just strengthens the bond with your target. If you're not careful, your magic will fizzle out—or worse, it'll rebound against you." Then something clicked in his memory. He looked Ayoka in the eye. "Your people don't seem to have that problem."

"There are ways to take ourselves out of the equation," she said. "Most people think the secret to powerful combat magic is *uhnalv*, which is simple, ordinary anger. But that can be tricky. *Ulonasti* is far safer—and far more powerful."

"And that word means...?"

"Anger at injustice."

Taylor was talking in hushed tones with Bryn and Évastre. William studied her martial stance, the flash of blue fire in her eyes. He couldn't hear the conversation, but he watched as Bryn nodded and the two of them embraced. Évastre stood beside them with a terrified expression on his face.

"She's not thinking about what Crom and Mara have done to *her*."

Ayoka shook her head. "Not anymore. At least, I don't think so. I think she has reached a state of *ulonasti*." She sighed. "I don't think you're going to talk her out of this, William. She'll take any risk, no matter the sacrifice, no matter the threat. The only thing she cares about is justice for Shanna. For Danny."

"She's going to Cair Cullen," William said, defeated. He remembered the imposing spires of the Winter Court's capital, the armies amassed in front of it. There must have been hundreds of warriors there—fae, trolls, ogres, goblins, and other things William couldn't even name.

"I don't suppose your people would be willing to lend a hand?"

"Right now? Tonight?" Ayoka said. "Doubtful. Tsuwatelda is vulnerable. There are too many wounded and dead after the fires. And you may not have heard, but the Summer and Winter Courts have gone to war. A lot of our warriors have already been sent to guard the border at Tobarty." Her face darkened. "If the sídhe decided to attack again...."

"Yeah," William said. He did a quick headcount: three little folk, a dog, a satyr, a woman with a tail (what in the world was *that* all about?), himself, Taylor, and...

"I've got to help her, Ayoka," he said. "What are you thinking?"

"I'm going too, of course."

"Of course." William's heart fluttered. If he was going to go storm a faery castle, having one reasonably competent warrior around sounded like a great idea.

But it was more than that. He was itching for a fight, and he couldn't put his finger on why. The last time he'd passed by Cair Cullen, something awakened inside him. Taking on those Autumn warriors was something he'd done on pure instinct. He wasn't fumbling with his magic; he wasn't even scared. It just seemed right.

"Are you okay?" Ayoka asked.

"Huh?"

"You look distracted."

"Well, it's my first war." He managed a wry smile.

"But not your first battle," Ayoka reminded him.

No, it wasn't. His mind drifted back to the day he first met Ayoka and the two of them held off an army of ectoplasmic bronze children. He chuckled at that. It was actually a lot worse than it sounded.

"And I see you're dressed for it."

"What? Oh." He remembered what he was wearing. It seemed like an eternity ago when he'd thrown on his University of Georgia tee shirt. He hadn't thought about it at the time, but he remembered what Ayoka had once told him.

"Red and black," he said.

"The colors of war." Ayoka nodded.

Chapter 23

Cair Cullen

Taylor, Ayoka, and William were the first to spill out of the ring portal. Just as they'd planned, they spread out quickly, ready to fend off any Autumn or Winter troops who took notice of their arrival. Taylor had almost hoped they'd get to blast somebody right away. It was better they didn't have to, though. They needed time to get ready if her plan had any chance at all of working.

She gazed to the east. Crom's forces had consolidated on the plain surrounding Cair Cullen. The sight of the camp in the distance, now swollen to five or six times the size it was when she was last there, filled her with dread, but it did nothing to damp her determination.

She took a look around. The hill with its petroglyphs was clear, but she and Ayoka had to keep it that way. The two girls quickly cast veils of glamour over the whole area. Hundreds of troops were camped only a mile or two away through the sparse trees, but a little bit of magic made Taylor and the others effectively invisible.

It was a gray, dismal morning, cold and damp. But they needed such light as the day provided. Securing their hiding place was only the first thing they had to do before nightfall.

Taylor and Ayoka had barely completed their magic when Bryn and Évastre appeared. Soon after that, the little folk stumbled onto the hillside with Mercy in tow.

"Are you sure this is the best place to be?" Évastre asked. "Something don't feel right."

"Maybe we should move on," Taylor agreed. She wanted to keep moving—and where to didn't really matter. She felt restless, agitated, and she didn't know why.

"Hang on," William said. He swept his foot over the ground, kicking away a reddish powder.

Taylor immediately started to feel more at ease.

"It's just my hot foot powder from yesterday," William said. "It's supposed to keep people away. Sorry about that."

"Don't be sorry," Taylor said. "It worked on the guards, or we'd have been surrounded by now."

"So now what?" Wasko said.

Taylor knelt down beside the little person. "When you and Haggler broke Pete out of there, I'm betting you didn't take him out the front door."

"Of course not," Wasko said. "There's secret passage next to the kitchen. It takes you out into the woods to the north. We was out before anybody thought to check it."

"A secret passage?"

"Most raths have 'em," Wasko said. "For quick escapes in case of a siege."

Taylor frowned. "But couldn't most fae just...I don't know... blink away?"

"You can't blink inside a rath," Bryn explained. "There'll be suppression charms all over the place. That's in case of a siege, too."

That actually made sense, as Taylor considered it. If somebody broke through your defenses, you wouldn't want them blinking around, going wherever they wanted. You'd keep them grounded, even if it meant you couldn't blink, either.

"Okay," Taylor said. "First order of business is to make sure that entrance is still there. Hopefully, it'll be unguarded. And then—" She choked back tears as she thought of Danny. "And then we'll need a diversion." She thought for a second. "What if—"

"Hold up!" William hissed. He was gazing down the gravel road in the opposite direction to Cair Cullen.

"What?" Taylor whispered.

"I don't know. It just feels..."

Six mounted fae came into view, their horses' hooves making no sound at all as they cantered over the gravel. Taylor and the others hunched down on the far side of the hill.

Now that she could see them, she could sense their magic: a subtle pulse rippling through the cloaking mist she and Ayoka had applied. Whoever these horsemen were, Taylor didn't want to face them in a fight.

"Scouts," Wasko said.

That also made sense. But were they Crom's men heading home from a patrol or Belas Wakefire's men spying out Crom's defenses?

"Any idea who they are?" Taylor whispered.

William peered into the distance. "They've got oak leaves on their collars," he said.

Taylor did a double take. "How can you—"

"I wish I knew," William said. He sounded almost apologetic. "But that's what I see, clear as day."

"Oak leaves mean Summer Court," Haggler offered.

Everyone watched in silence as the horsemen approached.

"What do you all think?" Taylor whispered.

"They might be willing to help us," Bryn said. Taylor wasn't so sure. Belas and Dubessa had their own reasons for opposing the Winter Court, but she couldn't imagine they'd ever accept her as an ally. And in the long run, their acceptance might be bad for her health.

"Let's just keep an eye on them," she said.

"By all means," a voice rumbled from behind them. Taylor instinctively flipped over onto her backside and summoned a shield spell. The others did the same.

A man on foot stood over them, musket trained on Taylor. Three others were at his side, dressed in forest green cloaks with oak-leaf brooches at the collar.

"In fact, perhaps you should get a closer look." He bored into her with steely gray eyes.

Taylor hissed a curse word.

The Summer camp was another mile or so to the west, cloaked beneath as powerful a veil of magic as Taylor had ever seen. The scouts—both mounted and on foot—escorted them into a make-shift village of scores of tents, both simple two-person tents and large pavilions festooned with green and gold bunting.

Everyone complied, grudgingly. They might have overpowered their captors with a little advance warning, but it would have been suicide to try anything lying prone on the ground. Even Mercy seemed content to trot along on William's short leash.

Taylor estimated the Summer army was about as big as the one defending Cair Cullen. It was mostly composed of various types of fae: spriggans, pisgies, and a dozen other types she couldn't place. Of course, her kinfolk, the daoine sídhe, were well represented among the officers.

Warriors stopped cleaning their weapons or filling their packs to watch as the ragtag bunch was herded through the camp. The scout who'd first captured them shoved them along, barking threats if anyone veered too far to one side of the path or the other.

Then Taylor heard a voice she thought she recognized.

"I'm merely informing you that the Chief Matron is waiting for my report," a woman was saying. "The Triad insists the rules of war be observed to the letter."

Taylor craned her neck this way and that.

"Move along!" the scout snarled.

"She'll get her report," another man said. "But if you haven't noticed, I've got a siege to plan—and I can't do my job until my giants get here!"

"I'm sure your giants are on their way," the woman said. "But that doesn't address my question—"

"Claudia?" Taylor called. She still couldn't see her, but there was no mistaking that stern, businesslike voice.

"Pipe down!" the scout ordered.

"Claudia Fountain!" Taylor yelled. Just then, the half-fae witch strode out from behind the side of a tent, deep in conversation with a sídhe officer with an ornate cloth-of-gold sash across his chest.

Claudia stopped in her tracks. "Taylor? Is that you?"

She turned back to the officer. "I shall submit a preliminary report at once," she said. "But I insist that you take time later this morning to answer Chief Matron Fairchild's specific questions."

"I'll do my job, Miss Fountain—if you'll let me." The man turned on his heels and marched away.

Claudia turned toward Taylor and her friends. "Taylor, what in the world is going on?" She addressed the scout who'd been minding them. "I'll take over from here."

"But they're prisoners," he said. "Probably Winter spies. I've got orders—"

"*I said I'll take over from here,*" Claudia said. Something rumbled through Taylor's body. Even though it wasn't directed at her, she felt a twinge of panic. She remembered what it was like to be on the receiving end of Claudia's father's thunderous presence.

The scout bowed curtly, eyes wide, and signaled for his men to disperse.

"This way," Claudia said. She stalked forward, and Taylor and the rest scrambled to keep up with her. They came to one of the smaller pavilions. Claudia held open the tent flap and urged everyone inside.

She only let her agitation show as she closed the flap behind them.

"Taylor? What in the world do you think you're doing, coming to Cair Cullen?"

"They knew," Taylor said, her voice barely louder than a whisper. Her lower lip quivered. "I don't know for how long... but they knew. They came for Shanna...." Her hands curled into fists. She could barely contain her anger. "Some of Mara's goons. They...got inside the city." She started to cry. "They burned it to the ground."

Claudia's eyes sparked green fire. "No."

Taylor could only nod her head.

Claudia looked toward the tent flap, as if assessing everything that was happening outside. "But...what are you doing here?"

"We're putting an end to this," Taylor said. There was fire in her eyes as well.

"Just the seven of you?" Claudia said. "You can't be serious!"

"Oh, I've never been more serious," Taylor snarled.

"Taylor, I know you can be very determined when you get an idea in your head, but you've got to think this through." Claudia looked over the group. She arched her eyebrows as if suddenly realizing something. "What does Danny have to say about this? He's not out there somewhere, is he? I can't believe even he would try anything this foolhardy—"

She stopped when she saw the tears flowing down Taylor's cheeks.

"Taylor, where's Danny?"

Taylor fell forward and wrapped her arms around Claudia. "Please tell me where Danny is!"

There were only two canvas chairs in Claudia's pavilion. Taylor and Claudia sat in them, knees almost touching. The others either sat on the floor or stood awkwardly, trying not to look at the conversation they couldn't help but overhear.

William sat in silence, scratching Mercy's head, as Taylor told the story of what had happened at Tsuwatelda. He'd heard part of it before, but Taylor shared more of the details now. Claudia rested a hand on Taylor's arm for support. When it came time to explain what the spriggans did to Danny, the gesture didn't seem nearly enough.

When Taylor finished, Claudia took several long, uncomfortable moments to digest it all.

At last, she said, "You can't go in there. You just can't. Your magic—"

"Somebody has to stop Crom and Mara," Taylor said. Her voice was hard but even. "They can't keep winning."

"Then let someone else—"

"No!" Taylor slammed a fist on her armrest. "This is my fight." She looked around the room. William's heart pounded when Taylor's gaze met his. What she had in mind was like nothing he'd ever done before. Of its own accord, his hand found the dracontia in his pocket. He wished he knew what it could do!

Then her gaze passed on to Ayoka, Wasko, and the others. "If this is going to happen," Taylor said, "I can't let them go in alone."

"You're not thinking," Claudia said. She sighed deeply. "I'm sorry, but you just can't stop them." She hung her head. "Nobody can." William could tell Claudia's heart and mind were still reeling from what Taylor had told her. She shook her head. "They're too powerful."

"I know a way," Taylor said. "And I don't care what it costs."

"Belas Wakefire has raised an army!" Claudia said. William felt her power rumble once more through the room. "What can you do that a thousand fae warriors can't?"

"There's a secret to Crom's power," Taylor said. "A kind of talisman he uses to store up magic."

Then Taylor explained her plan. Claudia listened quietly, gripping the armrests of her camp chair. Her eyes got wider and wider as Taylor spelled it out.

By the time Taylor had finished, Claudia was reeling. "You can't be serious," she said. She looked at Ayoka. "Can you even...?"

"I can try," Ayoka said. The defiant gleam in her eyes made William's heart surge with confidence. If Ayoka could buy into this scheme....

"And what about you?" Claudia said, this time turning her attention to William. Her voice was hard, almost accusing. William had to remind himself she wasn't angry with him. She just didn't want anybody else to get hurt.

He shrugged. "We've got to do something. I trust Taylor."

Claudia threw her head back and closed her eyes. "There's no point arguing when a sídhe has made up her mind," she muttered. A sob caught in her throat. "Worse than a pooka."

William bowed his head. Nobody else dared speak.

She sobbed once more, then straightened her back, wiping tears from her eyes.

Then she leaned forward again and look Taylor in the eye. "The Primus intends to begin his assault at dusk—assuming his giants ever get here from Mullandy. That should at least give you cover."

"Thank you," Taylor said.

"Don't thank me," Claudia said. "This is a foolish, foolish plan, and I'm a fool for condoning it."

Taylor stood. Ayoka and the others gathered around her.

Claudia marched to the tent flap and called for an attendant. "Bob," she called. "Find these children a place to rest for a few hours. They'll need someplace private. Somewhere they can practice magic."

As soon as the attendant left, she turned back to them. "Bob will take care of you," she said. "And I think..." she sniffled. "...I think I need to make a scry."

"Miss Claudia?" William said. It was now or never. "When you've done all that..." He pulled the clear crystal from his pocket. "What do you know about dracontias?"

Chapter 24

The Birthday Party from the Bad Place

Jill woke up Saturday morning still shaking from her run-in with Layla the night before. The Smarts were in trouble, not to mention the trouble William and Taylor were in somewhere up north.

She thought about Danny and let herself cry. It was all too much.

These people are killers, she told herself. *If anything else happens....*

In a few hours, some of her church and school friends would be coming for her birthday. She thought about cancelling. Let her mom tell them she wasn't feeling well.

But that wouldn't work. Her parents would want to know what was wrong—and they'd know in a minute if she tried to lie to them.

For about five minutes, she tried her best to convince herself Layla wouldn't show up. It would be too risky; Jill didn't think Layla wanted anybody to know who—or what—she really was.

"Who am I kidding?" she muttered as she sat cross-legged on her bed. "Of course she's coming. She's looking for more 'deathlings to play with'!"

So Jill began to prepare. She skipped breakfast. Fasting helped focus a witch's magic. She'd have to eat some treats with her friends later, but maybe a little bit of fasting was better than none at all.

She took a long, cold shower, letting the water wash away any magical residue that clung to her body. She couldn't risk her magical aura making things go haywire at a time like this.

She spent an hour in deep meditation, sitting cross-legged on the floor in her room and concentrating on a single votive candle in front of her. Waves and swirls of magic coursed through her, but she simply let them pass. The candle's flame burned a pure golden yellow.

She pondered her options. She had plenty of magical power, just not much control. She could probably blow Layla into the next county with a wind spell, but it would rip the side of the house off.

No, this called more for skill than strength. If everybody was going to get out of this unharmed, Jill was going to have to be smart.

She imagined what Taylor might do in her situation. She really loved Taylor, but she never wanted to get on her bad side! Then it hit her. Layla didn't just look like Taylor, she was the same sort of...being? Creature? It felt weird thinking of her best friend that way, but this was no time for sentimentality. Neither Taylor nor Layla were human, and maybe that was the key. If Jill was going to beat Layla, she couldn't play by Taylor's rules. She had to do something not even Taylor—or anyone like her—would expect.

The seeds of a plan took root in the silence after she finished meditating, as she allowed herself to ponder her situation. She knew she had all the ingredients. All it would take would be a little tweaking of a recipe she'd tried before.

She didn't like it. She'd always been taught to play fair, and what she had in mind was the opposite of fair.

But she could do it. She knew she could. More than that, she had no other choice.

And if it didn't blow up in her face, it ought to work just fine.

With that settled, she tried to work out the other details of the party. How could she keep herself and her friends safe?

Crooked lines could deflect magic. That was partly how her jet amulet worked to protect her from faery mind control. Could she somehow extend the effect over a larger area? Maybe she could tilt the pictures hanging on the walls of the den, move the furniture to odd angles—not a lot but hopefully enough to throw off Layla's concentration.

Another thought occurred to her, and she made her way quickly to the basement. She stood in front of the workbench with Maymay's spell book open in front of her. She pulled out the ingredients she would need: a half-dozen organza pouches, some lavender buds, a handful of crystals.

She frowned. There was only one amethyst; the rest were clear quartz—a classic, but not as powerful as amethyst. Would the spell be strong enough?

She'd have to hedge her bets. She ran back upstairs and returned with the copy of *Great Expectations* she had to buy for English class. She ripped out the first page and tore it into tiny shreds. Taylor would have probably said something about her ripping up a book, even if everybody in her class thought it was the most brain-crushingly boring book in the history of the English language. It didn't matter. This was more important than some stupid book she earnestly hoped never to have to read again.

She stuffed the crystals, the lavender, and the shreds of paper into the pouches, whispering an incantation as she worked. When everything was ready, she grabbed a vial from the top shelf and turned off the light. The subtle glow of moonbeams interrupted the darkness, and as soon as she opened the vial over her collection of pouches, that glow erupted into cold, silvery light.

The glow didn't last as long as Jill would have liked. Maybe William shouldn't have traded half of their moonbeams to Ocky and Fern. But it couldn't be helped. She would have to make do with what she had. She intoned her incantation until the light seeped into the pouches and faded away. When it did, the darkness in the basement was absolute. She crept to the lightswitch by the light of her phone. In a few minutes, she'd go back upstairs and tuck the pouches into the seat cushions in the den—and hope the magic worked.

She looked around, checking off a mental list of magical defenses. There was bound to be something more she could do. *Crooked lines*, she thought. *Mojo bags. What else?* She would definitely want to keep Maymay's blasting rod close by. She could hide it under the sofa or maybe in the umbrella stand in the front hall.

She sat on a folding chair at the card table and thumbed through the pages of Maymay's spell book, reminiscing about all the lessons she and William had received: channeling energy, the rules of contagion and correspondence, auras, equivalent exchange....

She might have stayed in the basement all morning long, but she needed to get ready for the party—and for any mayhem that might break out. She stretched and stood up. It was almost noon. She had wards to strengthen...and cookies to bake.

Abby was the first guest to arrive, a little past two o'clock. Jill waved at Abby's mom in the driveway and held the door open as the the happy, round-faced girl from school came in.

Mrs. Matthews took Abby's present and urged her to help herself from the spread of snacks on the dining room table.

"We'll start the movie as soon as everybody gets here," she said. "Then we'll have cake and Jill can open her presents when it's over."

Abby had filled her plate and was heading to the den when Jill's two closest church friends, Nyesha and Carla, arrived together.

Jill lingered by the snack table as Nyesha and Carla went to the den. She halfheartedly filled her own plate and once more hoped fake Taylor would skip the party. Maybe she wouldn't want to risk being discovered. Maybe she didn't think she could impersonate Taylor in front of other people who knew her.

Who am I kidding? she realized. *With her glamour power, she could convince them she's the Queen of England!*

The thought had barely entered her mind when the doorbell rang and nearly gave Jill a heart attack.

"I'll get it!" Jill called. She strode to the door and pulled it open. Sure enough, Layla was on the stoop, a hastily wrapped present in hand.

"Can I come in?" she said brightly. Taylor's pale blue eyes twinkled, but Jill could see the malice behind them. More than that, she could already sense the pulse of powerful glamour oozing out from her. Wispy green tendrils of energy wafted off of Layla. Jill took a second to rein in her Second Sight.

She wondered if saying no would accomplish anything. It probably wouldn't: Her folks had already given Layla permission to enter. She was just playing with Jill.

Still, she couldn't bring herself to say the word. She just gestured toward the screen door. Layla opened it and stepped inside.

"Happy birthday!" she said. Even her voice sounded like Taylor's. This girl was good; Jill had to give her that.

"Hello, Taylor," Mr. Matthews said from the doorway leading to the den. He smiled kindly. Jill reminded herself that her parents didn't know this was an imposter. She and William had only told them that Taylor was in some kind of trouble. That meant they'd probably bend over backwards to make fake Taylor feel at ease.

"What would you like to drink?" Mr. Matthews asked.

Layla studied the snack table and the selection of two-liters and the ice bucket at the end.

"How about a root beer?"

Mr. Matthews began to pour her a cup. It never registered with him that the real Taylor would have asked for a Sprite.

"Snack?" Jill said. "Pretzels? Potato chips?"

Layla scrunched her face.

Jill smirked. Maymay's notes said—and Jill's observation of the real Taylor's food preferences confirmed—that the Fair Folk had a thing about too much salt.

"Maybe you'd like some cookies," Mr. Matthews said, gesturing.

"What kind are they?" Layla said, reaching for one.

"Cranberry," Jill said.

Layla took a bite and grinned. "Delicious."

"Help yourself," Mr. Matthews said. Layla stacked three on her plate.

"Dad, you can tell them to start the movie," Jill said. "Taylor and I will be there in a minute."

As soon as Mr. Matthews walked away, Layla said, "Was there something you wanted to tell me?"

Jill swallowed. "These people have never done anything to you," she whispered.

"Your point?"

She looked into Layla's eyes. She leaned forward and said, "Just go, okay? I know your stupid mission is over. My brother told me last night. Shanna got away."

Layla grinned. "Did she, now?" She folded her arms.

Jill took a step back. "What do you mean?"

Layla shrugged. "I'm afraid your information is… incomplete. There were some last-minute reversals, I'm afraid."

Jill began to shake. "You're lying."

Layla gave Jill the look she might have given a little kid who couldn't figure out her math homework. "Do I really have to explain these things to you, Jill?"

And immediately Jill realized Layla was telling the truth. She hardly had a choice.

"Taylor…?"

"I don't have a clue about your friend. Though from what I hear, I'm not sure she'll be coming back." She took a nibble of her first cookie. She pulled her face into an expression of mock sadness, but immediately started to giggle. "I suppose I'll have to start building a fetch before long. I don't want to jump to conclusions, Jill, but I wouldn't be surprised if Taylor suddenly came down with a bad case of something rather fatal."

"No."

Layla nodded conspiratorially. "Not today, not today. To tell the truth, I have some vacation time coming. I thought I'd use some of it right here on human earth."

Jill clenched her fist. Sweat trickled down her neck.

"I told some friends to come by later. I hope you don't mind."

The room spun. This couldn't be happening! "M-my friends don't know anything about this," Jill said, her voice suddenly quavering. "They don't know anything about you."

"You should have thought of that before you started spouting the f-word."

Jill's dad came through the dining room. "The movie's started, girls."

"We'll be right there," Layla chimed. Mr. Matthews started upstairs. As soon as he was out of sight, Layla winked and whispered, "I'll save your parents for later. After I've warmed up a little." At a conversational volume, she said, "Now let's go have fun!"

Jill stood in place, not sure what to do, but she hoped the crooked lines she'd set up in the den would wipe that smug smirk off Layla's cheap knock-off of Taylor's face.

"We don't want to miss the movie, Jill," Layla said. She gestured for Jill to lead the way.

Maybe it'll be enough, Jill thought. The little changes she'd made to the den, tilting the picture frames and scooting the furniture out of place, would be a distraction at best. But if it meant Layla's magic was even a little impaired....

Jill entered the den and groaned to herself. Everything was perfectly neat and tidy: the pictures, the sofa and chairs, the lamps on the end tables. Nothing was out of place at all!

It had to have been her mom. She must have straightened things up while Jill was baking cookies. She sighed deeply and plopped onto the couch next to Carla and Nyesha. Layla took the empty easy chair where she got a good view of Jill. Abby sat cross-legged on the other chair and compared teacher stories with the girls from church.

On the TV, Cinderella's mom had suddenly fallen sick. They'd passed over that part in the animated version, but the live-action movie apparently spent more time on the heroine's childhood. Jill pretended to be interested.

Layla finished off a cookie and leaned back in her chair, grinning a satisfied grin.

Jill wasn't going to let her get under her skin. There was still the trick she'd worked on that morning. It ought to start working any time now.

As Jill waited for the magic to take effect, she subtly slipped her hand between the couch cushion and the armrest. The conjure bag she'd put there hours ago hadn't been moved. That meant the other five were in place as well. That was something, at least. If she had to take drastic action, she'd be ready.

It seemed, however, that Layla was content to wait. Jill sat on pins and needles all through the movie, waiting for her to try something. All she did was shoot Jill withering glances and go back to the dining room twice to snag more cookies.

She's building her reserves. Taylor always reached for dessert when she was planning powerful magic. That was in Maymay's notes, too. She didn't understand it, but she'd logged her observations about the Fair Folk and sugar. William thought it had to do with chemicals in the brain. However it worked, Jill had to be ready when Layla decided to act.

What are you planning? Jill thought. Should she open her Second Sight? No. It never seemed to work on Taylor, so she didn't have much hope it would tell her anything about Layla. Without her scrying bowl, she'd never be able to see the future to look for hints about Layla's plan.

So the two just traded evil glares while Abby, Carla, and Nyesha watched the movie. Jill crossed her arms and shot death glares at Layla. If she wanted to power up her magic, then let her.

"Hey," Carla blurted. "The fairy godmother is that evil woman from Harry Potter!"

"No way!" Abby said.

"No, look at her," Carla said. The others screamed and laughed when they figured out Carla was right.

"Man, I wish I had a fairy godmother," Abby said.

"Apparently they come in all shapes and sizes," Layla said. She winked at Jill.

"As long as they're not evil," Nyesha said, laughing. She pointed at the TV screen. "She don't look evil in this movie."

"Fairy godmothers can't be evil," Carla said. "Isn't that like a rule?"

Layla shot Jill a sly smile. Jill glowered at Layla.

"Having a fairy godmother would be awesome!" Abby said.

"You know what I'd wish for?" Nyesha began. "A sweet ride!"

"Girl, you don't even drive," Carla said.

"Then I'll wish for a driver, too!"

"I'd wish for a lifetime supply of makeup," Abby said.

"Or art supplies!" Carla chimed in.

"Don't you wish you had a magical godmother, Jill?" Layla said.

Jill scowled at her. She did have a faery godmother once. Thankfully, Taylor got her to cancel her contract, at the price of a favor owed to Mara Hellebore. That was what got her in trouble—and sent Layla to Macon, Georgia—in the first place.

"Not especially," she said. She slumped into her seat and tried to focus on the movie.

Layla finished the last of her cookies. She didn't say anything else until the movie was nearly over. As Cinderella's mouse friends worked to unlatch the window so the Duke could hear her singing, Nyesha said, "I like the mice in the cartoon version better."

"I dunno," Carla said. "These are cute."

"But they don't even talk. And Cinderella doesn't make them little outfits to wear."

"And they don't make Cinderella's dress," Abby said. "What do you think, Jill?"

"Huh?"

"About the mice."

"I think Nyesha's right," Layla said. "The mice were terribly underutilized in this movie."

"You see?" Nyesha said, playfully leaning into Carla.

"Mice never get old," Layla continued. "They're always good for a few laughs. Don't you think, Jill?"

Jill tensed her body. She didn't like the way this conversation was heading. "*Taylor*," she said.

Layla gestured toward Nyesha. "How about you, Nyesha? You said you like the mice, right?"

Before Jill knew what was happening, Nyesha leaped up onto the sofa cushion. Her whole body shivered.

Carla leaned away and shot her friend a bemused look. "What the—?"

"Layla, stop it!" Jill shouted, leaping to her feet.

"Who's Layla?" Carla said.

A second later, Abby had skittered to the floor. She squeaked at Nyesha, and Nyesha squeaked back at her. William had been right: Layla was really good at mind control! She had done something to Nyesha and Abby. She'd planted a suggestion that they were mice and not people.

"Now, what would be really fun," Layla said, giggling, "would be to throw a cat among the mice." She gestured to Carla, who pounced to the floor. On all fours, she arched her back and licked her lips.

Nyesha and Abby squealed with fright. Carla meowed and launched herself at Abby.

"I said stop it!" Jill yelled. But Abby had already bolted behind Layla's easy chair, knocking over a lamp. Layla jumped to the middle of the room. As soon as she got up from her chair, Carla leaped on it, tipping it backward as she slashed at Abby with her fingernails.

It's not working! Jill thought the trick she'd planned would have neutralized Layla's magic by now, but she wasn't even slowing down.

Jill dove for the sofa, where she'd hid Maymay's blasting rod earlier. At the same time, Nyesha trampolined off Jill's back and over the back of the sofa, squeaking and squealing. A couple of picture frames hit the floor.

Instead of retrieving her weapon, Jill got a face full of upholstery as Nyesha pushed the sofa out from the wall to scurry behind it. She fell back, seeing stars.

"What the blazes is going on in there?" Jill's dad called. She could hear his heavy footfalls on the stairs.

Jill raised her hands and intoned a spell. "Hush, little baby, don't say a word." Pulses of silvery magic exuded from the sofa and chair cushions all around the room. Her friends settled, at least a bit.

As her dad appeared at the entrance to the den, she continued the incantation. "Poppa's gonna buy you a mockingbird."

Mr. Matthews looked around the room, wide eyed. "What in the world...?"

"And if that mockingbird don't sing...." Abby, Nyesha, and Carla were sound asleep. The conjure bags worked, even if Jill's surprise for Layla hadn't.

Mrs. Matthews came in right after her husband. "Oh, my Lord!" she gasped.

"Jill," Mr. Matthews said. "Taylor?"

"That's not Taylor," Jill said. She kept her arms extended. Without her blasting rod, her options were limited. She began to mentally prepare a wind spell.

Amou aneme phthaneme pneuma ventibus thoou...

"What are you talking about?" Jill's mom said. "What's going on here?"

"Hey there, Mrs. Matthews, Mr. Matthews," she said, flashing a smile that was anything but innocent. Her face began to morph. Her skin turned darker and her hair went jet black, long and luxurious. At the same time, she grew two inches taller.

"Sweet Jesus!" Jill's mom blurted.

"Who are you?" Jill's dad demanded. "What are you doing in my house?" He took a step forward, hands extended as if to restrain the intruder.

"Dad, no!" Jill called.

Too late. Layla pushed out with her right hand and, wincing at the effort, thrust a shimmering arc of magic straight into Mr. Matthews's face. He groaned and crumpled to the floor.

"Charles!" Mrs. Matthews called. She was on her knees by his side in a heartbeat.

Jill took a defiant step forward. *Amou aneme phthaneme pneuma ventibus thoou...*

Layla's eyes perked up. "It's been fun!" she chirped. Then her body shrunk, her arms and legs drew up into her torso, and she became a small, green snake.

Jill jumped back. Nyesha, who'd been watching from behind the easy chair, squeaked and pawed at the wall.

In snake form, Layla slithered between Jill's legs and out into the hallway.

"No!" Jill shouted. She couldn't let Layla escape.

Before she could take a step, however, she heard Layla groan and curse. It sounded like she'd stumbled into a wall. Jill's heart raced. Maybe her trick was starting to work after all.

She stalked into the foyer. *Amou aneme phthaneme pneuma ventibus thoou...* A cool breeze now swirled around Jill's body, but she held it back. She might only get one shot.

Layla was in the living room, back in her everyday form. She looked out the window, smiling.

"This is over, Jill."

"You're darn right. Get out of my house—now!"

"You don't understand," Layla said. "This has been fun, and though I wish it could keep going, it's *over*." She glanced out the window again. Jill followed her gaze.

There were two strangers on the edge of the front yard. A wiry, black-haired man with glowing yellow eyes was kicking at the ghostly cat that paced back and forth in front of him. Jill and her brother had kept Maymay's warding spell up pretty well, it seemed. She wasn't sure what the cat actually did, but if it had materialized, it meant these strangers were not of this world.

The second stranger was a good seven feet tall, with warty skin and biceps as big as ham hocks. This man (or troll, or ogre—Jill had trouble keeping them all straight) snarled, baring his crooked, yellow teeth, as he eyed the living room window.

Jill was barely confident of handling one fae. There was no way she could deal with three of them at once.

"W-who's that?" Jill said.

"Like I said, Jill," Layla said. "I asked some friends to come by. That's my boyfriend." Jill noted beads of sweat on Layla's brow. *It's working, but not fast enough!*

"The little one is named Shagfoal. He's just a friend."

"Layla!" the big one growled. "We're hungry!"

"Coming sweetie!" Layla called from the window. She turned back to Jill.

"It looks like Eelick and Shagfoal would like something to eat," she said. She crossed her arms. "So, how about you invite them in?"

Chapter 25

Taylor's Plan

Mara peered into the scrying bowl, a shallow stone vessel resting on a table in Cair Cullen's trophy room. The water reflected the rippling image of Belas Wakefire's army advancing on the rath.

Let him come, she thought, smiling. As soon as the fool engaged with Crom and his Winter troops, he would realize he was in over his head.

Amber flames danced in lanterns along the walls between tapestries and Crom's mounted hunting trophies: elk, bear, panther, giant, and fae. One head in particular captured her attention, a pisgy who'd led an excursion against Crom the last time Summer and Winter went to war seventy years ago.

"Perhaps he'll put Belas's head next to yours," she told it.

"Ma'am?" the spriggan guard said.

"Nothing of your concern, Mr. Guenbrith," she said. She gazed once more into the water. "It seems Belas has brought giants."

Guenbrith betrayed no emotion.

"I expect our trolls will be able to keep them out of range."

"As you say, Ma'am."

She didn't look up, but continued to study the battlefield through the scrying bowl. The Summers advanced from the south and west, as if to force the Winter forces to fight with the setting sun in their eyes. But Crom had anticipated their strategy and positioned Kern Barrows and his Autumn troops at a distance from the rath, ready to ambush Belas from the rear. They had already engaged the enemy, forcing them to face into the sun instead.

Mara licked her lips, anticipating a slaughter.

Behind her was the mahogany desk. It had gone silent the night its twin was destroyed at Tobarty, which was only to be expected. But it had served its purpose. Crom knew more about the workings of the Summer Court than he could have dreamed—and had stolen more magic from Tobarty's bumbling Teyrnuses than he could possibly use. And it wasn't like the Winter Court didn't have other ways to discover their enemies' plans.

She passed her hand over the water. As it rippled, the scene changed and she surveyed the wide expanses beyond Cair Cullen in every direction. She doubted Belas was smart enough to use this initial advance as a diversion, but the Winter Court was nothing if not prepared. Mara would scan the area and inform Crom if she discovered any trickery.

The keep of Cair Cullen was located on the north end of the rath complex, with outbuildings, barracks, and craftsmen's houses mainly to the south and west within a series of walled-in courts. The main gate was to the south, but there were smaller gates to the west and to the northeast. Belas was apparently aiming for the western gate.

Mara turned her attention to the northeastern gate. Crom had pulled most of the troops from this portion of the wall to defend the western and southern gates. This, then, was a potential weak point, with little protection beyond the guards at the gatehouse itself. If Belas *were* to try anything clever....

She saw it at once, and arched an eyebrow. "Well, then," she said, and her smile stretched even wider. Could it be? She peered more closely, and her eyes widened as realization dawned.

"She wouldn't dare," she said, half-chuckling.

The guard stood at attention. "Ma'am?"

She didn't think the child would have the nerve, but she couldn't deny what her own magic was showing her. Shanna's insufferable little urchin was sneaking toward the rath! She studied the vision. It was definitely her, and she had a young man with her.

Mara recognized him almost at once. "Danu!" she hissed. He was the satyr, the child of Lorcan Redmane—but what was he doing here? The two crept along, avoiding soldiers, darting behind the cover of bushes and boulders under a half-hearted attempt at a camouflage of magic mist.

What is she thinking? If she enters Cair Cullen...

And yet, there she was. There was no mistaking the look of determination in those icy blue eyes of hers.

"Mr. Guenbrith," she said, "please send word to the northeast gatehouse to expect visitors shortly." If the child intends to destroy herself, what was that to her?

"Yes, Chief Matron," Guenbrith said. He set his blunderbuss on his shoulder and strode toward the door.

Mara frowned. "Surely the child can manage a better glamour than that."

She kept scrying, but hardly a second had passed before she called for her guard to halt. Something was wrong. Had her eyes deceived her?

She focused once more on the northeast gate, and there were Taylor and the satyr, skulking in the shadows. Then she returned her attention to the south gate...and there was Taylor again!

Her smile gave way to a giggle of disbelief.

"Ma'am?" the spriggan said.

She held up a hand as she continued to scry. There was Shanna's child—again—advancing on the southern gate. This time, though, she was with a little person: a native carrying a walking stick, wearing a bowler hat with a ridiculous turkey feather stuck into the brim.

"Oh, this is getting interesting!" Mara said. Two Taylors? Definitely some kind of trick.

"The same orders, Mr. Guenbrith," Mara said. "But please advise both the northeastern and the southern gates to expect company."

The door closed behind the spriggan. Mara was alone in the trophy room, absorbed in the scene playing out in the water of her scrying bowl.

Two Taylors, she thought. *One real, one an imposter.*

She leaned closer.

The real Taylor will never enter the rath, she decided. This was some kind of diversion. Mara scanned the southwest quadrant. Crom had caught Belas in a pincer with Winter troops in front and Autumn behind. Crom himself bounded across the battlefield on his white charger, directing his men with his mace of office.

The prospect of a massacre made her heart race.

A few minutes later, when Mara turned her attention back to the northeast gate, Taylor and the satyr were scrambling away, dodging a volley of elf-shot. Mr. Guenbrith had delivered his message, then.

At the southern gate, guards were advancing on the other Taylor and the little person. This Taylor extended her hand for a blast, and two soldiers fell stunned. She reached out her hand to the little person, who passed her his walking stick.

But it wasn't a walking stick. As soon as Taylor touched it, the knobby head burst into flames.

"A war club?" Mara gasped. Where had she learned to use such a weapon?

Taylor spun it around her body as she took a defensive stance, ready for the guards to advance.

What is your game, child?

The little person had pulled a knife from his belt and slashed it at the oncoming soldiers. Meanwhile, Taylor—whether real or fake, Mara didn't know—danced about, swinging her flaming war club at anyone who dared to come close.

Finally, a guard managed to reload his musket. He took aim at Taylor, but the little person flung a shield spell that deflected his shot.

"Get them!" Mara called. Four individuals were no match for Cair Cullen's guards, but it began to worry her that she couldn't see the point of this diversion. What was going on that she wasn't seeing?

She let the scene change again in the bowl. The other Taylor, the one with the satyr, was still dodging and weaving, circling around the rath as if to join her compatriots at the southern gate.

Belas seemed to be holding his own against Crom's men, but it was only a matter of time before he buckled.

Two spriggan guards burst into the trophy room. "Chief Matron!" one called.

Mara looked up at them.

"You need to come to the north tower, ma'am."

"Yes?"

"For your own protection," he continued. "There's been a breach."

"What? Someone's got inside the rath?"

"Yes, ma'am," the spriggan said. "Three of them. They're heading for the dungeons." He bit his lip. His eyes betrayed fear he was about to get in trouble.

"Well? Out with it!"

"It's just... The guards... They're saying Shanna's daughter is with them. And, beggin' your pardon ma'am, but they say she don't look happy."

William wondered what the guards of Cair Cullen thought when they saw a mortal teenager, a fat little person, and a sídhe girl in a black leather jacket storming through the dungeons. Thankfully, most of them didn't see them at all thanks to their glamour. William blasted anyone who did notice, robbing them of their magic long enough for his teammates to addle their minds or put them out with sleeping charms.

An explosion rumbled outside. Maybe that meant the Summer Court was turning things around.

Pete led the way through the corridors as quickly and quietly as they could, pressing ever downward into the belly of the keep and its dungeons. They made it to their first objective quicker than William would have hoped, but there were no guarantees the rest of Taylor's daredevil mission would go as smoothly.

Soon, the three intruders burst into Shanna's cell block, blasting at everything that moved. The dazed and befuddled guards didn't put up a fight when Pete pilfered their key ring and tried every one until they found the one to Shanna's cell door.

She seemed unhurt, but flummoxed to see them. William shushed her anxious questions and drew her into the corridor. Introductions were quickly made. Then William said, "Can you lead us to your dad's trophy room?"

Taylor helped William explain about the mummified head Crom had been using to stockpile magical power. Shanna quickly agreed to the plan—though William wondered if it weren't at least partly an act of desperation. She was through with her parents' abuse; that much was clear. Maybe she didn't expect to get out of Cair Cullen alive, but if she could bring Crom and Mara down with her....

William took a plastic bag full of beeswax from his jacket pocket. He motioned for Shanna to put some in her ears. She arched an eyebrow. "If things go bad, you might need it," he said.

Shanna pinched off two small lumps of wax.

"Ready?" William said, glancing at his team. Then he sensed movement behind him—a guard was coming around. He thrust his staff forward and yelled, "*Bazagra!*" The fae stumbled backward in shock. A second later, Shanna's blast sent him reeling.

"Ready!" she said.

They moved out. William took the lead, his heart pounding with the thrill of combat.

Take it easy, he told himself. *Save something for later*.

He settled his breathing and strode confidently forward. Hearing Claudia's explanation about dracontias and dragon's blood helped things fall into place he'd been feeling for days.

"Dragon's blood is highly poisonous," she had said—which William already knew. "But it sounds like you've managed to metabolize the dose you swallowed on the River of Night. Your body broke down the poison. When that happens, the substances that are left over have...certain effects."

William had explained how his eyesight had been dialed up to eleven. Claudia had nodded knowingly. "That's common. That and enhanced courage, coolness under fire."

"The danger makes me feel...more alive."

"And that's why you must be very careful," Claudia had said. "Dragon's blood will sharpen your senses, heighten your aggressive instincts—but it won't make you immortal, William. Always remember that."

They leaped up a flight of stairs and down a long, dim corridor that ended in a T. Taylor was disoriented.

"Which way?" William whispered.

"Left!" Shanna said. She hovered beside William's right shoulder, urging him on. The others followed close behind. He signaled for everyone to stop as he peered around the corner. All clear.

There was another explosion outside the keep. This one was so close William could feel the floor vibrate.

Being inside an actual faery rath made him giddy with excitement. He'd gone somewhere forbidden, and at least for now, he was getting away with it. He took in the sights—the tapestried walls; the odd, inhuman guards; the eerie glow of the lanterns and the twisted shadows they cast—with a mixture of dread and wonder.

On top of that, Taylor shouldn't even be there. She didn't seem to be suffering any negative results—yet. Claudia had been skeptical of Taylor's outrageous inspiration. "Not even you can lean that hard on the exact words of an oath," she had said. So far, though, the plan seemed to be working.

And yet, the whole thing could come crashing down at any second. He hoped Taylor knew what she was doing. If she suddenly lost her magic, or if her grandparents caught them there...

This is too easy, he thought. They should have faced more resistance than this.

You've got the dracontia.

Could that explain it? Claudia had said it worked something like a good-luck charm, siphoning tiny amounts of magic from the environment and putting it to use in a dozen different ways: causing someone to look the other way at just the right moment, making the basketball roll into the net instead of rimming out, deflecting or weakening curses, giving one's own magic an extra boost of strength.

William brushed his hand against his side. He could feel the magical crystal in the pocket of his denim jacket, against his stomach. He wondered what was happening outside. The others didn't have a dracontia. Was Ayoka all right? Or Wasko or the others?

Shanna grabbed William's arm. He whipped around as he stopped to listen, the others lurching into him.

The sound of footsteps echoed in the distance behind them. William readied his staff and gestured to Shanna. Which way?

Shanna pointed to the right, and they hurried forward under as powerful a glamour as three Fair Folk could conjure. They turned the corner—and nearly ran into a little person attendant!

There was an instant pile-up. The little person, a copper-skinned older woman, slammed into William. Before he could slap his hand over her mouth, she screamed.

The footsteps behind them broke into a run.

Taylor cursed. William's temple throbbed.

I knew this was too easy, he thought as a surge of adrenaline coursed through his body. He pushed the little woman out of the way as gently as he could. Shanna laid her hand on the woman's shoulder. There was a subtle pulse of magic, then she seized up and slumped silently to the floor.

"Get ready!" William hissed.

Pete pulled his secret weapon from his dusty traveler's pack. William pulled his from his backpack and wrapped the long leather strap around his left hand. He pulled a wad of crumpled paper from inside each of three cowbells looped together on the strap, but held them close to his body to keep them silent. He clutched his staff in his other hand.

Shanna checked her beeswax earplugs.

Three guards rounded the corner. The first fired his blunderbuss, but not before William smacked it down with his staff. The elf-shot sprayed the floor with greenish yellow sparks.

Pete rang his string of cowbells. All three guards winced. The ones that hadn't fired their weapons now did so on instinct, but both missed wildly. William dove into them, his staff spinning about his body.

"Halt!" More guards had appeared from the other direction—the direction they needed to go. Shanna loosed a stunning spell that sent them staggering backward.

"How much farther?" Pete called.

"One flight up!" Shanna cried. "There's a stairwell at the end of the hall. It's not far after that."

William laid out the last of the guards on his side, and the four pressed on. Before they could reach the end of the hall, though, two more guards burst out of the stairwell.

Pete and William rang their cowbells like there was no tomorrow. The guards staggered, but they didn't fall. William hadn't expected them to. The tolling of a good sized bell could make a fae pass out; the best a cowbell could do was disorient them.

A flurry of faery blasts took out these new guards, but the ones Shanna had stunned were coming to. William leveled his staff at the nearest one and snarled, "*Bazagra!*" He kicked away the blunderbuss the guard had been reaching for.

"They're still coming!" Pete cried, eyeing the stairwell. Terror darkened his face.

William's heart pounded. He jangled his cowbells like crazy. Pete did the same. Two guards spilled out of the stairwell, tripping over each other, hands clutching their ears.

His vision doubled; the cacophony was getting to him, but he pressed on. Shanna was now in the lead, storming up the stairs. William took up the rear, laying down a wave of sleeping magic on the stunned and bewildered guards behind him.

They walked over the heap of guards at the bottom of the stairwell and up to the next level. Then they spilled out into yet another dim hallway.

Taylor cursed again—and worse.

This corridor was packed with guards—at least a dozen of them. In front were two huge, warty, gray-skinned thugs that might have been defensive linemen for the Cair Cullen football team. The closest took a swipe at Shanna, knocking her into the wall.

"*MORE COWBELL!*" William hollered. He and Pete clanged furiously.

Shanna tried a blast, but it had no effect.

William began to conjure fire, but before he could complete the incantation, the second troll (or ogre, he could never keep those two straight) yanked his staff out of his hand and flung it behind him, where it clattered on the stone. Before he could ring his cowbells again, he was wrapped in the creature's hideous arms and was being dragged down the corridor along with the others.

"In here!" a woman's voice called.

Mara!

Someone ripped the string of cowbells from his hand. He heard Taylor's voice screaming threats. The temperature dropped.

The guards dumped William, Pete, and the rest onto the cold, stone floor. As he rose to his knees, he saw that he had to be in the trophy room. The walls were festooned with hunting trophies—including more than one human (or humanoid) head.

Mara Hellebore stood in front of a great mahogany desk, watching with cold satisfaction. She arched her eyebrow. With William's enhanced eyesight, he could just make out faded splotches of red where Taylor had splashed her with iron filings two summers ago. He grinned at the thought.

"*Does something amuse you?*" Mara said, and those cold, dark eyes bore into his soul. He felt a wave of presence washing over him. He stood up straight.

"No ma'am," he gulped.

Chapter 26

Will the Real Taylor Please Stand Up?

Mara still couldn't believe Shanna's daughter would dare set foot in Cair Cullen, but there she was, as plain as day, alongside Shanna, a pasty-faced little person, and a gangly deathling boy.

Guards placed their confiscated items on the desk behind her: a staff and a half-dozen cowbells.

She looked at Taylor. "I'd have thought you'd be dead by now," Her voice betrayed no emotion. She took a step forward. "I doubt you have much magic left after violating your oath."

Taylor said nothing. She glared at Mara, but the fire she had expected to see in her eyes wasn't there. She smiled.

"And all for some ridiculous rescue mission? Really, Selena, I thought you'd have learned your lesson by now."

She turned to Shanna. "And you! You insufferable little brat, you at least should have known better than to defy me."

Shanna spat and snarled as she twisted in the arms of the troll who restrained her.

The boy's eyes darted across the room, taking in every detail. His gaze landed on the table, and his expression darkened. "And who might you be?" she said. "I don't believe we've met, but I remember what you did to my pet." Ellen, her three-headed vulture, hadn't been the same since the boy had salted its feathers with banishing powder.

"I see you're looking for Crom's prize," she said matter-of-factly. "It's not here."

The boy glanced at the mahogany desk, and Mara could tell from his pained expression the instant he realized what she'd said was true.

"I'm afraid this little adventure of yours is ending in disaster. Oh, please. Don't act so surprised. I can't believe you actually thought it would work."

The boy struggled against the hold Mara's troll had him in. "Let us go!" he snarled.

"My, my!" Mara said. "Has Selena found a knight to fight her battles for her?" He nearly wrenched himself free, but the troll was far too strong. But there was definitely a fire in *his* eyes.

"Or perhaps...what do you young people say these days? A 'boo'?" Mara winked.

"She's not my girlfriend!" William shouted. "Look, she's a friend, and she's a girl, but..." He groaned against the troll's strength. "Why am I explaining this to *you*?"

"Why indeed?"

"Just let them go," Shanna said. "I'm the one you want!"

"My dear," Mara said. She could barely contain her fury. "I'm afraid we are well past the point of bargaining." She looked at the guard clutching Shanna's arms. "Take her back to...her room," she said. "The rest of you, stay here until I've turned these trespassers into something useful."

Shanna wrestled with her guard. A wave of cold rippled from her body.

The boy yanked his right arm free with a blood curdling roar. He stretched his hand toward the desk and shouted, "*Revenez à moi!*"

Taylor gasped. "William—?"

Another explosion rocked the keep, shaking the floor and the walls. The Summers' giants were still hurling boulders at the keep, it seemed.

But the shaking had another effect. The staff on the desk rolled forward and hit the floor with a clatter. Mara circled around the desk to pick it up, but didn't make it. Shanna let out a savage grunt and clasped the thighs of the troll who was guarding her. The troll let go, clutching his frost-covered legs and howling in agony.

Shanna dug the heel of her hand into the face of the guard holding Taylor. Spiderwebs of frost erupted across his nose and eyes, and he let go, screaming.

Taylor dropped into a crouch, gathering magic.

The boy—William—scooped up his staff and rammed it between his guard's legs. The troll doubled over in pain.

Mara had had enough. Taylor and her friends were mocking her, making her guards look like fools! It was time they paid for that. She waved her hand, unleashing a blast at Taylor, who flew backward into the arms of another guard, a spriggan who quickly grew until his head nearly brushed against the ceiling.

Only now it wasn't Taylor.

Her form had dissolved. In her place was a little person—an albino with wooly hair and fierce silver eyes. A decoy?

"Danu!" Mara hissed. "What is the meaning of—?"

Just then, William swung his staff into the spriggan's shins. When he dropped the little person who'd been impersonating Taylor, the boy shouted *"Bazagra!"* As soon as the spark of magic hit the spriggan, he deflated to his normal height.

The incapacitated guards were starting to pile up, bested by a deathling and two little folk!

"Enough of this!" Mara thundered. Her outburst was answered by another explosion outside. Dust fell from the ceiling.

The four intruders stood in shock before her. She turned her attention to the albino. Everything was finally beginning to make sense.

"Taylor is still somewhere outside," she told herself, her voice once more settling down. "She was never within the rath."

William chuckled. "That's right." Mara could see the rage swelling inside him. "She kept her oath—just like she kept the twisted promise you forced her to make. And you know what? She's still going to beat you, because it isn't about her anymore. It's about...everything." He took a defiant step forward, unfazed by Mara's presence. "She's going to stop you before you can hurt anybody else."

"We'll see about that," Mara said.

"And another thing," William said, his face betraying a satisfied smirk. "Did you honestly expect Taylor Smart to just walk in here and sacrifice her magic the one time she needed it most? You mean to tell me that was seriously something you thought she would do?"

Mara gathered magic. She suddenly felt on the defensive. It was not a pleasant feeling.

William cocked his head. "I really don't think you're as smart as people say you are."

In that instant, Mara understood.

"Taylor," she whispered.

William smiled. "You guessed it, *Grandma*."

Chapter 27

The Cavalry...and the Bison

"I'm waiting," Layla said. Jill watched a single trickle of sweat snake its way down the jinni's neck. Though she'd only seen her in her real face for a few minutes, she seemed paler than when she first dropped her Taylor persona.

Jill allowed herself a wry smile. "I'll bet you are."

The two circled around the living room. Jill kept meditating on her wind spell, but didn't unleash it.

"Things will be bad for everyone if you don't invite Eelick and Shagfoal in. I'll see to that personally." Jill had to hand it to her: Layla was a good bluffer. But it was clearer every second that things weren't going Layla's way. Maybe she didn't realize that herself yet, but Jill did.

"Uh huh," Jill said.

"You don't think I'm serious?"

"Oh, I believe you. It's just that, to be honest, you don't look so good. Are you feeling okay?"

Layla scowled at her. She had definitely turned paler in the last few seconds.

"Invite them in! Now!"

Layla shot out her hand to blast Jill. At the same time, Jill shouted, *"Amou aneme!"* A hurricane-force wind flung Layla out of the living room, into the foyer, and against the hall closet door, cracking the wood.

Layla fell to the floor.

Jill opened the front door. The troll and the pooka were still at the edge of the yard, ducking to and fro to see what was going on inside. The whole street was blanketed in fog: a tactic she'd noticed before when the Fair Folk wanted to shield their activities from mortal eyes.

"Now go." Jill grabbed Layla by the collar and hoisted her up. She was wobbly on her feet.

"I'm going to be sick," Layla groaned.

"That's the general idea," Jill said. She slammed her against the storm door and turned the latch. With nothing to hold her up, Layla stumbled onto the stoop, tripped down the steps, and landed on all fours on the grass.

"What have you done to me?" the jinni demanded.

"Nothing," Jill said. "Not one blessed thing."

"Love muffins?" Eelick the troll called. He tried to step forward, but an invisible barrier held him at bay. Maymay's spectral cat slashed at his shins. He jumped back, then tried to shoulder his way through the magical barrier again. It still held.

"Then why...?" She couldn't complete her sentence. Her whole body quaked as she heaved and then literally lost her cookies on the front lawn.

Jill's hopes soared as her stomach churned. "Ew."

Layla groaned. Eelick and Shagfoal paced.

Jill smiled broadly. "You did it to yourself."

Layla rolled onto her side to look Jill in the eye. "I never told you to eat all those cookies. How many did you have, anyway? Six? Ten?"

The jinni started to crawl toward her friends. She only got a few feet before she stopped to puke again.

"Turns out my grandmother was right. Rowan berries really are poisonous to the Good Neighbors."

Layla struggled to her feet, wide-eyed. "Rowan berries? You told me they were cranberry!"

Jill crossed her arms. "I lied."

She took a step forward. Layla flinched away. "A little extra honey and vanilla extract to hide the bitterness, some orange zest for flavor...."

"You filthy deathling," Layla spat.

"I told you to leave," Jill said. She raised her voice and called to the troll and the pooka. "Take her away," she said. "Get her to a doctor…or whatever you folks have. Now! Before this fog you all whipped up burns away."

The troll snarled. "I never made no fog, and I ain't ready to leave!"

Once more Jill shouted, *"Amou aneme!"* Layla rolled across the lawn and nearly took flight. She only stopped when she slammed into the mailbox. With a crack, it toppled onto the street. Layla screamed and clutched her backside.

"Layla!" Eelick yelled. He dashed to his girlfriend's side. Glaring at Jill, he hefted the mailbox and swung it over his head like a war hammer.

By the time Jill recognized the danger, it was too late. Maymay's wards protected the house and the yard against any kind of faery intruder.

It was never intended to deflect purely mortal projectiles.

Jill swore and dropped to the ground just as the mailbox flew over her head and crashed into the front window.

Her heart pounded. What else could that brute find to throw at her? He was already looking around for his next missile. Shagfoal came to his aid. He'd pulled down a tree branch from a neighbor's yard and wrapped it in a dingy handkerchief. Now he summoned fire in his hand and set the thing ablaze.

Jill let her wind spell spring to life, wrapping her in a miniature tornado of swirling leaves and dust. No matter how wildly the wind churned around her, it had no effect on the mystic fog.

She braced herself, ready to unleash her fury against Eelick.

The troll stalked back to the edge of the Matthewses' lawn, brandishing Shagfoal's makeshift torch. Jill glanced at the dried grass stretching out between her and them. The torch wouldn't stay lit for long, but if it caught the yard on fire…

Eelick wound up, ready to hurl his weapon straight at her.

And then he seized up and dropped the torch by the curb. A pair of arrows sprouted from his neck, then just as quickly evaporated into nothingness.

He wobbled in place. A second later, Shagfoal crumpled to the ground.

Eelick spun toward the Smarts' house.

On their lawn, a lone figure appeared: a Native American warrior with his bow drawn and nocked. He loosed another arrow. This one hit the troll in the middle of his chest.

Eelick staggered backward, then fell flat.

The warrior sprinted forward. Three others appeared beside him. All four were dressed the same, in buckskins and beribboned cotton trade shirts, with feathered topknots and multiple earrings in each ear.

With his bow still in his hand, the first warrior knelt down to check on his quarry.

"How dare you...?" Layla groaned, then rolled over and threw up again.

A second later the warrior stood up, satisfied. He gave a quick command in a language Jill didn't understand. One of the others pulled a Seeing Stone from a pouch at his belt and began to whisper an incantation.

The first warrior turned to Jill. "They won't give you any more trouble," he said. "My lieutenant is calling for someone to come remove them."

Jill realized she was staring with her mouth open. She cleared her throat and said, "I remember you." Her heart was still pounding, but now with relief. "You're Ayoka's cousin."

"Tsisgwa Imathla," he said, bowing curtly. "It's a pleasure to meet you again, Miss Matthews."

"But...how...?"

"Ayoka sent me word there was trouble here. Chief Coloma agreed it was worth risking our presence Topside. I've had a guard keeping watch at Taylor's house since daybreak."

Jill glanced at the house two doors up and across the street. Her heart skipped a beat. "Taylor's parents!"

Tsisgwa smiled. "We checked on them as soon as the imposter left this afternoon. They were heavily glamoured, but not any more. They'll be fine."

Jill sighed with relief. Then she frowned and looked behind her. "I wish I could say the same for our house. My dad's going to hit the roof when—Oh, God!" As soon as she said it, she remembered: Layla had blasted her dad, had done something to the minds of her friends. She had to do something!

She sprinted halfway to the house.

"Miss Matthews!" Tsisgwa called.

She stopped in her tracks and spun back around. "My dad and my friends are hurt. Can you help them?"

He studied the line of grass at the edge of the Matthewses' curb. "If you invite me in."

"Come on," Jill said. "Hurry!"

Jill's mom had fallen asleep draped over her husband. Tsisgwa's fellow warrior gingerly lifted her off and took her to the guest bedroom. A second warrior took up his post in the living room, where he collected the mailbox and the shards of glass and tossed them onto the yard.

"Muklasa Tasikaya will take care of your mother," Tsisgwa said. He knelt and placed a finger against Mr. Matthews's throat. Without looking up, he asked, "Is the sleeping charm your doing?"

Jill nodded. Then she realized Tsisgwa wasn't looking at her. "That's right," she said.

"Impressive." Only then did he notice the teenage girls snoozing behind the sofa and the easy chair.

"My secret ingredient is Charles Dickens."

Tsisgwa grunted noncommittally. "Perhaps we should leave it in effect until someone has had time to check on your friends."

"Good call," Jill said. She glanced back toward the foyer. "Any chance you know somebody who does home repair? Maybe a glass guy?"

Tsisgwa chuckled. "My man outside is sending someone."

"Is my dad okay?"

Tsisgwa stood up. "I think so. Blasts are unpredictable, but he seems to be in good health. That's to his advantage."

Jill let that sink in with a silent prayer of thanksgiving. "And my friends? Layla did something to their minds."

"Such things can be fixed," Tsisgwa said. "I'll ask Chief Efau, the Medicine Chief, to send a healer. The easiest thing will probably be to simply adjust their memories."

"What do you mean, 'adjust'?"

"They'll remember coming to your party, having a good time, and then leaving when it was over. Their own imaginations will fill in the details. Memories of previous get-togethers, expectations of what was supposed to happen. They won't remember the imposter or any of the mischief she caused. With a little luck, we can get your house put back to order before their parents come for them."

Jill thought about everything that had happened in the last couple of hours. "That sounds like a pretty good deal, actually." She looked down at her father asleep on the floor of the den. She watched his chest rising and falling. He seemed perfectly at ease.

"I suppose it was you that created the fog outside?"

"What do you mean?"

"The glamour. At first I thought it was Layla's friends, but they said they didn't do it. And then you showed up and—"

"Miss Matthews." He quirked an eyebrow. He shifted his weight as if suddenly on alert, waiting for something. "We assumed the fog was part of the house's magical defenses."

Jill's eyes shot wide and her mouth dropped open. If it wasn't Eelick and Shagfoal, and if it wasn't the nunnehi....

She bolted for the door, nearly running over one of Tsisgwa's warriors. Outside, the fog was just as thick as it had been before. The troll, the pooka, and the jinni had been removed, and the warrior who'd used the Seeing Stone earlier was standing watch in front of the Matthewses' with two newcomers.

264

"You all can go on inside," she said. "But first tell me what's going on with this—"

"Car!" a warrior called. He and his fellows stepped onto the edge of Jill's yard. Mrs. Dibney's white Honda rolled down Knottingley Drive and turned into the driveway on the near side of the Smarts' house.

Jill's neighbor stepped out of the car. Her little Pomeranian darted between her feet and began yipping at the nearest warrior.

"Thor! Come back here!"

Jill held her breath. The three nunnehi traded awkward glances. The one that had captured Thor's attention tried to shoo it away with his foot. The little dog growled, then sped back to its human.

"Sorry about that, Jill!" Mrs. Dibney called. "I bet he smells another dog."

"Yes, ma'am," Jill said. The fog—whoever had created it—was doing its job. Mrs. Dibney had no awareness of the supernatural beings congregating on her street.

Thor leaped into Mrs. Dibney's arms. Jill watched as her neighbor ambled up to her front door and went inside.

Jill let out a long, wearied sigh. Her shoulders slumped, and she turned to the nearest warrior. "This glamour isn't yours?"

"We thought it was part of the wards around your house," he said. "Or else something the troll called up." His hand went to the war club at his side. "It wasn't us." He barked a command. The other warriors drew their weapons as well.

The late afternoon sky suddenly darkened. The fog thickened. The nunnehi spun around, looking for signs of movement, but there were none.

The darkness coalesced into a churning ball in the middle of the street.

Jill gulped. Her mind raced, looking for a helpful incantation, but nothing came to her.

"W-what's that?" she finally managed. But when she looked at the nunnehi, they were frozen in place. At first Jill thought they were just surprised, but a second passed, and they didn't move at all.

A lumbering shape emerged from the darkness: at least eight feet tall, covered with shaggy brown fur, with a massive head set off with curved, black horns.

"Oh...my..."

The buffalo snorted and shook its massive body.

Jill lifted her left hand defensively. If this thing had a magical attack, maybe she could deflect it. If it decided to charge her.... She tried not to think about that.

The beast lifted its head. Its eyes glowed with amber light.

A pooka? Jill thought. *Some other kind of shape-shifter?*

"What do you want?" she challenged. She tried to look fierce and defiant, but she doubted she was convincing. Her legs were shaking, and her heart pounded so hard the beast could probably hear it at ten paces.

Make that eight paces. It was slowly making its way down the street in her direction.

She yelled, "D-don't come any closer!" but her voice gave out at the end.

"What would you do if I continued?" the beast said. Its voice was so deep and rumbly it would have made Avi from Pentatonix sound like a tenor, but it was perfectly human in its tone and timbre.

"I'm serious!"

"I'm sure you are, Miss Matthews," it said.

Jill gasped. "You know my name?"

It nodded its ponderous, devilish head.

It was more than Jill could take in. "I'm talking...to a buffalo... in the middle of the street."

"A bison," the creature corrected. "Buffalo are Old World creatures." It pawed the ground and snorted. Jill hoped she hadn't offended it. She glanced at the nunnehi. They were still stuck in place. She couldn't see that they'd moved an inch since the buffalo—the *bison*—had appeared.

"Time is wasting," the beast said. He twisted the whole front of his body around toward the shadowy vortex behind him. "Come."

If you think I'm going anywhere *with you...!*

Jill stood her ground.

Her friends were unconscious in the den. Without Tsisgwa's healer, they'd probably wake up still thinking they were small furry animals. Her dad had been blasted. Her mom—she didn't even want to think about what her mom would do when she came to! Everything was happening too fast. Her friends—her parents—needed her.

"I said, 'Come,'" the bison repeated.

"Don't I have a say in this?" Jill said.

"No."

Tendrils of darkness whipped out from behind the bison, wrapping around Jill, silently enveloping her in the shadows.

She tried to scream, but no sound escaped her throat.

And then everything went black as night.

Chapter 28

Exit Taylor

Ayoka buried the head of her flaming war club in the gut of another warrior. She spun around, ready for the next one.

"Behind you!" she shouted. Ten feet away, Wasko whipped around, slashing with his knife at an elfin warrior who'd come up from behind. The move threw the elf off balance, and Wasko deftly side-stepped him.

"Thanks!" he said.

Ayoka nodded. She waved Wasko on, and the two of them sprinted back toward the woods.

She knew her husk was slipping. Her once golden-brown hair was getting darker by the minute, as were her formerly pale skin and icy blue eyes. It was just as well: fighting her way through Cair Cullen's defenses would be hard enough without trying to impersonate Taylor Smart while she was doing it.

But hopefully she'd provided the distraction Taylor needed. Now she needed to concentrate on getting her and Wasko to safety.

If it weren't for the little person, she'd have just cloaked herself in a veil of invisibility and been off. But Wasko needed her, so she hung close and batted away any Winter warriors who impeded their retreat.

The opposing forces seemed evenly matched, though for the moment, Summer seemed to have the upper hand. Their forces were making slow progress toward the rath from the south and west. The Summers' giants lobbed huge boulders at the rath, softening the outer walls. A few lucky shots even managed to strike the keep.

As the Summer Court inched toward Cair Cullen, they pushed the Winter troops before them—which threatened to cut off Ayoka's escape route.

Ayoka muttered her war formula, the mantra she used to stir up aggression and keep her mind focused on the battle. With a throaty whoop, she plowed into a pair of redcaps before they could aim their tiny muskets in her direction.

In the distance, Crom Cornstack flitted through the lines astride a white charger. His blood-red cloak whipped about in the wind. His men pressed on as he barked orders, driving them against the enemy. His commanding presence made Ayoka take notice. His whole body seemed to crackle with magical energy, a subtle shimmer in the air that Ayoka could feel as much as she could see, even over fifty yards away.

She barely had time to ponder what that could mean before an explosion behind her captured her attention. Évastre the satyr stumbled into view, a trail of sickly green smoke rising from his back. His expression was dazed and hollow: he'd been elf-shot. A second later, Bryn appeared, still wearing her Taylor disguise.

Bryn and Évastre had been sent to the northeast entrance. It was clear things hadn't gone as well for them as it had for Wasko and Ayoka. The satyr fell to the ground face-first. Bryn shouted and launched a dazzling stunning spell against someone over her shoulder.

Wasko was on him almost as quickly as Bryn. He turned the satyr over onto his back and slapped him in the face.

Ayoka gathered magic as she sprinted to them. "Stay close!" she ordered. "This is only supposed to work for one person..." She extended her hands, calling on her magic to blanket the group and hide it from sight. The colors of the world, already muted in the failing light of dusk, washed away to gray. They were invisible.

"Come on, big guy," Wasko whispered, shaking Évastre's shoulders. "We gotta get moving."

"Trouble?" Ayoka said.

Bryn nodded. "Let's hope the others got in." She let her husk fall. Her hair became blonder, her eyes greener, her figure more mature. Her now-visible cow tail twitched apprehensively.

Évastre groaned.

Getting the others inside the rath was what this was all about. Surely they'd succeeded. "William is a fine witch," Ayoka said. "And a decent warrior as well. And from what I hear, Haggler is no slouch. If he and Pete can lead them to Shanna..."

A shot rang out. All eyes darted to where the thickest fighting raged. A jet of green smoke had rocketed over Cornstack's shoulder and was now dissipating. The Summers had a sniper in the woods!

A misshapen brown thing appeared in the Primus's hand. It turned in the wind, and Ayoka recognized it as a head.

She also saw that this head was the source of the Winter Primus's magical aura. His cold, blue eyes gleamed with malice as he displayed the head in the direction of the woods and his wood-be assassin. He uttered a simple incantation, and the entire battlefield grew suddenly dark. For a split second, there was nothing—no light, no magic...not even hope, it seemed. The whole world split apart to make room for a surge of malevolent energy that arced out of the Primus's talisman and into the woods.

Riding the surge was the smoky form of a giant boar that squealed as it tore through the Summer ranks and into the trees, snapping their trunks in half. In the gloom, the screams of agony and desperation told Ayoka the creature had found its mark.

"Danu!" Bryn gasped.

Then the Primus took aim at the giants. Once more, a wave of blackness—a void too terrible for words—crested over the battlefield. The boar charged out of the woods and into its next target. It gored the giants with its tusks and trampled on their bodies when they fell.

The Winter troops whooped and pressed their sudden advantage. The Summer troops, seemingly in shock, did all they could to hold their ground.

"By oak, ash, and thorn!" Wasko muttered. "What's that?"

"I don't know," Ayoka said. "But we'd better get moving." As soon as she said it, she realized her veil of invisibility was starting to collapse. It was like the Primus's talisman had left her depleted and demoralized, even though it had never even been trained on her. It was obvious the troops of the Summer Court felt it, too.

Bryn helped Évastre to his wobbly feet.

Shield! Taylor yelled inside William's head. He raised his staff in response to Taylor's command.

I know! William answered.

Taylor felt the strain of his muscles, the pounding of his heartbeat, the dryness in his throat. She reached deep inside herself to summon the magic for a shield spell. It formed just as Mara's blast erupted from her hand.

"Selena," Mara taunted. "You've entered my rath after all."

Taylor let loose a string of profanity that made William's ears burn.

"Taylor would beg to differ," William said. He trained his staff on an approaching guard and shouted, *"Bazagra!"* The surge of power erupted from the tip of the staff and sent the guard staggering backward.

"Enough of this!" Mara shouted, wide-eyed.

Taylor backed off, contenting herself to hover at the back of William's mind. If she wasn't careful, she'd interfere with his body—and the last thing he needed at a time like this was a back-seat driver. It was enough that she could feed him the words she knew would throw Mara off balance. Now she watched through her friend's eyes as he and the others used that moment of confusion in their bid to escape.

It looked like they were ready. Haggler's stunning spell came on the heels of Mara's blast, plunging the trophy room into a chaos of flashing lights and earsplitting explosions.

The guards reeled.

Pete lunged for the mahogany desk. Grabbing the cowbells, he threw one string to Haggler and kept the other for himself, even as he scrambled atop the desk, ringing with all his strength.

Mara clapped her hands over her ears and screamed orders at the guards. Filtered through William's ears, the noise still bothered Taylor, but not as much as it might have. Shanna, still wearing her beeswax ear plugs, gave a second dose of stun magic to the first guard who woke up.

And William...

Taylor hadn't quite known what to expect faring forth into a human being. Birds and small mammals were pretty jumpy; you had to move slowly or they'd knock you out of their consciousness awfully fast. William had been more accommodating—but no less anxious.

Taylor had told him over and over again that she didn't intend to take him over, she just wanted to be there as best she could. Maybe she could lend a hand. Based on Jill's past experience being ridden by Mara, she figured she could lend William some extra magical firepower, maybe even help him stay calm when all the weirdness began.

Her first surprise was William's sheer physical strength. His body was bigger and more muscular than hers, and he knew how to use it. She felt the surge of adrenaline coursing through him, sharpening his senses and dulling his pain, but there was something more, something even bigger at work; she didn't understand what.

When William spun about, swinging his staff like a baseball bat into the heads of the guards, it was like something wild raged through him, something that reveled in the danger, something supremely confident it would come out on top.

273

She hoped whatever it was was right, because her friends needed every advantage. Shanna and the others looked like they were near the end of their magical reserves. The guards in the trophy room were in no condition to fight, but William heard others tromping down the hallways. And Mara had barely begun to fight.

The Chief Matron gestured toward him dismissively. This time, his defenses weren't fast enough. He staggered, bent over with stomach cramps. He leaned on his staff to keep from falling to his knees.

Taylor willed more of her magic into William, just like she had when he had reclaimed his staff. As he steadied himself, Shanna conjured a shield to deflect a blast from Mara.

Meanwhile, Pete had snagged a blunderbuss from one of the guards. No sooner had he trained it on Mara than she hissed an incantation and the brass barrel froze solid and buckled.

"Oh, Brother Mike!" he cursed, dropping the useless weapon on the floor.

That was when the door to the trophy room burst open, and half a dozen more guards stormed in, fresh and ready for action.

William's heart pounded, eager for a fight.

Take it easy! Taylor thought.

I got this! he thought back. He swung his staff around and started to chant through gritted teeth. *"Sharba pesharba flammante fayah pyripeganyx."* Taylor felt heat coursing through her—or rather William's—body.

Don't be stupid!

"Get them!" Mara commanded. With another gesture, she blasted Shanna, who crumpled to the floor.

Haggler and Pete clanged their cowbells. The racket slowed the guards down, but it didn't stop them. What's more, the noise was slowly wearing Taylor down, making it harder for her to hold her connection to William. She'd managed easily before— William's Topsider ears made a pretty good noise filter—but now he was hurt, distracted.

Two guards, a spriggan and some sort of elf, charged at him. William leveled his staff. "*Sharba pesharba flam—*" The spriggan, suddenly eight feet tall or more, knocked the staff away and drove a meaty hand into William's ribcage.

The stabbing pain as William crumpled against the wall was enough to finally break Taylor's connection. She opened her eyes with a start, gasping for breath. She was back in her body, in Claudia's tent, seated cross-legged in the circle of power Claudia had cast for her.

"Something's wrong," Claudia said.

All Taylor could do was nod.

"Take your time. You've been away for almost two hours. It'll take a while to regain—"

"No!" Taylor managed. She steadied herself with one hand. Holding herself upright was an effort.

Claudia stepped forward, breaking the circle. She held out a cup. Taylor received it with shaky hands. Hot chocolate. Mercy nosed at her hands, tail wagging, and tried to lick her face. She gently pushed the dog away.

"William." She shook her head and squeezed her eyes shut. "Shanna..."

"Rest, Taylor."

"C-can't!" People's lives were on the line, and it was all because of her—again! This were her plan. She had been the one to convince them it would work, that they could rescue Shanna, destroy Crom's talisman, and get out alive. Now none of that was going to happen.

Why didn't anyone try to talk her out of this?

"The battle?" she groaned.

Claudia frowned. "Summer is pulling back."

Bile rose in Taylor's stomach. "Crom."

"The Primus has chosen to enter the battle himself," Claudia said. "I'm afraid it doesn't look good."

"He has the sacrum, doesn't he? The vessel?"

Claudia nodded. "He's used it to create a magical construct, a boar to trample the Summer forces."

Taylor started. "A boar?" She choked back tears. Anya Redmane had said Crom had conjured a boar to trample her father.

Claudia shook her head. "I've never heard of a construct so powerful."

"It's got hundreds of years of stolen magic behind it," Taylor said bitterly.

And now she was sitting safely a mile or more from the front while most of her friends were about to die.

She shivered. It hadn't been a week since she and William were fighting for their lives on the River of Night. The thought of William lying unconscious, his body spasming after swallowing a gobbet of poisonous dragon's blood, made her lower lip quiver.

"I've got to help them," Taylor said. This time, it wasn't just William in danger. Shanna, Haggler, and Pete were there, too, and none of them—not even all of them combined—were no match for Mara. "It's my fault..."

Taylor wiped away a tear.

Ayoka barged into the tent. She held the tent flap open behind her, and Wasko appeared, his bowler had in his hand. Its turkey feather had been singed to about halfway down. "We knew the risks," she said. As Taylor studied them, he saw other signs of struggle: a bloody gash on Ayoka's left pant leg, a burned spot on Wasko's buckskin jacket, mud and grass stains on both their knees.

Even so, their appearance at the tent flap was the first encouraging sign Taylor had seen in a while. "You made it!" she exulted. Her empty mug tumbled to the floor. Just as quickly, her face fell. "Where are the others?"

Ayoka knelt beside Taylor. "Évastre's been elf-shot," she said. Her expression was grim. "Bryn's with him in the medical tent."

"Is he...?"

"He's in good hands," Ayoka said. "The healers say no permanent damage."

Taylor sighed.

"Wasko and I thought you'd still be...away," Ayoka said.

Taylor felt her lip begin to quiver. "I think William passed out." She took a breath, working out how to say what she needed to say. "I couldn't hold on. It...doesn't look good."

"Then help me wrap my leg," Ayoka said. "I'll go see what I can do."

"You'll what?" Taylor's heart jumped again. She could tell from the look in Ayoka's eyes that she was serious. The nunnehi took to defending the underdogs like pookas took to mischief—and neither, it seemed, thought twice about what could go wrong.

Ayoka lowered herself into one of Claudia's camp chairs and dropped her war club at her side. She pulled up her torn pant leg. Taylor saw the swash of blood across Ayoka's shin and the long, thin gash that had made it. "It looks worse than it is," the nunnehi assured her.

"But you're still injured. You should stay here." It wasn't her fight in the first place. Taylor clenched her teeth. This was her battle; she should have been there at William and Shanna's side...

"And do what?" Ayoka challenged.

Taylor ignored her. "I'll go," she sighed. It's what she wanted to do in the first place. To hell with her oath!

"It could kill you," Claudia said. She brought in a washbasin, bandages, and a jar of healing salve from the back partition of the tent. "Forget about the guards, the simple act of setting foot in Cair Cullen could kill you. Listen to Ayoka." She knelt in front of her and began to clean her wound.

"But if Shanna or William—"

"You saw what happened to Mrs. Redmane," Ayoka said. Claudia positioned Ayoka's leg on her own thigh so she could wrap it properly. "How is that going to help your friends?"

"I've got to do something!"

"Why?" Claudia rumbled. She didn't look up from treating Ayoka, but Taylor could imagine the fire in her eyes, so much like her father's.

And she didn't appreciate her tone. "What do you mean, 'Why'?" She set her hands on her hips. "They're in trouble because of me, aren't they? I need to help them!"

"Okay," Claudia said. "*You* need to help them. So, you march straight up to Cair Cullen, maybe use the same secret passage they did. You get inside—and the minute you set foot in the rath, all bets are off."

Claudia now turned to face Taylor. With Ayoka's wound tended to, she rose to her full, imposing height. There was definitely a rumble of thunder in her voice. She continued. "Magic is all about vibrations. And now, because you've broken your oath, *your* vibrations are out of resonance with the rest of the universe. When's the last time you told a lie, Taylor? I mean a big one?

Claudia was getting more and more furious. But this wasn't about her, Taylor realized. Her mind was on Danny, and she was doing whatever she could to keep it together.

"An oath is even worse," she said. "It creates a feedback loop that's aimed straight at you."

"But—"

"Let's assume..." Claudia stopped and sniffled. The anger had given way to a mixture of terror and despair. "Let's assume you don't drop dead on the spot. You're going to lose at least half your magic. Maybe more. Maybe forever. So the first redcap or troll or spriggan that comes along... He's going to be a lot more than you can handle."

Taylor braced herself. It was all she could do not to lash out, to tell Claudia to mind her own business. And yet, she knew she was right, so instead she held her peace and stared at the floor.

"So explain to me how that helps Shanna and the others," Claudia said.

"You don't want me to do anything," Taylor spat.

"I want you to accept your limitations." She wiped away a tear. "Be smart. Do what you can do; don't try to do what you can't do. The whole world doesn't rest on your shoulders, Taylor."

Claudia rose to put away her medicine. "They call the daoine sídhe the Children of Pride for a reason, you know."

Taylor paused. Shanna had said something about that the first time they'd met. But this was an emergency!

And yet, Claudia had a point. Taylor took a deep breath. "So what can I do?"

"We'll think of something. The Winters are strong, but they're not invincible. If we could—"

She was cut off by an earthshaking explosion outside the tent. Then came shouting, a blast of wind, and the clanging of metal.

Claudia ran to the tent flap with Taylor right behind. Outside, cooks and farriers and others who'd stayed behind in the camp ran this way and that.

Someone—Taylor couldn't tell who—shouted, "They're coming! We've been driven back!"

Lieutenants barked orders, struggling to hold their retreating men in line.

Taylor looked toward the west. All she could see was a smoky haze punctuated by flashes of elf-shot. All she could hear were the war whoops of a thousand goblins, trolls, spriggans, and other nasties.

The Winter army was advancing.

Chapter 29

Crom's Head

Belas Wakefire managed to rally his troops from atop his dun warhorse, but not before the Winter forces ravaged the camp. Taylor, Claudia, and Ayoka scrambled through the trees a dozen yards behind the line of Summer troops, the confusion their only cover.

The air was full of smoke, thunder...and the cawing of birds. Taylor looked up to see a formation of female warriors mounted on giant ravens swooping down over the Winter troops. They dropped what looked like terra cotta softballs onto the battle-field, which exploded and sent Winter warriors flying in every direction.

"Hand grenades?" Taylor stammered. "They've got freaking *hand grenades*?"

The riders climbed and circled back over the Summer position.

"Th-they're on our side, right?"

"Must be," Claudia said. She stopped to catch her breath. "All the Courts use corvidry units." She pointed to the western sky. "Look." Sure enough, another squadron of flyers emerged from over the walls of the rath and engaged the Summers in the air. Both sides fired cavalry pistols (or corvidry pistols, Taylor supposed) before engaging each other directly with beaks, claws, and sabers.

The Summers had brought more hedge-riders than the Winters. Eventually, their superior air power drove the Winters back toward Cair Cullen. As the Summer forces advanced once more, Taylor and Ayoka rose to follow in their wake.

"Keep back," Claudia warned. Taylor ignored her. William and the others were still inside the rath. She had to get to them somehow.

Taylor strode forward. Ayoka tapped her war club against her heel. She pursed her lips and limped forward. Taylor might have known the nunnehi girl would be itching to return to the fight.

"Taylor, I'm serious!" Claudia called, now yards behind them. As they had fled the tent, she had grabbed a leather satchel from among her personal things. Now she clutched it tightly to her chest.

Wasko and Bryn, dazed and haggard, came up beside Claudia.

"I've got to help them," Taylor said. Her heart fluttered, half in determination, half in terror. The Summer forces were pushing the Winters back now. They were nearly to the southern gate. From the edge of the woods, Taylor had a clear view of Cair Cullen. The rath was only a few hundred yards away. Maybe everybody would be too preoccupied with the battle. She might not face any resistance at all. No need to use any magic. If she had the nerve, she could circle to the north, find the underground passage William, Pete, and Haggler had used, and then....

Belas thundered commands, urging his troops onward. The air exploded with the report of muskets and the acrid smoke of black powder and traces of whatever was used to make elf-shot.

A lone giant swung a stone bigger than a man's head in an enormous sling. He let go of one of its corded straps, and the missile sailed overhead like a cannonball, slamming into the parapets above the southern gate. A handful of Winter sharp-shooters screamed as they fell to the ground with the rubble.

In the sky above, the Summer corvidry troops had routed their Winter counterparts and were chasing them off to the north.

Taylor's heart raced. It looked as if Summer might actually breach the wall.

Her mind ran through the possibilities as she hurried her pace.

Claudia began to jog toward her with Wasko and Bryn close behind.

"Miss Hellebore!" Wasko called. "We don't want you to get in no trouble! You just stay back like Miss Fountain says, okay?"

"But Shanna...," she called over her shoulder. "William, Haggler...." Yes, it was stupid for her to keep moving toward the rath, but she'd never forgive herself if—

Crom Cornstack burst into the battle on his gleaming white charger. Wave after wave of magic flowed from the Winter Primus. It wasn't presence, Taylor decided, but something else that she could almost feel in her bones: raw, malevolent power.

At his side and eleven feet tall was Bledrus Dingle. His blasts and stun spells held men and horses at bay and cleared off a space for the Winter Primus.

The Summer troops stopped cold.

"Attack!" Belas Wakefire screamed. A Summer lieutenant added his own war whoop, and the battle surged forward—but only for a moment.

Crom's cloak and white-blond beard whipped in the wind. He gestured, and a pulse of magic rippled outward from his massive form. Taylor felt a sudden surge of wild, animalistic terror. He uttered an incantation, and a huge smoky apparition took shape: five feet tall at the shoulders, with a mouth full of tusks and eyes like embers glowing in a fireplace.

The boar pawed the ground, arched its back, and let out a hideous squeal. As the biting wind blew over the creature's back, it sent up wisps of black smoke, which made it look like the thing was smoldering with fires burning inside its massive belly.

Taylor's stomach twisted in knots. *That's how he killed my dad.*

The boar lurched forward, smashing into the nearest Summer troops and forcing them to retreat, some running, some blinking away.

"He can't get all of you!" Belas cried. "Attack!" This time, only a few listened.

The boar circled around for another charge. Summer troops retreated before it. Those that didn't fell, quickly and painfully.

Crom spurred his horse forward and to one side, exposing the southern gate of Cair Cullen. There stood Mara on the flagstones outside the portcullis. Behind her, flanked by four guards, were William, Shanna, Haggler, and Pete.

Mara sneered at Shanna and gestured to the battle. Taylor couldn't hear what she was saying, but she could guess her grandmother was gloating over the death and destruction, rubbing Shanna's nose in Summer's failure to take the rath—for it was obvious now that the Summer Court didn't have a prayer of bringing down Cair Cullen.

"You've lost, Belas," Crom said. He didn't shout, but his voice carried over the whole battlefield and to the edge of the woods. "Leave now, and I'll consider not destroying you for this indignity."

"*This* indignity!" Belas shouted. "This indignity is merely a response to the indignity *you* committed at Tobarty!"

Mara leaned in to say something to Shanna, who gave her a withering glare in return. Haggler, Pete, and William struggled against their guards, but even from this distance, Taylor could see that it was no use.

"You'll never learn, Belas," Crom said. "You're too stupid to know when you've been beaten."

But Taylor was barely listening. The guard closest to William was poking Haggler with William's staff.

She nudged Ayoka. "William's staff," she whispered.

Ayoka studied the scene playing out in the distance. "Yes?"

"We can't overpower them, but if we take them by surprise...."

Ayoka sized up the situation. Taylor continued. "We'd have to do it now, while the Primuses are arguing."

Ayoka hefted her war club. "I can't move quickly if you want me to keep you veiled."

"Just get up there as fast as you can and wait for my signal."

"What signal?"

"You'll know it when you see it. You go low; I'll be going high." Taylor ducked behind the nearest tree, kicking off her shoes. She repeated her true name to herself, letting the sounds of the syllables echo through her mind, as she formed a mental image of a blackbird. As she poured herself into it, she felt her clothes falling off of her. She shrank to half her normal size, a fourth, a tenth...and then she spread her dark gray wings and took to flight.

Taylor soared over the battlefield, flitting from tree to tree. Her tiny heart pattered with the thrill of flight.

She'd promised never to set foot in a rath of Arradherry, and she didn't. Instead, she flew high above it, looking down upon the keep, the courtyards with their craftsmen's shops, and the members of the garrison poised to spring into action at a moment's notice.

She never once alighted on any wall or turret—though she did take the time to void her avian cloaca over the keep.

She tried to estimate how long it would take Ayoka to reach William, moving invisibly and with a wounded leg. Surely a couple of minutes would do it. Of course, she didn't have a watch or her cell phone, so it was all down to how long it felt she was in the air—and how long it might be before more fighting broke out.

Perched on the branch of a poplar tree, Taylor gazed upon the scene. Crom was still strutting and crowing about his victory. He had dismounted so he could saunter closer to Belas's position. Dingle had shrunk to his usual size and drawn his silver sword. He took up his position at his master's side.

It's now or never, Taylor thought. She pushed off from the branch, flapped her wings, and soared high into the air. Below her were Mara and Shanna, still bickering. William and Pete struggled against their guards. Haggler's chin lolled against his chest, and his eyes were closed. Was he unconscious or just exhausted? Taylor couldn't tell.

William's guard stood a fair bit taller than William, which was to Taylor's advantage. The guard's smug face with its cleft chin and violet eyes made a clear target.

She spun into a dive. She wasn't a falcon or an eagle, so it probably wasn't as graceful as it might have been, or as frightening if anybody noticed her. She kept her wings close to her body, flapping them only to keep herself on course.

The guard didn't even notice her until she slammed into him, scratching at his face with her talons. He let out a frightened squeak and lurched backward, pulling William with him.

That's when Ayoka appeared behind him. Her war club burst immediately into flame, and she swept it against the backs of his knees, cutting his legs out from under him.

William's staff went clattering to the pavement. William himself rolled easily away. He grabbed the staff and came up thrusting it into the ribs of Haggler's guard. He spun around, aimed the tip at Mara and hissed, *"Bazagra!"*

Mara and Crom noticed the disturbance at the same time. Mara's shield deflected William's blast, but a second later, Haggler released a stunning spell that showered the pavement with smoke, cracks of thunder, and flashes of light in a dozen different colors.

Crom gathered magic.

Belas urged his men to attack. This time the Summer line surged forward.

Shanna went down in the tumult of Haggler's stunning spell, but Pete and William dragged her to safety. Pete stayed by her side as William stood watch in front of her. His eyes gleamed with glee as he spun his staff and began to whisper another incantation.

Mara stalked toward Shanna. Taylor wheeled about and then flew straight for her grandmother, squawking and chirping. The

Chief Matron made a swooping gesture and unleashed a faery blast. Taylor veered suddenly, falling from the sky and skidding across the grass, but she had avoided Mara's attack.

As Taylor hit the ground, Haggler unleashed a blast of his own. Mara staggered backwards, but didn't fall.

Crom once more summoned his boar and unleashed it against Belas's troops. It stomped and trampled through their lines, leaving a trail of darkness and dread wherever it went. It circled around, lowered its head, and charged straight for the portcullis where William and the others were fighting.

It was almost upon them when another misty figure tackled it from behind: a humanoid with a snarling, doglike head. It wasn't any bigger than a normal human, but it locked the boar in a headlock and pulled it to the ground.

Fifty yards away, Claudia stood on the edge of the battle with a painted gourd hoisted over her head. Her eyes were pools of sea-green fire, and her lips moved as she uttered her incantation.

Taylor took flight once more and sped to Shanna's side.

The boar shook off Claudia's hunter and stomped it into the flagstones. It shook its tusked head, pawed the ground, and bounded toward William.

But Claudia had bought him enough time to complete his incantation. The tip of his staff burst into brilliant golden light. The boar thundered forward. A jet of flame erupted from William's staff and caught it on the shoulder when it was still fifteen yards away.

The boar slowed to a halt, then slowly, purposely stalked forward, one cloven hoof at a time. Fourteen yards...thirteen. Ripples of dark, malevolent magic exuded from it.

William snarled and put his weight behind his staff, as if he were pushing against the boar with his muscles and not with his magic.

Crom had turned away from the battle to focus all his attention on his magical construct. Holding his sacrum aloft, the Primus channeled its magic into the boar.

In the confusion, Haggler pulled a length of rope from around his waist. With a tug, it stretched to twice its size. He blasted Mara one more time. While she was disoriented, he sprung to loop the rope around her wrists.

William was doing everything he could to hold Crom's boar-construct at bay. Over and over, he shouted his incantation: *"Sharba pesharba flammante fayah pyripeganyx!"* The flame grew hotter and whiter. The boar clawed its way toward him, but maybe—hopefully—more slowly. Ten yards...nine and a half...nine.

Shanna stood trembling next to Haggler and Ayoka. Soaring above her, Taylor saw the look of terror on her face. This was the magic that had killed her husband. It was her worst nightmare, and now Crom had turned it loose on her and her friends.

The Primus let out a low, rumbling growl as he urged his boar onward. Sweat trickled down his forehead, but it was nothing like William's pained expression. He let out a blood-curdling howl of anger—or maybe agony. His face contorted with the effort.

The boar vanished in a puff of black smoke. William's fire spell pushed him backward like a rocket until, a heartbeat later, the flaming jet subsided and he dropped his staff on the flag-stones. The end was cracked and blackened.

"Well, if it isn't the dragon-slayer," Crom said. A wry smile was just visible beneath his beard and mustache as he squared his shoulders and faced William. The geometric designs of his facial tattoo curled into an almost jovial expression. "You've been practicing."

William said nothing. He hastily dug a plastic zip-top bag out of his jacket. He kicked his damaged staff away and began to spread a white substance in a circle around himself.

Crom chuckled, but there was no mirth in it. "That was some exceptional conjuring you just did," he said. "Very impressive. Your magic is much stronger than it was on the River of Night." Crom pulled the sacrum from beneath his blood red cloak and held it aloft.

"I'll take it now."

He hissed an incantation, and the severed head opened its eyes.

Chapter 30

The Oathbreaker

William's knees were on the verge of giving out. His arms were leaden, and his hands were raw and chapped. The flame spell had burned hotter than he expected. That might have saved his life from the boar, but he was going to need something else against Crom, and his options were limited. He was exhausted. His magical supplies were low. His staff was damaged. It might not last much longer—not against Crom Cornstack, at any rate.

As Crom began to taunt him, his mind raced to form a plan. He had a little bit of salt in his pocket—perfect for a protective spell if he could work it in time. He kicked his staff away— cracked and burned as it was, he was afraid to trust it. He strewed the salt all around him, but his hands were shaky. He didn't come close to making a proper circle.

When Crom started talking about William's magical reserves, though, something occurred to him.

William's magical reserves were rubbish; it was the dracontia that had saved him, siphoning magic from all around him and giving it shape as he needed it. Whether Crom knew it or not, that's what he was after.

As Crom lifted that hideous severed head, William reached into his coat pocket and pulled out the crystal. It gleamed in the darkness with a pure, white light.

As the head's eyes opened, William thrust the dracontia forward.

A wave of darkness arced out of the head toward William. It wrapped itself around him, ripping through him as with a thousand icy needles. It was like he'd been stripped bare and dropped in ice-cold water, but he somehow maintained his focus.

He kept his thoughts on his dracontia while he brought his breath under control.

Long, shallow, in through the nose and out through the mouth, just as Maymay had taught him.

All the while, he mentally coaxed his dracontia to life, willing its power to manifest.

Soon the sensation of cold shifted from intolerable to merely excruciating. The pain was concentrated in his outstretched hand. Crom's magic was targeting the dracontia, not him. He took that as a good sign.

Of course, Claudia never explained what would happen to him if the dracontia were destroyed. Best not to think about it.

Instead, he fell to one knee. He didn't trust himself to stay standing for much longer. But he kept up his meditation. "*Eulamo*," he hissed with each exhaled breath.

Whatever Crom was doing, it was meant to steal his magic. He'd said so himself. That's what Taylor said his talisman did; that's why they risked everything to enter the rath to destroy it.

Well, fine. Crom had a magical doohickey that siphoned away magic. So did William. That's what dracontias did, too, after all.

Crom could steal his magic all he wanted to.

William would just steal it back.

It was just a matter of whose doohickey gave out first.

Get away from him! Taylor squawked. But it came out as a series of overwrought chup-chup-chups.

William's whole body was wrapped in what could only be described as a living shadow. Darkness billowed around him, churning and whipping about at the slightest movement. The protective sigils on his denim jacket blazed with golden light, criss-crossing his upper body with their cryptic designs and seemingly holding the shadows at bay...but for how long?

William knelt on the stones in front of the rath, his hand outstretched, the dracontia clutched in his fist.

Its white light arced back toward Crom.

It twined like the forgotten strands of a silver cobweb around the stream of darkness that emanated from Crom's sacrum.

That light seemingly infused the sacrum. Its dead-man's eyes glowed like tiny moons against the brown, lacquered skin of Crom's former enemy. William's magic wafted and rippled like the northern lights, racing around the sacrum, up Crom's arm, and over his gigantic form.

Taylor rocketed straight for her grandfather's face.

He barely flinched. With a wave of his arm, he sent a pulse of magic that flung her off course. She tumbled through the sky until she landed on the ground behind him.

She hit the ground and skidded across the frosty grass, growing heavier with each passing heartbeat. Her blackbird form had begun to grow, to morph back into her everyday, two-legged shape.

Oh, this sucks so bad! she thought.

She shivered and pulled herself up into a ball and looked around.

No one had even noticed what had happened to her. All fighting had ceased, and everyone's eyes were on Crom and William. Summer and Winter forces alike seemed mesmerized by the contest raging between the two of them. The scene reminded Taylor of a two-man tug-of-war: each one testing his strength against the other, seeing who would be the first to pull down his opponent.

Taylor didn't want to look away, but without a warm covering of blackbird feathers, she was about to freeze to death!

I am not shape-shifting again until July! she promised herself.

293

She spied a fallen warrior not five yards away. He was wearing a woolen cloak that would go very nicely with her current ensemble of chilblains, grass, and mud.

Bent over double, she scrambled to him. In the process, she nearly knocked over a Summer warrior, who simply grunted as she barreled past.

In my bedroom! she added. *With the blinds shut and the freaking door locked!*

She fell to her knees and tugged at the dead man's cloak.

Tramping feet came up behind her. Taylor looked over her shoulder and sighed with relief when she saw it was Claudia.

"Here!" She thrust a wad of clothing into Taylor's hands—everything she'd left behind the tree back at the edge of the woods, wrapped up in her black leather jacket.

Bless you!

She wanted to say thank you, but her teeth wouldn't stop chattering long enough for her to get the words out. She dressed as quickly as she could, her back to the two armies and Claudia blocking her from the front. She slipped on her tennis shoes and turned back toward William and Crom.

"Wh-what's hap-p-pening?" she finally managed to say.

"I think they're caught in some kind of loop," Claudia said, her eyes wide with alarm. "They're just...trading magic back and forth."

Taylor's jaw dropped. "William knows h-h-how to d-do that?"

"His dracontia does."

Taylor studied the scene once more. Through the enveloping shadows, she could read the strain on William's face. He was giving it everything he had, but the fire, the glee she had sensed in him before, was gone. He was barely holding his own, nothing more.

Across from him, Crom had braced his legs as if he were thigh-deep in the ocean and fighting for his footing against a succession of crashing waves. He held his massive muscles taut as he leaned into the magic pouring from his sacrum.

All around, people stood dazed. Some hefted their weapons as if poised to attack, but no one could tear themselves away from the contest playing out in front of them.

"N-nobody's fighting."

"They've never seen Crom struggle like this," Claudia said.

"Nobody's p-put up this much of a f-f-fight before?"

Claudia shook her head.

Taylor watched in awe and horror. William was in way over his head. She hoped he knew that. She brought one knee to her chest, then the other, stretching her limbs and trying to bring some more warmth into her body.

She took a tentative step forward. Even Bledrus Dingle stood amazed at the unfolding contest. He rested the point of his silver sword in the dirt and seemed confused about what he was supposed to do.

Crom growled and took a labored step forward. "*I...will... take you...boy!*"

William's other knee dropped. He was no longer holding his dracontia out from his body. Rather, he clutched it to his chest with both hands. Amid the crackling magic, Taylor could hear his whimpers of pain.

"*I...will...rip the magic...from you!*" Crom snarled. "*And... hang...your head...on a...pole!*"

He's not going to make it! Taylor looked about. There had to be something she could do.

"Daddy! No!" Shanna cried from the portcullis. Ayoka and Haggler stood at her side, though Haggler's attention was half on Pete, who lay dazed on the flagstones—the victim of one too many faery blasts.

"*You're next,*" Crom thundered, taking his concentration off of William to shoot his daughter a withering glare. His knitted brows could barely conceal the seething fury in his eyes.

Taylor scanned the gate. Where was Mara? Haggler had bound her with his enchanted rope, but now... There! The rope lay tangled on the stones. Mara must have gotten free; she was nowhere in sight. Taylor's heart sunk.

I could use Jill and her scrying bowl about now, Taylor thought. For just a second, her mind lurched home, to her parents and the imposter and Jill.

William groaned against Crom's onslaught. Taylor began to gather magic—but to what end? It didn't look there was anything anyone could do. William was about to buckle. His only hope was that Crom gave out first.

The Winter Primus roared and took a single ponderous step forward. He threw his entire weight behind his sacrum's attack.

William crawled backward, gasping in pain.

Suddenly there was a flash of superheated dust, and Mara appeared. She grabbed Shanna from behind and pulled her backward toward the portcullis.

"Shanna!" Taylor shouted. She darted for the rath. The crowds, engrossed in Crom and William's contest, hardly noticed her passing.

"Taylor, don't!" Claudia cried.

Mara and Shanna were only feet from the entrance to the rath. She could only follow so far before she would have to break her oath and enter Cair Cullen.

"Let her go!" she screamed.

Mara paid her no attention as she wrestled her daughter closer and closer to the gate.

A fierce, triumphant roar echoed in the night. Taylor whipped about, her temples pounding. *God, no*, she thought.

Crom had advanced another step on William. Her friend now lay on the flagstones, curled up in a ball. The glow of his enchanted jacket had faded away almost to nothing. Only the white light of his dracontia remained, but it looked nearly spent as well. The silver tendrils that had once infiltrated Crom's own dark magic had dwindled away to almost nothing.

Haggler flung his knife at Crom's head. The Primus deflected it with a wave of his left hand. He snarled an incantation. A second tendril of darkness lashed out from his sacrum and surged into the albino little person's chest. Haggler gasped and staggered backward. His whole body shook.

Still half-dazed, Pete lurched forward. Crom stomped his foot, and a crack opened in the flagstones that traced a jagged path directly to him. Pete fell.

Taylor could barely watch. She took a tentative step toward William. Shanna screamed defiantly behind her as Mara dragged her within Cair Cullen's southern gate.

"*Stop this!*" Taylor shouted. She let loose a blast in Crom's direction, but it veered away, spiraling into the dark shadows still swirling around the sacrum. The severed head seemed to grin with satisfaction.

"*Not till I've drained him dry,*" Crom growled. His facial tattoos danced with glee.

"He doesn't deserve this!"

Crom thrust his sacrum forward. William winced and whimpered. "He challenged my honor," he said. "Isn't that enough?"

Another pulse of darkness arced from the sacrum to the quickly dimming dracontia.

Crom's demeanor had changed. He wore the confidence of someone who knew the contest was over. He had nothing to fear. His sacrum was more powerful than William's dracontia. He knitted his brow and bored into William with his icy blue eyes.

"Let him go!" Taylor thundered. *I can't let it end like this!*

The Primus gritted his teeth, but said nothing. Maybe he didn't even hear her. He held the sacrum aloft. Shadowy tongues of magic licked out, wrapping themselves more and more tightly around William's motionless form, smothering him, ripping the magic out of him.

He let out a baleful cry.

Then there was a flash of light—the glint of metal reflecting the torches on the parapet. Something silvery-white slammed into the sacrum. It cut through the lacquered leather skin of the Primus's talisman, and the streams of darkness directed toward William recoiled and waved wildly.

The sacrum's lower jaw dangled freely, suspended by the slimmest strand of mummified flesh.

Metal clattered against stone. A silver sword had fallen to the ground.

Crom staggered backward, his eyes wide, his mouth open. When he shifted his position, Taylor could see who had attacked him.

Bledrus Dingle crumpled to the ground.

Chapter 31

Taylor Gets Angry

Crom began to shake—whether in terror or fury, Taylor couldn't tell.

Dingle looked suddenly pale and tired. Though his face didn't change, he now seemed impossibly old. His appearance reminded Taylor of Anya Redmane. As soon as she made the connection, she knew what it meant: the spriggan was sworn to the service of the Winter Court. Now he had broken that oath and had already started to fade.

William's body heaved with each labored breath. Taylor was at his side immediately, her hand on his shoulder, helping him sit up.

"Danu," Mara whispered, stunned. Her arms went limp. Shanna easily fought herself free from her mother's grasp.

A troll clutched his musket and mouthed a word Taylor couldn't hear. The spriggan beside him nodded and pointed a gnarled finger at Dingle. "Oathbreaker," he muttered. His voice cracked.

A Summer warrior echoed him. Soon, the word had passed through the lips of everyone at the gate, Summer or Winter.

"Oathbreaker," Taylor said with a revulsion she could barely understand. Dingle had probably just saved William's life—but that didn't make him any less a traitor. He had lifted a weapon against his lord. It didn't matter how glad Taylor was that he did what he did, her mind staggered at the very thought of going back on one's word.

The Fair Folk keep their word. She felt dirty even to be in Dingle's presence.

"*By Danu,*" Crom said. The initial shock had worn off, but he still looked dazed. Mara's face, already unearthly pale, had turned pallid and stony gray. Her dark eyes flashed outrage.

Robbed of his sacrum, Crom reached for the mace strapped to his belt. "*How dare you?*"

Dingle flinched. Crom's wave of presence was staggering, even yards away where Taylor stood. The spriggan had once bragged that his centuries of service to the Winter Primus had conditioned him to his powerful glamour. That protection, it seemed, had been stripped from him.

He tried to back away, but his body was weak. His massive strength, a strength that could uproot trees with one hand, was gone.

Crom towered over him. "*How dare you?*" he bellowed again.

"It...just ain't right," Dingle said, his voice barely above a whisper. "He didn't do nothing to you. She didn't, either." He gestured toward Taylor. By now, Shanna had come up behind her and knelt beside her and William.

He dropped his head. "Just...not fair...," he muttered. He twisted himself around and tried to crawl away.

Crom lifted his head and let out a furious roar. He raised his mace and, with a snarl of "Oathbreaker," slammed it against Dingle's exposed shoulder.

Lightning erupted from the sky. A jagged finger of blue-white light struck the tip of the weapon, which leaped out of Crom's hand with a jolt. The Primus clutched at his hand as if it had been set on fire. He brought his arm in close to his body.

Thunder cracked the sky. Taylor shrieked and covered her ears. Eyes darted in every direction as the sky grumbled and growled above Cair Cullen.

A figured appeared out of the shadows near the edge of the battlefield. A well-built man, nearly seven feet tall, strode confidently and purposefully toward the rath.

He was dressed in a crisp, pinstripe suit. Three tiny green will-o'-the-wisps hovered above his head, highlighting the turquoise green of his silk tie and handkerchief, his gleaming white dress shirt. As he approached, the thunder began to grow until Taylor realized it wasn't coming from the sky—it was coming from him.

Taylor gasped with recognition at about ten yards, when she could make out the man's features: his flashing slit-pupil eyes; his warm, chocolate skin; his woolly, salt-and-pepper hair with just a tint of green in it.

She realized he was barefoot. Finding proper footwear for long, webbed toes must have been difficult, although he didn't seem to mind the cold.

"Poppy!" Claudia called. Her face stretched into a bewildered grin.

Taylor smiled as well. When she had first been swept into the Wonder, she had asked Danny, "Why are we going to see Moe Fountain?" He had answered simply, "Because both sides are afraid of him."

Indeed, both Summer and Winter troops gave the approaching cymbee a wide berth. Some on either side stood at attention. Others backed away, afraid to turn and run but terrifed to be anywhere near the him.

The rumble of thunder was stronger than any presence Taylor had ever felt. When the daoine sídhe used their glamour, people fell in line. They showed respect—whether they really felt it or not. They found it hard even to imagine contradicting anything a Gentryman or Gentrywoman said.

What Moe Fountain inspired in the crowd wasn't compliance. It was terror.

Crom spun to face him, gathering magic.

"You've come a long way from home, old man," the Primus said. There was the slightest quaver in his voice.

"I won't be here long," Moe Fountain said. The wind picked up: an icy breeze that Taylor could feel in her bones. Thunder rumbled—this time, it was the real thing bouncing around in the clouds overhead. A storm was coming.

"I've come about Danny Underhill," he said. His faced turned into a stony frown, and his eyes blazed green fire. "I'd like to have a word with whoever it was that made my little girl cry."

Crom stood his ground. "Who the blazes is Danny Underhill?"

Lightning streaked down from the sky. Crom's conjured shield spell was quick, but the lightning strike was overwhelming. Bathed in electricity, he staggered to one side.

"Are you trying to kill me?" he thundered, gathering magic.

"I'm trying to show restraint," Moe said through clenched teeth. Another bolt of lightning landed in front of Crom. "You're lucky I'm weaker outside my domain."

"Danu's...pendulous..." He took a step backward. He gestured dismissively, addressing Mara. "Do you believe this nonsense?"

"Stand up straight, son," Moe said. "Have some respect for yourself."

Crom whipped back around to Moe. He clenched his fists. "It's not like you to stick your nose where it doesn't belong."

"You might say this time's personal," the cymbee said. Claudia kept a respectful distance, but there was no mistaking her expression of love and gratitude. Taylor shared the sentiment.

"I didn't think you did vendettas," Crom said.

"A man will do almost anything for his daughter," Moe said. "But I don't suppose you'd know anything about that."

Taylor glanced at Shanna, who stood bewildered with her hand in front of her mouth. Moe gave Shanna a kindly, fatherly nod. Then he winked at his own daughter before turning back to the Primus, and any trace of love or compassion vanished from his expression.

"Vendettas?" the cymbee continued. "No, Crom. This is bigger than my personal feelings. You're a threat to every domain and chiefdom in the region."

"You've been misinformed," Crom said. "The Summer Court has marched on *my* rath. I'm simply trying to defend it. Isn't that my right as Primus?"

"That depends on how you're defending it," Moe said, "and why the Summer Court got it in their fool heads to attack you in the first place—and during the Winter Assize at that."

Crom scoffed. "What are you going to do, old man? Convene the Deep Council on me?"

Moe grinned. "That would be the proper thing to do, wouldn't it?" He gestured, and another bolt of lightning fell. Once more, Crom deflected it with a shield, but gasped as the surge reached his left hand. He drew it back with a curse.

Moe frowned. "Yeah, definitely not as much oomph this far from home." He glared at Crom. "All right, then. We'll do this by the book." He lifted his voice. "Oronyatekha?"

A dark vortex opened beside him. Warriors dove or blinked away from it. It emitted a low, rumbling drone, like reverb in the subwoofer of a rock band's sound system. Three figures stepped out of it...and one of them was Jill Matthews!

Taylor's jaw dropped.

William perked up just enough to mutter, "J-Jill? What's she doing here?"

Taylor didn't know either, and the others who'd stepped out of the void left her speechless.

Leading the way was a Native American fae. He was no more than two feet tall, decked out in traditional, ornate buckskins—the kind folks would wear to important ceremonies and not just for a stroll through a battlefield. His jet-black hair was pulled back in a long braid, and his dark eyes compelled Taylor's attention. A drum was slung on his back.

Behind him was, of all things, a huge buffalo. Jill stood at its side. With a wary glance at all the soldiers filling the plain, she nudged closer and laid her hand on the enormous beast's side.

Surprisingly, it was the buffalo who spoke.

"Crom Cornstack," it said. Taylor could feel its deep, bass voice vibrating through her bones. "Mara Hellebore. The Deep Council would have words with you."

"You can't be serious!" Mara said.

"Brings Thunder With Him rarely jokes about such things," the tiny fae said.

"Y-you summoned the Deep Council?" Crom said, his pale eyes on Moe.

The cymbee waved off the question. "They were already on your tail," he said. "I just called in a favor so I could be here for the fun part." Moe nodded to the tiny fae.

"Shall we be going?" the tiny fae said.

He raised his hand, and the black vortex enveloped the battlefield.

Taylor held on to William, and Shanna held on to Taylor. Without warning, everything went utterly black. Taylor's ears popped, and her equilibrium shifted. The experience was disorienting, but it wasn't like her early forays into the faery rings. There was no sense of wild frenzy, no mind-bending flurry of sights and sounds. There was nothing but darkness.

Everything went still, so much so that it took Taylor a second to confirm she was still in her body at all.

Just as suddenly, it was over.

Taylor and her friends were in a sitting room, large and pristinely appointed with chairs and settees and a gleaming golden chandelier over her head. It could have been something from a Victorian TV drama, only...off. The wooden armrests and feet of the furniture were carved in grotesque shapes: dragons and trolls and wild-eyed unicorns. The curlicue pattern of the gaudy, yellow-green wallpaper slithered and twisted and twined about itself seemingly of its own will. The candles burning in the chandelier and the fire in the fireplace gave off a subtle greenish hue.

William slumped halfway onto a settee with his legs dangling off the edge, his staff on the floor in front of him. Shanna nudged him backward to keep him from falling off. She stroked his forehead and intoned a healing spell.

Taylor stood in the center of the room next to Claudia.

"What is this place?" Shanna said.

"A waiting room," Claudia answered. "I've never been here before...but that seems reasonable."

"Yeah," Taylor said. "But waiting for what?"

There was a peal of thunder. Taylor's attention turned toward a set of oaken double doors.

"If my Poppy's involved," Claudia said, "then we're probably guests of the Deep Council."

She found a chair in the corner and sat with her head down and her hands folded in her lap.

"I've heard of them," Taylor said. "Something like a United Nations for Our Kind, right?"

Claudia nodded.

The oaken doors rattled. Taylor could barely make out the sounds of shouting in the distance.

"What do you suppose they're..." With a jolt, Taylor remembered something. "Where's Jill? She was with the little person and the buffalo."

Shanna looked up from William, who was sleeping soundly. Claudia raised her head and looked around the room.

"And where's Ayoka?" Shanna said.

An uneasy lump wormed its way into Taylor's stomach. "Jill?" she called. "Ayoka?"

There were more sounds of shouting, more rumbles of thunder. Then the room fell silent. Taylor registered the tick-tock of a mantel clock flanked by silver clockwork griffins.

One of the double doors cracked open, and Jill appeared. She looked around the room wide-eyed. "What are you all doing here? William!"

She was at her brother's side in a second.

"He's fine," Shanna said. "Just worn out."

"Urnghsh," William said. He flexed the fingers of his left hand. Taylor could see where the dracontia had left deep, red marks across his palm.

"What about you?" Taylor said. "What are you doing here? When you showed up with that buffalo and that little person..."

"He's not a buffalo, he's a bison," Jill said. "Don't worry; it's a common mistake. And Oronyatekha isn't a little person, he's just...short. He's what they call a Drum Dancer."

"Okay," Taylor said. "But what are you doing here? Mom and Dad—"

"They're fine," Jill assured her. The two girls found a settee opposite the double doors and sat down. Only then did Taylor realize how exhausted she was.

Jill held Taylor's hand and filled her in on everything that had happened since Mara kidnapped her. The fake Taylor, the party, how Tsisgwa and his nunnehi warriors came to the rescue, and then how Brings Thunder With Him, the bison, appeared and whisked Jill off to who-knows-where.

"They're having some kind of trial," she said. "They called me as a witness."

"A witness? Wait... What? Who's on trial?"

"My parents," Shanna said. "Right?"

Jill seemed to register the person sitting next to her brother for the first time. "Maybe...?"

Taylor stepped in. "This is Shanna, my mom. And over there is Claudia."

Jill nodded to them both, then turned back to Taylor. "Yeah, it's your grandparents. It sounds like they're in a lot of trouble. Something about incursions into the Nunnehi Lands. Taylor, you never told me your grandfather tried to hunt you down last winter!"

"I guess it never came up," Taylor said. She found her eyes drifting toward the doors.

A howling winter wind rattled on the other side.

"So why are we here?" Taylor asked.

"They didn't think it would be safe back at the castle."

"They were probably right." For all Taylor knew, the Summer and Winter Courts had started back at it once the shock of Moe Fountain and the others showing up wore off.

"They're really going to do something about Crom and Mara?"

"It looks that way. The people in there... They had a lot of questions about Layla and what she was up to back home."

"Then maybe..." She could barely bring herself to think it, much less say it. "Maybe Shanna can finally be free." And maybe there wouldn't be any more of these awkward family get-togethers!

Her mind darted in a hundred directions, trying to imagine what that could mean. Shanna could be free! She could go where she wanted, do what she wanted.

She hoped and prayed it could be true.

The doors opened once more to admit a tall, barefooted, but otherwise impeccably dressed black man.

"Poppy!" Claudia said. She was in her father's arms before he had even pulled the door completely shut. She buried her face in his chest and sobbed silently.

"Claudia, I'm so sorry," the cymbee said. "I know he meant a lot to you."

Taylor tried not to watch. The pain of losing Danny was still raw in her own heart. She couldn't imagine what Claudia was going through.

"Taylor, you and your friends are free to go," Moe said. "I'm to take you all home right away."

"What's going to happen with Mara and Crom?" Taylor asked.

"Arradherry is going to pay reparations to the nunnehi for the destruction at Tsuwatelda. And they're going to forfeit some territory along the border."

"That won't go over well with the other Courts," Shanna said.

"Not at all," Moe agreed. "I wouldn't be surprised if Summer got the Bardic Curse imposed against them."

Shanna's mouth fell open. "Oh, my!"

"What's the Bardic Curse?" Taylor said.

"Open mockery," Shanna said. "Poets and satirists have free reign to shame them any way they want, and the bearer of the curse is forbidden to retaliate."

Moe nodded. "Most daoine sídhe think it's a fate worse than death."

"But what about Mara and Crom?" Taylor pressed. "Is anybody going to stop them from coming after Shanna?"

"I'm afraid that's not something the Deep Council can decide."

Shanna hung her head. "Oh."

A chill raced down Taylor's spine. "Wait, are you kidding me? They're not going to do *anything*?"

"Taylor, the Deep Council doesn't get involved in inter-personal disputes."

"*So that's it?*" The temperature in the room began to drop. "*Some land and a couple trips to Home Depot, and they're off the hook?*"

"You have to understand..."

"*Well, I don't!*" Taylor snapped. Crom and Mara were going to go free. The Deep Council's punishment was barely a slap on the wrist! How long would it be before they made another grab for Shanna?

This was unacceptable!

Taylor stalked toward the double doors and threw them open, barging into the corridor on the other side.

Chapter 32

The Deep Council

It was a short corridor with walls of dark, paneled wood, lit by some orange and yellow orbs of faery fire floating near the ceiling. It ran the length of the waiting room, but there was another set of oaken doors directly across.

"Taylor!" Moe called. "Don't go in there!"

"Taylor, come back!" Shanna shouted.

She didn't care. She stormed through the second set of double doors. Through clenched teeth, she hissed, *"You're going to do something about Crom and Mara and..."*

She was suddenly in an ancient stone keep that looked nothing like the waiting room. "...you're going to do it..."

The ceiling was forty or fifty feet high, and the room was at least that long in any direction. Nine figures sat in a semi-circle in a great apse to her right. Crom and Mara sat behind a rail to the left and, separated by a wide aisle, Ayoka with her grandfather, Chief Tewa of Tsuwatelda, and another nunnehi Taylor had only met once before: Nocosi, the White Chief of Ichisi. Chief Tewa, dressed in white from head to toe, leaned forward. His eyes flashed surprise and irritation.

Taylor lost her train of thought.

She realized she was a mess. Her black leather jacket was torn and dusty. Her jeans were covered with mud and grass stains. Her hair was all over her head.

Maybe she should have taken a minute to freshen up.

Moe appeared at the door but didn't come in. Shanna ducked around him to see what was going on. Restless shadows told

Taylor that William and Jill were hovering in the background as well.

"And you would be...?" An old woman said, pronouncing the word "would" as if it started with a v. She sat at the center of the semicircle, a lean, steel-haired woman with black, beady eyes. She was knitting something out of blue and silver yarn. It was just a small patch, barely the size of a potholder. Beside her ornate alabaster chair was a basket from which the yarn snaked its way up to her knitting needles.

The others spread out to the woman's right and to her left on similar thrones, yet not quite as large or ornate. To her immediate right was another woman with blazing eyes and fiery red hair that poked out from beneath a headdress of shimmering gold coins. Next to her was a foul-looking man, a troll if ever there was one. His hair stood up on top like a hedgehog. He licked his lips when Taylor appeared, baring a mouth full of wolf-like fangs.

Then was a young brown-skinned woman with black wavy hair. She seemed much younger than the others, dressed in what looked for all the world like a loose-fitting, multicolored beach cover-up. She brushed her hair as if she were bored with the proceedings. Finally there was a bearded, well-muscled man in colorful silks and pointed shoes. He looked to be five feet tall at the most. His clothes and overall appearance reminded Taylor of something from the Arabian Nights.

To the knitting woman's left was a petite fae woman with brilliant blue hair and a matching dress of diaphanous silk. Beside her was a bald man with almond eyes who sat in a lotus position and levitated several inches above the purple cushion of his throne.

Next to him sat the Drum Dancer—Jill had called him Oronyatekha. His throne was just as large as the others, but a smaller copy rested upon it. That's where he sat, his arms crossed in front of him.

Finally, a place had been cleared and adorned with plush green pillows for Brings Thunder With Him, the bison.

"Mother Nadezhda!" Crom grumbled. He held his left hand, blue and charred from Moe Fountain's last lightning bolt, close to his body. "This child has no standing before the Deep Council! I insist—"

The old woman silenced the Primus with a steely glare. Though it wasn't directed at her, the wave of presence she sent toward her grandfather nearly made Taylor's ears pop.

The old woman then lowered her eyes to Taylor. "Young lady?" she said. Her address jolted Taylor back to reality. Or whatever this was.

"I'm Taylor Smart," she began, hesitantly. The fury was still in her gut, but she realized it wouldn't do any good to lash out. Something deep inside her, something that was too primal for words, warned her it might even get her killed. "I mean... My lords...and ladies... I'm sometimes called Selena Hellebore, and I'm *their* granddaughter."

"This could be interesting," the spiky troll said with a grin.

"Be good, Yaghmuur," the red-haired fae scolded.

"Y-you...You've got to do something," Taylor continued. She focused on her true name and tried to express presence. There was no way she could ever intimidate these people, but she feared if she didn't project self-assurance, she'd crumble into a heap.

She glanced to Moe Fountain, who was half-shielding himself with one of the great, oaken doors. He nodded encouragement but said nothing.

The Drum Dancer spoke. "What is it you would have us do, Miss Hellebore?"

"I don't know. Just...something. They can't keep treating Shanna like she's their property. She's a grown woman, for goodness sake!"

"Shanna?" the woman with the mirror said.

"You remember, Courantine," Yaghmuur the troll said, "the Hellebore whelp we all thought was stuck in the bowels of Cair Cullen."

"That's right," Taylor said. "If you don't do something, they're going to go after her again. They won't give up until they've succeeded."

"And how do you know this, child?" Mother Nadezhda said.

Taylor did know it, as surely as she knew anything. And with a twinge of self-consciousness she understood why. "Because...," she began. "If I were in their shoes...if I thought someone had roasted me that bad...I wouldn't give up, either." She cast an icy glare at her grandparents. "I'd make them pay."

Mother Nadezhda kept knitting, but her eyes never left Taylor.

"Members of the Council," Crom said, waving his powerful hand dismissively, "are we actually entertaining this child's argument? Don't your esteemed personages have better things to do?"

Ayoka clutched her grandfather's arm. She looked as frightened as Taylor felt.

Behind Moe Fountain, she heard Shanna's exasperated sigh. She had a right to be used to her dad's bluster, but it seemed to unsettle everybody else.

"The Primus has a point," the blue-haired fae said. Brings Thunder With Him snorted. Taylor couldn't decide if it was a grunt of agreement. She hoped it was just allergies.

The blue-haired fae's eyes flashed. "The child has no standing at this tribunal, Mother Nadezhda. Perhaps we should just turn her into something and send her on her way."

"No, wait!" Taylor blurted. Everyone on the Deep Council turned to her. She could almost feel Crom's and Mara's eyes burning holes in her back.

"Yes?" Mother Nadezhda said. Her knitting needles went still.

Taylor had to think fast before Blue-hair decided what to turn her into. She and Crom were probably right that she had no business even being there. The Eldritch Law was mostly a mystery to her, but she definitely got that there was a right way and a wrong way to do just about everything.

She needed to find a loophole she could exploit.

"She's stalling," Yaghmuur whispered to Courantine. Courantine shrugged and went back to combing her hair.

Blue-hair tapped her fingers on her knee.

Taylor needed to find a loophole fast. She glanced to Moe for help. He nodded encouragingly, but didn't seem disposed to say anything. Then again, the way everybody was acting, he probably had his reasons for not barging in.

Taylor wondered how much trouble she was already in for interrupting the meeting.

Nothing I can do about it now, she thought. She might as well keep going. She cleared her throat and said, "You've already decided that Crom and Mara—"

"You will address us by our proper titles!" Mara snarled.

"...that the Primus and the Chief Matron," Taylor corrected herself, "are guilty of messing with the nunnehi, right?"

"Again, Mother Nadezhda," Crom said, "what is the relevance of any of this? I respectfully request that—"

"Why?" Taylor blurted.

"Why what?" the red-haired fae said. The coins on her head-dress jangled as she leaned forward.

"Why are they in trouble for moving against the nunnehi?"

"The Nunnehi Lands are a sovereign power in the Wonder," Yaghmuur explained. He took the tone of someone explaining matters to a simpleton. "Their claims must be respected."

She stole a glance at Chief Tewa, who was whispering with Chief Nocosi. Both of them stole furtive glances her way. Chief Nocosi shrugged in response to something Chief Tewa asked him.

"How did they get to be a sovereign power?"

"They simply *are*, child," Blue-hair said with a dramatic sigh.

"Indeed," Chief Tewa interrupted. Taylor spun around, startled to hear the ancient fae speak. The members of the Deep Council looked his way as well. "Anyone who questions this will find we are quite capable of enforcing that claim."

313

Chief Nocosi nodded in agreement. Chief Tewa patted Ayoka's knee. He looked at Taylor and gave her a sly wink.

That was for me, Taylor surmised. *You're trying to help me...but how?*

"Are we through here?" the short, bearded fae asked. "I don't see anything to be gained from belaboring this child's incoherent babbling."

"Nor do I, Besammon," Blue-hair said.

Taylor turned Chief Tewa's words over in her mind. The nunnehi are capable of enforcing their claim to sovereignty. So what? What does that have to do with anything?

"Chief Tewa, Chief Nocosi," the floating almond-eyed fae said, "please share the Deep Council's regards to your people. If there is anything else we can do..."

"For which we are truly grateful, Master Li," Chief Tewa said. He glanced once more in Taylor's direction.

Taylor glanced back, then once more toward Moe Fountain, biting his lip in the doorway.

Think, Taylor!

"I move to adjourn," Yaghmuur said.

"Yaghmuur moves to adjourn," Mother Nadezhda said. "Is there a sec—?"

"*Then what do we need* you *for?*" Taylor shouted.

Blue-hair gasped. Courantine dropped her mirror. Crom cursed under his breath.

"*I beg your pardon?*" Mother Nadezhda said through clenched teeth. Her presence was palpable, but Taylor stood her ground, repeating her true name to herself.

I am Neunhiri. I am Laughter in Winter.

Her knees nearly buckled, but she didn't collapse into a quivering puddle of sweat. So that was something, at least.

And she had to go on. For Shanna's sake—and for her own—she had to put a stop to Crom and Mara's irrational vendetta against their daughter. She had stood up to them before, after all. And to Osaa the king of the tie snakes. And to Anya Redmane. And even to Mrs. Markowitz, her former English teacher.

She could handle Mother Nadezhda the same way: by not backing down, by speaking her mind...and by getting under her skin.

"Why do we even need a Deep Council if people like the nunnehi are supposed to stick up for themselves?" she asked. Her throat was dry and her heart pounded, but she kept on. "You say I have no standing here. Fine, maybe I don't. But why do the nunnehi even need to be here? Aren't they supposed to fight their own battles? Chief Tewa just said that's how it's supposed to work." She looked over her shoulder at him. "Right?"

"Would you plunge the Wonder into chaos?" The redhead with the golden headdress said.

"Unej speaks truth," Brings Thunder With Him rumbled. "Rival herds need ways to settle their grievances."

"Well, who's going to settle *my* grievances?"

"Certainly not us," the short, bearded fae said. "The Deep Council has far more important issues to deal with than some insignificant family squabble."

Taylor had reached the boiling point. *"That's not good enough!"* she thundered.

"What do you expect us to do?" Yaghmuur said, throwing his arms wide. "Declare you a sovereign domain so we can adjudicate your rights?"

"If that's what it's going to take to get Crom and Mara off our backs, then you better believe it! Where do I sign up?"

"Danu!" Crom hissed.

Ayoka blurted something in Cherokee.

The members of the Deep Council erupted into a hornet's nest of murmuring, finger-pointing, and shouts of "Unprecedented!" "Who does she think she is?" "She's nothing but a child!" and "The very gall!"

Taylor turned to see what was happening among the nunnehi. Chiefs Tewa and Nocosi were huddled together, whispering and gesturing at each other. Ayoka sat very still, almost in shock, and couldn't take her eyes off Taylor.

I don't think this is what Chief Tewa had in mind.

With some effort, Mother Nadezhda restored order in the Council chamber.

"Miss Hellebore," the steely old woman said, "surely you weren't serious...were you?"

She glanced to her right. Shanna had crept around Moe Fountain and was now standing just inside the door. Taylor could read the bewilderment in her expression but also, maybe, a glimmer of defiance in her eyes.

Whatever it takes, Crom and Mara don't get to win, she thought. *Not today.*

But as soon as the thought crossed her mind, she remembered Claudia's words: Accept your limitations. Be smart. Do what you can do; don't try to do what you can't do.

Taylor strode to the railing and stood before the White Chief of Ichisi.

"Chief Nocosi," she said, bowing at the waist. "I live in the Topside world. I know that's not your territory, but...but there's a little patch of the Wonder where I go to practice magic and meet with my Wonderling friends.

"Yes?"

"I don't know anything about running a sovereign domain. I mean, literally. Not a clue. But...maybe you could claim my Topside neighborhood as part of the Nunnehi Lands?"

Chief Nocosi whispered something to Chief Tewa. Then he looked up at Taylor. "You understand the nunnehi defend the weak, the oppressed?"

Taylor bowed again. "I'm yours to command."

"And what is this Topside neighborhood called?"

"Knottingley Drive, I guess."

Chief Nocosi said something else to Chief Tewa. Chief Tewa shrugged and gestured his permission: *Have at it, old buddy.*

Chief Nocosi stood up. "Mother Nadezhda," he said, gesturing expansively. "I rise to sponsor the claim of Taylor Smart, also known as Selena Hellebore of the daoine sídhe, to sovereign dominion over the Topside region known to her people as Knottingley Drive."

"*WHAT?*" Crom slammed his fist against his armrest so hard it broke off.

Shanna's mouth fell open—but no wider than Taylor's!

The Deep Council murmured, but Chief Nocosi pressed on. "In the name of the city of Ichisi, and with the assent of Chief Tewa..."

"What is this game?" the blue-haired fae, demanded.

"You were right, Yaghmuur," Unej said. Her headdress tinkled as she leaned toward him. "This *is* interesting!"

"With the assent of Chief Tewa," Chief Nocosi repeated, "who speaks today on behalf of his brother, the Great Falcon of the Nunnehi, I further claim the right to administer this domain as regent until such time as Miss Smart reaches the age of maturity."

The members of the Deep Council turned toward each other, each shouting to be heard. It sounded to Taylor like she had at least a few allies among them: Unej, the levitating Master Li, and maybe Courantine, who had retrieved her mirror from the floor where she'd dropped it.

Taylor leaned against the railing, suddenly exhausted. Not ten feet away, Crom Cornstack and Mara Hellebore glowered and bristled.

"Thank you," she told Chief Nocosi. Ayoka sprang up and put her arm around her from the other side of the rail. "I...I don't know what all of that means."

"In due time," Chief Nocosi said.

"We had hoped you would simply claim the nunnehi's protection," Chief Tewa said. "The way we had claimed the protection of the Deep Council."

"Yeah," Taylor said, "I didn't think you were trying to make me a faery princess or something."

"No, we weren't" Chief Nocosi said, his visage suddenly stern.

"I cannot believe that they are even considering such a hare-brained..." Crom muttered. He wasn't even trying to keep his voice down.

Chief Tewa winked at Taylor, pretending not to notice Crom's outburst. "But Yaghmuur gave you an opening and—to the amazement of all of us—you took it."

Chief Nocosi leaned in and grinned. "Then we decided we liked this idea better."

Chapter 33

The Teyrna of
Knottingley Drive

Master Li, Courantine, and Unej convinced Oronyatekha and Brings Thunder With Him to vote with them to recognize Taylor as Teyrna of Knottingley Drive, with Chief Nocosi as her regent until the age of one hundred.

A couple weeks later, in mid-December, there was an official ceremony in the faery woods behind Taylor's house. Wasko, Pete, and Haggler set up a straight-backed wooden chair near the fire pit they had dug the summer before and draped it in blue silks and pure, white linen. Silas Bludgitt was there with both his dogs. So were a little folk couple Taylor didn't recognize, who introduced themselves as Ocky and Fern.

Chief Nocosi and the other Chiefs of Ichisi came with a dozen or more attendants. They sang and danced into the night, weaving protective spells around the clearing. Some even went invisibly into the Topside world to extend their protection to Taylor's entire domain.

Shanna stood beaming at Taylor's side along with William and Jill. The Smarts even ventured to attend the festivities, wide-eyed and slack-jawed. Mrs. Smart cried and held her husband tight as Chief Nocosi placed a circlet of silver on Taylor's brow.

Then, before the swell of magic got to be too much for them, all the mortals returned to their own realm. Mr. Smart later said he'd never been more proud of his little girl.

A week later, Riverview High School hosted a holiday party for the ninth- and tenth-grade classes. Taylor usually avoided such things, but after everything she'd been through, the thought of getting away for a few hours had a distinctive appeal.

She sat at a table sipping punch with Jill, William, and William's friend Jalen Harris, when somebody called her name.

It was Tommy Morgan. "Over here," he called, waving eagerly. So eager, however, that he tipped his paper plate, and a handful of nuts fell on the floor. He dropped to pick them up as Taylor, curious, got out of her seat.

Taylor took a step in Tommy's direction. When she saw the nearby karaoke machine, she got a pretty good idea what he wanted.

"Come sing something!" he said.

"I...I don't know." Taylor bit her lip.

"Come on, Taylor," Abby Dillard called. "Some of these kids who didn't go to Bulloch don't know how good you can sing."

That was the problem. The last time Taylor really let herself go, her singing managed to glamour an entire auditorium full of Topsiders. She'd gained a lot more control since then—thanks to Mara's glamour boot camp. And she did love to sing...

"Just one song," Jalen called.

In the end, something Wasko had told her that morning made the decision for her. The Courts of Arradherry had leveled the Bardic Curse on Mara and Crom. That was the last blow: word was already spreading through the Wonder that the Winter Court was about to kick them both out of office. That gave Taylor all the incentive she needed to break into song.

When she reached the dad who was running the karaoke machine, she said, "Do you have 'Call Me Maybe' by Carly Rae Jepsen?"

He scrolled down the computer screen until he found the right one. He selected the file and clicked play. The music started, but Taylor didn't bother looking at the lyrics on the video screen. She had something else in mind.

"You threw your kid in the cell,
Just ask me, I'd love to tell.

A crooked crew has a spell
'Cause she was in the way.

"Won't trade my oath for a wish,
Plenty of time for a switch
I wasn't looking for this,
But you were in my face.

"Your glare was holdin',
Dead heat—glamour flowin'
Not right
Winter's blowin'
Why do you think you're gonn' enslave her?"

Some of the kids caught on right away that the words were different. Most just sang along with the lyrics they thought they were hearing. Even the ones that noticed Taylor's changes looked like they enjoyed the song, even if they didn't understand it.

Jared McCaughey shot Taylor a bemused grin. Jill and William were laughing themselves silly. Taylor winked at them and launched into the chorus.

"Hey, I don't get you,
Your thinking's hazy,
To do a number
On the nunnehi!
You tried to look right but your baby
She had your number,
So now you're fading!

"Hey, they just caught you,
... Misbehaving,
Must be a bummer
To call me Lady!
And all the other Courts

Just okayed it,
So hear me taunt ya,
And go to Hades!"

The crowd ate it up, and when she came to the end, everybody cheered. Taylor studied the crowd. They were clapping and smiling, and none of them looked even a little glamoured. And that made her smile.

She'd never had any problems with accidentally bewitching her parents or even Jill. Over the past few months, even William had developed some immunity to her mind-controlling magic. She'd guessed long ago that presence didn't work on people she really cared about, the people she counted as family. That gave her hope.

Especially when her eyes wandered to a table in the far corner of the gym.

Her heart raced. Should she risk it?

She figured impulsive decisions had been working pretty well for her in recent weeks, so why not?

She walked over and sat in the empty chair next to Jared McCaughey.

"Hey," she said.

"Hey."

"So..." she began. She looked him in the eye and willed herself to keep her presence in check. "We haven't really talked since the dance back in September."

"I guess not."

"We should do something about that."

He smiled. "Sure. I mean...I thought you weren't..."

"I wasn't," Taylor said. She winked at him. "Maybe things have changed."

He smiled even wider. "I'll call you over break."

Taylor returned his smile. "That would be nice."

Her dad appeared at the door. Jill and William had already seen him and were heading his way.

"I've got to go," she said.

"Merry Christmas," Jared said. "I'll call you, for sure."

They rode home in Mr. Smart's minivan, filling him in on all the fun they'd had.

When they pulled into the Smarts' driveway, Taylor said, "I'll be inside in a minute, Dad."

Mr. Smart left them in the driveway. William and Jill hung around to say their goodbyes. A cold wind blew across the lawn. Above them, clouds blotted out the stars.

Taylor sensed something at the edge of her consciousness. Walking into the middle of her front yard, she said, "Hello?"

Tsisgwa and two other nunnehi warriors appeared in front of her. One was tall and grim-faced, the other smaller and with a playful gleam in his eye.

"I will never get used to that," William said.

"Tsisgwa Imathla," Taylor said, smiling. "You're on guard duty tonight?"

He gestured toward his comrades. "Imejiska Hajo and Asin Yahola will be taking the night shift. I'm showing them around."

The grim warrior bowed curtly. "Imejiska Hajo at your service, my lady. Asin Yahola and I will secure your domain until dawn. You will not die tonight."

"Good to know," Taylor said, trying not to giggle. She addressed Tsisgwa. "If you see Shanna, remind her I'm coming by tomorrow. I'm looking forward to seeing her new house in Ichisi."

"I'm sure she's looking forward to it, my lady."

"Any news of Dingle?"

Tsisgwa frowned and squirmed a bit. "The spriggan doesn't seem to be anywhere in the Nunnehi Lands."

"The spriggan's name is Dingle," Taylor said. "And should he turn up, I want him to know he's welcome here." She bit her lip and glanced at Jill and William. "We owe him at least that much."

"As you say, my lady," Tsisgwa said. He gave a signal, and the three nunnehi vanished into the night.

"My lady?" William said. He could barely suppress his snicker.

"I know, I know," Taylor said, rolling her eyes. "I've tried to tell them that's not necessary. They don't seem to believe me."

"Come on, Taylor," Jill teased, "just admit you love the fawning adoration."

"Nobody's fawning," Taylor said testily. But it was hard to stay in a bad mood tonight. "Wanna come in for a while?"

"We've got to pack," Jill said.

"We're leaving for New Orleans in the morning," William added. "Two whole weeks at Maymay's house for Christmas!"

"Tell her hello from me," Taylor said.

"I just wish I could figure out how to get my hanbo on the plane," he continued. "I sawed off the cracked part and treated the wood with costus root extract. Now I just need to re-carve the sigils and—"

Jill shook her head, laughing.

"What?"

"Bro, just enjoy your time off from school for a change."

"But I'm almost finished!"

"It'll wait. Good night, Taylor." Jill waved. She dragged William toward their house. "And don't even think about packing any index cards."

"That's cold, sis," William said. "What if Maymay wants to teach us something new?"

"It's Christmas, bro. Maybe you've heard of it? Presents? Homemade fudge? Sleeping in till noon?"

"But...but..."

Jill and William crossed the street, playfully arguing.

Taylor watched them walk up the steps and go through the front door. They turned off the porch light as they went in.

Tomorrow, Taylor would have lunch with Shanna and help her get settled in. It looked like her two worlds were finally coming together the right way.

She took deep, cleansing breath and let it out with a satisfied sigh. It was a cold winter night, but she wasn't anxious or afraid. Not anymore.

It started to snow.

And Taylor began to laugh.